THE SICK MAN'S
RAGE

AMIR TSARFATI
AND STEVE YOHN

TEN PEAKS PRESS®
EUGENE, OR

On page 90 is a citation from Tanakh: The Holy Scriptures (1985), Deuteronomy 25:17-19, Jewish Publication Society, Logos software edition.

Cover design by Faceout Studio, Jeff Miller

Cover images © klempa, STILLFX, ZeynepTirpan, JOGENDRA KUMAR, ltummy, OSTILL is Franck Camhi, Reddavebatcave, photolinc / Shutterstock; Ensup / iStock Photo

Interior design by KUHN Design Group

This book is a work of fiction, yet some elements of the story include mention of real people, events, and places. These real aspects, however, are used in the context of an entirely fictional storyline with fictitious characters, incidents, and locations, all of which are a product of the authors' imaginations.

For bulk or special sales, please call 1-800-547-8979. Email: CustomerService@hhpbooks.com

 TEN PEAKS PRESS is a trademark of The Hawkins Children's LLC. Harvest House Publishers, Inc., is the exclusive licensee of the trademark TEN PEAKS PRESS.

The Sick Man's Rage
Copyright © 2024 by Amir Tsarfati and Steve Yohn
Published by Ten Peaks Press, an imprint of Harvest House Publishers
Eugene, Oregon 97408

ISBN 978-0-7369-8836-0 (pbk)
ISBN 978-0-7369-8837-7 (eBook)

Library of Congress Control Number: 2024931125

Printed in the United States of America

24 25 26 27 28 29 30 31 32 /BP/ 10 9 8 7 6 5 4 3 2 1

AMIR DEDICATES THIS BOOK TO...

God, the true giver and sustainer of life.

My family who is always there. The Lord has walked us, and our nation, down some difficult paths this last year. I am so thankful that we are taking the journey together.

STEVE DEDICATES THIS BOOK TO...

The God who remains by my side. There is so much peace in knowing that no matter the path, I am never traveling it alone.

Nancy, who is as much a part of this book's creation as anyone. Before, during, and after my recovery, you were always there carrying me through without complaint. God has greatly blessed me by placing you by my side.

TOGETHER, WE DEDICATE THIS BOOK TO...

The many victims of October 7. Whether you were killed, brutalized, beaten, taken hostage, or forced to run for your lives that day, we remember you and honor you. And for the families and friends of the victims, we acknowledge the daily suffering you go through knowing what your loved ones endured. Originating from a wounded place, this book was created to ensure that the world never forgets your torment, your sorrow, and the reason for your anger.

ACKNOWLEDGMENTS

God, what a year You have brought us through. We thank You for protection, health, creativity, and direction. Our prayer has been and will always be that You are glorified through what we write.

Amir thanks his wife, Miriam, his four children, and his daughter-in-law. Steve thanks his wife, Nancy, and his daughter. We've both walked through the valley this past year; they were just different types of valleys. We could not have navigated our way without the love and support of our families.

Thank you so much to the Behold Israel Team—Mike, H.T. and Tara, Gale and Florene, Donalee, Joanne, Nick and Tina, Jason, Abigail, Kayo, and Rebecca. You are so diligent in your work and so faithful in your prayers. The ministry is a reflection of your character. We also thank the CONNECT team in Israel. What a blessing it is to have you on board.

Thanks once again to Ryan Miller for your military and weapons expertise. Finally, we are so grateful to Bob Hawkins Jr., Kim Moore, Steve and Becky Miller, and the whole Harvest House team. You have become part of our family, and we are so thankful to be partnered with you.

"Turkey seems to be falling to pieces…We have a sick man on our hands, a man gravely ill, it will be a great misfortune if one of these days he slips through our hands, especially before the necessary arrangements are made."

TSAR NICOLAS I OF RUSSIA
(1853)

"Thus says the Lord GOD: 'Behold, I am against you, O Gog, the prince of Rosh, Meshech, and Tubal. I will turn you around, put hooks into your jaws, and lead you out, with all your army, horses, and horsemen, all splendidly clothed, a great company with bucklers and shields, all of them handling swords. Persia, Ethiopia, and Libya are with them, all of them with shield and helmet; Gomer and all its troops; the house of Togarmah from the far north and all its troops—many people are with you.'"

EZEKIEL 38:3-6

"Sovereignty is not given, it is taken."

MUSTAFA KEMAL ATATÜRK,
FIRST PRESIDENT OF TURKEY (1881–1938)

"We must be strong so Israel won't be able to do these things to the Palestinians. Just as we invaded Karabakh and Libya, we will do the same to Israel."

RECEP TAYYIP ERDOĞAN
(JULY 29, 2024)

GLOSSARY

HEBREW

abba – "father"

achi – "friend, bro"

achla – "wow, great, cool"

ahabal – "idiot, moron"

al hapanim – lit.: "on the face"; "awful, terrible"

Avarnu et par'o, na'avor gam et zeh – lit.: "We got through Pharoah, we'll get through this too"

balagan – "mess, disaster, confusion"

b'chaiyecha – lit.: "in your life"; "oh, come on"

betach – "of course"

boker tov – "good morning"

bul – "to the point; bingo"

chai b'seret – lit.: "living in a movie"; "to have unrealistic expectations"

dohd – "uncle"

ein li musag – lit.: "I don't have a concept"; "I have no idea"

ein matzav – lit.: "there isn't a situation"; "not a chance; impossible"

elef ahuz – "1,000 percent right"

esh – lit.: "fire"; "awesome"

goy – "Gentile"

habibti – fem. "my dear"

ima – "mother"

layla tov – "good night"

l'chaim – lit.: "to life"; used as a Jewish toast

mashu mashu – lit.: "something, something"; "great, fantastic"

motek – "sweetheart"

saba – "grandfather"

sababa – "cool, good"

safta – "grandmother"

tachles – "bottom line; in reality"

ta'ut sheli – "my mistake; I'm sorry"

tembel – "jerk, idiot"

tuches – "backside"

walla – "wow"

yaldah – "girl, daughter"

yalla – "let's go"

yeled – "boy, son"

yesh matzav – lit.: "there's a situation"; "it's possible"

yutz – "fool"

ARABIC

abni – "my son"

haji – lit.: "one who has made the pilgrimage to Mecca"; used to refer to an Arab

kam assaa'ah – "What time is it?"

sayyida – "ma'am"

umm – "mother"

FARSI

bodo – "hurry up"

gast-e-ershad – "guidance patrol; morality police"

inshallah – "if God wills"

mersi – "thank you"

negarani nadareh – "no concerns; no worries"

rāndan – "drive"

TURKISH

durmak – "stop"

eller yukarı – "put your hands up"

giriş – "entrance"

mavi vatan – "blue homeland"

CHARACTER LIST

ISRAELIS

Shaul Arens – minister of foreign affairs

Dima Aronov – Kidon operative

Avi Carmeli – former Kidon operative

Efraim Cohen – assistant deputy director of Caesarea

Irin Ehrlich – Kidon team leader

Yaron Eisenbach – Kidon operative

Farzat – Unit 504 operative

Adira Halevi – Yossi Hirschfield's girlfriend

Gil Haviv – Kidon operative

Yossi Hirschfield – Mossad analyst

Dan Hurvitz – minister of defense

Ira Katz – *ramsad*; head of Mossad

Tommy Libai – Kidon team leader

Aryeh Neeman – Kidon team leader

Asher Porush – deputy director of Mossad

Yariv Rabin – Mossad analyst

Liora Regev – Mossad analyst

Elias Rochman – Nir Tavor's brother-in-law

Shayna Rochman – Nir Tavor's sister

Dafna Ronen – Mossad analyst

Eli Rosen – minister of interior

Idan Snir – prime minister

Stavro – Unit 504 operative

Yoram Suissa – director of Caesarea

Lahav Tabib – Mossad analyst

Adah Tavor – Nir Tavor's mother

Eliana Tavor – Nir Tavor's niece

Ezra Tavor – Nir Tavor's father

Hannah Tavor – Nir Tavor's sister-in-law

Michael Tavor – Nir Tavor's brother

Nir Tavor – Kidon team leader

Imri Zaid – Kidon operative

AZERBAIJANI

Elnur Isayev – former assistant deputy head of the Azerbaijani Foreign Intelligence Service

BELGIAN

Mila Wooters – executive assistant at Yael Diamonds

HAMAS

Emad al-Natsheh – Hamas's representative to Iran

Khaled Mousa – cofounder of Hamas; former head of the political bureau

KURDISH

Mustafa Nurettin – colonel in the Kurdish People's Protection Army

RUSSIAN

Vladimir Putin – president of Russia

SOUTH AFRICAN

Nicole le Roux – Mossad analyst

SYRIAN

Burhan Bakir – masseuse at Hotel Sultanahmet, Istanbul

Sabra Bakir – Burhan Bakir's sister

TURKISH

Oltan Dogan – minister of defense

Recep Tayyip Erdoğan – president of Turkey

CHAPTER 1

Fire burst over the desert as the sun broke the horizon. Bright orange at the edges, blood red below. The heat radiating from the glow cut subtly into the cool of the desert. Crisp, fresh, unpolluted air bit at the lungs, reminding one that they were alive and it was another day.

"There is nothing as beautiful as a desert sunrise," Adira Halevi said, leaning tighter against her man. "You were right, *motek*."

Yossi Hirschfield, who was the back half of the spoon on the dusty ground, squeezed her bare shoulder a little tighter, replying, "I always am."

Adira chuckled and turned her head to give him a little kiss.

This is a moment, Yossi thought, as the bass thumped from the speakers behind them. *The only thing that could make this better is if it was just the two of us. This might even be the time I'd finally ask her to make things a little more permanent.*

But it was far from just the two of them out in the Western Negev. Three thousand other sun worshippers surrounded them; some were dancing in front of the stage, some slept or had passed out on the ground or in tents, some were huddled with Yossi and his girlfriend, watching the birth of a new day.

Behind him, someone started swearing, totally breaking the mood. He turned to tell the guy to shut up but saw him pointing into the sky. Dozens of bright lights were soaring through the air, seeming to float toward them from the direction of Gaza. Yossi was so glad that he and Adira had that moment with the sunrise because it was suddenly quite evident to him that the party was at an end.

It had been just over two months ago that Adira had told him about the Supernova Sukkot Gathering, better known as the Tribe of Nova Festival, down in the Negev. He had heard of Nova and its ties into the drug-laced trance culture. Electronic music, black lights, love, peace, and nature, all blended with a dose of Eastern mysticism and a steady supply of Molly, or MDMA.

Initially, Yossi was unsure about going. The event seemed kind of weird, and he wasn't sure he wanted to be around a bunch of drugged-out hippies. This was despite the fact that, if asked, he would likely admit to being a bit of a hippie himself. But his greater concern was that it was being held only about five kilometers from the border with Gaza. After wrestling with the decision a bit, he came to the conclusion that, based on history, the worst that might occur is that they'd have some rockets fired their way. If that happened, they'd all bug out and head home. Besides, he'd been forced to say no to Adira so many times lately because of his job, sometimes at the last minute. She always seemed to understand, but still. It was obvious that she really wanted to go, and he kind of owed her this one.

Yossi Hirschfield was an intel analyst for the Mossad, assigned to assist a specific team of Kidon agents. When the Israeli intelligence service, Mossad, wanted a person or persons eliminated, it passed the operation down to Caesarea. And when Caesarea needed the job done immediately and with absolute finality, it passed the assignment on to Kidon. Yossi was not part of Kidon's tip-of-the-spear wet work. His job was back in CARL. He always smiled when he thought of CARL. He and his offbeat fellow analysts had spent a lunch hour wrestling with what to call their workroom. At the end of the break, they had settled on the acronym CARL. What did the letters stand for? Absolutely nothing. But those in CARL were the only ones who knew that, and as a result, the cryptic acronym had been the subject of many water-cooler discussions throughout the Mossad compound.

The couple made the 90-minute drive from Tel Aviv to Re'im on October 6, arriving a little after dark. The rave was already in full gear, and it took them about 15 minutes to hike in from where they had to park their car along the side of the road. It would have been impossible for anyone to miss the location of the party—as they trekked the dirt path, a glow rose into the sky and the rapid, steady beat from the electronica carried through the cool desert night.

A couple minutes was all it took for Adira to start getting a little groove to her walk. Turning, she grabbed Yossi's hands, and they danced as they hiked. She was beautiful—jet black hair, olive skin, her face showing heavily her father's Grecian background. When she moved, it was with a dancer's grace, showing off her long legs and bare torso. For his part, Yossi's long, light brown hair and matching hipster-length beard caught the wind as he spun her and dipped her.

The two moved and swayed until Yossi took hold of her shoulders and kissed her. They stood that way in the middle of the road with their lips locked and their bodies pressed together, until he once again felt her hips begin to move back and forth. She pushed him back with a laugh, lifted her arms above her head, and started grooving to the beat. Yossi, who was no slouch on the dance floor, joined her, and they continued on their way.

The festival was mayhem, but it was a controlled "everybody loves each other" kind of mayhem. It made Yossi think of the spirit of Woodstock, only with glow sticks and ecstasy instead of mud and LSD. Everyone was moving, everyone was smiling—one big happy family.

There were two dance floors, and Adira and Yossi made their way to the larger one. Very soon, they were jumping and bumping with hundreds of their new best friends as a DJ he had seen on viral TikTok posts controlled the crowd from up on stage. They had been there only about ten minutes when Adira said something to him that he couldn't understand, then slipped away.

Fifteen minutes later, she was back, carrying two small drink cups. He took one from her and was about to toast her when she reached into her pocket and brought out two little green pills with a yin-yang symbol pressed into them. She raised her eyebrows at him, and he shrugged his shoulders. Neither one of them regularly took drugs. In fact, if Nir Tavor, Yossi's boss at CARL, knew about him popping this tablet of MDMA, he would probably force him to type "I will not take Molly" 10,000 times on his computer without the benefit of cut and paste. But his team had just finished an operation, and he wasn't due back to work for three more days. When in Nova, might as well do as the Nova-ites do.

CHAPTER 2

Yossi popped the pill into his mouth, then swallowed it down with whatever horribly sweet alcoholic drink was in his cup. Taking Adira's cup and adding it to his, he crumpled them and tucked them into his crossbody waist pack. These love-and-nature Nova events were probably the only mass parties where the sites looked better when everyone left than when they first arrived.

Several years back, Yossi and a group of his friends had gone backpacking in the Italian Alps without allowing their systems time to acclimate to the altitude. The weird, floaty euphoria he felt from that oxygen deprivation was like the wimpy little brother to the effect the Molly brought on him. He was laughing. He was dancing without any inhibitions. At some point, he met a guy from Morocco, but then the dude ran off. Then this girl came up and kissed him full on the lips before dancing to the next guy and kissing him. Later, he found himself very upset and scrambling around on his hands and knees, looking for the rubber band he'd lost while resetting his man bun. Hours later, when his head began clearing and the synapses in his brain started firing to the needs of his body rather than the beat of the bass, his first thought was *Yeah, I'm never doing that again.*

Sometime during the night, he had lost Adira. Their designated meetup for such an occasion was an artists' tent where people were getting their nature on through paint. Pulling back the flap, he spotted her stretched out on a blanket next to some old guy's easel. Yossi walked over.

"She yours?" the man asked without taking his eyes from his canvas.

"She is." Yossi squatted down to brush her hair back from her face.

"When she came in, she wasn't making too much sense. Said something about her boyfriend calling the Mossad to track her down. You the boyfriend?"

Yossi cringed when he heard "Mossad." Being part of Israeli intelligence is like being part of Fight Club; the first rule of Mossad is that you don't talk about Mossad.

"Yeah, and I've got Eli Cohen infiltrating the rave," Yossi answered, saying the last part in a whisper. Every Israeli knew about Eli Cohen, who, in the early 1960s, penetrated the shell of the Syrian government and was later hanged for doing so.

The old man smiled at the reference, then nodded to Adira as he swirled his brush into a dollop of sea blue. "Keep her away from the pills. I know this is rookie night, but they aren't doing her any favors."

"Her and me both," Yossi said, reaching up to fist-bump the man's brush hand. He gently shook Adira's shoulder until she opened her eyes. Her first words were, "Never again."

He smiled as he helped her to her feet. The two of them were so much alike. She had to be the one for him. After Adira hugged the old artist, the two young lovers left the tent. Both were pretty much done with the party, but Yossi insisted they stay for sunrise. They could not make the long trip down to the Negev without watching the sun break the plane of the desert floor.

The next several hours passed slowly. They stayed for the most part on the edge of the action, although every now and then a groove would get them going and they'd step back onto the dance floor and into the fray. But mostly they sat on the ground, leaning against each other and talking about the future.

When it was time for the new day to begin, Yossi walked Adira to a place east of the grounds, where they could get an unobstructed view of the earth's personal star making its grand entrance. It was perfect.

But then the idiot Gazans decided to fire off a barrage of rockets.

Seriously? What were they hoping to hit with their trash missiles? Most will probably land on their own homes.

Adira had done her mandatory military service in the north near Syria, so she was used to seeing these Katyushas. "That's a pretty heavy salvo," she said. "Not their usual five or ten."

They watched as the bright lights arcing through the dawn sky went out abruptly one by one. Seconds later, boom, boom, boom echoed across the open land from the Iron Dome missiles intercepting their targets.

A voice called out over the sound system's speakers. "Red alert! Red alert! Everyone down!"

Red alerts had become commonplace in Israel. Whenever one of Hamas's or Hezbollah's rockets actually made it across the border, a siren would sound in whatever city, town, or kibbutz might be in its way. That would be the signal for every Israeli to drop what they were doing and find the nearest bomb shelter. If you weren't in a place that had bomb shelters—say, at a rave in the middle of the desert—you knew to drop to the ground and lie flat.

Yossi and Adira obediently lowered themselves to the dirt. But rather than going flat, Yossi laid on his side facing east. He pulled Adira close to him and they spooned there on the desert floor, watching what remained of the sunrise.

That's when the guy next to him swore and pointed to the sky.

CHAPTER 3

06:25 (6:25 AM) IDT

The party was over. That was confirmed when the voice came back on the speakers a couple minutes later. Everybody had to go home immediately.

A collective groan sounded throughout the crowd. Nobody wanted the good times to end. As the sun had been rising, Yossi had felt a weird certainty that it was an omen of sorts. It spoke of his future with Adira and the life they could share together. It spoke of new life and children and maybe even grandchildren someday. He had been formulating in his mind just the right words to let her know what he was thinking. But now that would have to wait for another time.

He kissed the back of her head as it lay on the arm he had stretched out as a pillow for her. "I guess that means us."

"Can't we wait a little longer?" she asked, pulling his other arm tighter around her body. But already, people were on their feet and moving.

"I'd love to, but if we stay here much longer, we're liable to get trampled to death." He stood, then helped Adira to her feet. As they both stretched, Yossi got his bearings.

Unsurprisingly, no one was rushing. The chances of one of those rockets reaching them was miniscule. How would Hamas even know about Nova? It wasn't like the producers of the rave would have blanketed Gaza with posters. No, if there was anyone targeted, it would likely be the nearby Kibbutz Re'im.

Then again, anyone within five miles of the target of a Hamas rocket better watch their back. There's a much better chance of them being hit than the place where it was aimed.

All around, people were talking and laughing as they made their way toward the edges of the camp. There were no loud complaints about the cancellation. No yelling or screaming. Early shutdowns were eventualities that Israelis experience throughout their lives. Everyone had felt the sadness of a picnic in the park being shortened or a concert being canceled or a school play getting shut down because one terrorist group or another felt that it was the appropriate time to send off another rocket.

"I don't want this moment to end," said Adira, taking Yossi's hand as they walked.

"Well, we need to go. But there's nothing that says we need to do it quickly." He imitated the deep bass line and the two of them began dancing. Soon, three or four others joined them. When he ended, the strangers fist-bumped him and went on their way.

Adira grabbed Yossi's arm with her other hand. "Hey, let's go by the artists' tent again. I want to thank that man one more time. I can't imagine what I was like when I stumbled in there."

They made a slight shift to their trajectory and weaved their way through the slowly moving mass of people. When they arrived in the tent, most of the artists were still in the process of packing up their gear. They spotted their new friend and went over to him.

"If it isn't my little lost desert flower," the artist said with a smile.

Adira answered him with a hug.

"Well, that's a greeting I'll take any day," he said, wrapping his arms around her but not quite touching her. Adira, though, went in for the full grab, not noticing the stray paint blotches that decorated his shirt.

"Thank you again! I don't know what I would have done without you," she said.

When she stepped back, Yossi held out his hand. "Yeah, thank you so much, Mister…"

"Sharabi. Asa Sharabi," he answered, without taking Yossi's hand. "Sorry, I still haven't cleaned myself off. And you, little flower, may take back your gratitude after you see what hugging me has done to your clothes. I tend to get a little messy when I work."

Yossi looked at the fresh blue, red, and green blemishes that now flecked Adira's tan shirt and bare torso.

"I don't know. It looks kind of fashion forward to me," he said. He began with his bass line again, and Adira broke into a runway strut across the floor of the tent.

"Beautiful," laughed Sharabi as she walked back. "Maybe instead of painting, I should be designing clothing."

Yossi introduced himself and Adira, then offered to help carry the artist's equipment to his car. Sharabi readily accepted, saying it would save him a second trip.

Ten minutes later, Yossi was gently placing a wooden easel in the back seat of Sharabi's vehicle, while Adira and the artist filled the trunk with his supplies and a still-drying canvas. Once all was closed up, they met by the driver's door.

Sharabi pulled a card from his wallet and offered it to Yossi. "I have a gallery in Ein Hod near Haifa. If ever you are in the area, I'd love to show you around."

Adira snatched up the card. "I know Ein Hod. We'd love to come."

"Then I look forward to seeing you there." They said their good-byes and Sharabi got in his car. Unfortunately, the traffic had become so backed up by that time, it was unlikely he would be moving anywhere soon.

They were about five minutes south of the party site, and Yossi's car was a fifteen-minute walk north of Nova. He turned to begin the journey, but Adira didn't move.

"*Motek*, what are those?"

Yossi turned and looked to the west. When his eyes finally focused on what she was pointing at, he realized that their situation had just gotten much more dangerous. He quickly began unzipping his waist pack. "We need to move, Adira. Now," he said, as he pulled out his phone and speed-dialed a number.

CHAPTER 4

The taller masts were just becoming visible in the distance. Probably only another kilometer until halfway. Once Nir Tavor reached the marina on the southern edge of Herzliya, he'd swap out the sandy shoes he was wearing for the clean pair in his backpack. Then he'd jog cement paths and roads for the five-and-a-half kilometers back to his car parked just this side of the power station at the north end of Tel Aviv. When he first attempted this route, he had run barefoot in the Mediterranean sand. It took less than two kilometers before his calves burned and he felt like his ankles were going to break. Lesson learned.

Later this morning, he was booked for a flight back to Brussels. From there he'd take the train to Antwerp and his European home. In the past, he'd always relished his times not too many kilometers from the eastern shore of the Atlantic, where he lived his life dealing in precious stones. But the appeal was wearing off. There was so much going on in his home country of Israel. Every time he had flown out lately, he felt as if he was shirking his duty by going off to live the good life in Europe.

The music in his earbuds faded as an electronic voice alerted, "Call from Yossi."

Nir double tapped his right earbud, sending the call to voicemail. The music, a song by an Israeli rapper named Tuna, rose back up.

But it wasn't like he was abandoning his country. Hadn't he just two days ago returned from leading a Kidon operation in Cyprus? Some Turkish mechanical engineer needed to be encouraged to offer his talents to someone other than the Iranian government. Nir and his team had employed their own brand of persuasion, and the man had quickly acquiesced. But now, while the rest of the team stayed here in the country, their leader was jetting off once again.

Maybe it's time to get out of the diamond business. I already have more money than I need. I claim that it's my cover, but really, it's become my comfort. When's the last time I used my diamond-broker alias? Almost a year ago in Russia. And before that? At least a few years.

Tuna faded again, and the electronic voice repeated, "Call from Yossi."

Dude, I'm working out.

He double-tapped the earbud. The rapper came back up.

It used to be that Nir took every call that came his way. That led to his workouts becoming hours long, filled with starts and stops as he dealt with issues that could easily have waited. Out of frustration, Nir decided that only two people would be allowed to interrupt his jogs— Efraim and Nicole. Efraim Cohen was his best friend and his superior at the Mossad. Nicole le Roux was…

What is she? The best analyst I know. The most beautiful woman I've ever met. The only Jesus-follower I can tolerate listening to for more than five minutes. The love of my life, who is breaking my heart because she's letting her Christian convictions come between us.

Nir shook the thoughts from his mind and focused on the music. This guy had some deep lyrics. Besides, it was too beautiful a morning to let himself go down the Nicole rabbit hole. As soon as the Cyprus operation ended, she had hopped a flight back home to Milan, where she had a photo shoot for some cosmetics company. He had no idea when he would see her again.

Half a kilometer to go. Nir took a sip from a straw that led to a water pouch in his backpack.

The music faded and a voice said, "Call from Yossi."

Nir tapped the earbud once. His frustrated tone showed a little more than he intended when he blurted, "*Achi*, I'm in the middle of a workout. Can I call you back?"

"Sorry, boss, I wouldn't be bugging you if I didn't think it was important," Yossi replied.

Nir sighed. "You're right. *Ta'ut sheli*. What's up?"

"Adira and I are down at the Nova rave in the Negev."

"Heard about it. You staying away from the Molly?"

Yossi's pause was as good as an admission of guilt.

Yeah, we're going to talk about that when I see him next.

"Let's just say it's been a crazy time. Anyway, we were watching the sun come up when suddenly a huge barrage of rockets came flying out of Gaza. Not unusual, I know. But some of them seemed to be coming our way, which was weird."

Nir slowed his pace down to a walk. "Why would they target a party? Did anything make it through?"

"Not that I could tell. Looked like the dome took most of them down. So they called a red alert, then told us all to bug out."

"Probably smart." Nir tried to picture the notice about the rave that had popped up as an ad on his social media. "You're where? Re'im, right? I'm going to give Efraim a call and see if he knows what's going on."

"Yeah, Re'im. But there's something more. We're looking toward Gaza and we're seeing these things in the sky coming our way. They're too low and slow to be rockets. They almost look like parachutes. But they're moving parallel to the ground instead of vertically. And the weirdest thing is that there are people on them. They've got me a little creeped out."

Parachutes traveling parallel to the ground? What the heck?

Nir began cutting up toward the road. "*Achi*, I'm not liking this. Can you hear anything?"

Again, Yossi paused. "There's too much noise here. Everyone is trying to head out, so it's all car engines and horns honking."

What kind of parachute travels parallel?

All Nir could picture were the parasailers off the shore in Tel Aviv. But Yossi was in the desert.

His analyst's voice interrupted him. "Nir, some guy here just said they're gliders. I think he's right. Again, it's too loud here to hear them, but it looks like there's an engine below the parachute, and someone is sitting in front driving it."

Why would gliders be carrying people from Gaza?

Then it hit him. "Yossi, you and Adira get out of there now! Tell me, do you have earbuds?"

"*Motek*, we need to move faster. Hurry!" Nir heard Yossi's breathing begin to accelerate. "I've got earbuds, boss."

"Put one in and leave this call open. If we get cut off, call me back. If it sounds like I'm gone, it's because I'm talking to Efraim. Run, brother, and don't stop until you're out of there."

Nir heard Yossi tell Adira to hold his phone for him. After finally reaching the road, Nir stopped and got his phone out of his pocket. He was about to switch lines to call Efraim when he heard the pop of gunfire through his earbud.

CHAPTER 5

06:50 (6:50 AM) IDT

Nir speed-dialed Efraim Cohen. As the Mossad's assistant director of Caesarea, his friend had to know what was going on.

The phone rang once, then twice, while Nir waved to a passing car. With a frightened look, the woman driving passed him. Nir's call went to voicemail.

"One thing I can be sure of with Efraim. He's not out jogging," Nir muttered to himself, picturing his friend's gradually softening physique.

The second car he waved to pulled to the curb just past him. Opening the door, Nir found a man who appeared to be in his sixties wearing a button-down shirt and a yarmulke.

"I need you to take me to my car immediately," Nir said.

"Get in," the man replied with a deep voice that spoke of years of tobacco addiction. Nir obeyed. The smell in the car confirmed the man's long-standing habit. Odor aside, the interior was spotless and Nir got the impression that the man had probably bought the 20-year-old-plus Toyota when it was new.

Nir dialed again and listened to the ringing. The driver remained silent. That was one thing that Nir knew he could count on. Every Israeli had served in the military. Thus, every Israeli had at some time received unexplained orders they were expected to obey, a mindset that typically carried into civilian life. This wasn't simply blind obedience to authority. Instead, it came from recognizing that Israel is a country surrounded by enemies, who every now and again will get on the wrong side of the border and attempt nasty things. It was obvious Nir's driver understood this was one of those times, and that his passenger was involved in doing something to stop it.

Nir swore. The call had gone to voicemail again.

Quit screening my calls, ahabal.

He ignored the twinge of irony as he dialed a third time. "I'm parked by the power station. You have to take a few dirt roads to get there," he said to the driver.

"I know the area," the man replied, keeping his eyes on the road.

When Efraim finally answered, his tone made it perfectly clear that he had stuff to do and whatever Nir had to say was not part of it. "I can't talk. We've got something going here." Shouting voices on the other end of the call made it difficult for Nir to hear his friend.

"Let me guess. Gaza is popping off and you've got border breaches."

"How…?" Efraim paused. Nir heard a door open and slam, immediately shutting out the surrounding din. "Tell me what you know."

Nir filled him in on Yossi's situation.

"Gliders?" Efraim asked. "Like towed-by-airplanes-then-released gliders?"

"No, the parachute kind with the three-wheeled thing underneath holding an engine."

"They're called powered parachutes," said the man behind the wheel. Nir turned to him, but he kept his gaze forward. "I saw it on TV. They're powered parachutes."

"My driver says they're called powered parachutes."

When Efraim responded, his volume and pitch both increased. "Your driver? Where are you, and why do you have someone listening in on this call?"

Nir's voice matched his friend's. "I'm about fifteen minutes away from you, and I don't have much choice. Now, tell me what you know."

Efraim hesitated. "Can he hear my side of the conversation?"

"I'm on an earbud," Nir assured him.

"Okay. All of our southern observation posts were hit simultaneously, taking out our eyes on the border. Then the rockets started flying."

"So you thought diversion for the north," Nir said. "Makes sense." He glanced at the driver, who continued looking straight ahead. *Oh well, in for a shekel...*

"Right. We both know the Gazans can't coordinate their efforts enough to field a short-handed football team. So, we've been rolling assets north. Only..."

"Only there's nothing going on up in the north, is there?" Nir interrupted.

"*Bul.* Not a sound. We don't even have an indication that Hezbollah has a clue that Hamas is getting stupid in the south."

"So, what is the...?"

"Shut up a second." The door that Efraim had ducked out through had obviously been opened again because the shouting was back. The ambient sound was muffled, but not enough for Nir to miss Efraim beginning to curse.

Nir pointed to where his car was parked, and the man angled toward it.

Suddenly, the sound through his earbud cleared up. When Efraim spoke, Nir could hear panic in his voice. "I've got to go, *achi.* They are pouring across the border and heading for the kibbutzim. Dozens of them, maybe even hundreds."

"What about Yossi?"

"Feed me everything he reports to you. And, Nir, tell him he needs to run." Efraim hung up.

The driver had stopped, and Nir reached for the door handle. Before he could pull it, he felt the man's hand grab his arm with a surprisingly strong grip.

"I don't know what is happening, and you know that I will speak to no one of this chance meeting. Just tell me, I have family south in Sderot. Will they be okay?"

Nir looked at the man, wishing he had hope to give. But the fact was he was so deep in the fog of war that he could neither give worry nor hope.

"Just pray, my friend. Just pray."

Nir tugged the handle and jumped out of the car. As he did, he hit a speed-dial number.

After one ring, Yaron Eisenbach, the number two on his ops team, answered, "Go."

"I need you to get everyone together," Nir said as he slid into his Mercedes. Immediately he cursed himself for forgetting to lay down a towel as a barrier between his sweaty body and the leather seats. "Ops and analysts. Get everyone to CARL immediately."

"Got it."

"And don't bother with Yossi. I'll tell you about him when I get there."

Yaron hung up. Nir tossed his phone onto the passenger seat and took a second to breathe and think.

Re'im is about 90 minutes away. That's a long drive if this actually does turn into anything. Maybe I can convince Efraim to requisition a Blackhawk for us, or even just a police chopper.

He glanced at the phone and wondered if he should call Nicole. There was nothing she could do, but she did like to pray, and prayer never seemed to be a bad thing. But, ultimately, he decided against it. The news would only make her worry, and she had her own work to do.

Taking a deep breath, he picked up the phone and clicked back into Yossi's call.

CHAPTER 6

NOVA MUSIC FESTIVAL—07:00 (7:00 AM) IDT

The dusty road was filled with cars, and not one of them was moving. Dozens of young men and women were half-crouched around their vehicles, confused about what to do or which way to run.

Where's Nir!

Yossi glanced at his phone again, just to confirm that the line was still open. It was. Another series of gunshots sounded back at the party site, causing everyone to drop lower. By the sound of it, a massacre was taking place in and around the dance floors. The cracks of the rifles had begun right after Nir had clicked off and were steadily increasing as more and more terrorists were arriving.

As an analyst, subtle variations in data or visuals stood out to Yossi. That's what made him so good at his job. Being able to tune in to the details, unfortunately, also carried into what he now heard. Squatting down by the cars, he could distinguish three different kinds of screams coming from the festival grounds. The first was terror. It echoed out but was typically silenced by gunfire. Groaning and cries for help accompanied the second kind. These had to have been the wounded and the dying. Many of them, too, were silenced mid-cry. The third type of scream, though—those were the ones that made him pull Adira closer. They were mostly female and were haunted with anguish, pain, and misery. It was these screams that lingered on and on and on.

His earbud pinged.

"Yossi, sitrep," Nir inquired, looking for a situational report.

"It's *al hapanim*, man. A total nightmare. There are dozens of gunmen here and they're slaughtering everyone still left at the site. Constant gunfire. And, *achi*, it also sounds like they're taking their time with some. Torturing. Raping. The screams, dude…" Yossi's voice caught.

"Stay with me, *achi*. What's it look like for getting out of there?" Nir's voice exuded confidence, and Yossi tried to strengthen himself with it.

"*Ein matzav.* There's no way. The roads…" A small explosion back at the rave site caused everyone to drop to the ground. "The roads are backed up. No one is driving out. A few minutes ago, I heard the sound of dirt bikes, and I saw a lot of dust in the air on the other side of the grounds. I think the dirties are completely mobile."

"Where are you?"

"We're on the side of the road. Maybe ten minutes north of the site. I know there's security back there, but I think they're overwhelmed. I feel like I need to go back in there and try to do something." Adira spun around and looked at him with wide eyes.

"No," Nir yelled. "You will not go back in; do you hear me? The numbers are impossible. You have one person to save in all of this, and I'm assuming she's right next to you. She is your only responsibility, and I expect you to protect her with your life. Do you understand?"

When you can't save them all, save who you can.

Yossi remembered that from a late-night session in the IDF between his squad and his sergeant. If he went back in, he would certainly die, and it was likely Adira would too. But he had a chance now to save her and maybe some others.

"*Avarnnu et par'o, na'avor gam et ze,*" Yossi replied, pulling Adira into an embrace. "I'll protect her the way Moses protected the people."

A wave of partygoers began sweeping past them from farther up the road. Adira grabbed a girl to ask her what was going on.

Yossi missed the girl's reply as Nir said, "Good. Now tell me, do you see any other dust clouds anywhere, either near or far?"

"Hang on, Nir. Adira, what's going on? Why are these people coming back this way?"

"The road is blocked ahead. People are being killed up there. There's no getting through to the north."

Yossi passed the information on to Nir.

The analyst could hear his boss pound the steering wheel. But when Nir came back on, his voice was calm. "Okay. Tell Adira good work." A car horn blared through the earbud. "*Ahabal*," Nir called out. A moment later he was back on. "Sorry, *achi*. Listen, I need you to be my eyes and ears there. Anything remotely interesting, you report to me. Then I'll pass it along to Efraim. But remember—and I want to make sure you fully understand this—information gathering is your secondary job. What is your number one responsibility?"

Yossi put his arm around his girl one more time. "Get Adira home safely."

"*Sababa*. Now, you've got to get away from there. You need to run to the east. West is Gaza, and north and south…It's looking like Hamas is smarter than we've given them credit for. If they have any brains at all, they'll have blocked the road south, also. Then they'll slowly close the noose until you're all fish in a barrel. Your only chance is to outrun them to the east."

"We can't outrun dirt bikes," Yossi replied, seeing more dust clouds approaching the Nova site.

"You're right, you can't. If you sense they're catching up to you, then hide in the scrub. Staying where you're at now, though, will certainly get you killed. North, south, and west will get you killed. East is your only option. Now get going and keep this call open."

A click in his earbud told Yossi that Nir had switched to another line.

"We've got to go east," he told Adira, pointing to his right. Then, cupping his hands around his mouth, he called out, "East! We've got to go east!"

Some people immediately began running into the fields in the direction of Yossi's finger. Others yelled angrily at him, saying that his way would get them killed. "No, listen! I swear! I'm on with special forces," he called out, pointing to his earbud. "Our only way out is east!"

A handful more listened and took off running, but there were still many who cursed him and his recommendation, vowing to stay with their cars until they could drive to freedom.

Adira tugged on Yossi's arm, and he began running with her. The field felt like fallow farmland. The dirt was loose but not deep. You had to watch your step so that you didn't twist your ankle in a rut. They were maybe a minute into traversing the open space when gunfire erupted, and Yossi watched as one, two, four, six people dropped to the ground.

"Run, *motek*, run," he called out to Adira, shifting his position so that he was between her and Nova.

The gunfire increased. Shot after shot. Every step Yossi took felt like it would be his last. Then Adira cried out and plunged to the ground, her momentum rolling her over and over.

CHAPTER 7

Yossi dropped to the dirt next to Adira. She was screaming, which brought an odd sense of relief. At least she was alive.

"I've got you, *motek*. I've got you," he said soothingly as he reached for her right leg. He hadn't needed to look hard for her wound. The rear part of her foot between her ankle and her heel was pretty much gone. What was left brought bile up into his throat. Around him, the gunfire continued. Adira wasn't the only one screaming.

Think, think!

There was no way she could walk. They were in the middle of an open field. Behind them, terrorists were firing automatic weapons in their direction. Ahead of them, the field was open for the next 500 meters, at least.

Adira was saying something to him, and he looked down at her. "Am I going to die, *motek*? Am I going to die?" She grabbed him by the shirt as she repeated the phrase over and over.

Smoothing her hair back, he took her head firmly in his hand. "You are not going to die, my love. I will not let that happen." Then his voice softened, and he held her cheek with his hand. "But it's going to hurt, babe. There's nothing I can do about that."

As evidence, a fresh wave of pain caused Adira to cry out. Yossi held her to his chest.

When he laid her back down, she pleaded, "Promise you won't leave me here, Yossi!" Her eyes were big, and her breathing was rapid. Unless he calmed her, she would begin to hyperventilate. "I heard the screams, Yossi. I know what they're doing. Please don't leave me."

Locking with her eyes, he said, "I will never leave you. Do you hear me? Besides, Nir gave me one job, and I always follow my orders." He winked, and she smiled weakly.

Another wave of pain hit her, and she wrapped her arms tightly around his neck. He held her firmly until her breathing began to slow again. Finally, she released him and said softly, "So, you're just following orders?"

"What?" Yossi saw a strained smile on Adira's face, and his love for her grew even more. He kissed her on the forehead, then on her lips. Then he put her back down.

"I'm sorry, *motek*. This is going to hurt," he said as he pulled his T-shirt over his head. "I'll do what I can, but there is no way around the pain. Try to think of something different. Think of our future house, and what our firstborn will look like." He tried to ignore the sounds of the gunfire as he used a pocketknife to cut the shirt into strips. Then he began to wrap up her foot. Adira shrieked and her hand grabbed tightly onto his calf. "I'm sorry, baby. I'm sorry," he repeated as he wound the strips around her destroyed heel.

When he was done, he turned back to her.

"*Tembel*," she said, trying to force a smile.

Yossi feigned offense, then returned a sad smile. "Yeah, I deserved that one. Okay, now we need to go."

She shook her head. "I don't think I can walk."

"Don't worry, *motek*, I'm your personal Uber." Reaching under her back and legs, he lifted her up. She stiffened with the pain as she slid her arm around his neck. "Oof, you had to have those falafels at the snack tent, didn't you?" Yossi groaned.

"Oh, don't make me laugh," she said, wincing as he took his first step.

Yossi was a strong surfer with lean, muscular legs and a well-toned upper body. He also had an incredible sense of balance, which was helpful as he made his way across the uneven ground.

The gunfire began to fade, an indication that they were not being followed. All around, others were hurrying past. Every now and then, one would say, "May God bless you and strengthen you," and other words to that effect.

Yossi didn't know how long Adira would survive without getting to a doctor. Already she had bled through the makeshift T-shirt bandage, but at least the wound hadn't started to drip yet. He also didn't know how long he had. His superhuman adrenaline strength was wearing thin. While Adira was on the small side and very fit, carrying anyone for a long period over uneven ground took its toll.

Nir's voice echoed once more in his thoughts. "You have one job." *Yalla! Let's go!*

He pushed on.

It took about ten minutes to make it to the far end of the field. From this point on, it was trees and scrub. Yossi stopped under an acacia tree and set Adira down against its trunk. There were tears in her eyes, and her moaning had been steadily increasing in volume.

As he held her close, she wept into his shoulder, "Oh, Yossi, it hurts so bad." She held him tight, her fingernails digging into his bare skin.

"I know. I know," he said. But the fact was, he didn't know. He couldn't imagine the excruciating pain she was feeling. Judging by her blood loss, he figured she wasn't far from going into shock. He wasn't exactly sure what that meant physically, but based on all the TV dramas they had watched together, he knew it wasn't good.

If only I could ease her pain somehow. Wait…

"*Motek*, listen to me. Do you have any more of the MDMA?"

At first his question didn't quite register with her. Again, he asked, "The Molly—do you have any more?"

There was a guilty look in her eyes as she nodded to her left. "In my pocket."

He reached in and felt two tablets. Resting under the tree had allowed Adira to calm some, and in a strained voice, she said, "I'm sorry. I bought four in case we liked it. But I don't ever want to do that stuff again."

"I know you don't, but listen. I remember reading an article somewhere about people using MDMA as a pain reliever for PTSD patients. I have no idea if it will help you with what you're going through. But it's worth a shot, isn't it? Just this one last time. Then, when we're home, we're done with it forever. Okay?"

Adira whimpered but nodded.

"Okay, work up some spit." Then when she nodded again, he slipped a pill into her mouth. The other he put into his pocket. She swallowed, gagged, then swallowed again. "Good job. Who knows, maybe we'll meet another nice old artist—a sculptor this time?" Adira didn't respond, other than to continue straining through her pain. "Okay, bad joke. Listen, we've got to get going. Hold tight and let me do the work."

Yossi lifted her and began moving. It didn't take long for her groaning to quiet down. Within ten minutes, she hung limply like she was asleep. He couldn't be sure that she wasn't overdosing or hadn't gone into shock, but her breathing seemed okay. Rapid, but steady.

He could still see people running up ahead. As long as he kept them in sight, he figured he was going the right way. But not only was it the right way, it was the only way. Behind them, the dirt bikes had started up again, and he could hear them drawing closer.

CHAPTER 8

CARL, MOSSAD HEADQUARTERS, TEL AVIV, ISRAEL—
OCTOBER 7, 2023—07:15 (7:15 AM) IDT

Nir zigzagged through the halls of the Mossad. It seemed as if everyone alive who had worked for the Mossad at one time or another was in the headquarters and directly in his path. Confusion and desperation showed on many faces. On others, there were tears. Whatever was taking place right now had caught everyone off guard, and it appeared that a lot of innocent civilians were dying as a result.

Arriving at the door of CARL, Nir pressed a card to a pad, and the lock clicked open. As he stepped in, he heard, "Hold that!"

Turning, he saw a late-twenties man with thick black frame glasses and side-parted hair that could probably use a good washing. He wore Birkenstocks, a gift from his friend and fellow analyst Yossi, and a white T-shirt that declared in English, "Vote for Pedro."

"Thanks for rushing in, Lahav," Nir said, propping the door open with his foot.

Lahav Tabib, a brilliant mind who often kept a rather tenuous hold on legal convention, was one of the four offbeat millennials who made up his analyst team. The young man didn't say anything as he passed, but Nir could see that his eyes were red.

Liora and Dafna were already sitting at the conference table, and they gave him tentative waves as he walked in. Liora Regev was a tiny brunette whose sweet was often overpowered by her spicy. Dafna Ronen, however, was pure sharp edge, with enough ink on her body to write a novella.

"Where's ops?" Nir called out.

"They're coming," answered Liora.

Just then, the door burst open. Imri Zaid and Dima Aronov rushed in. Imri was young, bearded, and fit. He kissed Liora on the top of the head as he sat next to her. The two had gotten engaged two weeks earlier, a large group affair, apparently, that Nir had ensured he was out of town for. Dima sat across the table by Lahav. An enormous Russian emigrant, he fit his nickname, Drago, in both looks and attitude.

"Where's Yaron?" Nir asked.

"Just a few minutes out," answered Imri.

"Got it," Nir said, crossing the room to his office door, which he opened long enough to toss his keys on his desk. When he turned back around, the fourth operator entered the room—the new guy.

When Nir had lost a man in Damascus last year, it had taken some time to find someone to fill the cherished teammate's shoes. They were looking for an experienced operator who was tough, unafraid, had strong medic skills, and wasn't a stickler for regulations. After several duds, Efraim had finally sent them Gil Haviv. The assistant deputy director had spotted his name on a roster of recent retirees from Shayetet 13, the deadly batwing special forces of the Israeli Navy. Eighteen months ago, Gil had resigned, deciding that he was done with constant deployments and life-threatening situations. He soon realized that sedentary life didn't suit him. Within three months, his wife had given him an ultimatum: Either he signed up with something or someone that would get him out of the house and out of her hair, or she was going to divorce him. When he heard that the Mossad was looking to replenish their ranks after losing so many agents the previous year in Syria, he put his name in.

Nir had taken to Gil right away, as had the rest of the team. His courage, skill, loyalty, and, most importantly, ability to hold his own with the quirky analyst team had cemented his place as part of the family. As Nir approached the table, he locked eyes with the newbie. What he saw beneath the well-coiffed, precisely shaven exterior was exactly what was reflected in all the others—sorrow mixed with rage.

"Where's Yossi?" asked Dafna, with touches of concern and accusation in her voice.

"I'll get to him when Yaron gets here," Nir answered. "Now, tell me what you know."

"Why can't you tell us about Yossi?" asked Liora.

"I said I'll tell you when Yaron's here," Nir snapped. Then he stopped and took a breath. When he spoke again, he forced calm into his voice. "When Yaron's here, okay? Now, please, fill me in."

Dafna spoke first. "There are reports of kibbutzim being attacked all along the southern fence. There is no estimate on the size of the enemy force, but it's at least in the hundreds."

"Is the IDF engaging them?"

Lahav spoke up, although he kept his eyes on the phone he was scrolling through. "IDF? What IDF? No one was expecting this. The government and generals were all too busy plotting how to get rid of the prime minister, and now those poor settlers are having to fight off an invasion. They don't stand a chance."

Nir knew this was true. Israel was a divided country with a growing number of angry leftists seeking to topple the government.

Maybe that will change now.

"Tell me about what's happening in the north."

As Nir said this, he heard the door lock disengage. Yaron, the bald, weathered veteran of more operations than Nir could count, came storming in, and as he did, he said in his gravelly voice, "The north! There's nothing going on in the north." Getting to his usual chair, he stood gripping its back. "I was just talking with someone in the command chain. He said that when it all started going down, the generals thought Hamas was playing a fake for a northern invasion. Apparently, they forgot that Hamas is too stupid for that kind of strategic thinking. If they look like they are invading from the south, it's because they are invading from the south. *Ahabalim!*" He pulled out his chair and dropped into it.

Nir already knew about the confusion that had sent troops north, so he decided not to pursue it.

"Okay, Nir, Yaron's here. Tell us about Yossi. He's at Nova, isn't he? He told us he might be going," Liora said. Nir assumed the "us" meant her and Dafna.

Nir took another deep breath before answering. Rarely was he emotional, except when it came to his people.

Come on, man, they need to see strength. Suck it up!

"Yossi is at Nova. He's alive, and so is Adira." He paused to let the relief spread through the group. "But it's not good there. He's on the run. There's a massacre taking place. And it's not just killing. They're torturing and they're raping before they kill."

Everyone reacted to that. Dima slammed his fist so hard on the table that an empty metal snack bowl that had been left in the middle of the table bounced up and flipped over.

"Can they get to his car?" asked a surprisingly emotional Dafna. Rarely had Nir seen much out of her other than snark and snarkier.

"The road is blocked north and south, and they're shooting people who reach the roadblocks. Right now, Yossi and Adira are on foot running east. There are hundreds of others who are with them." Pulling out his phone, he said, "Listen, I've got Yossi connected right now. He's keeping his side of the line open. If I put him on, then only encouragement and positive words for him, got it? Dafna, hook my phone into our coms."

Dafna rolled in her chair across the cement floor to her workstation. After a brief flurry on the keyboard, she said, "Go."

"Again, if you feel you have to say something, be brief," said Nir. "He needs to keep situational awareness. Chitchatting with you will just distract him. Understood?"

Nods all around. Nir switched his phone back to Yossi's line.

Immediately, they heard his heavy breathing. "Nir, is that you?"

"I'm here, Yossi. I'm with the gang at CARL."

Everyone shouted a greeting or a "We love you" or a "Hang in there."

Yossi responded with a brief "Hey, guys," then continued, "Nir,

Adira's been hit. Her right foot took severe damage. I'm carrying her now. I gave her a tab of MDMA to help with the pain, but I don't know if that is going to help or hurt."

Lahav clapped his hands, then said, "You did good, *achi*. It won't help with the pain, but it will keep her from being able to fully process what she's feeling. That's bound to help."

"Okay, thanks," said Yossi. "Listen, we got beyond the gunfire, but in the last couple minutes I heard the dirt bikes revving up again. If they come our way, there's no chance I'll outrun them."

A picture popped up stretching across two large monitors hanging above Liora and Dafna's side-by-side workstations. Nir hadn't noticed that Liora had rolled away from the table until she said from her desk, "This is Google Earth of the area east of the Nova site. Fields, then scrub."

Yossi said, "Yeah, exactly. We're in the scrub now. Mostly bushes and acacia trees."

"How many are with you?" asked Nir.

Yossi paused, then said, "At least 300 spread around. Maybe more."

"Can you separate out? Put some distance between yourself and the main pack?"

Yossi was again quiet for a moment, then said, "I…I think so. We're spread pretty wide already, but I suppose I can move to the edges."

"Do that. Then, if you hear them coming, take cover before they see you. Remember, you will bring that girl home."

"Yes, *hamefaked*." Then after a few more exhausted breaths, Yossi added, "Nir, is anyone coming to get us?"

The question stabbed Nir in the heart. As he looked down at the table, he could feel everyone's eyes on him.

"Listen, brother, the IDF is coming your direction. Meanwhile, we're working on a way to get there ourselves. We're not going to leave you there. Got it? You just keep running. I'm going to leave this channel open but muted. If you need me, you just say something."

When Yossi answered, Nir could hear the disappointment in his voice. Despite the logistical impracticalities, it seemed like desperation had him hoping that his brothers on the ops team would somehow come rolling in to save them. "Okay, Nir, I understand. We'll be waiting for you."

Nir picked his phone up off the table and pressed mute.

"Come with me into the hallway," a voice said behind him.

Nir spun around and saw Efraim Cohen. He hadn't heard him come in.

There was so much to do to prepare a rescue operation that normally Nir would have pushed back on his friend. But the look in Efraim's eyes told him that this time, the best course was obedience. He nodded and followed him through the door.

CHAPTER 9

I know what you're going to say," Nir told Efraim as soon as the door closed behind them. The halls were still a flurry of activity, so he kept his voice somewhat quiet.

Efraim spun around to face him. Early forties with a growing paunch, Nir had recently commented to him that he was the perfect illustration of people and their pets looking alike if Efraim's dog happened to be named Ariel Sharon. "Tell me what I'm going to say, Nir."

"You're going to tell me that I can't take a rescue team to get Yossi. Then I'm going to tell you that I am going to take a team. Then we'll go back and forth a little until you give in and arrange a helo for me. So, let's just skip all that crap for time's sake and jump to where you start making calls to requisition what I need."

"Not this time," Efraim said. He crossed his arms as if to emphasize his resolve.

"I thought we were going to skip this part, but okay…Yes, Efraim, we are going to rescue Yossi, and I need a helo."

"Nir, for once just shut up and listen." There was a look in his friend's eyes that he hadn't ever seen before. Sorrow mixed with anger and steel-hardened determination. His arms now uncrossed, and a finger bounced against Nir's chest, emphasizing each pertinent word.

"You cannot, I repeat, cannot take a team out. It won't happen, and I don't have the time for that back-and-forth stupidity you talked about. Instead, let me simply inform you that if you push me any more about taking a team, I swear I will have you escorted out of this building."

The two men stared at each other. Finally, Nir broke and asked, "Why? *Achi*, that's Yossi out there!"

"First of all, I doubt there is a single helo in all of Israel that is not being requisitioned at this very moment by people much farther up the 'I need a helo' chain than you. But it's more than that. It's different this time. Everything is different, and I don't think it will ever be the same." Efraim's hands slid into his pockets. "The stories that are coming in—brother, it's a nightmare. There are thousands of dirties down there and it's free rein. It reminds me of the stories of Rwanda—or even, God forgive me for saying it, the Holocaust death camps. It's a massacre. And that's just from the few reports we've gotten in. I think what we're going to hear and see in the hours ahead will be beyond imagination."

All the news Nir had heard made it clear the situation was bad. But to hear these words from his friend, a man who was not prone to exaggeration, was almost beyond grasping. "Then why aren't we stopping it? Where's the IDF?"

"They're trying to get going, but they got caught flatfooted. It was like when we watched that NBA game a couple nights ago with that one dude. What was his name?"

"Who? Curry?"

"Yeah, Curry. Remember when he did that one move, and the defender collapsed because Curry got him leaning one way, then he cut back the other. Remember what the commentator called it?"

"An ankle-breaker," Nir said, picturing the move. The two of them had jumped up in awe at the fake.

"Somehow, Hamas pulled an ankle-breaker on us. Whether it was on purpose or not, they got us leaning to the north, then they poured over the south. We're just now getting back on our feet and turning our forces around."

One of the most powerful and most advanced militaries in the world, and we let ourselves get fooled by a bunch of genocidal, half-witted terrorists. There's no excuse!

Nir leaned forward so his whisper could still be heard amongst the hallway bustle. "Listen, if the IDF is struggling to get their act together, then isn't this the perfect time for Kidon to do what we do? How many terrorist attacks have we thwarted or turned around?"

Efraim rested his hand on Nir's shoulder. Using the same level whisper, but with a greater intensity, he said, "That's what you're not getting, *achi*. This is not a terrorist attack. This is an act of war! This is an invasion! I don't know if Hamas is thinking, *Oh, we'll finish up then melt back across the border like we always do. Then it will be back to business as usual.* I'm telling you—there will be no more business as usual. This is war!" Efraim declared emphatically.

"Okay, I get it. It's war. But if this really is war, then the IDF needs all the guns and intelligence it can muster. They need us!"

Efraim shook his head. "That's where you're wrong. War is a military venture, and you are not military. We're about to see a massive force going in with big vehicles, large weapons, and thousands of soldiers. You are a small team carrying sniper rifles and very sharp blades. They kill their thousands. You kill the one who leads their thousands. Your time is coming, brother. I promise you that."

"I understand, but what about today? What do we do today, right now?"

Efraim shook his head and leaned his shoulder against the wall. "Today is not your day. It's not your team's day. Today is for taking back our towns and securing our borders. Today is for the IDF. Soon will come the time for vengeance. That will be your day."

Nir knew he was right. But still...

"I made a promise to Yossi, man. We can't just leave him out there. What do I tell him?"

"Tell him the IDF is coming. Tell him to find shelter. Tell him to pray."

The two friends stood still in the busy hallway, staring down at the floor. Finally, Efraim tapped Nir twice on the chest with his fist. "I'll keep you up to date."

"Yeah," said Nir, not looking up as Efraim walked away.

How do I tell Yossi we're not coming? How do I tell my team? The guilt and uncertainty left him rooted to the floor tiles just outside the door to CARL. He might have remained there all morning had not someone barreled into him from behind, almost knocking him over. He twisted in time to catch a young lady from stumbling to the ground. She muttered an apology as he stood her back up and she hurried to catch up with her small group.

I guess that's my sign. God help me—this is not going to be pretty.

Nir pressed his card to the reader and the lock clicked open. He sighed, then walked in, expecting the worst. But nobody seemed to notice his return. All the analysts were at their stations working. Imri had his chair pulled up behind Liora and Dafna and was watching their screens over their shoulders. Dima was standing with one hand on Lahav's chair, leaning over as the analyst pointed to his screen and explained something to him. Yaron and Gil were each absorbed in what sounded like news reports on their phones.

All was quiet except for one sound that echoed through the room. As Nir sat in his chair, folded his arms on the table, and put his head down, the steady sound of Yossi's labored breathing carried through his phone and cut deep into his heart.

CHAPTER 10

NEAR RE'IM, ISRAEL—07:50 (7:50 AM) IDT

How long could he last? Already, Yossi could see that he was lagging behind. The mass of those fleeing were pulling away from him, leaving him a sitting duck.

Fear was setting in, making him anxious and paranoid. Before, he had been acting on adrenaline and instinct. No thinking, just moving. But now he couldn't get out of his mind what it would feel like when the first bullet hit him. Would it be in his back or in his leg? Would it be a gut shot? He had always heard those were the worst. Or would it be to his head? A split second of pain, then you're no more. A little more than a month ago, he and Adira had watched a movie about people who hunted other humans for sport. As they snuggled close to each other with a large bowl of popcorn, they joked together about what it would be like to be human prey. Now, that's exactly what they were.

The chatter of gunfire sounded somewhere behind him—a long burst of automatic weapon fire. His insides clenched as he waited to be hit. *Please don't let it be a gut shot. I don't want to bleed out while I try to keep my intestines in my body.*

Although Yossi wasn't a praying man, he found himself muttering, "If they catch us, please let her die right away. Keep her from their torture and abuse. Then bring your vengeance down on them! Make them pay for their sins."

The roar of motorcycles and staccato of small arms came at him again. But this time it was from his left. A fresh wave of screams carried across the landscape and reached his ears. He cut to the right.

"Nir, you there?"

Adira, who had been passed out in his arms, stirred at the sound of Yossi's voice and opened her eyes.

"That's okay, *motek*, go back to sleep," he said, giving her a reassuring smile. Looking down at her caused him to stumble, but he managed to keep his feet.

Nir answered in his earbud. "I'm here, brother. How're you holding up?"

Ignoring the question, Yossi answered, "Listen, up until now the gunfire has been behind us. But I just heard bikes and guns to my left. Like to the north. And not just back and to the left, but directly to my left." His voice dropped to a forced whisper. "I cut right because, with carrying Adira, I'm falling behind the main group. I'm getting left alone in the open."

"Nova is to the right? I mean, the way you just turned?"

"It is. But that's maybe two or three kilometers back. Maybe a little less."

You idiot! Why didn't you think of Nova being this way instead of just reacting? You're going to get both yourself and Adira killed.

"I don't know, Nir. Maybe it was stupid—"

"No, you did good. You've got to get away from the threat you know so you have time to address the threat you don't know. It's just…" Nir trailed off.

Yossi had heard that sound in Nir's voice before. He got it whenever a thought suddenly occurred to him, and it usually wasn't good. "It's just what? What are you thinking?"

"*Achi*, I'm concerned about a pincer. The fact that they are parallel with you in the north makes me think that they're going to get ahead of the herd and push you all back. I wouldn't be surprised if they're somewhere right ahead of you to the south also. Once they get you surrounded, it'll be a slaughter."

Yossi slowed, then stopped. All around him he heard the sounds of gunshots and engines and screams.

"Then what do I do, man?"

He could feel the panic welling up inside. He was already breathing hard, and now he was starting to have a difficult time getting a full breath.

It's hopeless. We're dead already.

He dropped to his knees and laid Adira down on the rocky ground. He had an overwhelming desire to lay down next to her and wait for the moment when the bullets stole their lives. Closing his eyes, he began to mutter a prayer that he had learned back when he was a kid.

But something was keeping him from focusing on the prayer. A sound buzzing in his ear. Shaking his head, he snapped out of his panic and realized that the noise was Nir's voice.

"Yossi! Yossi!" In the background, he could hear others in CARL calling out his name too.

"I'm here, *achi.*" As he spoke, he slid his arms underneath Adira once again. He stood, groaning as he did so. "Sorry. I think I bugged out there for a minute."

"Understandable, brother. Listen, here's what I want you to do. I want you to find the best hiding place you can in the scrub. You need to get down in there, as deep and as hidden as you can. Then cover yourselves up and wait for the IDF to come."

Yossi started moving, scanning his surroundings for someplace where the brush and the grasses and the trees all met. "What about you guys? Am I going to get a special Kidon operation? Operation Adossi or Yossira or something?"

He meant it as a joke, but when he said it, he knew he sounded desperate. Still, he would have given all he had to hear, "You bet. We're already on our way."

Instead, he heard Liora's strained voice. "Maybe Operation Adira. You'd just be along for the ride." She choked on the last couple words, barely able to get them out.

"*Elef ahuz,*" he said, trying to get the courage back into his tone. "Like you told me, Nir, I've got one job, right?"

"Right, brother. Bring that girl back home. Now find yourself cover. They'll be looking for easy targets, so their eyes will be on the vertical. Get yourself horizontal and you'll be below their sight line."

"On it, *hamefaked.*" Up ahead in the distance, Yossi heard engines.

The southern half of the pincer. Please, God, help me to find cover and find it now!

CHAPTER 11

CARL—08:30 (8:30 AM) IDT

I t's okay, my love. They'll be coming for us soon. I know it hurts. I know. Just hold on. Maybe for our wedding you can roll down the aisle on one of those knee scooter things. Your sisters can decorate it with flowers and ribbons. Maybe we'll even put a little bell on the handlebars."

Yossi's whispers of love to Adira provided a beautifully discordant bed to the analysts' flurry of activity in CARL. Liora and Dafna were scouring all social media sources trying to gather as much information as possible about the attacks. Video posts from the many kibbutzim peppered various platforms, as did video updates from those near Yossi who were also fleeing Nova.

The ops guys had surrounded Lahav's station. They had begun working out potential scenarios for taking out Ismail Haniyeh, the political leader of Hamas who now lived in Qatar, and Yahya Sinwar, the head of Hamas in the Gaza Strip. No directive had been given from the *ramsad* for them to do so, but they figured it wouldn't be long before the head of the Mossad tasked Kidon with those targeted killings. Besides, it gave them a direction to funnel their anger as they listened to their friend try to comfort his wounded girlfriend.

Sitting at the conference table by himself, Nir stewed. If only a fraction of the reports they were hearing were true, this would be the worst terror attack in the history of his country. Incredibly, however, it was becoming more apparent with each new report that not only was more than a fraction true, but that what they were hearing only scratched the surface of what was really taking place in southern Israel.

"Call from Nicole," said a digitized voice through the headquarters' speakers. Nir quickly sent the call to voicemail.

Liora scowled at him from her workstation.

"Not now," he growled. Normally, screening a call from Nicole would have been the perfect opportunity for a heavy dose of Liora's trademark snark. But no one was in a joking mood. The analyst returned to her work.

"Baby, I know. I'm so, so sorry. Just take my hand and squeeze as hard as you can." There was a pause. "Ow, you're breaking my hand with that grip. Maybe that means our sons will be wrestlers." Adira made a soft reply. Yossi laughed quietly. "*Mashu mashu.* You're right. Our daughters will be wrestlers." The sound of a soft kiss was followed by a hushed love song, one Nir had heard on the radio recently.

How did I not know Yossi had such a beautiful voice?

Nir stood abruptly, sending his chair rolling backward across the room. This was ridiculous. They were Kidon. They were one of the most lethal squads in all of Israel. Yet here they were, passively trying to get information and planning out theoretical operations while their team member—their family member—was being hunted by crazy, bloodthirsty terrorists.

"Yaron, phone," he called out.

The ops man reached into his pocket as he turned from Lahav's station and tossed his phone. Nir caught it with one hand then dialed a number.

Efraim answered, "Hey, Yaron, did Nir put you up to calling me with a rescue plan?"

"Where's the IDF?"

"Oh, hey."

Nir perched on the edge of the table. "Yossi is still out there sheltered under a freaking bush. A freaking bush! Where is the IDF?"

Efraim paused. Nir knew he regularly employed this tactic because he thought it would help calm the discourse. What he didn't know was that this subtle manipulation only made Nir angrier.

"Efraim…" he warned.

Beginning his tirade with a curse, Efraim blurted, "I don't know where they are. We're all asking ourselves the same question. It was no more than ten minutes ago that they finally got around to even declaring 'a state of alert for war.'" Nir could picture his friend doing those stupid air quotes like he always did when he used that tone of voice. "I'm telling you, *achi*, they got caught with their pants down. Now they're scrambling to coordinate a response."

"Coordinate a response? What does that bureaucratic horse crap even mean? All I'm asking is that you coordinate me a Yanshuf helicopter, and I'll bring the response."

Apparently that was one step too far, because when Efraim responded, he was matching Nir in tone and volume. "What helicopter? Seriously, what helicopter are you talking about? You think I have a spare one in my garage? Maybe you can get me a pumpkin and I'll bib-bidi-bobbidi-boo it into existence. Quit being an idiot and think for once. When you fly your imaginary helicopter south and you land at the Nova site, what are you going to do against hundreds of terrorists?"

"Oh, I don't know. Maybe before we land, we'll send them a few strafing passes and a couple rockets to get their sorry butts turned around and running for the border fence?"

"Brilliant! And who are you going to shoot at, you *ahabal*?"

"Let me think. How about the terrorists? Yeah, maybe I'll shoot at the terrorists. That sounds like a good plan."

Efraim sighed. "You see? You don't have all the information, so you're just talking out of your butt. Tell me, how are you going to tell the good guys from the bad guys? They're all dressed like civilians. And the ones on the motorbikes and in the trucks? They've got hostages with them. That's why this is such a *balagan*!"

This time it was Nir's turn to pause.

Efraim continued, "*Achi*, this is bigger than Nir Tavor and his Jericho 941 pistol taking on the world. You are as helpless to save Yossi as he is to get to safety."

Nir dropped into a chair. He pushed "end" on his call and dropped the phone onto the table. *Helpless.* What a terrible word. Last time he had felt this powerless in a situation, he was chained to a wall enduring the skills of a master torturer. But he had willingly put himself in that position. He had allowed himself that lack of personal control to further a mission.

Today, helplessness had been forced upon him. This time, it was a team member he was unable to rescue, someone he loved.

He snatched up Yaron's phone and hurled it across the room. It struck a wall and shattered to pieces. He leaned back in the chair and spun to the left. Everyone was looking at him.

Crap.

"Sorry, man," he said to Yaron, who nodded and turned back to Lahav's screens.

You really should call Nicole, he thought. *She always gives you perspective. Besides, she deserves to know about Yossi.*

"Liora, does Nicole know about Yossi?"

Without turning, the analyst answered, "She knows. She said to call when you're ready. She said she's praying."

That's why I don't want to call. I don't need someone to tell me this is God's plan, and it will work out okay. No God would allow this to happen. And, if He did, I want no part of Him.

But he knew he wasn't being fair to Nicole. He wasn't sure how she would explain all this, but it wouldn't just be "Suck it up, Buttercup. He's God and you're not." She'd figure out some way to blend a good God and a bad world, just like she always did.

But there will be time for that later. I just can't right now. And, God, if You are back to listening to my prayers, protect Yossi and Adira. They really need Your help.

Nir put his hands behind his head and stared up at the ceiling. Yossi's soft, melodic voice was letting Adira know that she was his sunshine on a cloudy day. Bringing his hands from the back of his head, Nir covered his face.

CHAPTER 12

NEAR RE'IM, ISRAEL—09:10 (9:10 AM) IDT

I wanna go! I wanna go!"

Yossi covered Adira's mouth with one hand while he held her tightly to his body with the other. "Hush, *motek*, we must be quiet."

Her hands clutched at his shirtless back, tearing deep streaks into his skin.

Twisting her head, she got her mouth free. "We need to go! They'll kill us if we stay! They're going to kill us!" She pushed hard against him and began to scramble up, but he pulled her back down. "Let go of me! We have to go!"

The panic had resurfaced several minutes ago. This was the third time in the last hour she had awoken from a restless sleep with one goal in mind—escape. Thankfully, the field around them had been free of Gazans during each episode. But that was just lucky happenstance.

Motorbikes had passed through the area at least ten times since they'd gotten buried down in the scrub. Two of those drive-bys sounded like they were within meters of the couple's hiding place. Adira's panic, whether it was coming from pain, fear, or a bad reaction to the MDMA, had him panicked. If she freaked out at the wrong time, they were both dead.

"The army is near, sweetheart. They're coming to find us. Nir has sent them on a special mission to rescue us and bring us home. Aren't we lucky to have a friend with such great authority?" he said, brushing her hair with his hand and holding her face to his bare chest. He felt no guilt lying to her. Even though what he said was false, he was still giving her a form of hope. And hope was what was needed to calm her down.

Their hide was horribly uncomfortable. Branches were jabbing his body from all angles and uneven rocks burrowed into his ribs and hip. His back and side were scarred with little pocks and scratches from thorns and briars. Then there were the bugs. He wasn't sure what they were, but evidently there were a lot of them, and they weren't thrilled he and Adira were there. Where his body wasn't hurting, it was itching.

Still, he knew that he was feeling nothing compared to the misery that Adira was experiencing. For the most part, her body was on top of his. He wanted to make sure that she wasn't suffering the same kind of terrain discomfort as he was. He couldn't imagine the pain her wounded foot must be causing her.

Slowly, Adira began to calm down as he whispered words of love and optimistic expectation. Then a burst of gunfire sounded from the distance, and her breathing accelerated again.

"Nir, any news?" He tried to allow gaps between his pleas for updates. But time was so fluid in this small thatch that he didn't know whether he was asking every fifteen minutes or every five.

"Nothing new, brother." Yossi figured there wouldn't be. But hearing Nir's voice strengthened him. It was his one link to the world outside this scramblewood hide. As long as Nir was still there, he knew they were not forgotten. Someone was working to bring them home.

Nir continued. "You got anything to report?"

"Close call not long ago. Still a lot of gunfire. But instead of it being constant, it's coming in bursts. Usually, it's accompanied by screaming. I'm guessing the mass of moving targets has either gotten clear or they're all dead. Now the terrorists are hunting the rest of us like we're gazelles."

As if emphasizing the point, a burst of gunfire erupted, followed by two more series of shots back to back. Once again, Adira tried to push herself up from Yossi, but he held her tight to his body.

"It's okay, baby. They're a long way from here." That was another lie. Those shots sounded no more than 200 meters away. The faint sound of screams and laughter carried across the landscape.

A distant female voice sounded over the phone. Nir passed on the question. "The girls are asking how you and Adira are holding up."

"Me? I'm doing my best to stay strong. But when I hear those bikes coming close, I have a hard time controlling my shakes. Adira, though, is the one I'm worried about. I know the pain is terrible, and I'm having a hard time controlling her panic."

There was a pause, and he could hear another voice in the background. "Lahav is asking if you have another MDMA tab."

"I have one more, but I don't know if what I've already given her is contributing to her anxiety."

"Last time it put her out for a while, didn't it? Maybe that's what's needed to give the IDF time to get there."

Yossi took his hand from Adira's back to reach into his pocket. When he did, two things happened. First, Adira pushed up from him again, shifting the branches he had spread on top of their bodies. Second, the sound of motorbikes reached his ears. Wrapping his arms around her, he pulled her down hard. Adira cried out.

The motorbikes paused.

Adira was in full panic mode again, even as Yossi felt his own pulse increasing.

"I don't want to die! I don't want to die! I don't want to die!" He could feel her body shivering uncontrollably as she repeated this mantra over and over.

"Oh, baby, please be quiet," he whispered into her ear, as he pulled her face even tighter into his chest. "Please be quiet. They're going to hear us."

The throttles on the bikes slowly increased and they drew closer.

Adira began screaming; Yossi's body muffling much of the sound but not all.

The bike engines idled, then shut off.

There were voices speaking Arabic. Yossi heard them saying, "Right there. I saw movement."

"Shhh. Listen…"

Rifles were racked. "You there! Come out!"

Adira cried out.

Yossi heard a hoot. "It's a woman! About time!"

Footsteps approached. Suddenly, the branches were pulled off. Hands reached in and Adira was pulled off Yossi. He grabbed for her, but a rifle butt slammed against his forehead. He fell back to the ground. He didn't stay long. Hands took hold of him, pulled him up, and threw him to the ground outside of the hide. A boot drove into his gut, then another to his chest. Gasping for air, he curled into the fetal position. Another kick connected with his forehead, snapping his head back and graying his vision.

Through the fog he could hear Adira's screams and men's laughter. A hand grasped his hair, lifting up his face. A fist drove into his cheek, driving his head back down. Another lift and another punch. Again, then again. On the fifth punch, he felt bone cracking around his eye. He laid on his side, blood leaking from his nose, mouth, and left eye.

In his right ear, he could hear Nir crying out, "Yossi! Yossi! What's happening?"

A new voice spoke into his left ear. "Want to see what we do to Jewish whores?"

The hand was in his hair again and he was lifted from the ground. A second man was there to help heft him and hold him up.

"Look, doesn't it look like she's enjoying it?"

Yossi closed his eyes, but not fast enough. What he saw…

He cried out and spun free of the two men. This was his last chance to save Adira. But his equilibrium was still gone from the beating. He lost his balance and fell to the ground.

There was laughter, then the kicking began again. Over and over and over.

Finally, it stopped. With Adira moaning behind him, he opened his eyes and tried to focus through the swelling and the blood. When his vision became clear, he saw that he was looking down the barrel of an AK-47.

CHAPTER 13

Y ossi! Yossi! Are you there?" Nir frantically called his friend's name, praying for a response.

Everyone in CARL was still, eyes focused on the giant speaker mounted to the wall as if it could somehow give a glimpse of what was happening near that little patch of scrub in the Negev. Nir could make out the laughter and the voices of the terrorists, but the words were indiscernible. The sound of Adira's torment, however, was crystal clear.

Then there was Yossi. "Umph…Umph…Umph…" With each blow, his reaction was weaker. Finally, the beating stopped, and the room resounded with one rasp followed by the next as the young analyst labored to draw in each successive breath.

Then he spoke, pushing out a phrase after each grating inhalation. "One job…I…I failed."

A gunshot distorted the speakers, followed by a second. When the sounds dissipated, the rasps were gone.

Crying and cursing filled the auditory void. Each analyst and ops member expressed their anger and grief in their own way, with all of them vowing revenge on the pigs who had done this.

Nir continued to stare at the speaker. He knew this wasn't over. Through the expressions of sorrow, he could still hear the assault of Adira.

He sat. Silent. Still. He could feel the tears trailing out of the corners of his eyes.

Gradually, the others began to take notice. When they did, they, too, quieted their heartache. They remained there out of respect for the next 20 minutes. With each cry from Adira and every outburst of laughter from the murdering rapists, Nir's grief grew and his hatred deepened.

Finally, blessedly, there were two shots. Soon after, engines fired up, then faded away.

Everyone remained still where they were.

After several minutes, Nir said, "All of you go home. Your families need you. Make sure you're back here first thing tomorrow. We've got work to do."

Liora and Imri were the first to walk out. The others filed out behind them. Yaron and Gil each placed a hand on Nir's shoulder as they walked by. Then the door closed, and he was alone.

Now that he was by himself, he placed his head into his hands and broke down. Sorrow, guilt, helplessness, anger—it all poured out of him. He allowed himself a few minutes to get it all out before he lifted his head up. Slamming his hand on the table, he shouted, "Enough!"

Deep breath, followed by another, then another.

"Get control of yourself." Nir wasn't in the habit of talking to himself, but he needed something to break through the violence of his thoughts. "You've got people to lead. You've got people to kill. Use the pain to make yourself better, smarter, more determined, more lethal. Make them pay. Every last one of them. Make them pay."

Seeing that his phone still had an open line, he pressed "end." When he did, it brought up his missed calls. There she was.

Nicole. She needs to know. Just please don't give me optimistic happy God crap.

After a couple more breaths to make sure the emotion was all out, he pressed her name on his call list. She answered on the first ring.

"How's Yossi?" she asked. Her South African accent was stronger than usual, as often happened during stressful times.

When he didn't answer right away, she said, "Oh, Nir. And Adira too?"

"They found their hide. He was beaten, then shot. Adira was...these people are animals. It got to the point that I was relieved when they killed her. How sick and twisted is that?"

There was silence. Then Nicole spoke. "No, I get it. I understand. I just...I just can't believe they're gone."

"I know. First, what happened in Damascus last year losing Doron, and now this. I mean, why Yossi? He was such a good guy. Quite literally he'd give you the shirt off his back. And the best analyst I've ever seen at processing through all the data."

"Yeah, he was a bright light in CARL. Always making us laugh. Always watching over Lahav to make sure he didn't get himself fired or arrested."

Nir laughed bitterly. "Yeah, he did a good job of that." They paused in their reminiscences. "I just don't get it. From what I'm hearing, Yossi and Adira are just two stories of hundreds today. Murder, rape, torture, kidnapping—it's all over the south. Today, evil is having a field day, and the bad guys get the win."

Nicole took a breath to talk, but Nir interrupted her. "And please don't give me some optimistic, 'Well, God is still in control, and He'll make it all good.' There is no good in this and I don't know what God was doing today, but He sure wasn't protecting Israel."

There was an edge to Nicole's voice when she replied. "That isn't what I was going to say, Nir. And there is no reason that today of all days you should turn us into adversaries."

Nir leaned back in his chair and rubbed his forehead. "You're right. Sorry."

When Nicole spoke again, her voice was much softer. "You may be surprised to hear that I was going to agree with you. Evil is having a field day today. But from what I've seen in my Bible, especially in the Old Testament, every time someone comes out against God's people, there is a reckoning. Even if it starts as God using some nation to teach Israel a lesson, He'd later punish them for hurting the people He loves."

That set Nir off. "Wait, wait, wait. Are you trying to say that this is all happening because God is teaching Israel a lesson?"

"Nice job completely missing my point, you *yutz*. What I'm saying is that God loves Israel. There's a verse somewhere that says the people who mess with Israel mess with the apple of God's eye. Hamas just poked God in the eye. How do you think He's going to respond?"

Nir pictured God getting poked in the eye. "I can't say exactly, but I certainly look forward to being part of it. Which brings me to another reason why I made this call. I need you here, Nicole. It hasn't been passed down the chain yet, but I have no doubt that while the IDF goes after the snake, we'll be chopping off the snake's head."

"Well, isn't it convenient that I just got off with my agent telling her to cancel all my modeling gigs until further notice. It's not just that you need me there. I need to be there."

Relief filled Nir as he pictured her sitting at her workstation in the corner behind him. "That's great. Thanks, Nicole. First plane out. We'll have your computers booted up and ready when you get here."

"Good," Nicole responded. Then she paused. "I know that I can never fully feel the pain of what you and your fellow Israelis are experiencing. Just know that I am grieving with you."

Nir disconnected the call and set the phone down on the table.

CHAPTER 14

15:45 (3:45 PM) IDT

Nir wasn't sure how long he had sat in the dark listening to updates from the intel department on the secure line through his phone. He knew that hours had passed since he had shut everything down and turned off the lights. His intention had been to go home, but instead, he had found himself back in his chair. Now, he couldn't bring himself to get up from the table. He felt like if he did, it would make the day's events all real. But as long as he stayed where he was, Yossi and Adira would be okay. The families in the kibbutzim would be laughing and playing together. No one would have been kidnapped or tortured or murdered. All he had to do was remain planted in his seat.

The door opened, and a wedge of light entered the black room.

"Nir, you in here?" It was Efraim. Nir had silenced about a dozen calls from his friend over the past few hours.

"Yeah."

"How about I turn on a light so that we're not in the dark?"

"No."

"Fair enough," Efraim said as the wedge of light narrowed, then disappeared. Nir wasn't sure if his friend had left or if he was still in the room. His question was answered when he heard the casters of a nearby chair roll back. Efraim settled in, and the two sat in the darkness.

But only for a minute. It wasn't long until Efraim said, "Okay, this is weird."

A light appeared, and Nir could see that it was coming from the flashlight on his friend's phone. Efraim pulled a ring from the back of the case and propped the phone up with the beam pointing away from them. "That work? Gloominess without the creep factor?"

Nir's gut told him that he wanted to be left alone right now. But a different voice, one coming from his heart, told him this was probably what he needed right now.

"It works," he answered.

They were quiet a minute more. Then Efraim said, "I heard about Yossi. *Achi*, I am so sorry. I loved that guy. Such a free spirit."

"Good lord, I hated that man bun. You're a grown man. Get a haircut."

"Brother, you're just jealous. You grow your hair out, you'll look more like monkey boy than Fabio. And his beard. Perfection. It's no wonder you shaved yours off, having to get shown up by him every time you walked in the office."

Nir nodded. "You're right there. And the guy's balance. I went out surfing with him a few times. *With him* is a relative term. I'd still be trying to paddle myself out and he'd already be on the waves. He was a natural. More graceful on water than on land."

Silence filled the room again.

"Are the reports I'm hearing true? Is it really as bad as it sounds?" Nir asked.

"It is, and it's only going to get worse the more we learn."

Emotion filled Nir. He'd already had his unmanly cry earlier, but he could feel his eyes welling up. "I just don't get it. It's just so barbaric. It's stuff you read about from olden times, like with the Mongols or the Huns. This isn't how you act in the twenty-first century."

"Undoubtedly. The stuff I've seen them doing. The cruelty…"

"Wait—the stuff you've seen them doing?"

"Oh, yeah. You haven't heard? These animals livestreamed the slaughter. We've shut down the internet, but the videos are out there. Cold-blooded murder. Tossing grenades into roadside bomb shelters filled with terrified people. Families getting pulled out of cars and shot down in the street. Homes being invaded. The beatings. The torture. The rapes. The kidnappings. Oh, and do you know what makes this even worse? It wasn't just Hamas doing it. They invited civilians on the border to come along. So you've got old Everyday Ali rushing through the fence, running into a kibbutz, and cutting people down."

Nir's eyes were drying, and he clenched his jaws. "We need to go in and level Gaza."

Efraim shook his head. "How? Remember, we're the ones who don't kill innocents."

"But you just told me there are no innocents. The civilians were part of it. They all joined in, so they should all pay."

"They didn't *all* join in. What I was saying was that some civilians joined Hamas in the butchery."

"You can't tell me, though, that the vast majority of Gazans weren't celebrating the massacre."

Efraim remained silent.

"Yeah, what I thought. So, how long will it be before they attack again? They surprised us once; they can surprise us again. It's not like anyone in Gaza is going to warn us. They're raised on hating Jews."

"That's true. But, seriously, it's not everyone. It's just like we see in every country—there are a few good ones amidst all the bad. It's like Abraham with Sodom and Gomorrah. 'Perchance there be ten good people?' or whatever it is."

"Well, if there are, then it sucks to be those ten good people, because we've got a job to do, and that's to make sure this never happens again."

Efraim leaned back in his chair. "And we will. Hamas is going to pay, but it's going to take time."

"Time," Nir said derisively. "Don't talk to me about time."

More minutes passed as the men were lost in their own thoughts. Finally, Nir spoke. "It just seems so surreal. I remember wondering how Americans felt after 9/11. I know it brought the nation together, but only for a time. Now they're back at each other's throats again. This is so much worse. It's so much more personal. It's not just planes ramming into buildings and killing random people. This is hands on. It's guns and knives and pipes and whatever weapons they could find. It's shooting and stabbing and beating and beheading. It's raping and torturing. Again, it's just barbaric."

"No doubt. What is the mindset that lets you torture and kill a child? A freaking child! It's pure evil. It's demonic. And, again, we still don't know the half of it. The stories will come, and with each new report, the nation is going to be thrown right back into mourning."

Rage was fully cycling in Nir's mind. He wanted to lash out at someone, but he forced himself to calm down. The time for vengeance would come.

"You talk to your family yet?" Nir asked his friend.

"No. I can't bring myself to call. I know everyone is okay, or else I would have heard."

"What's stopping you?"

"I don't know, *achi*. I just feel like I let this happen. I wonder if I missed some piece of intel or some communication that would have tipped us off."

"Join the club. While I'm sitting here in a dark, air-conditioned room in Tel Aviv, Yossi's body is somewhere under the hot sun in the scrub of the Negev." Efraim began to say something, but Nir cut him off. "And yes, I know in my brain that it's not my fault that he's dead. But a huge part of my heart is wondering what I was doing sitting in this chair while he was out there taking a bullet."

In the ensuing quiet, the light from Efraim's phone went out. Nir heard him lift the phone and tap it a few times, then curse Apple for the device's lack of battery life.

"Just tell me that we'll be going in hard," Nir said.

"The prime minister is determined to make them pay. For now, everyone is on his side. But he's going to have to do it fast. If he gets bogged down in Gaza, the same idiots who were trying to push him out of office will turn against him again."

"Have we heard anything from Iran or Hezbollah? Are they in on it?"

"It's too early to tell. Hezbollah sent rockets over the border, but they almost seem late to the game. It's like there was no coordination between Hamas and anyone else. They launched, and everyone else was forced to play catch-up."

"What about the Palestinian Islamic Jihad in the West Bank? Any word from them?"

Nir heard Efraim sigh. "Yeah, nothing from them yet. But if we don't move fast, they'll be emboldened, and we'll find ourselves fighting in both Gaza and the West Bank."

There was only a short pause this time before Nir responded, "Don't leave me out of this, *achi*. You know what my team and I can do. Promise me you'll put us to work. I need you to put me to work."

"My brother, you know that I've never lied to you, other than in cards and my weight. There will be plenty of opportunities ahead for you to get your hands wet. You are always first on my list. So don't force it. Just wait. I will call."

"Thanks."

"You got it. Now quit being a freak and sitting here in the dark. Go home and get some rest. You're going to need it."

Activating the flashlight on his own phone, Nir used it to find his way to his desk to grab his keys. Once outside, the two friends pounded fists and then parted.

It was a short drive for Nir to get to his flat. By the time he arrived, he was looking forward to some rest. But after walking through his front door, he made the mistake of turning on the news. Another eight hours would go by before his body finally shut down and he fell asleep on the couch.

CHAPTER 15

Nir looked out the window of the Gulfstream jet at the green mountains below. From his elevation, the area looked so quiet and pastoral. It was hard to believe that only a few months ago there were thousands of Armenians fleeing across those same heights from the oncoming Azerbaijani army. When the long-running tensions had reached their apex with the breakaway Republic of Artsakh—the name the ethnic Armenian population had given to their autonomous government—the Azeri government decided they'd had enough. They invaded the Nagorno-Karabakh region and forced the president of Artsakh to dissolve all government structures. With a few signatures, the republic ceased to exist.

As the president was signing papers, the Armenian population took off while they still could. Of the 150,000 who lived there, two-thirds now resided back in Armenia. Those remaining behind were scattered far and wide.

Mulling over the history of the region, Nir began to see parallels with what was happening in his own country over the past few months. Both Nagorno-Karabakh and Gaza were autonomous portions of a larger entity. Both had populations that were hostile toward the larger nations. Both had experienced or were experiencing major military actions from their host countries. And the populations of both had been sent fleeing.

But there were also glaring differences between the Armenians of the Republic of Artsakh and the Palestinians of Gaza. The Armenians hadn't gone on a day-long rampage of murder, rape, torture, and kidnapping. The Armenians hadn't vowed to drive the Azeris into the sea. The Armenians hadn't taught their children from the time they were old enough to walk that the best thing they could do with their lives was to die a martyr while committing an act of terrorism against the Azeris.

Nir drained the last of the energy drink that he was holding and crumpled the can in his hand. No, that was the Gazans. It is only from their generational, murderous hatred that a vile organization like Hamas could be born. Israel had been putting up with extremist terrorist acts and intifadas long enough. How can a nation have peace when there are hundreds of thousands of people wanting to kill you just on the other side of your border? A case could be made on both sides of the Azerbaijani-Armenian debate. But there is no rational argument that could be devised for the actions of Hamas or against the subsequent response of Israel.

For Israel, there had never been a day like October 7, 2023. As Nir sat on his couch at home, he saw videos of helpless civilians being kidnapped and carried away on the backs of motorbikes. Bloodied bodies were transported in the beds of trucks and taken back into Gaza. When the IDF had finally reached the kibbutzim, all they had left to do was to document the carnage. The same was true when they arrived at the Nova site. Body after body. Many had obviously been brutalized. Mercifully, many more had been murdered in cold blood without any of the pre-death cruelties.

What kind of a world is it when I feel relief at seeing those of my people who were only shot and killed? I'm old enough to remember both intifadas and all the bombings over the years. I can remember when I was a teenager and a bus blew up on Dizengoff Street in Tel Aviv. Then there were the ones at the Jerusalem bus station and on Jaffa Street. Then the restaurant

*bombings. The blast at Ben Yehuda Square and at the Dolphinarium disco
and at the Sbarro restaurant and at the Passover celebration at the Park
Hotel. Time after time—there have been dozens, hundreds. But nothing
has ever made me feel like this.*

Maybe it was because the other attacks were carried out by individ-
uals or small groups. Sure, they were part of a larger organization like
Hamas or the Palestinian Islamic Jihad. But this was different. This
was a massive wave of evil that had poured over the border. It was as if
the devil himself had infiltrated the soul of every individual perpetra-
tor, creating in them a bloodlust, a desire to cause maximum suffering.
He had seared their consciences so that they were unable to feel com-
passion or mercy or guilt.

Nir's emotions were building up again, and he took a few deep
breaths to calm himself. Catching the eye of the flight attendant at the
front of the cabin, he lifted his empty energy drink can and gave it a little wave. The black-haired, olive-skinned, middle-aged woman smiled
at Nir and nodded, then rose from her seat.

"Too many of those will make you jittery."

Nir turned back toward the small row of seats diagonal from him.
Yaron Eisenbach was giving him the same look Nir's mother had given
him when she used to scold him for taking an extra cookie.

"Says the old man on his sixth cup of coffee," Nir replied, nodding
to the empty mug next to his teammate.

"You two bicker like a couple of old aunties. I'm going to start calling you *Doda* Beardy and *Doda* Baldy." Gil Haviv had his Jericho 941
9mm in pieces on a tray in front of him and was in the process of adding a little oil to the slide. *That's got to be contrary to some sort of flight
regulation*, Nir thought as he turned a little more so he could glare at
the operative.

When Gil saw Nir looking, his eyes got big. "Uh-oh, are you going
to throw me out of the plane like you did to that militia guy in Syria?"

"It wasn't a plane; it was a helicopter. And I didn't throw him; he
jumped."

Gil went back to his work. "Yeah, that's much better. I appreciate
the clarification."

A snort escaped from Yaron's direction. Nir turned and saw the man beet red and shaking with laughter.

"You shut up," Nir said, pointing at him.

The old man composed himself long enough to say, "It'll never get old," before another fit of laughter took him.

"Did I miss the joke?"

Nir turned the rest of the way around and saw the flight attendant holding a can and a glass of ice in one hand and a carafe in the other. The can and glass were on a trajectory for the small table next to him.

"You let one prisoner jump out of a helicopter, and they never let you live it down," he said with a shake of his head.

"Ah, I see," she replied. Then she leaned closer. "When I was active, do you know what we called a prisoner flying out of a helicopter?"

That was not a question he expected from this pleasant, mom-ish looking woman. "Uh...no."

"The first," she said with a wink. Then she turned to refill Yaron's coffee mug. Nir stared after her.

In Israeli intelligence, you can never assume anyone's background. Who knows what kind of operations are in her history?

After she had finished with Yaron and asked Gil if he needed anything, she started heading back toward the front.

"Excuse me," Nir said. The flight attendant stopped. "May I ask what branch you served with?"

Pressing her hand against his cheek, she answered. "*Motek*, you can *ask* me anything you want." Then she turned and walked back to the front of the plane, where she sat down and began flipping through a magazine.

Nir smiled, but the moment was short-lived. A mental picture of Yossi Hirschfield with the right side of his cranium missing popped up in his mind. Yossi and Adira had been found on October 8. He had been beaten before being finished off with two shots to the head. Miraculously, Adira was still alive, barely. She was taken to a hospital to begin the slow process of recovery. Then, three weeks ago, Nir got the call that she had taken her own life. Tragically, that wasn't unusual for Nova survivors.

That never should have happened. Yossi and Adira could be planning their wedding right now. Registering for gifts or picking out curtains for their house or whatever it was that soon-to-be-wed couples did. Instead, their futures were stolen from them in an act of cowardly violence.

Nir could feel his anger rising again. His passion for revenge was at a peak. He breathed deeply, trying to bring himself back down.

The plane began a noticeable descent. Nir popped open the can and chugged its contents, ignoring the glass of ice. He rubbed his chin as he looked out the window.

Doda Beardy, I only wish.

Nir had begun growing his beard again, but the acumulating scars on his face were making it look like a toddler had gone crazy with an electric trimmer. Looking out the window, he saw the city of Khankendi below. Up until a few months ago, he would have been looking at Stepanakert. Back then, it had been a bustling city of 75,000, a hive of Armenian cultural and political activity. However, now that it had its old Azeri name back and people had fled, its empty streets made it look like a ghost town.

It's always the people who pay. The innocent civilians were just doing their day-to-days, getting by the best they could. Meanwhile, the politicians were living high while they threw their threats back and forth. When everything finally popped off, who were the ones who paid? The people. It's always the people.

The same was true in Gaza. Hamas's leaders had planned their heinous operation against Israel. Now, it was the people who were paying for their leaders' sins. The soldier-terrorists of Hamas were also paying, as they should. The ones who were getting off scot-free were Hamas's leaders. They were continuing to live their best lives in five-star hotels in Turkey and Qatar and Iran.

Well, that's about to end. Me and the boys are coming to get you.

CHAPTER 16

KHANKENDI, AZERBAIJAN—
DECEMBER 30, 2023—11:05 (11:05 AM) AZT

The pilot of the modified private plane gently set the wheels down on the runway at Khankendi Air Base. Azerbaijan had made several of its bases available to Israeli military planes in the past. Some were even closer to the Mossad team's ultimate target. But Khankendi had the benefit of being far enough off the beaten path that no one paid close attention to what went on there. Some of the town's residents might notice a Gulfstream jet flying overhead and making a landing. But they would likely chalk up its appearance to being a few more Azeri politicians coming in to rummage through some of the belongings that the more wealthy of the fleeing Armenians had left behind.

As the plane taxied into a hangar, Nir spotted the man he was here to meet. Although his hair was now all white, Nir would have recognized his thick mustache anywhere. He had first come across Elnur Isayev more than five years ago during a very successful operation to steal Iran's nuclear secrets out of a Tehran warehouse full of vaults. All had gone perfectly until Nicole got herself arrested after breaking the nose of a handsy policeman.

I do not want to revisit that event, Nir thought, shaking the memory from his mind. *Not now. Not ever.*

The former assistant deputy head of the Azerbaijani Foreign Intelligence Service had proven himself to be a reliable ally during that operation. Nir hoped that nothing had changed in the man's trustworthiness over the intervening years. He and his men were depending on this aging fellow intelligence operator.

Once the plane came to a stop, Nir lifted his bag from the seat across the aisle and made his way to the front. The stairs had already been lowered, and as he mounted the first one, he heard the flight attendant's voice behind him.

"Have fun storming the castle, boys."

That woman has got a story. Maybe I can coax it out of her if she's still here for the flight home.

But he had no time to think about her now; Isayev's voice was already booming out from the bottom of the stairs.

"Welcome! Welcome, my friends!"

Even before Nir reached the bottom of the stairs, he was assaulted by the harsh odor of the nasty Turkish cigarettes the man chain-smoked. Back when he had first met him, Nir had wondered how the man hadn't yet keeled over from cancer. Now that he had to at least be in his early seventies, Isayev was a walking miracle of nicotine resistance. Dressed in a dark blue business suit, the old man held a cane in both hands like a staff, almost as if he were trying to mask the fact that he needed it for walking.

"Deputy Isayev," Nir replied, holding out his hand.

Taking the proffered hand, the deputy said, "Elnur, please. I'm too old for formalities."

As Nir stepped aside, Isayev said, "And I recognize you. You were Tavor's right-hand man even back then, right?"

"I was, and I am. Yaron Eisenbach." The two shook hands.

"Still together after all these years. That never happens in Azerbaijan. Inevitably, one or the other winds up captured, court-martialed, or killed. And you are?"

"Gil Haviv. I'm the new guy."

As they shook hands, the old man said, "New guy, huh? That wouldn't have anything to do with that nasty business in Damascus, would it?" Then he waved his hands. "No, forget I asked. None of my business. Tell me, how was your flight?"

He began walking across the hangar toward a row of offices. The three Israelis followed.

"I've flown enough commercial coach to never complain about a private jet," answered Nir.

Isayev roared with laughter. Ten or twelve steps along, the old man gave in to necessity and the cane began tapping the ground with his steps. "We will eat, and then I will send you to your friends. But let me say to you, I don't like these Kurds you are meeting. They are unsavory and obnoxious. Most loathsome of all is that colonel friend of yours. I promise you—for the right amount of money, he would betray you in a heartbeat."

That colonel was a major when Nir had met him. And, under normal circumstances, he wouldn't have trusted him either. "I recognize your concerns. But this one owes me a debt."

Isayev grunted. "For being such dishonorable people, the Kurds do tend to honor their debts."

The smells reached Nir well before they arrived at a certain office with an open door. So strong were they that they even overpowered Isayev's cigarette stench.

Standing at the entrance with his arm extended in, Isayev said, "Come. Eat and enjoy. Then you may go to meet your Kurds." A tablecloth covered an office table. There were four place settings, and each man took a seat. Along with a plethora of side dishes, the men feasted on dolma stuffed with beef and spices, dushbara dumplings in a broth, and an oversized platter of kourma plov with the most tender mutton that Nir had ever tasted. When the baklava and pastries came out at the end, the three operatives tried to politely refuse. Isayev was adamant, however, and an international incident was averted only when the men agreed to take a bag filled with the desserts.

With their stomachs filled and their heads more than a little groggy from the long flight, the Mossad agents thanked Isayev for the feast and got up to leave.

As they stepped outside the hangar, Gil said, "Oh, I recognize her."

Nir smiled. He, too, had a history with what was waiting for them in the lot. A Plasan SandCat armored vehicle sat idling, taking Nir back to his days in the IDF. Plasan was a manufacturing company headquartered in northern Israel that specialized in armored vehicles and robotics. The SandCat was one of their more widely disseminated models, reaching Central Europe, South America, and, apparently, here in Azerbaijan.

Isayev laughed. "You like her? I thought you would. A little taste of home away from home. Your driver, Jafarov, will take you to the Kurds. From what you have told me, they will get you the rest of the way to your destination."

Nir stopped at the front passenger door and turned. It took a few moments for Isayev to limp up to him. Reaching out his hand, Nir said, "My friend, thank you for arranging all this."

Isayev leaned his cane against his body and enveloped Nir's hand with both of his. "Listen, after hearing what those motherless sons had done to your people, I wanted to trade this cane in for a rifle and go down there myself. When you called me for help, I couldn't help but say yes. I don't know what you're here to do, but I'm thankful to be part of it. Now, go, be safe, and make them pay." The old man's grip became surprisingly firm as he said those last words.

"We'll do it. And I'll say your name when they go down."

The former spook's eyes moistened. He shook Nir's hands up and down several times, saying, "Yes, do that. You do that." Then he released Nir and turned to go.

The others had already climbed up into the back of the vehicle. As Nir opened the front passenger door, he heard Isayev's voice again.

"Hey, Tavor, whatever happened to that feisty South African? She was certainly a spitfire. Broke the Iranian dog's nose! Did you ever marry her?"

Nir turned. "She's still around, and as feisty as ever. And, no, I haven't married her."

"Why not?"

This was not a conversation that Nir wanted to have right now in front of his team as he was setting off on a mission. "It's complicated."

"Complicated?" Isayev waved his hand dismissively and turned around. As he walked, he said, "Israelis! Brilliant at making war; fools at making love."

Nir stared at the old man's back for a moment before sliding into the front seat of the armored vehicle. As he did, without turning around, he snapped, "Shut up. Just shut up."

CHAPTER 17

HOTEL SULTANAHMET, ISTANBUL, TURKEY—
DECEMBER 30, 2023—11:45 (11:45 AM) EEST

Nicole opened the door. A man stood in the hall holding a stack of towels.

"I am Burhan Bakir. I'm here for your massage." He was slight, but with surprisingly well-developed arms that showed through his uniform.

Nicole pulled the soft lapels of her hotel robe tight against her neck and said, "Ooo, yummy! Please come in."

The man smiled and nodded. Hefting his table, he followed her into the main room of the suite.

Nicole turned, letting her recently dyed blonde hair cascade over her shoulders, and swung her arms open, indicating the room. "Will this work?"

"This will be perfect, ma'am." He set down his bag and began to move aside a long glass-top table.

Meanwhile, Nicole flopped into an overstuffed chair and crossed her legs in front of her. "You said it's Burhan, correct?" At his affirmation, she continued, "Listen, Burhan, if I'm going to be comfortable, I need you to call me something other than ma'am. Would you please call me Nicole?"

Burhan looked at her for a moment before saying, "Of course, Miss Nicole." There was still a little hesitancy before he said her name, but it was progress.

As she watched him set up his massage table, her mind went back to an evening four weeks ago at Yaron's house. He and his wife had a little bit of property east of Netanya with a couple dozen fruit trees and too many chickens. Everyone from the ops and analytic teams were there, except for one. Much less rowdy than their gatherings of the past, it was still a nice time to get away from the office and stretch one's arms a bit.

It was nearing 9:00 p.m. The burgers, lamb kebabs, and a few of those pesky chickens had all been polished off by that time. A healthy fire was burning in the pit, taking off the chill of the evening. Everyone had a beer or a soft drink in their hand and toasts were being offered up to Yossi and Doron.

Nicole had been keeping her eyes on the long driveway, and when she saw headlights, she got up and went inside to the kitchen. A foil-covered plate sat cooling on the top shelf of the refrigerator. She pulled it out, unwrapped it, and walked out the front door.

"Miss Nicole, the table is ready," said Burhan, shaking her from her revelry.

She smiled.

Miss Nicole. I suppose I can live with that.

As she stood, Burhan continued, "I will go into the next room so you may lay down and prepare yourself."

"Sounds swell," Nicole said. Then, with a wink, she added, "And no peeking."

Burhan flushed. "Of course. Never," he said as he hustled out of the room.

Once the room was clear, she let the robe slip from her bare shoulders and lay face down on the table. Her cheeks cushioned into the soft face pillow. And even though she was wearing bikini bottoms, she still tucked the sheet up above her waistline.

"I'm ready, Burhan."

A moment later, she heard the Syrian's accented voice next to her.

"Please let me know if there is anywhere in particular you need me to work on as I go."

"You bet."

Over the years, Nicole had enjoyed so many Swedish massages that she knew the process by heart. As Burhan began the effleurage focusing on her circulatory system, her mind went back to Yaron's house.

Nir was just stepping out of his Mercedes when she reached him. Rising up on her toes, she gave him a peck on the cheek.

"Long meeting," she said, not as a question.

"Yeah, but good. Very, very good." Taking the plate she was holding, he added, "This is perfect. They brought food into the office, but it wasn't difficult to pass on dry falafel and hummus knowing that Yaron's barbecue was waiting."

"Figured as much. Now, come on. Everyone is dying to hear what you have to say." She slid her arm in his and they walked around the side of the house. Cheers and greetings met them as they rounded the back corner.

Nir spotted Yaron and held up a skewer that was already nearly empty. "*Achi!*"

Other cheers went up for the host of their feast.

Someone jumped up from the group and rushed to Nir. Passing his plate to Nicole, Nir wrapped him in a bear hug. "Avi, I'm so glad you came." Avi Carmeli had been a member of Nir's ops team before being severely wounded in the arm during an operation in Dubai. At first it looked like they'd be able to save the limb, but an infection a few months later took it from him. Avi was a brilliant strategist, and his heart was already with the team.

"You couldn't keep me away. Riding a desk sucks. Got any jobs for a one-armed man?"

"I think we're short a bandit," called out Yaron.

"I'm pretty sure we have some paper that needs hanging," added Dima.

Avi gestured his lack of appreciation.

Nicole was startled from her reminiscence by a hand very near her thin, cotton no-go zone. But then she felt Burhan's hands stop their traveling and begin to knead. This was the beginning of the petrissage. "Please make sure you really get my lower back. Those carry-ons are a nightmare."

"Yes, Miss Nicole."

As the Syrian's hands began to work her lower back, Nicole once again went back to that night at Yaron's. Nir had tried to eat, but everyone wanted the news right away. Finally giving in, he nodded to Dima, who apparently was overseeing the alcohol distribution. He reached into a cooler, pulled out a Goldstar, and tossed it over. Nir pulled a tactical knife from his boot, popped the cap, then closed the blade.

"I'm assuming that everyone knows about Operation Wrath of God. If you don't, you probably shouldn't be in the Mossad."

"Or even in Israel," added Liora.

Operation Wrath of God was Israel's response to the murder of 11 athletes and coaches at the 1972 Munich Olympics by the militant Palestinian group Black September. Over the next 20 years, at least 18 members of the terrorist group were hunted down and killed by the Mossad. Wrath of God was the operation that solidified the reputation of Israeli intelligence as the best and most ruthless in the world.

Nir continued. "We aren't calling this Wrath of God 2.0 or anything. However, the same attitude exists from the prime minister to the *ramsad* and on down. Everyone involved in the leadership of October 7 has got to go."

Words of affirmation and commitment sounded throughout the group.

"The IDF is doing a great job with Hamas down in Gaza. The problem is that those who are really responsible—Haniyeh, al-Natsheh, al-Arouri, Mousa, all those guys—they're all living it up in luxury hotels in Qatar and Turkey and Iran. You all know that."

Nir paused. All eyes, including Nicole's, were on him.

He took a long swig of beer to draw out the anticipation before finally saying, "That, my friends, is about to end."

Cheers and whoops sounded out from around the fire pit. Everyone was not only ready, but excited to bring revenge against the terrorists who had taken their friends, their families, their peace.

Nir continued. "In the same way we talk about Operation Wrath of God, the next generation at Mossad will talk about you and Operation Amalek. Yariv, tell us about Amalek," pointing to the new guy with the mouth of his bottle.

CHAPTER 18

A pain around her shoulder blade pulled Nicole back to the present. She was so deep into her thoughts that she had completely missed the tapotement phase and was on to friction. Part of her hoped she hadn't dozed or, worse, snored.

"You do a remarkable job, Burhan."

"Thank you, Miss Nicole."

She was still trying to get a good feel for Yariv Rabin. Tall, thin, with a dark beard that reached the top of his chest, he was a good-looking guy who had been brought in as a replacement for Yossi. But he was different. She didn't know much about Orthodox or ultra-Orthodox or Hasidic Judaism or any of that stuff, but somewhere on that spectrum you could find Yariv.

In some ways, he fit in. He was definitely brilliant, and he had been on the verge of being tossed from the Mossad for puncturing all four tires of an assistant deputy in the cryptography department. No one was quite sure why he had done it, but, as usual, it was suspected that a girl was involved. Efraim had saved him from being tossed into the dustbin of Israeli intelligence history, assigning him to the analysts in CARL.

Still, Yariv was also very different. He was the only one around that firepit wearing a yarmulke on his head, tassels at his waist, and who had brought his own food because Yaron insisted that a good burger could not be achieved without the addition of cheese. He didn't swear, which she appreciated. And the man knew his Scripture.

"It's a brilliant name for the operation," Yariv said, answering Nir's question. He spoke with a rich baritone voice that sounded like it belonged to a man decades older than his 27 years. "When Moses led the people out of Egypt, the Amalekites came up against them. That was the battle when Aaron and Hur had to hold Moses' arms up as he directed God's power to the army below. Later, when the Hebrews were about to enter the land, God reminded them that they had a score to settle with that people." Closing his eyes, he quoted, "Remember what Amalek did to you on your journey, after you left Egypt—how, undeterred by fear of God, he surprised you on the march, when you were famished and weary, and cut down all the stragglers in your rear. Therefore, when the LORD your God grants you safety from all your enemies around you, in the land that the LORD your God is giving you as a hereditary portion, you shall blot out the memory of Amalek from under heaven. Do not forget!"

"Wow, you must have gotten beat up a lot as a kid," Lahav snorted.

"It's actually pretty impressive," said Nir. "Do not forget what they did to you. We are not going to forget, and we are going to blot out the memory of Hamas from under heaven."

Again, there were cheers around the fire.

"But don't get me wrong. Operation Amalek is not the whole plan. In fact, Shin Bet has tasked NILI to do the exact thing we're doing, only with different targets."

"NILI. Man, that's a throwback," said Imri.

"It is. For you who don't know, NILI stands for *Netzah Yisrael Lo Yeshaker*." Turning to Nicole, Nir said, "That means 'The Eternal One of Israel will not lie.'"

"From the writings of Samuel," added Yariv.

"Exactly. NILI operated against the Ottoman Empire way back during World War I. Eventually, they were discovered, tortured, and most were either hanged or committed suicide. This reconstituted NILI is the tip of Shin Bet's assassination spear against Hamas. Caesarea continues to be the Mossad's. And we continue to be Caesarea's. Operation Amalek is just one part of our plans against Hamas. In fact, Amalek is just one day. One twenty-four-hour period during which Kidon is going to take out four of Hamas's leaders in four different locations in a simultaneous action."

Operation Amalek was what had sent Nir to Azerbaijan and eventually down into Tehran. It was also what led Nicole to this hotel room with this masseuse.

I think I got the better of the deal.

"Tell me about yourself, Burhan," she said. He was on to the vibration part, thumping on her back.

"There is not much to tell, Miss Nicole."

"Well, you don't sound like you're from Turkey. You sound more Egyptian or Saudi or someplace less European."

Burhan's pace on her back slowed just a touch, then picked up again. "I am Syrian. Most people don't know, but a great majority of migrant workers here in Turkey are from my country."

"Fascinating! Up on my right shoulder, please. That's where the strap was. Yes, perfect! Do you have family here or in Syria?"

Again, a brief slowing as Burhan thought. "I have no family here. Back home, only a mother, a sister, and two young brothers."

"A sister? Interesting. What is her name?"

The masseuse paused longer than he should have before replying, "Rabia."

Nicole let out a long sigh. "Burhan, just when we were establishing such a great rapport. Suddenly, you lie to me about your beautiful sister, Sabra."

The hands left her back. Behind her, nothing but silence.

Nicole knew she was completely vulnerable. But she pressed on, her face pushed into the tiny pillows. "My darling Burhan, the decisions you make in the next few minutes will make all the difference for you, your mother, your brothers, and especially for sweet Sabra. I know how she suffers, and it breaks my heart."

Quiet filled the room while Nicole waited Burhan out. Finally, after a couple minutes, he asked, "And what would you require from me?"

Another voice answered this question. It was deep, with a heavy Russian accent. "Please sit, my friend, and I will tell you all about it."

CHAPTER 19

12:35 (12:35 PM) EEST

While Nir's operation was generated mostly from within the walls of CARL, Nicole's was pretty much handed to them by Mossad strategists. There were three Kidon teams left after the tragedy in Damascus and four hits to make. CARL agreed to take the extra targeted killing in Turkey with the understanding that they were essentially just supplying the manpower. Most of the hard work had already been done by Unit 504, which had been collecting data on foreign Syrian workers for years.

Burhan Bakir was an opportunity just waiting to be exploited. He had a fatherless family back home with an extremely hardworking mother. His training as a masseuse allowed him to migrate to Turkey, where the pay was better than back home. As his skills increased, so did his opportunities. Finally, he was given employment at the prestigious Hotel Sultanahmet. That is where he suddenly found himself with access to the leadership of Hamas.

Sure, he was a Syrian, but the political side of life had never interested him. All he wanted to do was to help provide for his mother and his siblings, especially his sister. Sabra suffered horribly from cystic fibrosis—a terrible enough disease in a first-world country, and one that was unsurvivable in third-world Syria. Once he proved to Hamas he could be trusted around the organization's leadership, his family was given a very small monthly stipend by the terrorist group. That extra income was enough to provide for only the most essential of medications that Sabra needed.

Thus, Burhan was a trapped man. When his life and predicament were presented to Nicole and company, the operation came together quickly.

Nicole pulled the sheet from her waist up over her shoulders before sitting up. Behind her, she heard the Russian and the Syrian stepping toward a seating area.

She turned to see Dima sitting in a large, overstuffed chair. Diagonal from him, Burhan perched tentatively on the forward edge of a couch.

"Excuse me, boys," she said as she purposely walked in front of them and settled back deeply into the other end of the couch.

"That woman," Dima said with a laugh, letting his eyes follow Nicole. Then he turned back to Burhan. "You are at a disadvantage because I obviously know you, but you don't know me. My name is Dmitry Kobylkin. I serve as an ambassador of sorts for the Russian government. Nicole is my wife and acts as my…"

When Dima paused to search for a word, Nicole piped in, "Nemesis? Antagonist?"

"I was going to say partner, but you may be closer to the truth."

Nicole tucked herself tighter into the couch and blew Dima a kiss.

"She believes that because she is not from Russia, she has more heart. I believe it simply means she has less brain." Dima roared with laughter as he dodged a throw pillow. Meanwhile, Burhan sat quietly, trying to process the show that was taking place in front of him.

As Dima leaned forward, wagging his finger at Nicole, the masseuse eked out, "What is it you want from me?"

"He speaks! And such an apropos question," said Dima, leaning back in his chair. "What is it that we want from you, Burhan?"

Dima let the silence hang for a moment before leaning forward again. "We need you to play a little trick on someone for us."

Nicole watched as the Syrian's eyes opened wide. That was not what he was expecting to hear. "I'm afraid I don't understand. A trick? Of what sort?"

Once again, Dima sat back in the overly cushioned chair. "Listen, you know what happened back on October 7—what Hamas did to the Jews, right? Well, I've got no love for the Jews. With a little more brainpower, those idiot Palestinians could have gone a long way to finishing the job."

"Mitya," scolded Nicole.

"Don't *Mitya* me. It's how I feel," he roared at Nicole, who shrank back into the couch. Turning to Burhan, Dima stopped, took a deep breath, then continued. "No one cares what the Palestinians did to the Jews. The world cried its crocodile tears and is now moving on." Putting his hand on Burhan's arm, he said, "But what they did was just plain stupid. They went in like a band of hooligans, raping and killing anything they could find. It was reckless. It was unplanned, and it forced us to draw resources back into Syria, from where they were more needed in Ukraine. We cannot let an action like that go unpunished."

"I will not kill anyone," Burhan said quietly.

Dima leapt to his feet, towering over the masseuse. "Did I say to kill anyone?" He turned to Nicole. "Did I say to kill anyone?"

"No, Mitya, you did not," she answered, still feigning hurt feelings over Dima yelling at her.

Turning back to Burhan, Dima lowered himself again. "I need you to listen to the words I say and not jump to any ridiculous conclusions. I said we want to play a little trick on someone. He must be reminded who is boss. Maybe he gets uncomfortable. Maybe his skin gets a little hot. Maybe he cries a little bit until we show him how he can be better. But no one said anything about dying."

As Dima spoke, Burhan was shaking his head. As soon as the Russian paused, he spoke up. There was heavy emotion in his voice. "I cannot do anything like that. Hamas has already told me that if I bring any harm to any of their people, my family will die. They know where my mother lives. As soon as the man you are targeting feels any reaction to anything, a call will be made to Syria."

Nicole scooted over so that she was next to Burhan. She put her arm around his shoulders. "*Habibi*, do you think I would let that happen to your family? When Mitya shared this with me, I asked, 'But what about his family?' Mitya said, 'They will be taken care of.' I asked, 'How?' And he said, 'We will bring them out.' And I said, 'What about the daughter? What about Sabra?' And do you know what my Mitya said?"

Burhan, who was watching this beautiful woman speak to him, shook his head slowly.

Nicole nodded to Dima, who said, "I told her, 'We will get Sabra the best doctors Moscow has.' And do you know what she said back to me?"

Again, Burhan indicated his ignorance.

Nicole replied, "I said to him, 'Oh, no, you won't take her to any of your horrid Russian doctors! This sweet girl deserves better than that. You must send the family to Europe. Hungary or Estonia or someplace like that.' And Mitya said he would. Isn't that right, dear?" Leaning across Burhan, she gave Dima a kiss on the cheek.

"Did I not say she has a big heart?" Dima said with a laugh. "We will move you and your family to a place in Hungary, where you will be given new identities. You will be given a job, as will your brothers. It will not be luxurious, but it will be much better than how they live now. But best of all, Sabra will be admitted to their children's hospital, where she will receive the best treatment available."

Burhan's eyes were big with possibility and disbelief. "How can I believe this to be true? This is so much, especially for a simple trick."

Dima leaned back into his chair and pointed at Nicole, answering, "You know it first of all because she says it is true. Can you imagine living with her if I screw you over?"

"It would not be pretty," Nicole confirmed.

"But I understand your reticence. You may understand our willingness to go through so much effort when I tell you who the target is. The victim of our little prank is none other than Khaled Mousa."

Burhan blew out a lungful of air and sat back. Born in the West Bank back in 1956, Khaled Mousa was a cofounder of Hamas. Later, he became head of the terrorist organization's political bureau until he passed that role on to Ismail Haniyeh. Now he was a kind of diplomat, spending most of his time living luxuriously in Doha, Qatar, with occasional trips to Syria, Lebanon, Russia, and Turkey.

"I received word this morning that he is coming. I was told to schedule him for hammam therapy," said Burhan.

"We know all this, Burhan," said Dima. "We have it all planned out. When to play the trick during the therapy, how to do it, all the details. You just need to do exactly what we tell you, and all will be good."

Burhan's head was slowly moving back and forth. Dima was about to say something more, but Nicole gave him a barely perceptible headshake. The Syrian knew that his sister's life would be short no matter how much he earned in Turkey. And, although the details of their new life would be different than what they were presenting—new identities in Denver, Colorado, instead of Budapest, Hungary, and an "in" at National Jewish Health, which was one of the premier hospitals for respiratory ailments in the world—the results would be the same as they were promising. In fact, likely far better. Better lives for his family and hope for Sabra.

There was one minor detail he didn't know, however. Yes, he would be playing a trick on Khaled Mousa, but that trick would be lethal. Burhan himself would not know the extent of the deadly prank—at least until long afterward. And even then, he could at least have the comfort of knowing that he never intended to truly harm anyone.

Small consolation. But it is the best we can do in this situation. Mousa is guilty of his crimes. Burhan is simply the innocent executioner.

"And you promise you will protect my family?" Burhan asked suddenly.

Nicole took Burhan by the chin. "I'll make sure they treat sweet Sabra like she is my own little sister."

As Nicole pulled her hand back, Burhan began to nod. "Okay. Tell me what I need to do."

CHAPTER 20

Nir slid down from the front seat to the pavement below as the Sand-Cat was coming to a halt. Off to his right stood four men, one in heavy green camouflage and the other three in civilian clothes. The three in the back, he didn't recognize at all. The one smiling in front, however, was a relief to see.

Catching his feet under himself, Nir strode up and took the man in a bear hug. "Mustafa! So good to see you."

"May Allah bless you and keep you," replied the Kurd, returning the embrace. When Nir had first met Colonel Mustafa Nurettin, the man had been a major in the People's Protection Units, a Kurdish militant group that operated mostly in Syria. Nir, Dima, and the late Doron Mizrahi had found themselves on the ground in northern Syria due to an operation that had devolved to the point that a certain prisoner had jumped out of a helicopter. The sound of gunfire led them over a hill to a place where they witnessed a small battle taking place. Unfortunately, the major and his team were pinned down and hopelessly outnumbered by a Syrian army patrol. The three Israelis decided to even the odds, and the Syrian soldiers were quickly dispatched. When the battle was over, a grateful Nurettin promised Nir that he would return the favor whenever and in whatever way possible.

The colonel continued. "What those Hamas animals did to your country was unconscionable. What is done to combatants is fair game. But the way they treated the innocents—no one should get away with that. From my leaders to yours, you have our condolences and our support."

"That is what I would expect from a true Kurd who has been under oppression for many years. It's also why I called you." Nir noticed that Yaron and Gil had joined him. "Colonel Nurettin, this is my team. Yaron Eisenbach and Gil Haviv."

Nurettin shook the men's hands. Then, indicating the three men with him, he said, "Behind me are three of my most loyal men. They are also three of my greatest undercover assets in Iran, so you'll pardon me if I withhold their names."

"Of course. Will they be seeing us to Tehran?"

Standing up straight, Nurettin replied, "I will be seeing you to Tehran. Your request came to me, and I accepted it. I will ensure that all goes according to plan."

This was unexpected, but also a huge relief. You can trust the Kurds only as far as the Kurds can be trusted, which wasn't always that far. Knowing the colonel would be with them gave Nir a much stronger sense of security. "Thank you, Mustafa. I am truly honored."

"You saved my life once, *heval*. I owe you. My goal is to finish my life with no debts but those owed to Allah."

Nir shook the man's hand once again. "Fair enough. Are we in the box truck?" His eyes went to the stained, white vehicle with faded lettering parked behind the Kurds.

"Accommodations fit for a king," laughed Nurettin.

The three Israelis went back to the SandCat to get their gear. Then they dismissed Jafarov, the driver, and hauled their bags to the back of the truck. After tossing everything in, they climbed up.

Nurettin jumped in with them, moving to the rear of the cargo area. "Join me—this will be where we stay. Sadly, my Persian is not at the level where I won't raise suspicion. So, you are stuck with me. But don't worry; we will not be alone." Then he pulled a bottle out of a bag already tucked into a corner. Nir recognized it as Lebanese arak, something he hadn't expected from a devout Muslim.

Nurettin caught Nir's eye and winked. "Allah understands that warfare allows for certain indulgences that aren't normally accepted. Twelve hours in the back of a truck to get to Tehran will require more than cards and stories."

"Fair enough," Nir said with a smile. If this man trusted his crew enough to sip a little spirit, Nir felt he had no choice but to do the same. The four men got themselves comfortable in the small space up against the rear of the cab. Then two of Nurettin's men put a false wall in place, while the third started up the truck. Within minutes, they were bouncing along the broken road.

This ride probably would have been a lot smoother a few months ago before the tracks of Azerbaijan's armor had rolled in. War is the great destroyer, even of the mundane.

Nurettin splashed drinks into four plastic cups and passed them around. They toasted Israel. They toasted the Kurdish People's Protection Units. They toasted vengeance and their friends who had passed before them. An hour and a half later, when they reached the Iranian border, the four men in the back were each feeling a glow. But Nurettin had promised them that they need not worry. His men were the best, and within ten minutes, they were through.

It took another 90 minutes for the Kurdish colonel to start running out of stories. Another 15 passed before he began snoring in his corner of the cramped space. Nir tilted his head back against the frame of the truck and closed his eyes.

That man has way too many words. But we couldn't do this without him.

As the glow of the Lebanese spirit lubricated Nir's joints, his mind went to their upcoming target. Emad al-Natsheh was born in Jordan in 1970. Balding and bearded, most people would dismiss him as a mid-level CPA. At least, if they didn't know his strong terrorist ties. In reality, as Hamas's representative to Iran, al-Natsheh was a stone-cold killer. If Tehran was a faucet of terrorist funding, this man was the handle that twisted open the flow of money and weapons to Gaza.

Without al-Natsheh's tireless advocating, Hamas could not have pulled off the October 7 attack. It was his constant promotion that drew in cash for small arms, rockets, and the parachute rigs that the first wave of attackers used at Nova. His hands were as bloody as if he were pulling the triggers himself. That blood was about to be avenged.

Despite his violent work, rather than hiding in fear, al-Natsheh lived a very comfortable life in Tehran. Home was a large, well-furnished apartment. He ate well and played very well. All of this was done with little fear of repercussion, due to the well-armed guard team that accompanied him wherever he went.

Your guards will not be enough to protect you. You came into our homes and destroyed our peace. Now I am coming to you to destroy you.

When Nir had sat with the team in CARL, they had weighed their options. The Hamas man stuck very closely to his routine. For most, that would be a fatal flaw. But for al-Natsheh, that routine was what protected him.

"It's like he's using all of Tehran as his personal human shield," Dafna said. "You can't hit him without taking out about a dozen others."

Which was true. The man was never by himself—ever. He never traveled out of the city, nor did he ever take any less-used back roads. Truly insulated, he was surrounded by his bodyguards, who were surrounded by Tehran. Because of his routine, it would be child's play to give him the Soleimani treatment and send a Hellfire down his gullet. But, as Dafna had pointed out, a dozen or more innocents would instantly lose their lives with him. That was unacceptable.

"We will not kill any innocents," Nir had told his team at CARL. "That's exactly what Hamas did to us. We will not sink to their level."

Gil asked, "Can we run someone into him on the street? Give a VX hit like what Kim Jong-un did to his half brother?"

"*Ein matzav.* Security is too tight," answered Lahav. "You may get someone in, but you wouldn't get them back out. It would be a one-for-one death swap."

"What about a magnetic mine, like an anti-tank mine?" asked Imri. "I know they've learned to direct charges a whole lot better."

That opened up some good discussion until Yaron shut it back down. "Ultimately, it is too fine of a line. Too little explosion, and you risk your target's survival. Too much explosion, and you face collateral damage. Trust me, I'd love to go and slap a magnetic mine under the fool's car, but it just isn't feasible."

The meeting had gone long into the evening until Avi Carmeli came up with an idea. They talked it through, building and destroying several iterations. But the more they worked it through, the better chance it seemed to have of success. This plan was what brought Nir, Yaron, and Gil into the wolf's den of Tehran with two magnetic mines, a couple motorcycle helmets, and a few other little surprises. They wouldn't leave until al-Natsheh was dead.

Nir rehearsed the plan over and over in his mind until he fell asleep. He woke up a few hours later, disappointed to see they were still more than eight hours away from their destination. The men passed time playing cards, checking their weapons, and listening to Colonel Nurettin, who was back telling his stories.

By the time the false wall was pulled out at the safe house, they were all ready to stretch their legs before getting some real sleep.

CHAPTER 21

Closing his eyes, Nir tried to let sleep overtake him. But he knew it was an impossible task. The sense of oppression from the enemy surrounding the safe house was so strong that he kept finding himself hopping up from his cot and walking through the home every ten or fifteen minutes, checking locks and glancing out windows. This was their second night here and, for Nir, it was no better than the first.

The day had been productive. He, Gil, and Yaron had driven al-Natsheh's route in an old Toyota Corolla, looking for places they could hide if it all went upside down. There were certainly some options, but they wouldn't last long. The targeted killing would go down in the heart of the federal district, and the police presence would be great. What Nir wouldn't have given for a nice, quiet, out-of-the-way alley where he could simply blow up the terrorist.

Slipping off his cot, he moved to the door.

"*B'chaiyecha!* It's all locked, you *yutz*. Same as it was ten minutes ago," said Yaron from his cot against the opposite wall.

"There go *Doda* Beardy and *Doda* Baldy again. If I knew you two bickered like this, I would have joined Unit 504," grumbled Gil from where he was stretched out.

Ignoring them, Nir slipped through the door. The house was small, a typical residence for the ten million or so Kurds living in Iran. Most had arrived as refugees during the diasporas from the Iran-Iraq War and the Persian Gulf War in the '80s and '90s. Although a large minority, they had little power and even less money. Much of their role in Iran was to make the lives of the Persians more comfortable.

The matriarch of the house, an old woman in her seventies, sat at a chipped table in the kitchen working on something requiring a needle and thread. She side-eyed Nir briefly as he passed by before returning to her work. The kitchen still held the spicy fragrance of kofta and the homey scent of naan from dinner. It wasn't much, but it was what they could offer. When Nir tried to pass some currency to the man of the house, the old woman had stopped him.

"These men you are looking for deserve what they get. I will not profit from their demise," she had declared.

The man, her son, nodded and withdrew his hand. Later in the evening, Gil had suggested tucking away some cash where the man would find it after they were gone, but Nir had nixed the idea. This family was not acting out of humility, but on principle. Nir's team had to respect that.

He passed one closed door, where the old woman would sleep. Behind the next were the man, his wife, and their two toddlers. The last door was the front, and Nir twisted on the deadbolt to ensure that it was still engaged.

From there, he stepped into a small living room with seating for everyone if the children didn't mind the floor or a lap. Reaching into his pocket, he pulled out a satellite phone before dropping into a stiff armchair. Because of the way the phone was rigged, there was only one button on the keypad that worked. Nir pressed it.

After two rings, a smoky alto voice answered. "Guido's Pizza. We've got the best gelato in town."

Nir smiled. "Gelato sounds good tonight."

"I agree. I think I may room service some right up," Nicole answered. "Why would I do that? Because I can."

"You are reaching new levels of rudeness, *motek*. You better be careful, or I just might find myself someone new. In the next room there's a single woman who may be a little long in the tooth, but she would make sure that my socks never had holes."

"Ouch. Hard to go up against competition like that. How are you doing, Nir?"

Normally, Nir would never talk shop over a satellite phone in an enemy country, but Lahav was the one who pieced together the device before Nicole encrypted it. There was no entity, human or AI, that could break in.

"We're doing okay. We've driven the route. It'll be tight. But as long as no one screws up, we'll get it done."

"What about getting out? What's the police presence like?"

That was the rub, wasn't it? Taking the guy out would be tough, but doable. Getting away after? That's where the real challenge came. But Nicole didn't need to have that on her mind.

"I think we'll be alright. Got a few good options."

"Liar." That word hung in the air for a few moments before Nicole added, "Aren't you going to ask me about my operation?"

Thankful that she had pushed on, Nir responded, "And how is Operation Full Body Rub going?"

"Yuck! I asked you not to call it that. It sounds so smarmy. Anyway, I don't know the view you have from where you are, but I'm standing out on my balcony with a full panorama of the Blue Mosque below."

Nir looked at the small television balanced on an end table in front of him. "You may have me slightly bested."

"Yeah, well, you could have been here with me, mister, and let Dima go to Tehran. But you had to run off to get your adrenaline rush."

There was no way Nir could have sent others on his team to Tehran while he luxuriated in Istanbul. "Listen, Nicole, I'm the leader…"

"Oh, stop it," Nicole laughed. "I was just poking the bear. You're so easy sometimes. Besides, you should see Dima in a tailored tux. It's a good thing I don't have roaming eyes."

Nir was quietly laughing now. This was exactly what he needed tonight. It was a reminder that there was a real world outside of this Kurdish enclave in Tehran. "Tell me how it's coming together with Bakir. Is he willing to play ball?"

Nicole sighed. "Burhan's in. Whether he suspects anything or not, I don't know. Because he thinks we're Russians, it's likely he does wonder if this is more than just a trick on Mousa. But I don't think he feels like he has any other choice."

"He really doesn't."

"Which kind of sucks. I mean, that's my struggle, Nir. We're tricking a man into killing someone. What about the moral culpability he'll feel? Because he will find out. He's too smart of a man not to realize when he sees the news that it was his hand that took Mousa's life."

"And if he does find out, he'll deal with it. He didn't choose to do the wrong thing. He was tricked into it. Whether that makes things better before God or not, I don't know. That's more your purview. All I know is that we had to get to Mousa, and Bakir was our one shot."

Nicole gave an exasperated grunt. Nir could picture her dropping onto some well-cushioned couch. "I know. I get that. I just wonder if we could have been honest with him?"

"Absolutely not," said Nir, standing and pacing the small room. "We couldn't have taken that chance. What if he just disappeared? Packed up and left? Listen, Mousa has to die, and Bakir is the man to do it. And by doing it, he will give his mother, his brothers, and most of all, his sister a new life filled with opportunities. There was no hope for them back in Syria. Remember, I was there. I saw the devastation of the Damascus earthquake. This will save their lives."

"I know. I know."

Nir sat back down in his chair. "Listen, Nicole, I don't know how much longer we have left to take these people out. Already, all the goodwill people had toward us is fading. First, we'll see our enemies turn back against us. Then our friends. And after that, our own people. The prime minister has the country with him for now, but the longer we go without getting our hostages back, the more the nation will turn against him. Eventually, we'll be back to how we were, with a divided country—one side wants safety through victory, while the other just wants to get along with the rest of the world. This is our window— right here, right now."

"I hear you, Nir. You're right. I just…hang on." It sounded like she was moving. Nir could hear a sliding door close on her end. He waited for her.

"Chilly night," she said. He continued to wait. The door opened, and she said "No thanks" to someone, probably Dima or Imri. Then he heard a door close.

There was a soft sigh as she settled on something cushiony. "I'm all in on this, *motek*. So don't worry about me. You focus on yourself. There are things I want to say to you—things about your spiritual life. But you've heard them all from me before."

"Yes, I have. And I appreciate them all."

"Just promise me you'll be careful. Think again about what I've said. Maybe in the midst of Tehran's darkness, you'll see a great light."

Nir chuckled softly. "Maybe. You never know. Take care, *motek*. I love you." The words were out of his mouth before he knew what he was saying. He knew they were genuine, but he hadn't planned on letting them out on a satellite call from the heart of Tehran. Once they were out, though, there was no taking them back.

Silence hung in the air before Nicole finally responded. "And I love you, Nir. Take care."

The line went dead.

Nir sat for another 15 minutes thinking about the mission, thinking about God, but mostly thinking about Nicole. Finally, he got up and retraced his steps. The deadbolt on the front door was still secure, and the matriarch of the family didn't bother to notice him this time as he passed by. Slipping quietly into his room, he laid down on his cot. He closed his eyes and didn't open them again until morning.

CHAPTER 22

TWO DAYS LATER
JANUARY 3, 2024—16:35 (4:35 PM) IRST

The last two days had been a lot of hurry up and wait. They didn't dare go back out and drive the route again. That would have been dangerous and would have signaled uncertainty. Anything they didn't learn during their first go-round wasn't worth knowing. He had no idea where Nurettin and his men had gone. They had disappeared the first night, promising to return in time for the extraction. Once again, he found that his life was depending on the word of a Kurd.

Nir shifted on his seat. For all the motorcycles he had ridden over the years, this was the first time that he had found himself sitting back in shotgun. There were other names that Gil and Yaron had for his seat position—none of them polite, none appropriate for mixed company.

Thankfully, Gil was masterful in his driving, and even the weight in Nir's backpack didn't pull him backward when his partner accelerated. Both men were dressed identically—black leather from top to bottom with black helmets lightly streaked with red to match their bike. The motorcycle was a TVS Apache RTR 200. It was very maneuverable and had a quick ramp-up speed. Although the kilometers per hour maxed at 127, they wouldn't need more than that. If they ended up in a chase, it would be in the city. So they would count on Gil's driving skills to get them clear, not the bike's speed.

They had been cruising the streets for about 30 minutes when Liora's voice sounded in Nir's ear. "Target is exiting the building." Nir tapped the back of Gil's helmet with his own to make sure he had heard the report. Gil squibbed a quick left/right to acknowledge. They weren't far away, so they continued going the opposite direction. They waited for the next update on Emad al-Natsheh's location.

"Target is confirmed in second vehicle." There was a pause, then Liora continued, "Eyes on the ground put him in the Lexus SUV." She then read off a license plate.

Gil revved the engine twice and veered. Nir confirmed they had received the message, simply saying, "Check."

Traffic was heavy this time of the evening, which was exactly what they had counted on. As the bike made a lazy circle around Topkhaneh Square, Nir pictured in his mind the three-vehicle convoy zigzagging its way through a busy alley system until it found Sadat Sharif. After turning left, they would cruise a few blocks south to Imam Khomeini Street, where they would point themselves to the west.

It was at that junction that Nir had initially wanted to do the hit, but Yaron felt the surrounding buildings weren't quite right. After some discussion, they decided to let the convoy pass through Hasan Abad Square, travel up a block or so, then hit them there.

Gil finished his lap around the old artillery building and merged into the traffic on Imam Khomeini Street. Up ahead five or six blocks, the convoy should be approaching the main thoroughfare. Gently, Gil feathered the accelerator, keeping their speed without gaining any ground.

"Target is on Khomeini," said Liora.

Nir tapped Gil's side, letting him know not to make any sudden moves. Slipping his arms from the backpack, he brought it around to the front. Another tap let his partner know he was holding on. Gil began to twist up the throttle.

"Target is passing through Hasan Abad Square."

If all went according to plan, they wouldn't get much farther. As he hoped, Nir heard, "Decoy deployed. Looks like three of four lanes blocked. Traffic is stopped. Target is twelve cars back."

The one thing the Israelis had been missing was a diversion. It would be too easy to get caught in traffic and lose their chance at the hit. A quick call to Nurettin had provided what they needed. From the sound of things, he had made the right decision bringing the Kurds in. A van driving north on Bastiyun-e-Garbi had just plowed into the west-flowing traffic, bringing it to a standstill.

Next bottle of arak is on me, Mustafa.

As Nir unzipped the backpack with one hand, Gil wove between the cars that had come to a standstill.

"Two blocks ahead," said Liora.

Inside the bag, Nir felt two buttons, one on top of each mine. He depressed them, knowing that they would trigger blinking green lights.

"One block ahead," said Liora.

Nir slapped Gil's side, letting him know that he was ready.

Ten seconds later, Liora said, "On your right. On your right."

Nir pulled the two mines out of the backpack. He hit one hard against the tinted rear passenger window of the SUV carrying al-Natsheh to make sure he got the attention of all inside. He waved the first magnetic mine in front of them, then slammed it down hard onto the roof. The second he slapped up against the door. Staring into his own reflection in the tinted window, Nir aimed a finger gun and pulled the trigger.

CHAPTER 23

HOTEL SULTANAHMET, ISTANBUL, TURKEY— JANUARY 3, 2024—16:05 (4:05 PM) EEST

Because of the humidity in the room, there was a slight fog covering the camera lens. But the picture was still clear enough for Nicole and Dima to see Burhan laying out all he needed for Khaled Mousa's hammam treatment. Even through the haze, Nicole could see the man's hands shaking. She prayed that he could keep it together.

Mousa was in the next room over, warming up his body temperature in preparation for the massage and cleansing. Imri couldn't get a camera into that well-used area, but the fact that Burhan was as nervous as he was told Nicole that he hadn't ratted them out.

Just hold on, Burhan. This will soon be over and your life and that of your family will be so much better.

"Pod is in position," came Yariv Rabin's voice from CARL. Nicole was still startled every time she heard him. The team had been made up of her, Liora, Dafna, Yossi, and Lahav for so many years. She used to feel like the outsider—like a South African in a world of Jews—which was quite accurate. But now the outsider position belonged to Yariv. She wondered if they would ever get totally used to him and his Orthodox ways.

Nicole's eyes shifted to a second laptop she had set up on a small rack in the back of their rented Fiat Doblò van. She and Dima had checked out of the hotel that morning and taken a shuttle to the airport. It was there they were picked up by the vehicle and driven by a local asset back to their place in the hotel garage.

Positioned alongside the first computer, the laptop Nicole now focused on showed a street view. Actually, it was a street-ish view. The road was lined on both sides with tents and some makeshift hovels. Located outside the city limits of Damascus, this camp, Al-Hariqa, was one of hundreds that surrounded the borders of the once-great city that was now demolished.

"Pod in position," Nicole acknowledged. *Pod* was the name for the Unit 504 team that was prepared to spirit Burhan's family out of Damascus—and out of Syria—should all go well.

It has to go well—for Burhan, but especially for Sabra.

Nicole had seen pictures of 15-year-old Sabra. Black hair, amazing smile, a little small for her age, which isn't unusual for sufferers of cystic fibrosis. In the camp, she probably had less than a year to live. In America, she could have decades.

"He's positioning the Novichok agent," Dima said, pointing to the hammam screen from next to Nicole. Up behind the wheel of the van, the local Mossad asset, Aydin, kept his eyes on the street around them.

Nicole turned her eyes back to the shot from inside the hotel and watched as Burhan slid heavy gloves onto his hands. Next, he took a small metal container from his right pants pocket. He stared at it without opening it. Then his eyes turned up toward the camera, and Nicole felt like they locked with hers. All his faith was in Nicole and Dima. If he went through with this, it would mean life or death for him and his family. If they abandoned him, he would be arrested, and Hamas or Hezbollah would round up everyone he loved. They would do unspeakable things to his mother and to Sabra, and, judging by October 7, to his brothers too.

Staring hard at the screen, Nicole tried to instill courage and determination into the Syrian.

Just get this done, my friend. We've got your back and we've got eyes on your family. It will all work out, I promise you.

Turning his attention back to the container, Burhan rested it on the large marble bed in front of him. Reaching to a shelf below, he removed two large brass pitchers. He set them on the bed, opened the metal container, and poured half the contents in one and half in the other. Once again, he looked at the camera before putting the pitchers back under the table.

Quickly, Burhan moved to a corner of the room where there was a sink. He pulled off his long gloves and vigorously scrubbed his hands. Then, before turning back around, he lifted his hands in front of his chest in prayer. As Nicole watched him pray to his god, she prayed to hers. She prayed for his courage. She prayed for his success. She prayed that God would punish those responsible for October 7. She prayed that she was doing the right thing.

Once Burhan was done, he passed his hands over his face, took a deep breath, and walked to the door.

"Snare is collecting the rabbit," said Dafna, using the code names for Burhan and Mousa.

"Snare is collecting the rabbit, copy," answered Nicole. "Gath, stand ready."

"Standing ready, *root*," answered Imri.

Nicole watched the empty room for three minutes before she saw Burhan return through the door with Khaled Mousa. The exceedingly hairy man was wearing only a towel around his waist, and he was talking and laughing as he walked in. Burhan appeared to be doing his best to keep with the conversation.

A large marble bed sat in the middle of the room, which the Syrian had covered with towels. With a little help, Mousa was able to hoist himself onto the hard surface. Once balanced on top, he turned face down.

Yariv's voice came over the coms again, giving a real-time translation of the Arabic conversation.

"Is the bed comfortable enough?"

"It isn't supposed to be too comfortable, is it? Just give me one more pillow for my face."

Burhan complied. Once Mousa was relaxed, the Syrian lifted two large pitchers of hot water and poured them over Mousa from his head down to his feet. Then, from a compartment in the table, Burhan lifted a small brass bowl containing dried clay. He proceeded to sprinkle it over the man's body. For the next five minutes, he massaged the newly formed clay into the Jordanian's hairy back and legs before rinsing it off with two pitchers of hot water that he had retrieved from a nearby pool.

Next came a thick, black lava soap followed by a round with rough exfoliating salts. Each time, Burhan would finish the cycle by dipping the pitchers into the hot-water pool and letting the water luxuriously cascade over the man's back.

The second-to-last application was the eye-opener. Much like applying aftershave on a freshly groomed face, an astringent was splashed over the open pores of the back and legs to close them down and protect the skin. There were many who skipped this final step because it could be like a hard slap after a soft kiss. But Mousa insisted on the whole treatment. Burhan took the applicator, which looked much like a small mop, dipped it in the astringent, and painted it onto the Hamas man's back. Mousa let out a howl and a laugh.

"If I hadn't asked you to do that, I would kill you," the Jordanian joked through clenched teeth.

"I'm very sorry, sir. There is no good way to do this."

"I know, I know. I'm only joking. But I can think of five or six people I'd like to give that treatment to."

Burhan then waved a towel over Mousa's back to try to cool it down. "Are you ready for the water before the suds?" The Hamas man grunted his affirmation.

Once again, Burhan looked up at the camera, and Nicole felt like his eyes had locked with hers. This was the decision point. He could dip the pitchers he had been using all night into the cold-water pool, and his life would go on as before. Or he could reach below, retrieve the pitchers he had prepared earlier, and trust that life would change for the better. It all depended on whether he trusted her or not.

Burhan didn't move.

"Gath, get ready," said Dima.

There was going to be an attempt on Mousa one way or another. If Burhan didn't do it, then it would be up to Imri to take out the guard at the front of the hammam spa, then the two guards who were posted outside the *hararet*, or hot room, where the treatment was taking place. Once inside the hot room, he would dispatch Mousa with two shots to the heart and one to the head. The backup plan was risky and could likely get both Imri and some innocent bystanders killed.

Nicole touched Dima's arm. "Give him a second."

The moment hung in the air until Mousa growled, "Well?"

Burhan reached under the table and collected the deadly pitchers. Quickly, he dipped each into the cold-water pool and poured them down the length of the man's body.

Mousa sighed and tensed at the iciness of the bath.

"Please give me one moment as I prepare the special soap."

Burhan moved quickly to the sink, where he washed his hands thoroughly once more. Then the Syrian poured soap into a large, thin bag. Next, he dipped the bag into the hot-water pool, mixing the soap with water. Then he swung the pouch around, creating a sudsy froth. Soon, he had a huge sack of bubbles. Starting from Mousa's head, Burhan squeezed the froth through a small opening in the bottom of the bag until there was a thick layer of suds covering the man like an overly frosted birthday cake. As the bubbles effervesced and popped, life would be brought back to the skin.

It was then that Mousa began to convulse.

CHAPTER 24

Nir slapped Gil's side, then held on for dear life. The engine throttled up and Nir felt the g-force trying to pull him off the back of the bike. Over the din, he could barely hear the panic as the passengers attempted to escape the SUV. But that wasn't the sound his ears were tuned for. A crack sounded through the air, followed two seconds later by a second.

"Target is down," said Liora. "Confirmed, target is eliminated."

Across the street from the traffic jam stood the multistory Etka Store. While a department store for the families of armed forces would not normally be the best sniper lair, there weren't a lot of options on Emad al-Natsheh's route home. So, in the middle of the previous night, Yaron had climbed up the outside stairs of the building to the roof carrying a long case, a camouflage tarp, a full water flask, and an empty water bottle for when his body processed the contents of the full water flask.

In the case was a gray Barrett MRAD bolt-action rifle chambered in 338 Lapua Magnum. Nir knew how much Yaron loved that gun. He had often seen him on the range hitting long-distance targets dead-on using an MRAD. There may have been more expensive guns available, but to ensure he made this shot, Yaron needed the gun that he knew best. After prepping the gun and arranging his camouflage against the side of the roof, the old man had settled in for what turned out to be a 14-hour wait.

Nir and the team at CARL knew that using real mines was out of the question. In a traffic jam on a busy street, there would have been at least a dozen unintended casualties. And when it came down to it, most of the people outside al-Natsheh's SUV hated the people inside the SUV as much as they did. Making civilians pay for the sins of their governmental tyrants and the regime's toady militias was a nonstarter. They had to flush the terrorist out into the open.

It was Avi Carmeli who came up with the idea to use dummy mines. There had been enough real-life stories and movie scenes of bikers blowing up vehicles with magnetic explosives that no explanation would be needed for what was happening. A bike rides up, attaches two devices, then speeds off—your car is about to crack open like a tin can. So what do you do? Get out while you can.

The plan had apparently worked to perfection, as Liora had confirmed when she reported that al-Natsheh was no longer among the living.

That's one more we're sending to you, God. Give him what he deserves. And please help Yaron to get away.

The hope was that in the confusion, Yaron would be able to quickly slip down the back of the Etka building and into his nondescript Saipa Tiba and roll away. But Nir couldn't worry about his old partner now because as they wove through the accident site Nurettin's Kurd friend had created, a police officer was rolling up. Neither Gil nor Nir looked at the man, but he had obviously spotted them. He turned his lights on and angled his vehicle to block their path.

Skirting around him was no problem. But as Nir looked back, he could see the officer on his radio even as the man punched his accelerator. Racing up Imam Khomeini Street for a few blocks, they neared a major intersection with Valiasr Street. But from that intersection, two police cars rounded the corner and aimed directly toward them. Gil clamped down on the brakes, skidding around the first car, then the second. Twisting the throttle, he brought them back to speed before turning right onto Valiasr. On their left were the grounds of the Quran Museum and the Iran Art Museum. On the right were office buildings. And on the sidewalks were dozens of pedestrians pausing their commute, watching and wondering what was going on.

Two blocks up, Gil slammed the brakes and turned right. Half a block more, he cut into an alley.

Nir had already begun unzipping his jacket by the time Gil came to a stop. Over behind a dumpster waited two other motorcycles. Unlike the high-end TVS they were riding, these were designed to blend in. Gil stripped off his black leathers and helmet, leaving him in jeans and an olive-drab T-shirt. He jumped onto the nearest bike—a scaled-down Bajaj Pulsar with a 150cc engine. Pressing the starter, it jumped to life.

Nir, now in jeans and a black T-shirt, straddled what was supposed to be his Honda CD 100, but which he greatly suspected was some other off brand onto which someone had slapped a Honda label. He kicked down on the starter, and nothing happened. Gil looked back at him impatiently. Nir kicked the starter again. A little sputter, then nothing.

Suddenly, up at the entrance to the alley, two police cars turned in.

"Get on," yelled Gil.

"No! Go! Now!"

It was evident by Gil's look that he was not happy with Nir's order, but he was a military man. So he gunned it and drove out the alley's exit. Nir cranked the starter two more times. Not even a sputter. The police cars were almost to him. Rolling the bike so it blocked the center of the alley, he ran.

Behind him, he heard tires screech to a halt and words yelled in Farsi. Ignoring them, he ran up to a row of doors and tried the handle on one, then another. The third handle turned as he heard gunshots behind him. They pinged off the metal door.

He found himself in a kitchen with five sets of surprised and hostile eyes on him.

Thinking quickly, Nir shouted, "*Gasht-e Ershad! Gasht-e Ershad!*" He knew very few words of Farsi, but he did know the name of the guidance patrol or morality police. Again, few Iranians had any love for the Islamic regime. And for most, the lowest of the low were the morality police, who made it their duty to punish people, mostly women, for perceived slights against the Quran. It had been only a year and a half since the Kurdish Mahsa Amini had been arrested by the religious thugs for not wearing a hijab properly, and she had died in custody after a beating. Huge protests had swept the nation before being violently put down by the regime. Nir had no idea who the officers were that were after him, but the only way to get these people on his side was to make them think it was the hated guidance patrol.

When they heard the words, all five snapped to action.

"*Bodo! Bodo!*" said an older man dressed like the head chef. He waved Nir through to the dining room and pointed to the front door.

Behind Nir, there was a crash and a very angry exchange. It sounded to him like maybe his kitchen friends were buying him time. He came out on a main street. Sirens sounded to his left, so he ran right. He had made it only half a block before two more police cars rounded the corner ahead.

"Cross the street and enter the building directly opposite you." It was Avi's voice. He was so in the moment that he had forgotten that there were eyes watching from overhead. "Gil is clear. So is Yaron. You're the only one left, and we're going to get you out."

"You're on now, Avi? What have you been doing?" Nir called out as he ran, relieved to hear his friend's voice.

"Sorry, just warming up my coffee. Do you know how hard it is to open those sugar packets with just one hand?"

Gunshots cut through the din of the street and a windshield next to Nir shattered.

"If I make it back, I'll buy you one of those sugar dispenser thingies and have your name stenciled on it. Just get me out of here now."

CHAPTER 25

HOTEL SULTANAHMET,
ISTANBUL, TURKEY—16:35 (4:35 PM) EEST

I mri, go," Nicole called into her coms.

"*Root*," came the reply.

Mousa's reaction to the poison should have taken longer. The plan had been for Burhan to slip out and tell the bodyguards that their boss was on an important call and demanded to be left alone until he texted for the masseuse to come back. That would give the Syrian the chance to slip from the warmup room through the welcome area and out the front, where Imri would meet him to skirt him away.

So much for the plan.

The first problem they now faced was that a bodyguard remained outside the front doors, leaning against a wall and looking at his phone. Nicole watched the hotel's in-house security camera as Imri walked toward the front door.

"*Kam assaa'ah?*" Imri asked the man.

As the man looked up, Imri punched him hard in the solar plexus, doubling him over. Imri then brought his knee up into the man's face, putting him out. Grabbing the man under his arms, he dragged him to a bench. He positioned him so he was sitting up, but the man's busted nose was pouring blood.

"Just let him go. Get Burhan," Nicole commanded.

"*Root*," answered Imri, letting the man fold over and finally drop to the ground.

Turning back to the heavy wooden doors, Imri pulled them open. Nicole switched her view to another camera. A pretty, young Filipino girl began to greet him, but he smiled, said "Excuse me," and continued onward like he belonged there.

The girl seemed unsure of what to do, which allowed Imri time to get through to the preparation room. Nicole had no cameras there, so she listened intently.

"Should I go help him?" asked Dima, who was extremely antsy at being trapped in the van next to Nicole.

"Wait just a second," she responded. As she did, her eyes caught sight of Mousa twisting in agony. It was brutal to see.

Remember what he commanded his people to do to the innocent parents and their precious children. He deserves what he's getting!

Pointing to that screen, she said to Dima, "You watch that and make sure he dies."

The Russian Jew angled the laptop so that Nicole would have to intentionally lean over to see it.

Suddenly, Imri's voice spoke English in Nicole's ears. "Mr. Bakir, I'm so glad I found you. You have an urgent call from the management."

Someone spoke some angry words that Nicole couldn't understand.

In his most pleasant voice, Imri replied, "Well, I'm sorry, sir, but this is urgent business."

There were more angry words, then the sound of a scuffle. Screams sounded from a distance, which Nicole assumed were other patrons awaiting their turns in the hot rooms.

"Let's go! Now," shouted Imri.

Imri and Burhan appeared in the welcome area, rushing through to the front doors.

The girl at the front desk quickly picked up the phone. As she did, Nicole pressed three keys on her keyboard. The girl put the phone to her ear. Then she pulled it away and looked at it. She set it down and picked it up again. She listened, shrugged, then put it back down.

Always got to keep a little something up the sleeve.

Shutting down the hotel's phone system was an emergency plan Nicole had hoped to not use. But, once again, preparation was the greater part of wisdom.

Imri and Burhan had made it far enough up the hall to where they could cut left to the stairs. Two flights down put them on ground level. One more level down put them in the garage, where the van waited.

"The dog is dead," said Dima. "Do you want to confirm?"

Nicole didn't want to, but she did anyway. Mousa had fallen off the marble slab and was splayed on the floor in a very uncomfortable-looking angle. His eyes were opened wide in terror and there was no movement in his chest or abdomen.

"Confirmed."

"Target down and out," said Dima.

"Confirmed. Target down and out," replied Dafna.

The side door to the van slid open and Imri and Burhan climbed in.

"What was that? He was dying," yelled the Syrian.

"He's not dying," said Dima. "He's already dead." Nicole elbowed the Russian hard in the ribs.

Burhan was near panic. "What? How? I told you that I would not be party to killing anyone."

"And, as far as you knew, you weren't," said Nicole. "Your conscience can remain clear."

"My conscience! What do you know about my conscience? You just tricked me into killing a man, and now you say that my conscience can still be clear. And now what will you do? I know how you Russians work. Mousa will not be the only dead man today." The terrified Syrian backed into a corner of the van.

Nicole reached out her hand. "Listen, your work is not done yet. Right now, I need you here next to me."

Ignoring Nicole's hand, Burhan remained in the corner.

Undeterred, Nicole stretched her hand out farther. "Please, Burhan, come. I'm going to need your help."

Anger and bitterness filled the Syrian's words. "What? Do you have someone else you need to kill?"

"No, I'm going to need you to convince your family that it is okay to go with my friends. I told you before, we are people who keep our word." Turning a laptop toward Burhan, she gave him a live view outside his family's temporary shelter in Syria.

CHAPTER 26

Nir burst through a door and into a small lobby.

"Which way?" he called out.

"How would I know? I'm watching from a drone, *tembel*. You just need to keep moving. Three police cars are braking hard out front," replied Avi.

Nir ran down a hall, trying door handles as he went.

"There's an alley out back if you can get through," said Avi.

At the fifth door, the handle pushed down. Nir burst through the door as he heard yells coming from the lobby. He ran through a small entryway into a family room where three young children sat around a small television, watching a cartoon.

Someone shouted something behind him.

Nir turned. A large man was directly in front of him in the kitchen with his wife. He snatched a cooking knife from nearby and stood to block Nir.

Seriously?

Nir had too much momentum to stop and not enough time to draw his gun. He dove at the father's knees as the man took a swipe at him. The Iranian toppled and cracked his head on the ground. Nir jumped to his feet, spotted the knife, and kicked it down a hall toward what must have been the bedrooms. The man had twisted on the ground and was grabbing at Nir's legs. Nir leaned over the man with his hand cocked to punch him when he felt a clang on the back of his head. He stumbled forward, trying to regain his balance. When he turned, he saw the wife standing with fire in her eyes and a large, shallow pan in her hand.

Nir felt as if the room were spinning. The husband was back on his feet, but very unsteady. Before Nir could do anything about the wife, the husband lunged at Nir. But he was sloppy, and even in his fogginess Nir could see it coming. He flopped against a wall, letting the man glance off him, then gave the man a hard punch to the back of his neck so that he went sprawling down the hallway.

Nir turned back to the woman, who was holding up the pan defensively. She looked terrified and determined.

"Out," Nir said in Arabic. The woman didn't understand him. Nir pointed to himself, then made his fingers walk fast. "How do I go out?"

Recognition crossed the woman's face, but she didn't lower the pan. She pointed to the front door. Nir shook his head. "Back door." He made his fingers run, then jump.

Again, the woman seemed to understand. She lowered the pan a little and pointed past her husband's sprawled body to the back rooms.

"*Mersi,*" he replied.

"Three more cars pulled up out front. Get out of there now, Nir." It was Avi again, telling him what he already knew.

He ran, leapt over the crumpled husband, and went through the door at the end of the hall. It opened to a nicely kept master bedroom with windows at the back. The stars had cleared from his vision, but he still felt a little uneasy on his feet. Pulling open the window, he was grateful not to find iron bars blocking the exit. Upper body first, he pulled himself through the window.

As he did, Avi said, "Be careful coming out the back. I see two police cars and two motorcycles turning up the alley."

Nir cursed. "That's information that would have been helpful ten seconds ago."

"Okay, I see you. There's a cut-through across the alley, two buildings to the right."

Nir ran. He could hear the engines of the motorcycles rev up as he made the turn. The cut-through was narrow—too narrow for a car, but unfortunately not for a bike. Nir was only halfway through when he heard the bikes turn in and gun it. There was no way he would make it out to the street.

Spotting a wood pallet among some restaurant trash, Nir snatched it up, spun, and let it fly. It hit the lead driver squarely in the chest, doubling him over and sending him down. The second motorcycle cop had no time to react and plowed into the first bike. He flew over the handlebars in Nir's direction and hit the ground. Nir dropped hard with his knee onto the man's chest, feeling a bone break. He flipped the man over and secured him with his own cuffs. The first man wasn't moving, so Nir didn't worry about him. Instead, he lifted his bike, pressed the start button, and was relieved to hear it come to life.

Voices called down the alley. A high-pitched whine flew by his ear followed immediately by the sound of gunshots. Nir twisted the throttle, spun the bike in the opposite direction from the gunfire, and raced out of the alley.

"You've got cops coming from both sides. Go straight through to the next alley," Avi said over the coms.

Nir obeyed, hearing the sirens racing up behind him. Unfortunately, this passageway was wider, and he heard cars turn in after him.

"Okay, you're going to do a quick right, left, left, right, and left."

"Seriously? How about I do some calculus in my head while I drive? Just tell me when to turn."

"Now!" A narrow alley appeared and Nir angled the bike hard. There was trash all around and he almost lost traction as the rear tire skidded.

"Left, now! Go left!"

Nir obeyed. This alley was wider, but dead-ended about 100 meters ahead.

"Left again, then stop and try to blend into the wall!"

Blend into the wall? What?

Then right in front of him, one police car, then two, then three and four sped past.

"Nice blending. Now, as quietly as you can, take your bike across the alley and go up a few buildings. I'll tell you when to turn right."

Barely twisting the throttle, Nir eased across the alley.

"Wait!" Avi yelled, but it was too late. Another police car turned into the alley. Nir saw the cop looking right at him. He twisted the throttle as the officer punched down on the accelerator.

"This is ridiculous, Avi! Get me out of here!"

Avi swore. "I'm trying! The cops are everywhere!"

There was no way he was going to escape on the bike. He was too easy to recognize—a tall civilian without a helmet on a police motorcycle. Nir could hear other police bikes in the alleys nearby. It was just a matter of time before they found him.

"Where's the nearest busy street?" he asked.

"It's to your right. Any of the alleys will take you to it."

"Okay, I'm going to try something. Let me know if you see cops turning onto that street."

Going up three blocks, Nir took a right. Seeing the back door to a restaurant, he dropped the bike in front of it. He opened the door, but didn't go in. Then he ran ahead to the street. Before stepping out of the alley, he breathed deeply and calmed himself. A row of cars were waiting for a red light to turn green. He scanned the drivers before striding to an old green car to his right.

Inside was a man in his fifties in a business suit. Nir knocked on the front passenger window to get the man's attention. Then he smiled and did a cranking motion with his hand, indicating for the man to lower his window even through there probably hadn't been hand-cranked windows on cars for maybe a decade or two. Obviously curious, the man obliged. When the window lowered, Nir reached in, popped the lock, opened the door, and sat down.

He slid his Masada Slim 9mm from his ankle holster and pressed it against the man's side.

"*Negarani nadareh,*" Nir said, still smiling and trying to assure the man that he shouldn't worry. "*Rāndan,*" Nir added, continuing his butchery of the Farsi language by trying to tell the man to drive.

Apparently the command was clear enough to get the man moving.

"Where am I?" Nir asked Avi in Arabic.

"You're heading west on Pasteur Street. If you can go up through the Pasteur Square roundabout with Kargar Street, a few blocks past there I can have one of our Kurd friends pick you up in front of the Tahid Mosque. But you're going to have to do something about your driver."

"Hang on. I'm going to try something." Nir looked at the driver, who was stoic yet kept looking down at Nir's gun. "Hey," he said. When the man turned to him, Nir said, "Raisi," referring to the current president of Iran. Then he turned his thumb downward.

The man glared at him. He said, "Raisi," and pulled his thumb across his neck.

Nir nodded. "Me," he said, pointing to himself. Then he held up his gun and pointed to it. "Raisi."

The man stared briefly at Nir, a light of recognition appearing in his eyes. He turned back to the road, muttering, "*Inshallah.*"

As they approached the mosque, Nir pointed to the roadside. The man pulled over. "*Mersi*," said Nir as he stepped out of the car. The man just grunted and drove off.

Of all the cars parked along the street, there was only one that had someone standing outside. Nir went his direction, and the man slipped into the driver's seat. Nir joined him in the car and found a blue-and-gold embroidered kufi hat on the dash in front of him. He settled it on his head and nodded at the driver. That began a 45-minute journey of main thoroughfares, side streets, and alleyways. Police cars with their sirens blaring passed them often for the first half hour, but gradually diminished in number. Occasionally they saw a roadblock, but the driver was adept enough to weave through the backways to avoid them.

At last, after turning a corner, the man abruptly pulled to the side of the road. Nir looked and realized he was back at the safe house. He thanked the man, who didn't respond. Exiting the car, he went through the front gates and into the courtyard where Gil and Yaron were waiting for him, as were Colonel Nurettin and his small group of men.

Before Nir had time to deliver his "Sorry, guys, I got sidetracked shopping for truncheons at the morality store" line—which he had been practicing in his mind for at least 20 minutes—a frantic Nurettin stepped forward and grabbed his arm. As he dragged Nir toward an idling box truck, he said, "You're finally here. We are running far behind schedule. Quick, we must get into the truck and on the road. They'll be closing down the highways soon."

Submitting to the Kurd's lead, Nir allowed himself to be pulled along. "What happens if they close the roads before we get through?"

"I am killed immediately. You will be kept alive for a show trial before you are killed."

Nir turned to see if there was any indication that the man was joking. There was not. He glanced at Gil and Yaron, who both looked equally tense.

Glad I didn't get the truncheon line out. You've got to read the room.

Nir climbed first into the back of the truck, followed by Gil and Yaron. A heated argument with the driver delayed Nurettin a minute before he, too, pulled himself in. The four men tucked themselves into the front of the box and the false wall was secured to block them from prying eyes.

"Everything okay?" Nir asked, sitting down on the metal floor.

"Persian Kurds are just a little softer than those of us who live in the war zone," answered the colonel. He seemed exasperated, but Nir didn't sense it was with him.

"Are you sure that they won't sell us out?"

"That's what I was reminding them of. They don't need to think just of themselves, but of their extended families. They'll be fine."

"Interesting. I've had to use that 'kill your family' line on quite a few enemies. Never on a friend."

As he spoke, Nurettin retrieved a long piece of fabric from next to him and began to unwrap it. "There are many kinds of friends among the Kurds. Most don't need reminding. Some do. We'll be fine."

Once the soft covering was removed, the colonel lifted an M16A4. He pulled the mag to make sure it was full, then slammed it back in and chambered a round.

Nir nodded toward the gun. "And that? What kind of friend is that for?"

"We Kurds learn early that anyone who is not a friend is an enemy.

There are few Kurds in this world. That means there are many, many enemies."

"So what does that make me? I'm not a Kurd."

Nurettin laughed. "No, you are not. But I have declared you to be an honorary Kurd."

"Cool. Do I get a medal or a certificate or something?"

"Still the funny man. Being an honorary Kurd just means that I help you and you help me, and we'll try not to kill each other while we're doing it."

"Sounds like a good deal to me," said Nir, sliding across the floor toward the cooler. He tossed bottles of water to each of the men.

As he did, Nurettin said, "With men like you, we could do great things. Who knows? Maybe we could take over Iraq."

"Who'd want it?" grumbled Yaron.

"Ha! Despite how he looks, he's a funny man too! We have to have the grumpy one along with us. We could take over the world!"

The roads were still passable as they exited the city and began their long trek north. Nurettin spent the time talking about ways they could invade Baghdad and topple the Iraqi government. At first, the three Israelis barely paid attention, but soon they were all engaged. Anything to pass the long, monotonous hours riding in the back of a box truck.

Elnur Isayev, the former Azeri intelligence man, had already left Khankendi by the time the team arrived back in Azerbaijan. This allowed Nurettin's men to drive the Israelis all the way to the air base. After saying their goodbyes, Nir's team boarded their agency Gulfstream. Nir was disappointed to see they had a new crew.

On the way back, the plane stopped in Tbilisi, Georgia, where Nir left the rest of the team. His flight plans didn't have him going south, but west. He'd be back in Tel Aviv soon enough. But for now, there were a few things he needed to wrap up back in Belgium.

CHAPTER 27

HOTEL SULTANAHMET, ISTANBUL, TURKEY— 16:43 PM (4:43 PM) EEST

Don't harm them. Please, I will do anything. Just don't do anything bad to them." There was fear and desperation in Burhan's voice as he rambled on and on.

Nicole slapped Burhan hard across the face to get him to focus. The man closed his mouth.

"Calm down! We had a deal. You help us; we help your family. But for us to help your family, you need to chill out. Do you understand?"

Burhan nodded, his hand against his cheek.

"Good. We have men there who will enter your family's dwelling when we give the word. It will be up to you to convince your mom and siblings to go with them, okay? We will not take anyone by force, and we will not make a scene. Either your family calmly walks out, or we leave them. Do you understand?"

Burhan's eyes were still wide, and his hand hadn't left his cheek.

"I need to hear you say it, Burhan. Do you understand?"

"I understand."

Nicole turned to Dima and nodded. Dima spoke into his coms system. "Go! Go!"

Another laptop sat on the shelf in the van. Nicole opened it up, and the screen revealed the video feeds from the five Unit 504 operators. Each man had a tiny camera and microphone threaded from their collars at the right side of their necks to packs in the small of their backs. The doors of two cars opened, and the men got out and made their way to the door of the rickety lean-to.

Without bothering to knock, the men entered the home, drawing their weapons as they did so.

"Quiet! Quiet!" they told the family in Arabic. Imri leaned toward Nicole and gave her a real-time translation.

Nicole's heart broke when she saw the conditions they were living in. There was just enough room for a cookstove and two cots. Burhan's 19-year-old brother, Rifar, was on one cot, while his tween youngest sibling, Nizar, sat on the ground. Lying on the other cot immersed in a coughing fit was Sabra. His mother, Nurul, was squatting next to the small stove, cooking.

As soon as the men stepped in, Rifar reached under his pillow, then leapt to his feet holding a knife.

"Get out of here! Now!" he yelled.

One of the 504 men grabbed his wrist, twisted the knife away, then pushed him back onto the cot.

"We are not here to harm you," said the leader of the squad to Burhan's mother, who had turned and was holding a metal spoon in front of her like a weapon. "We have been sent by your son, Burhan, to help you. You must come with us."

"Go with you? Who are you? Burhan's not here. Go, go, before I cry for help," said Nurul.

Sabra, who had briefly gotten control of her coughing, once again broke out in a deep, rattling fit. Her mother instinctively turned, which gave the lead 504 man time to snatch the spoon from her hand. This caused Rifar to jump up again, only to be pushed back onto the cot by a hard shove. Nizar just sat big-eyed and mute on the floor.

"Please, *Sayyida*, we do not have much time." The man removed an iPad from a waist pouch. As he did, Nicole clicked on the camera in front of Burhan and herself. "Please look. Here is your son."

The man lifted the iPad to the woman, and Nicole changed the view on the laptop to that of the handheld device's camera.

"*Umm?*" Burhan said.

"Burhan? Is that you?" Nurul burst into tears.

On the other laptop, Nicole saw the youngest child, Nizar, leap to his feet to look at the screen. "Burhan!" he cried.

"*Umm*, it's me," said Burhan through sobs. "Please listen to these men. They have come to help us. They have promised to help Sabra."

"And you trust the Israelis?" It was Rifar's voice. "They will stab you in the back as soon as look at you."

"These aren't Israelis," said Burhan. "They're Russians. They've already done for me what they promised. We must trust them."

Rifar was up at the iPad now, and Nicole could hear Imri's voice tense up as he translated. "You are such a fool! These are not Russians. These are Israelis, and if we go with them, we will end up dead in a ditch somewhere." A hand grabbed the back of Rifar's neck, and he went flying back to the cot.

Burhan's mother spoke. "Rifar is right. You have been fooled. The ones in our tent are Israelis, not Russians. Oh, *abni*, what have you brought upon us?"

"Time is running out," said the leader of the Unit 504 team.

Nicole had been watching the action with Rifar. When she turned back, Burhan's eyes were on her. "Is this true? Are you Israeli?"

"No, I am not Israeli. However, I work for them."

Burhan slid on the van floor away from her. In response, Nicole slapped the shelf holding the laptops. Two of them tumbled to the ground, which Imri quickly snatched up to put back in place.

"Listen, Burhan, nothing has changed. If we were going to use you and toss you away, would there be any of our people in Syria right now? Would you even be breathing? Everything we have promised you, we will do. I gave you my word—not as an Israeli or even a South African, but as a person who wants your sister Sabra to have the best chance at life she can have."

Burhan looked away, trying to process everything.

"Look at me!" Nicole slid over next to him and grabbed his chin.

Turning his face toward hers, she repeated, "Look at me! I give you my word. Everything that I promised you will take place. For the sake of Sabra, you must trust me!"

Her eyes were locked with Burhan's for several seconds before he moved back to the shelf and the iPad. "*Umm*, please, you must go with them. They have promised me that they will give us new lives and will provide Sabra the best doctors available. For her sake—for her life— we must take this chance. Please, *umm*, I told you when I left Syria that I would find a way to help Sabra. Here it is. You must take it, and you must do it now!"

Rifar's voice carried across the small lean-to. "You are a fool, Burhan! You are leading us to our deaths."

A hoarse shout broke through. "Stop!"

The iPad angled toward the other cot. Sabra was trying to stand. Rifar raced over and helped get her upright. "I will go with them. If I stay here, I will die."

With his arm still around her shoulders, Rifar said, "But if we go with them, we may die."

Sabra's hand reached to her brother's cheek. "Riffy, here there is no hope. The only chance I have is to go with them. Please don't take this from me."

There was silence for a moment. "We need to go now," said the 504 leader.

Rifar spoke to the man. "We will go with you." Then, turning toward the iPad, he added, "But if we are killed along the way, Burhan, our blood—your mother's and your sister's blood—will be on your hands."

"So be it," said Burhan quietly.

The iPad went dead. Imri switched the laptop back to the 504 men's camera feeds. There was a flurry of activity as the mother and three siblings each packed a small parcel. Then they were rushed to the lead car and helped in. Once the vehicles began to move, the feed cut out.

Nicole was exhausted. "Thank you, Burhan. I know that was tough, but you just saved your family's lives."

But Burhan was not relieved or even grateful. He was angry, which Nicole thought was totally understandable. He had been fooled three ways from Sunday. Every time he turned around, there was a new revelation—a new "gotcha." In his place, she would also be fuming.

"What now? I'm assuming there is no clinic in Hungary for Sabra."

Nicole explained to him that he would meet his family in London. Then, from there, they would fly to Denver in America. She told him about National Jewish Health, explaining that the name came from its roots and not from its clientele or doctors. There, Sabra would find the help she so desperately needed.

When Nicole was done, Burhan responded quietly, "*Inshallah*, Sabra will be made well." Then he went back to the corner of the van. He remained there until they reached Istanbul Airport. Once there, he and Nicole stepped out of the side of the van. Each had a rolling suitcase packed by someone at the Istanbul Mossad station. They checked in under false papers, then two hours later, flew first class to Heathrow in London.

Burham was quiet during the flight. He spoke only to ask necessary questions. Once they were on the ground in London, Nicole assisted in getting the Syrian cleared through immigration and customs. Near the bag check was a man she didn't recognize, but who apparently was on the lookout for her.

"Is yours the red bag, ma'am?" he asked when he walked up to her.

"No, mine is the blue," she replied, giving her half of the introduction. "This is Burhan Bakir."

The man held his hand out. "Burhan, my name is Tommy Stotts. Let's get your bag and be on our way."

Burhan shook the man's hand tentatively, looking at Nicole for reassurance. She nodded. The Syrian turned away from her and never looked back. Even after he and Tommy had his bag, he never acknowledged her again.

Can't say I blame him. It was a rotten trick we pulled. But, hopefully, once he and his family are settled in Denver and Sabra gets the help she needs, he'll at least be able to forgive me.

Spotting her bag circling on the conveyor, she pulled it off, extended its handle, and began walking toward the trains. She already had a ticket for a ride that would take her east through the Chunnel to the mainland. From there, she would catch another train that would take her north.

CHAPTER 28

A frying pan?"

"Flush on the back of my dome. I literally saw stars spinning around my head." Nir reached for his glass of pale Duvel ale and took a sip. Nicole continued slowly rotating her Diet Coke on a cocktail napkin. Both were laughing.

They sat next to a floor-to-ceiling window, beyond which was the city of Antwerp. Even though the Lindner Hotel was only 12 stories tall, it sat in a city with few skyscrapers. So the Skybar at the top of the hotel gave a beautiful view of the chilly Belgian city below. On their side of the window, though, the temperature was warm, and the company was great. Nir loved to see Nicole laugh. The flash in her green eyes lit up the room.

He continued to speak softly, knowing this conversation might raise the eyebrows of anyone listening in. "Before I could neutralize the cooking elements, the husband came back at me. I dodged him and put him back down as gently as I could. Then I somehow managed to communicate to the wife that I just wanted to get away. She pointed to a back room, where I dove out a window."

Through the rest of the beer, Nir told her about the motorcycle chase, then getting in the car with the Raisi-hating man.

"How'd you decide on him?"

"He was the oldest guy I could see and he wasn't wearing any religious kind of outfit. I figured he'd remember the old days before the regime and not be too happy about what his country had become. Folks like that are not hard to find in Iran. Even though I kept my gun on him, I think we had kind of an understanding. He knew that I was there to deal with the same people he wanted dealt with."

"So, you used your spidey senses to find a grumpy old curmudgeon and you bonded on some unspoken grumpy old curmudgeonly level. And he drove you to safety. You are truly the master." Nicole sipped her soda, which had gotten watery by that time.

Nir got the attention of the server and ordered refreshers on both their drinks.

Shaking her head, Nicole continued. "I don't know, Nir. I don't like the decisions you have to make. They're so spur of the moment. Too life and death."

Nir drained the last of his beer, setting the glass aside to make room for when the new one came. "I don't like it either. But quite honestly, I don't really think about it until I go back over it when it's all said and done. I go in with three goals in mind. One, deal with the target. Two, minimize collaterals. Three, get out alive."

"Most people would put your number three up at number one. How do you think you did with your goals on the mission?"

"Well, I know that numbers one and three worked out. Number one, al-Natsheh was very definitely dead. Yaron took him out with one shot to the chest and another to the head."

Nicole waved her hand. "Yeah, I don't need details."

"Understood. As for number three, I'm here talking to the most beautiful woman in the world. So that worked out well." Nir reached across and took her hand for a moment before drawing it back. "As for number two, I think I did okay. I'm not sure all the policemen made it, but I tried to be careful."

"Wouldn't be a bad thing if a few of those Iranian cops met their Maker," Nicole said, looking down at her heavily condensated glass.

The change in Nicole's mood was sudden, but it wasn't surprising. A number of years back, she had run afoul of some Iranian cops, which had led to a pretty rough interrogation. Thankfully, Israel was able to call in some favors from international diplomats that eventually set her free. But the wound still remained, and it didn't take much to pull the scab from it.

"Sorry, *motek*, I should have been more careful with my words," Nir said.

Nicole began to say something, probably to try to blow the whole thing off, but she was saved by the server. He cleared their old glasses from the table and replaced them with new ones on fresh cocktail napkins.

When the server left, Nir said, "Listen, I made sure that those who didn't deserve to die were okay. But those who did? I didn't give them a second thought." He lowered his voice to just above a whisper. "Like those Hamas guys we're going after or all the terrorists in Gaza. Let them die and die with a vengeance."

Nicole had been raising her glass to her lips, but she set it back down as Nir spoke. "I don't know, Nir. I know that Mousa got what he deserved. But I still couldn't watch him as the poison was destroying his body. I had to turn away."

Nir saw how watery Nicole's eyes had become, and he reached to take her hands. "Listen, I understand. Watching people die is not for everyone. In fact, it's not really for anyone, except for some freaks. But you...you weren't created for this. You were brought in through no fault of your own." But then he paused. "Okay, maybe through a little fault of your own."

Nicole affirmed his words with a raise of her eyebrows and a tilt of her head. It had been her hacking into the Mossad system all those years ago that had first caught the attention of the Israeli spy agency. They had given her a choice—join us, or...well, they had never fully defined the "or," but she knew it would not have been pleasant.

Nir continued, still leaning forward, but with his hands now wrapped around his glass. "But you have to realize my perspective and that of most Israelis. Every cry I hear from a Mousa or an al-Natsheh or an al-Arouri or a Zaaroub—any of those guys we took out with Operation Amalek—I hear in those cries the suffering of the innocents. I hear the fathers weeping as their wives and daughters are being raped in front of them. I hear the helplessness of the children as they watch their parents killed and of the parents as they watch their children killed. The horror of the torture and the mutilations and the beheadings. Then the hostages—men and women—who were taken to Gaza and raped day after day after day before being slaughtered. And who's to say that those hostages killed weren't the lucky ones? Can you imagine trying to survive day after day after what so many of them went through?"

Nir lifted his glass and took a long draw. Nicole waited him out.

Nir looked out the window at the city below. "There is not enough suffering in this life for those who planned and who carried out October 7. I only wish they all suffered like Mousa. Al-Natsheh and al-Arouri and Zaaroub, they died too quickly. Just like that. Snuffed out. No anguish. No lingering pain."

"You know their suffering doesn't end there," said Nicole.

Nir turned back. "So you've said. And I want to believe it. But how do I know they aren't just eliminated from all sentience? You know, cease to exist. Back to the dirt."

"In the book of Hebrews it says, 'Just as man is destined to die once, and after that comes judgment.'"

"Yeah, but what does that even mean? Is it eternal suffering? Is it purgatory? Again, is it just extinction? There's no way to know."

Nicole lifted the maraschino cherry out of her Diet Coke and used her teeth to pull it from the stem. "But we do know, Nir. The Bible talks tons about the eternal state of those who follow God and those who don't."

Now Nir sat back. This was turning into one of "those" conversations. "Listen, Nicole, I understand what you're saying. But I've told you before, I'm a Jew. I'm not one of your New Testament acolytes."

Nir saw a little glint in Nicole's eyes. "Did you just say New Testament? I'm sorry, my surly, frying-pan-dazed friend, but I'm also talking from the Old Testament. Daniel 12:2 says, 'Many of those whose bodies lie dead and buried will rise up, some to everlasting life and some to shame and everlasting disgrace.' And Malachi 4:1 talks about the coming day when the wicked will be burned like stubble. And Isaiah, one of the greatest of the Old Testament prophets, ends his book talking about new heavens and a new earth and how those who sin against God will go to 'where the worm does not die and the fire is not quenched.' So, what do you think about that, Jack?"

She finished by flicking the bright red stem of the maraschino at Nir, hitting him in the cheek.

Nir couldn't help but laugh. Nicole had an amazing way of taking the most depressing of conversations and making them not only interesting but entertaining. "*Walla!* Someone's done a little studying." Spotting the offending stem on the table, he flicked it back her direction.

Leaning forward with a big smile, she said, "Yeah, I'm not just some Bible noob anymore that you can push around with your grumpiness and snotty attitude."

"Color me impressed."

Nicole leaned back. As she did, she lowered her head and her voice turned serious. "This is why I keep bringing this up, Nir. You have done so much good in this life. I want you to be rewarded when it's over."

She's truly a master. She can make the most depressing conversation enjoyable, and in the next moment make the most enjoyable conversation miserable.

"Listen, *motek,* I've tried to reconcile what you believe with who I am as a Jew, and it just doesn't work. And what kind of hurts in the whole thing is that not only are you sending me to hell because I don't believe in your New Testament, but you're saying I'm going there because I believe something different than your newfangled interpretation of the Old Testament."

"Nir, nobody is sending anyone anywhere, and two thousand years is long enough to shed the *newfangled* label. Listen, it's not your belief in anything that determines what happens after your life is over, but your lack of belief in the Messiah."

Nir turned back to the window. The view of the city was spectacular. Off to the left, he could see the building in the diamond district that held his office.

Don't let this turn into an argument. This has been too good of a day, and we have too much left to do. Please, give me a way out without having to hurt Nicole's feelings.

His quiet prayer was answered by a vibration in his pocket.

CHAPTER 29

Nir stifled what Nicole was about to say by holding up his finger. "Hang on just a sec."

Sliding his phone from his front pocket, Nir saw a message from Efraim:

Turn on the news

He thumbed back:

kinda hard. im at a bar

Dots appeared on his screen, which transformed into another message:

Put it on now!

There was a link attached to Efraim's message.

"Who is it?"

"It's Efraim. Who else? He wants us to watch this link."

Nir pressed the link and his browser opened onto a news channel. Filling the screen was Recep Tayyip Erdoğan, the president of Turkey.

He was giving a speech, and he was in full lather. The link was from a Hebrew news station that was providing closed captioning at the bottom of the screen. Knowing that neither Turkish nor Hebrew was of any help to Nicole, Nir began to translate the captions into English.

"He's saying, 'They cannot say they weren't warned. We told them to keep their assassins out of our country. We warned them that bloodshed on Turkish soil would not be tolerated. So, what do they do? They assassinate a Palestinian businessman, Khaled Mousa, while he was having a massage. What kind of people do that? A man comes to Turkey to do business, and when he seeks relief from his stressful life, the Jews strike.'"

A picture of Mousa appeared in the top corner of the screen. Even though it was too tiny to make out any details, Nir noticed Nicole turning away.

"Businessman, my *safta's tuches*. He was a businessman as much as I'm a diplomat."

"Just translate."

"Right. Uh…'They pretend to be the victims, but when we look at the violence in the Middle East, whose hand is always behind it? Look at the genocide they are perpetrating in Gaza. Look at the huge number of innocent women and children they have killed in pursuit of so-called terrorist tunnels. Look at the way they are starving the people and destroying all the hospitals so that the wounded can receive no medical care.' Yeah, and why are we going after the hospitals? Because they're being used as human shields."

"Nir, please. I want to know what he is saying."

"You're right. You're right. 'In the north, there are constant airstrikes. The Lebanese, who have done nothing to Israel, are being slaughtered by the thousands due to their warplanes and missiles and killer drones. Yes, Hezbollah is there, but they are playing a defensive game against Israeli aggression.'"

Nir slammed the phone face down onto the table, took a long pull from his glass, and sucked in a deep breath. When he noticed that people at other tables were looking their way, he gave a polite wave and picked up the phone again.

"Uh, Damascus. Erdoğan's talking about Damascus now. Hang on."

He slid the time bar back 15 seconds. "Okay. There was no active tectonic fault that we are aware of in the Damascus area capable of the destruction that city suffered. Instead, there was another kind of disaster. Israel sent teams there in a futile search for weapons of mass destruction. None were found. Instead, there was a massive earthquake that leveled the city. Is that a coincidence? Can we really believe that? Did Israel set off an explosion of their own? Do they have secret weapons capable of that kind of devastation? Knowing their history, it all seems too coincidental to me.' *Oy*. What a—"

"Nir, please. Stay on task for once," Nicole chided. Looking at Nicole, he saw concern in her eyes. He realized that this was her life that this man was talking about. She had fronted the team. If they put her and Dima together with the assassination, she might have to look over her shoulder for the rest of her life.

"Sorry. He's saying, 'Now they've used their hyperbolized victimhood as an excuse to ignore Turkish sovereignty. They shed blood on our soil—on my soil. We will not stand for this. They were warned. They ignored the warning, and now there will be retaliation. To you Israelis who are watching, your blood is on your own hands. Even more so, it is on the hands of your prime minister and his cabinet. When the time comes to pay the price, just know that you only have yourselves to blame. And to those of you who were involved in the killing of this innocent man, understand that we will hunt you down and bring you to a swift and certain justice.'"

Erdoğan continued to stand at the podium as his audience stood to applaud. The news service soon cut away to a panel of talking heads.

Nir clicked the phone off, but before he could return it to his pocket, another message appeared from Efraim.

> *Not just bluster real deal you*
> *guys watch your backs*

Nir replied:

> *any indication nicole cover blown?*

Efraim's message came through a moment later.

Not so far but can never know for sure

When Nir looked up, he saw Nicole was back to slowly spinning her three-quarters full glass. Her eyes were glistening as she stared at the brown liquid.

Nir reached over and gently lifted her chin. "You're safe. Efraim said there is no indication that they have any idea about you."

"As far as he knows."

"Of course," Nir admitted. He looked back outside at the fading winter sun, noticing the reflection of the full tables around him. Suddenly feeling a bit too out in the open, he said, "Let's get over to my office. We can talk there."

Nicole stood quickly, like she had been waiting for him to release them. He peeled off a 100-euro note from a stack in his pocket, slid it under his glass, and the two walked to the elevator.

CHAPTER 30

16:50 (4:50 PM) CET

When they exited the front doors of the hotel, Nir began to lead Nicole to a taxi.

"No, I want to walk," she said.

"It's five degrees. You'll freeze! I'll freeze."

"Please, Nir. We'll get to your office before it's dark," she slipped her arm in his and began walking. He followed along. "Besides, I need to stretch my legs. There was some creepy guy in the hotel gym this morning, so I shorted my workout."

"Sounds lovely. Did you shoot him?"

Nicole chuckled. "No, I avoided the Tavor approach and ran away. Now, tell me—is Erdoğan really as mad as he seems? I mean, he's got to just be posturing. He'd be crazy to come after Israel right now."

They came to a corner and paused as Nir pressed a button for the crosswalk. "Unfortunately, I would have to disagree with you on both counts. I don't believe he's just posturing, and with most of our military resources pouring into Gaza, this may be the best time to come after us. And if he were to do that, I'm afraid of what might happen. We have no troops to send to Turkey. There is no option for conventional warfare. If it pops off with Turkey, it'll be a very big pop. In fact, depending on how big he goes, it could be a nuclear pop."

The light turned and they began walking again. "But I still don't get it," said Nicole. "Israel kills someone in your territory. Yell at them. Sanction them. Cut trade with them. But it sounds like he's planning on some sort of military retaliation. That makes no sense."

"You're right, *motek*. It doesn't. But that's because you're ignoring the other part of our prime minister's threat. When we are trying to find a motive for any action, what is the first thing that we do?"

"We follow the money," Nicole replied like she was reading from a script. "But what money was there with this Hamas guy other than exorbitant hotel bills?"

Nir pointed ahead to the left and asked, "Remember that place?"

Large lettering spelling out "Hoffy's" stood over a doorway. Just below the English name were the Hebrew letters כשר, letting patrons know that the food inside was all kosher. The bright lights inside showed a long deli counter leading back to the restaurant where Nir had brought Nicole and Efraim less than a year ago.

"Hoffy's!" exclaimed Nicole. "I didn't realize this was where we were. Should we stop and get Mila a turkey bone?"

Mila Wooters was Nir's office secretary and surrogate mom. She hated Hoffy's, using the menu item called Turkey Bone as the prime example of why no one should ever eat there. As they watched, two Orthodox Jewish men walked out of the restaurant wearing long coats and wide-brimmed hats.

Pulling Nicole forward, Nir said, "Nah, I'm already in her doghouse. Don't want to make it worse. So, back to Erdoğan. When our prime minister first challenged him, he said that if Turkey harbors Hamas leaders, we'll do what?"

"Come and kill them?"

"Right. But think: What else did he threaten?" After Nicole remained silent, Nir answered his own question. "He said that we would cut our gas deal with them."

"He did? I think I was too caught up in the first part because I knew that probably meant us."

"Totally understandable. But the discovery of Mousa in Turkey and his subsequent elimination means that our prime minister is making good on his threats. The pipeline deal to get Israel's natural gas to Europe that we were working on with Turkey and Cyprus will now belong only to Cyprus. Not only is this a financial disaster to a country that is currently one big financial disaster, but it defies the entire Turkish concept of *mavi vatan*."

"You know, sometimes I think you throw out foreign phrases just to make me feel dumb," Nicole said with a punch to his arm.

"What? Like when you call me a *dwaas*?"

Nicole laughed. "Well, if you're acting the fool, you need to be called out as a fool."

"True, true. *Mavi vatan* simply means 'blue homeland.' It's a grand Turkish philosophy that says they own all the waters around them in the Black Sea, the Aegean Sea, and the eastern Mediterranean."

"Well, that's fair, isn't it? Every country has territorial waters."

"Yeah, but it's a question of the extent of those territorial waters. Their idea of territorial waters has brought them into conflicts with Greece, Cyprus, and even Italy. So, picture this. They tell Greece, 'Sure, the island of Crete is yours, but the water around Crete is ours.'"

"That could be a problem."

"It is a problem. Still, Turkey is set on their *mavi vatan*, and they've even tested it out. About five years ago, they conducted some major naval exercises with over one hundred ships and twenty thousand soldiers throughout what they say are their waters. People swore and complained, but no one did anything about it. So, Erdoğan says, 'See? They're our waters.'"

Nicole slipped her arm out from Nir's. "Hold that thought." She hurried across the narrow street into a bakery, returning a few minutes later holding a pink box.

Nir narrowed his eyes and shook his head. He took the box from her so that she could slide her arm through his again. "If this is what I think it is, Mila's going to flip."

"She deserves it after putting up with you for so many years."

They began walking again. "Back to *mavi vatan*," said Nicole. "Turkey sees most of the eastern Mediterranean and Aegean Sea, and a good portion of the Black Sea, as theirs. So, if Israel skirts around their blue homeland with their pipeline, they lose a huge chunk of change."

"But that's the problem. Israel can't skirt around the waters Turkey claims are theirs. Let me take a step back. There are a couple main focuses for *mavi vatan*. First, there is heavy militarization at home and in their foreign policy. That is why you see these major armament deals taking place between Turkey and other NATO countries. The second focus is expansion into cross-border areas. You'll find a strong Turkish presence in places like Somalia, northern Iraq, Qatar, and Libya. In fact, in Libya, they've even taken control of the country's maritime territory."

"Wait, wait," Nicole said, stopping. Nir saw that she had her eyes closed and was concentrating. When she opened them, he could see that she was having an "Aha!" moment. "I was just picturing the Mediterranean. You've got Cyprus, which has a Turkish presence in the north."

"And which, except for its southern border, is surrounded by 'Turkish waters.' And I'm talking extending down below the island on either side."

"Okay, got it. But then you have Libyan waters coming up from Africa toward the island of Crete. Essentially, in the eyes of Erdoğan, Israel is cut off from Europe without the help of Turkey."

Nir kissed Nicole on the forehead. "Smart girl. Cutting out Turkey is denying *mavi vatan*, which is telling the Turks, 'You and your perceived destiny? Yeah, we're not buying it. We're going to go through your so-called waters with or without your permission.' That is why Erdoğan is having such a conniption. He's offended. He's hurt. His economy is tanking, and his big hope for financial solvency through Israeli gas has just been pulled out from under him."

"Makes sense. Crazy. It really does all come down to money."

CHAPTER 31

17:10 (5:10 PM) CET

They walked for a while quietly. Something Nicole said was bothering Nir, and he was trying to work it out.

Did it really all come down to money? Sure, money was a major part of it. Turkey was nearing financial ruin and would need to be bailed out by Russia or China or someone if something didn't change. But it seemed so much of it came down to Erdoğan himself. He was paranoid of overthrow, which made sense after the failed coup back in 2016. But was that even real, or was it actually a created opportunity for the man to get rid of some troublesome or threatening enemies?

They rounded a corner and began to move north.

Erdoğan had to know that Turkey didn't have the firepower to go against Israel alone. If they collected some alliances, maybe they could. Russia and Iran were probably ready to go. Turkey already had Libya in its pocket, and they had major inroads into Somalia. But still, the timing doesn't make sense. It's almost like it's an ego thing with him. Like he's a little sick in the head.

That's when all the pieces fell into place. Foreign pundits around the world would likely argue with him, but to Nir, this was what made sense. He was about to share his brilliance with Nicole, but she beat him to the punch.

"Let's sit," she said, directing him to a bench that faced the beautiful, winter-bare Stadspark across the road. Nir sat and set the pink box down next to him. After Nicole sat, she unzipped her handbag and pulled out two foil-wrapped bundles. "These looked so good in the hot case at the bakery, and since we didn't get a chance to eat at the bar, I figured I'd get us a little dinner."

Nir took his, then paused a moment to let Nicole say an internal prayer. The package he held was warm and smelled delicious. "Okay, open it up," she said when her green eyes were back on him.

He pulled back the corners, then let the package unroll. Inside was a croissant, split in two, with he didn't know what kinds of cheeses melted between the halves.

"Just smell it," said Nicole with a grin. "It's downright decadent."

Nir inhaled deeply, then took a bite. Somehow the cheeses inside were still hot, scalding the roof of his mouth. The flavor matched the scent perfectly. It was like eating a cheese festival. "Oh, that is so good," he said, his mouth still full.

Nicole looked like she wanted to reply, but instead was waving air into her mouth to cool it down. When she could finally speak, she asked, "Is that some sort of kosher magic getting food to stay that hot for that long?"

"Ve haf our veys, *yaldah*," Nir said, taking on the voice of a Yiddish mother. Changing back to his regular voice, he said, "Amazing call on dinner, *motek*. The only thing that could have made it better was a little ham in the mix."

Nicole snorted with a mouthful of food and put a napkin to her mouth. "Nice try. You're the one who decided to walk me through the Jewish quarter."

They finished their sandwiches. Nicole gathered up their trash and stuffed it back into her bag, then leaned up against Nir. He pulled her tight, letting their combined body heat ward off the night chill.

Remembering his earlier revelation, he said, "Hey, I was about to say something before our incredible dinner. Back in the mid-nineteenth century, Tsar Nicolas I first called the Ottoman Empire a 'sick man.' Later, some newspaper picked up the phrase, calling Turkey 'the sick man of Europe.' That title has stuck ever since. Imagine Erdoğan, who is an egomaniac as it is, knowing that the world views his once-mighty country that way. I mean, at one time that area was considered the center of the civilized world. It was the link between East and West, between Asia and Europe. If you wanted to trade goods, you went through Constantinople."

"Or Byzantium before and Istanbul after," Nicole agreed. "But then shipping became more popular and merchants weren't confined to the coastlines anymore. Who wants to walk thousands of miles when you can sail?"

"But the reverse is true too. The only way to the Black Sea from the rest of the world is through what's now Istanbul. But if Turkey is going to be a pain, then we'd rather walk to avoid the water and travel by caravan up to Black Sea ports and sail from there."

Nicole pulled a little tighter against Nir and began fingering a button on his jacket as she spoke. "It's geography as destiny. It's like how the railroad killed so many towns in Europe and in the United States. For a long time, you're needed. Then they build the railroad two towns over from you, and—boom—you're nothing."

"Exactly. So, now picture Erdoğan. He's the president of the country that has what was once known as the Queen of Cities, as *Nova Roma*—the New Rome. And how does everyone picture you? As the sick man of Europe. No wonder he's so angry. But now he has a chance to make it right. Maybe the Bosphorus Strait is no longer the link between Asia and Europe, but the Turkish waters—the *mavi vatan*—can be the link between the energy suppliers of the eastern Mediterranean and the desperate consumers of Europe."

"True, until one man, the Israeli prime minister, says, 'Sorry, Jack, but you're out of luck.' All his hopes come crashing down, and the sick just keeps getting sicker. No wonder he's being such a turd."

Nir sat there, enjoying the moment. His Mediterranean blood was turning to ice in the chill of the air, but dealing with icy veins was worth it. Using his best Texas accent, he said, "You know, you're kinda smart for being so purdy."

She lightly punched his gut. "You ain't so bad yerself, pardner."

They enjoyed the warmth and the closeness for a few more minutes before getting up to finish the trek to Nir's office.

CHAPTER 32

N icole!"

As soon as they walked through the entrance to Yael Dia-monds, Mila Wooters jumped up to wrap Nicole in a warm hug. "It's so good to see you, Mila," said Nicole, her voice slightly muffled by Mila's neck.

"Let me look at you, girl." Mila stepped back and put her hands on Nicole's cheeks, but just as quickly pulled them away. "What? You're freezing! You're like a block of ice! Did this one make you walk all the way here?" she asked, punching Nir in the chest as she did. "What are you doing to this poor girl? You can get anywhere in the city for less than a forty-euro Uber ride."

"It's not his fault," Nicole broke in. "I wanted to walk. Besides, I had to make a stop on the way here." She took the pink box from Nir and presented it to Mila.

"Oh no. Is this…?" Mila opened the box to find an assortment of a dozen eclairs. "Oh my, they're perfect! But what are you doing to me, sweetheart? If I eat these, I'll start looking matronly and before I know it, I'll stop getting likes on my dating app."

"Whoa, there's a backstory I want to know nothing about," said Nir, his hands up in the air.

"I'm sorry, Mila. I thought you liked them." Nicole looked a little crestfallen.

Mila leaned forward and whispered, "I love eclairs, and I'm going to eat every last one of them. But how would it look if I accepted them without at least a little protest?"

"Got it," Nicole said, taking hold of the older woman's arm. Nir just rolled his eyes.

As Mila put the box on a credenza behind her desk, Nicole asked, "So, how is the packing going?"

Mila turned with a surprised look. "Didn't Nir tell you? I'm not going anywhere."

Nicole pivoted toward Nir, who said, "The man I sold the business to asked if I could recommend anyone for the front office. I told him there was no one better than Mila. I guess they hit it off."

Mila walked toward Nir. "You need to give the whole story." When she reached him, she put her arm around his waist and turned toward Nicole. "First of all, the severance package this one gave me could have allowed me to retire to the south of France, or at least rent a villa there for a few years. But more importantly, I love to work. So, when Mr. Levy presented me with an offer with the same benefits and nearly the salary that Nir gave to me, I jumped at the chance."

Nicole creased her forehead and stuck out her lower lip. "Does this mean you're not going to fly with me to Milan so you can be my mom?"

Mila rushed over and wrapped Nicole in another hug. "Oh, I'm going to miss you so much, dear." Suddenly, she stepped back again. "Wait a second. That box says that the eclairs are from Heimisch Bakery. Does that mean he took you back to that horrid turkey bone restaurant again?"

Nicole laughed. "No, we went fancy this time. The Skybar."

Mila turned toward Nir. "Oooo, up on the Lindner. Nice work, young man."

"Every now and then I get it right."

Nir's surrogate mother stepped back and admired the two of them for a moment. Then, suddenly she was moving back to her desk. "Now, as much as I love catching up, I know you're not here just to see me.

You two go off and talk about whatever you need to talk about. I'll be in with coffee in a few minutes."

Nir and Nicole excused themselves, then moved into his office. After closing the door, Nir took a chair set at an angle to the soft couch that Nicole stretched out on. She lifted a thin blanket out of a basket on the floor and threw it over her legs.

"Still a little chilly," she said.

"January in Belgium will do that to you."

"Are you sure you want to give all this up?"

That was a difficult question. After the operation in Damascus, Nir had felt the pull to come home. The world was becoming a more dangerous place, particularly if you were Jewish. He wrestled with his decision until October 7. That one day cemented in his mind that his era of splitting time between Belgium and Israel was at an end. He needed to be ready to fight for his country at a moment's notice, and he couldn't do that while evaluating the cut of a ruby in Antwerp.

"Admittedly, there are parts of this job that I'll miss. But it's time for me to be home, and this isn't home."

Lifting her eyebrows, Nicole asked, "Is it wrong that I don't feel that way yet? I mean, I'm going to be there whenever I'm needed, but I'm not feeling anything that's saying, 'Hey, give up modeling and be an Israeli spook full time.'"

Nir laughed. "I'm sorry. There's just something funny about hearing you call yourself an Israeli spook. Maybe it's the accent. Maybe it's that you look anything but spooky."

Nicole laid her head back on the couch and sighed. "Always the *goy* in a roomful of Jews."

"Hey, don't knock it. Sometimes we need someone to tell us that the glass is half full. That's something you won't find in a roomful of Jews." They laughed together. "Besides, Nicole, you don't have the same reasons to be in Israel. For you, it's still safe to go everywhere. For me, the list of people who want to hurt me just because of who I am is growing every day."

"You see, I don't get that antisemitic mindset. I thought it died off in 1945. But now I'm hearing people say things about Israelis that blow my mind. And the stuff I see on social media? Who are these people? They have to be bots spewing the words of a small handful of hateful freaks, don't they?"

Nir shook his head. "No doubt there are bots out there that aren't helping the situation. But what happened in 1945 with the revelation of the Holocaust and the freeing of the concentration camp survivors didn't kill antisemitism. It just pushed it underground, where it lay dormant waiting for an opportune time to rise up again. That's what we're seeing now. October 7 gave people a chance to show that they weren't antisemitic. 'Oh, poor Israel. What happened to them was tragic. Kidnap, rape, murder, mutilation? Just horrible.' But now that we are fighting back against the killers in Gaza, these very same people are saying, 'Look at those Jews! They're baby-killers! They're targeting hospitals! They've always been bad, and now they're showing their true colors!'"

"Not only that, but they're now saying, 'Rapes? There were no rapes. There was no brutalization. That's just the Israeli government making up stuff to get sympathy.' It makes me so angry when I hear it!"

There was a knock on the door. Nir invited Mila in, who brought them both a Nespresso cappuccino. "Thanks, Mila," Nicole said, squeezing the hand that Mila had placed on her shoulder.

"Yeah, thanks," said Nir, his emotions still high. Mila raised her eyebrows at him, then walked back out the door, closing it behind her.

Nicole spoke first. "Okay, before we both get into too much of a froth, let me ask you this. Do you think that antisemitism is a high motivating factor for Erdoğan?"

"Good question," Nir said, pausing for a few moments. "I'd say yes and no."

"Hmmm, thanks for clearing that up," Nicole said with a wink.

"Just hold your horses and let me explain. I would say yes because as Jews, we are Semites and he hates us. But that is a technical answer. A more nuanced look might say no because it wouldn't matter if we were Arctic Inuits. He'd still hate us."

"Why? What's he got against you guys?"

"A lot of years of bad blood. First of all, the Turks are Ottomans, and they aren't happy that they lost our region in World War I. But it's more than that. We've been trading barbs back and forth for decades. Have you ever heard of the *Mavi Marmara* affair?"

Nicole shook her head.

"So, back in 2010, a six-ship flotilla set out from the waters of Northern Cyprus for Gaza. They were filled with people, building supplies, and humanitarian aid. The problem was that Israel had a shipping blockade against Gaza. These ships, filled with members of the Free Gaza Movement and the Turkish IHH, which stands for something like the Foundation for Human Rights and blah blah blah—these boats were planning on running the blockade. Israel wasn't having it, so they sent some folks out after the ships, including some from Shayetet 13. Well, some of these batwings got aboard the MV *Mavi Marmara,* and they were met with people carrying pipes and knives."

"Not an ideal way to meet the Shayetet boys."

"For sure. Not surprisingly, things went south quickly and nine activists were killed, with a tenth dying about four years later from his injuries. It turned into a big deal and Prime Minister Netanyahu ended up having to call President Erdoğan to apologize because it was all Turks who died."

"That had to hurt."

Nir nodded. "Undoubtedly. The Turks made huge hay out of the incident, rubbing Israel's nose in it time after time. They even convened a court, demanding that Israel give the names of the commandos involved. Israel refused. So, the courts instead went after the Israeli chief of staff, a navy commander, and a couple intelligence guys. They convicted them and gave them ten life sentences each. Needless to say, none of them have plans to visit Turkey anytime soon."

"I kinda wonder about that one," Nicole said, looking up at the ceiling. "Yeah, they met armed guys on the boat, but was there a better way to stop them? Or would it even have been more politically expedient to let them through to Gaza?" Her eyes shifted to Nir's. "Although I get that too. You let one flotilla in, you're going to have forty more launching the next week."

"Exactly. But let me tell you one more. And with this one, you won't have to think. We were definitely in the wrong and it was beautiful! Throw me a few of those pillows from the couch."

Nicole sat up and tossed Nir a few pillows, which he put on the seat of his chair. When he took his seat again, he was staring down at Nicole, who was a couple feet below him on the couch.

"Okay, that's a little weird," she said.

"Just listen and let me explain. About five months before the flotilla incident, Turkey, and Erdoğan in particular, had been going after Israel mercilessly. Constantly criticizing the prime minister and the government in the press over their handling of the Gaza situation. Then came the coup de grâce. A Turkish television station broadcast a drama depicting Israeli soldiers as brutal and evil. In the program, they were shooting old men and kidnapping children. It's essentially the same stuff that the American left is accusing us of now."

Nicole snorted a laugh.

"The prime minister was not happy. So he had his deputy foreign minister call in the Turkish ambassador. When the guy arrived, the deputy foreign minister didn't even shake his hand. The ambassador was directed to a low couch, where he sat. The deputy and his contingent then took their places on full-sized chairs. They were looking down on the ambassador like I'm looking down on you. Then the deputy chewed the guy out, up one side and down the other. The ambassador left humiliated."

Nicole was full-on laughing now. "What a beautifully awful political move."

"Yeah, we ended up sending a letter of apology for that one too. But the point was made, and it will never be forgotten."

Nicole raised her finger up and said formally, "Because nothing is ever forgotten in the Middle East."

"Exactly!"

They talked a while longer. Then Nicole asked, "So, you're heading back to Israel now?"

"In a couple days. Where are you off to from here?"

"Well," she said, dragging out the word, "I had thought of maybe tagging along with you."

"No shoots lined up? Aren't there clothes that desperately need modeling?"

"There may be, but it feels like my family needs me. I can't be ready to jump in the fire if I'm modeling a swimsuit on a beach in Saint Tropez."

Nir didn't answer. Instead, he stared up at the ceiling.

Nicole followed his gaze. "What are you staring at?"

"Nothing. I'm just picturing you in a swimsuit on a beach in Saint Tropez."

A pillow flew through the air and hit him in the face. "Stop. Don't be a creepy stalker freak."

With skill and great accuracy, Nir flung the pillow back at her, following it up with the three that he was sitting on. "Don't mess with a sharpshooter, little missy."

Nicole had her hands up. "I surrender. I surrender."

"Good decision. Now, how about we invite Mila in and spend a little family time?"

Without answering, Nicole popped up from the couch and moved toward the door.

CHAPTER 33

Nir peeked around the corner, then ducked back. His target's head was barely showing over a low wall. Taking a quick breath, he slid into the room and fired two shots from his Jericho 941 9mm. His target went down.

Serves him right. These are the idiots who took out Yossi. They all deserve what they get.

Yaron, Imri, Dima, and Gil fanned out around him as he pressed forward. He heard two shots from his right and two from his left. By their positioning, they would have come from Imri and Gil.

"Room clear," he said into his coms.

"Clear," came the responses from his team.

"Yaron, Imri, kitchen. Dima, Gil, hall."

"*Root*," came the replies.

The room ahead of Nir led to what appeared to be a back storage room. His gun in firing position, he moved steadily forward, step by step.

Two shots sounded from behind him.

"Target down," said Dima.

Good. One less to worry about. Hopefully, you'll find someone in the room in front of you. Chalking up the body count.

Nir didn't stop. He didn't acknowledge. He kept advancing on the closed door ahead. When he arrived, he lowered his left hand from the grip of his pistol and carefully twisted the knob. It turned.

Once again, he breathed in and brought the handle down until there was movement in the door. He pushed it just enough so that the latch cleared the jamb, then he returned his left hand to cover the fingers of his right around the Jericho's grip.

Okay, let's play.

He counted down in his head, *3, 2, 1…*

Nir bumped the door with his hip. It swung open. Immediately, he saw a man to his right. Two bullets burst from Nir's gun, hitting the man center mass. More movement caught his eye to his left. He spun and fired again. Two more bullets hit his target.

The little girl fell to the ground.

A buzzer sounded and the duskiness of the course was illuminated by white light.

"A civilian is down," said a husky voice over the loudspeaker.

Nir walked toward the target. There were two holes in the pretty dark-haired toddler—one in her chest, and one just under her left eye. Without looking away, he released his mag from his pistol, slipping it into his tactical vest. Then he racked back the slide, catching the flying round with his left hand in a motion he had carried out hundreds of times before. That, too, went into his vest.

"Dude, it happens," said Gil, who had walked up next to him. He put his hand on Nir's shoulder.

But then a shove to his back sent him stumbling forward. It was Yaron, and he was hot. "That's the second time you've done that in the last four weeks. *Yeled*, you've got to get your head back in the game. If you can't tell the difference between a *haji* and a little girl, then you need to rethink whether you're the one to lead this team."

Anger welled up in Nir, but he pushed it back down. Yaron was right, and if it had been any of his men who had taken out a civilian twice in a month, he would have been saying the same thing. He stood there staring at the older man, not knowing what to say. Was he unfit? Had he let October 7 get so deep into him that he was now trigger-happy?

The confusion on Nir's face must have softened Yaron a bit. "Listen, I get it," he said in a calmer voice. "We're all wrestling with it. But these are people's lives we're talking about. You've got to think it through, *achi*."

"No, you're right. You're right."

Dima stepped up and grabbed Nir by the arm, leading him off the course. "We trust you. You've just got to get your head together. This may be personal for all of us, but you've got to find a way to stop making it *so* personal. You've got to get Yossi out of your head. We don't have the luxury of vengeance. We've just got a job to do. *Comprende?*"

Gil spoke up. "*Comprende?* What's a Russian Jew doing speaking Spanish?"

Dima looked offended. "That's not Spanish. That's pure Russian Cubano."

Nir couldn't help but laugh quietly. "Dumb Cossack," he said to himself.

"Let's go regear and run it again," Gil said, putting his arm over Nir's shoulders.

But Yaron stopped him. "You guys go ahead. We'll catch up with you in a few minutes."

"Oh, Nir, you are in deep now," said Imri as the group walked off.

Yaron walked Nir another direction out of the practice house. A couple dozen meters away, they found a bench. "Sit," said Yaron. Nir obeyed.

"You know that there's no way you could have saved him," Yaron said, settling down next to Nir.

"Who?"

"What do you mean, 'Who?' Who do you think?"

Nir did know who he meant. He just felt foolish admitting it. "I was the one he called, *achi*. When he was being shot at and he had to find a way to escape, he turned to me. He didn't call the cops. He didn't call his folks. He didn't call you or anyone else on the ops team. In his mind, he thought, 'If there is one guy who can get me out of this, it's Nir.' And now he's dead, and so is Adira."

Yaron was quiet for a moment. Then he swore under his breath. "That's rough. No doubt. Brother, I am never going to knock you for feeling like crap over this. But you do know that there was absolutely nothing you could do to help him, right? You had no way to reach him, no way to extract him, no way to get him to safety."

"But he was counting on me."

"Of course he was. You were his hero. You're Nir Tavor, the guy who can get anything done. But guess what? You're just a mortal man. It's like me being trapped on the moon and saying, 'Help, Nir. Get me off of here!' You know what? Try as you might, there's nothing you can do to help me. You've got no rockets to send. You can't transport me off there like Scotty or Spock. As much as you want to help, you can't, and I'm just plain screwed."

"Scotty and Spock? Exactly how old are you?" Nir asked, looking to divert the conversation.

"Listen, *achi*, just because you got the call doesn't mean you're the only one hurting. We all loved Yossi, and we all lost him. And not just him. You know that I lost two cousins at Kibbutz Be'eri, and one of my best friends growing up was killed with his wife, daughter, son-in-law, and two grandbabies at Kibbutz Kfar Aza. You think I'm not pissed? Their faces come to mind every time I pick up a gun, and I see them every night when I close my eyes."

"Then how do you do it? I mean, how do you tamp down the anger? Or, more so, how do you get past the guilt for not doing something about it?"

"I keep reminding myself that I didn't fire the guns that killed the ones I love. However, I do have the honor, privilege, and responsibility of firing the gun that will kill the ones who pulled those triggers. The past is the past. As much as I wish I could, I can't do anything to change what's happened. So my focus now is on making it right. And it will only be right when every one of those Hamas dirties are dead and rotting on the ground."

Nir breathed in the cool March air and thought about what Yaron had said. Undoubtedly, he was carrying guilt over Yossi's death. It had led to some strange decisions. When he had been asked to read a eulogy at Yossi's funeral, Nir had kept his words generic, saying he was a good worker and a friend. Then, later that night, he had gone home with only a bottle of arak as a companion. It took several hours and nearly the whole bottle for him to drink himself to sleep. The next morning, when he had called Liora to tell her that he would not be in that day, he felt he could hear an accusatory tone in her voice. She had said, "Don't worry about it, Nir. You get some rest." But what he heard was, "Are you going to let me down one day like you let Yossi down? Am I going to get killed waiting for you to rescue me?"

That kind of thinking was stupid, and Nir knew it. But it didn't matter. He had switched from liquor to beer and polished off a 12-pack of Gold Star before passing out until the next morning. The only positive to come from that 36-hour period was a commitment to never drink like that again after he finally woke up around 9:00 the next morning. He forced himself to do a 15-kilometer run as both penance and to help sweat any remaining alcohol out of his system.

Yaron was right. He had to let the past go. If he kept hanging on to it, he would end up making a major mistake and the consequences would be huge. One of his teammates could get killed or an innocent civilian might get seriously hurt. In either case, he would come up for disciplinary review and likely be removed from his position. Then he would be no good to anyone.

"What do you do when they come into your mind?" he asked Yaron.

Yaron let out a long sigh. "When I see their faces, I thank God for them. For the life He gave to them and the time they had on this earth. Then I pray the *Hagomel*. *'Barukh ata Adonai, Eloheinu melekh ha'olam, ha'gomel l'chayavim tovot, she-g'malani kol tov.'"*

As he prayed, Nir joined him in his mind: *Blessed are You, Lord our God, ruler of the world, who rewards the undeserving with goodness, and who has rewarded me with goodness.*

When Yaron finished, Nir offered the traditional response: *"Mi she-g'malcha kol tov, hu yi-g'malcha kol tov selah.* May He who rewarded you with all goodness reward you with all goodness forever."

Yaron gave a weary smile. "Yeah, I don't know if it's appropriate or not. My synagogue attendance has been spotty at best over the past three or four decades. But it makes me feel good, and it seems to fit."

Nir put his hand on his friend's shoulder. "It's good, *achi*. It's good."

They met the rest of the team back at the entrance to the house. Another Kidon group was completing the exercise, so they waited for them to finish and for the course to be reset. Nir knew that the targets would all be different this time, but he was also pretty sure that the trainers who ran the course would make certain that he had at least one civilian within his purview area.

When their turn came, they entered the house with their IWI X95 assault rifles at the ready. Immediately, targets popped up, and each man cleared their assigned sector. Nir quickly dropped his magazine and slammed in a new one. Because the X95 is a bullpup, designed to be more compact, this took place behind the rifle's trigger instead of in front. Formerly known as a Micro-Tavor, this had long been Nir's gun of choice for well over a decade and a half.

After clearing the entryway, Imri led the way to the next door off to their right. As soon as he opened the door, Gil and Yaron tossed in flash-bang grenades. After they blew, Nir led the way in. They cleared this room, and, after a mandatory switch to their Jericho sidearms, they did the same in the next.

Now came the time for them to split up. Nir called out their assignments, receiving an acknowledgment from each man. This time, however, as Nir moved toward the door, he saw Yossi's face in his mind. And rather than letting the rage rise in him, he thanked God for the time he'd had with his friend.

As before, the door was unlocked. Nir prepared for entry. When he pushed in, there was movement to his right again. His finger tightened on the trigger, but he held back. The little girl cutout with the two holes in it was staring right at him. There was movement to his left. Dropping to his knees, he spun to where the girl had been before. Again, he prepared to shoot, but this time he saw a mother holding her baby. Nir let up the tension from his trigger. Clearing the rest of the room, he saw that there were no threats.

Nice try, trainer guys.

Into his coms, he said, "Lead, all clear."

CHAPTER 34

Nir leaned against the doorframe of his office. After showering at the training facility, he had taken his ops team out for a noodle lunch. Between the five of them, they had polished off three large edamame appetizers, which Nir then followed with a spicy miso ramen. While the other guys cooled off their mouths with Gold Stars, Nir settled for sparkling water knowing that he had a 13:30 meeting with the team at CARL.

Now, five minutes before the meeting was to begin, he watched his analyst team at work. Liora and Dafna were talking and typing at their conjoined desks. Some of their dozen or so screens flashed pictures. Others scrolled code. It amazed him that what seemed to him to be utter chaos was all part of an analytical melody they danced to every day.

Next to their workstation was a desk holding several computers and a five-screen spread of monitors. Unfortunately, they were all dark. After the Tehran operation, Avi had been called back to the Caesarea main analyst department. Nir had fought hard to keep him, but he was denied. His relationship with his old operative would be forced to revert back to a monthly beer-and-bluster with the rest of the ops guys.

At Yossi's old desk sat Yariv Rabin. He was still a bit out of place with his yarmulke and curls, but he was beginning to lighten up. A mutual affinity for Eastern European klezmer music had provided a link between him and Lahav, while Nir convincing the girls to stop calling Yariv *rabbi* had helped to soften their relationships. Because Yariv didn't have the history with Nicole that the rest of them did, it seemed to Nir that Yariv still struggled with what she was doing on the team.

Well, that's something he's going to have to work out himself, because if he gives her any hassle, especially when I leave her in charge, he'll have to deal with me.

That wouldn't be a problem right now, though. Paris Fashion Week had just finished a few days ago, and now Nicole was off to New York for some other shoot. When Nir had talked to her by Zoom last week, it almost sounded like she was pleading for a reason to have to cancel her New York dates and come to Tel Aviv. Unfortunately, there was nothing going on that demanded her attention. After Erdoğan's great bravado, the president had faded to the background apart from a fresh threat every week or two. His failing economy was eating him alive, and it seemed like he didn't have any spare time to worry about revenge against Israel.

Sliding off the doorjamb, Nir made his way toward Lahav's desk. To do so, he had to skirt around the full-sized Chewbacca mannequin that the analyst kept in his workspace. In the past, the rapidly shedding Kashyyyk native's headwear had been regularly updated by anyone who found a hat worthy of the Wookie. But once he had been crowned with a pale-green bucket hat discovered by Liora as she was cleaning out Yossi's desk, that rotating tradition was discontinued. He now proudly wore the ridiculous-looking head covering permanently.

"Got any of those pistachios left?" Nir asked the analyst.

Without looking up from his screen, Lahav opened a drawer. Nir looked in and saw a bag. Reaching in, he lifted it out and set it on the analyst's desk. It amazed Nir that the man could type almost as quickly one-handed as he could using both hands.

"Thanks." Taking a handful of the nuts, he dropped them into his shirt pocket. Near the front door was a water cooler minus a tank.

These days it served solely as a cupholder. He walked over, pulled out a cardboard cup, sat at the head of the conference table, opened his first nut, and tossed the shell into the container.

"You've got two minutes," he said.

Grumbles sounded from the analysts while Dafna showed a more tangible sign of her disapproval.

Nir shelled another nut and popped it into his mouth. He was anxious to hear from his team. He had divided them between the three biggest second-tier threats, or threat-countries that were not along their borders. They were Turkey, Russia, and Iran, not necessarily in that order.

So many Mossad resources were being directed at Hamas, the Palestinian Islamic Jihad, Hezbollah, and all the psychos in the militias. But Nir didn't want to lose sight of the puppet masters who were pulling all the strings. So he had set his team to work on Sunday and gave them two-and-a-half days to do a deep dive. Today, he was going to get his payoff.

Nir let out an obnoxious whistle.

The team grumpily made their way over. Liora, who almost always brought snacks to their meetings, tossed a metal bowl onto the table. It was filled with green bags. Nir lifted one.

"Kale chips? Are you serious?"

Liora shrugged. "I figured with my wedding coming up, we all probably wanted to watch our weight."

Nir tossed the bag back into the bowl. "We're not fat."

"Well, not at present. But I could see you really pushing maximum density," Liora said with a smile.

"*The Breakfast Club*," cried Yariv. "Very funny, Liora."

That was another problem with the new guy. While old movie quotes were part of the lingua franca of the analyst team, he felt it necessary to point out every line that he recognized.

The girls rolled their eyes, but Lahav said, "Hey, give the guy a break. He's just being social. True, he's demented and sad. But he's social."

"That, too, is *The Breakfast Club*," said Yariv, reaching out his fist to pound knuckles. "Well done, Lahav."

Nir was already wishing that he was back shooting things on the range. "Is this really all you have for us?" he asked Liora.

She sighed. "You guys are pitiful and you're going to turn into blimps." She pulled the bowl over, tossed the kale chip bags in Nir's direction, then dumped the remaining contents of the bowl onto the middle of the table. Hidden under the healthy option had been a stash of mini-bags of M&M'S—plain, peanut, peanut butter, and caramel. "They were supposed to be a surprise for after you guys ate the healthy stuff."

"How can you have your pudding if you don't eat your meat?" said Lahav in a terrible British accent as he reached for a few bags.

"Thanks, Liora, but I don't need another mother," Nir said, sweeping the kale bags to the floor. He then picked through the candy bags and pulled out four packages of peanut M&M'S. "Okay, Lahav, what's going on with Turkey? What's the mustache-man's great plan of revenge?"

The analyst was prepared to dump a full mini-bag of caramel candies into his mouth, but stopped short. "Dude isn't doing jack," he said, before completing the transfer of the M&M'S bag.

"Any chance you can elaborate on that insightful statement?"

Lahav held up a finger as he chewed. Nir could hear Liora and Dafna snickering as he waited. Yariv was scanning the packaging of a bag of peanut M&M'S in what Nir could only assume was a double-check to ensure they were kosher.

Nicole, where are you when I need you?

Finally, Lahav was able to start forming words, albeit very thickly. "He's doing nothing. Nada. Between his embarrassingly crappy economy and the regional elections at the end of the month, he seems to be one hundred percent focused on protecting his own butt. Sure, every now and then he says he's going to bomb us or invade us, but I haven't seen squat militarily from our Turkish friends."

Nir leaned back in his chair. He hadn't expected to hear that. "So he has nothing going on internationally? Nothing with Russia or Libya or anyone?"

"He's always got stuff going on with them. But I'm not noticing anything major; at least not anything major that's also electronic. They could be passing secret notes on the benches outside the Blue Mosque, but that's a human intel issue. *Ein li musag.* I wouldn't know."

"Interesting," Nir said, rocking in his chair. "So the sick man appears to be sleeping. What about the great bear?" He turned toward Yariv.

The new guy sat up straight, arranged two stacks of papers in front of himself, and said, "There is much more activity in Russia. Undoubtedly, you have read about President Putin's expected spring campaign possibly beginning at the end of this month. In preparation, he is swapping out his weary troops with fresh ones. However, rather than furloughing the ones he is bringing back, he is moving them south to Lebyazhye Air Base near Kamyshin, along the Volga River, just one hundred and eighty kilometers from Volgograd."

"*Betach.* That's no surprise. We know that Putin has been hesitant to diminish his military at all due to how poorly the war is going," said Dafna.

"That's true," said Yariv. "What's interesting is the location. Up until recently, the air base had fallen into disrepair. No one was guarding it, and locals were coming in and looting the place. But suddenly, there's a full staff there and they are building the place back up."

Nir shook his head. "I still don't understand. If the president is giving soldiers leave to rest and recuperate, he's got to have a place to put them."

"Begging your pardon, *ha'mefaked*, it is not the fact that they are doing it. It is the location where it's being done." Lifting a paper from his right stack, Yariv slid it over. Pulling it toward him, Nir saw that it was a map of western Asia from the Caspian Sea to the Mediterranean. In the north, a red circle had been drawn around Kamyshin. The same-color line passed over Georgia, Turkey, and Syria to another circle around Beirut. Above that line was written "3½ hours."

"You know we have screens mounted pretty much everywhere so that all of us can see at once?" Nir asked.

Without seeming to hear the question, the analyst continued. "Whether his motives are benign or not, it is evident that Putin is amassing a sizable force less than a six-hour air-then-road journey from our border. This may be nothing, and it likely is. However, there is a second factor."

Nir put the map down. "Is this going to be on paper, too, so you and I can just share it between ourselves?"

The analyst looked confused.

Waving his hand dismissively, Nir said, "Never mind. Go on."

"Russia has been making a very big deal about the humanitarian aid that they shipped into Beirut, bound for Damascus. However, some of the back-channel talk—and I'm talking about stuff that could never be admissible in court, absolutely nothing official. It's just whispers here around the Mossad. Some of that talk is saying that what's being sent is not aid but weapons. A lot of weapons. High-grade weapons. And not the kind that Russia provides for other countries. This is the stuff they keep for themselves."

Nir swore under his breath. "So you're telling me that it's possible that Russia is preparing for an attack on Israel."

Yariv put his hands up. "No, *ha'mefaked*, I'm not making any conclusions. I am an analyst. I tell you what I see. It is up to you as to what you do with the information."

Liora let out a derisive laugh, while Dafna blurted, "What a chump." Lahav might have added his own response if he had not just poured another two packs of M&M'S in his mouth, and he was now chewing furiously.

Nir leaned toward Yariv. "Listen, my young friend. I don't know what you were taught in junior analyst school, but let me make clear to you what your job is. I expect you to think. You are incredibly smart, maybe the smartest one in here."

Lahav cleared his throat.

Nir corrected himself. "You may be one of the smarter people in here, but if you are not going to look at this information and draw some actual conclusions, then you are of no more use to me than a trained monkey in a party hat. So, using that brain of yours and the information in those two stacks of paper—which, by the way, is surprising enough to see since I didn't know they still made paper in this electronic age—I want you to tell me whether you think that Vladimir Putin is planning an attack on Israel."

The analyst's eyes were big at first, but then they narrowed. He leaned back in his chair and thought.

"The suspense is terrible," said Liora.

Dafna nodded. "I hope it lasts."

"Willy Wonka," mumbled Yariv. A few moments later, he sat up. "I'm sorry, but I can't tell you for sure. What I do know is that Putin is still furious for what you did against him in Damascus, thwarting his plan against our country. I also know that he wants our gas fields one way or another. So, what I can say is that it is possible. Is it probable? I can't answer that yet, but I will continue to dig."

"Excellent. Can't ask for more than that." Nir stuck out his fist, which Yariv bumped.

Liora and Dafna each gave a verbal or physical thumbs up, and Lahav said something that sounded like "Woo wob" or "Ooo wad."

Nir now turned toward the girls. "What's happening with Iran?"

Liora piped in. "It's fashion season in Tehran. I hear they're going all in with the burqa this year."

"They've expanded to two colors to choose from," added Dafna. "There's black and there's the new ebony."

Nir didn't want to laugh, but they had spoken with such conviction that he couldn't help himself. "You two are a *balagan*. Now, seriously, tell me what our moral betters are doing."

"They are not happy with the US," said Liora. "And with the physical state of the American president, they feel they have free rein to do what they want. Attacks on the United States's army in Iraq by Iranian proxies have increased massively. Most aren't large—pretty much just UAVs that fall short of their targets, but some have broken through. It seems like they keep increasing the strength and effectiveness of the attacks just to see how much they can get away with before the US strikes back."

"The same is true, to an extent, down here near our borders," said Dafna. "Rocket attacks are increasing, as you know from your Red Alerts. The difference between us and America is that every time we're hit, we strike back ten times harder. This all reminds me of an MMA fight. So often the two fighters circle each other jabbing and leg kicking, feeling each other out. But then, when one finally sees an opening, they dive in for the takedown. With Hamas, we were in a fight with an enemy that we didn't take seriously, and we got taken down and beat to crap. We need to take our northern enemies very seriously, because one of these days they're going to shoot for our legs to take us down. We need to be ready to counter them so that we can tap them out."

Nir poured the last couple peanut M&M'S from an open bag into his mouth and said, "*Achla*, nice fight metaphor."

Dafna smiled broadly.

"And good report, girls. Lahav, seriously, I have to believe that Erdoğan has something going, so keep digging. Yariv, I want to know what is in those boxes marked 'Humanitarian Aid.' Dafna and Liora, I need a fashion report from Yemen next. See what you can get me."

"You got it, boss," Liora said, laughing.

"And collect all those bags of kale from the floor and give them to Efraim. If anyone needs them, it's him."

Nir got up and headed for his office. Closing the door behind him, he pulled out his phone. He glanced at the clock on the lockscreen.

Excellent! We're still in the window.

He hit one on his speed dial. A moment later, a dusky voice answered, "Hello, stranger."

"We encrypted?"

"Do chickens have lips?" Nir could picture Nicole's smirk as she said it.

"Umm…maybe? Yes? I don't know. Anyway, get yourself comfortable. We just had a meeting, and I've got some stuff I need to run by you."

CHAPTER 35

The Mercedes rumbled as Nir downshifted. Angling the wheel left, he pulled into a long drive. He was late, as usual, and he could see the cars of his brother, Michael, and his sister, Shayna, already pulled off onto the grass in the front yard. His oldest brother, Aaron, was an importer in Perth, Australia, and his youngest sister, Ava, lived in Geneva, getting by however a young, very pretty divorcee got by in Switzerland.

I don't know, and I don't want to ask.

It had been 15 years since he had seen Aaron. The only time his brother had been home in the interim was when their *safta* on their mother's side passed away. Unfortunately, Nir had been on assignment in Greece at the time and missed him. Ava would pop up every now and again at their parents' house. She was shallow and flighty, and Nir did his best to not be available when she was around.

Nir parked next to Michael's SUV and stepped out of the car, only to be mobbed by two boys and two girls, all under ten. "*Dohd*," they all called out, wrapping him in their arms. Laughing, he made sure each one felt his arm on their back before he stepped back. Squatting down, he looked at them, and silence filled the air.

"Why do I feel like you're expecting something from me?" he asked, suppressing a grin.

Menashe, his three-year-old nephew, said, "It's Purim. You're supposed to give us candy now." The others giggled at his brashness.

"Candy? Nobody told me to bring candy."

Menashe was crestfallen, but the others were used to Nir's games, so their grins widened more in anticipation.

Reaching back into his car, Nir pulled out a bag filled with mini packages of M&M'S. Earlier in the day, he had stolen the candy from Liora's desk, substituting it with a note that promised replacement. Holding the bag in front of Menashe, he said, "It's a good thing I just happened to have this in my car."

Menashe beamed as the other children cheered. Nir tore open the bag and gave each one just enough little packs of candy to make their parents unhappy. "Thank you, *Dohd*," they each said, taking turns at giving him a hug before running off toward the side of the house.

"Always the hero."

Nir looked up, knowing by the voice who he would see. Slowly moving down the front steps of the house was his oldest niece, Eliana. She was a younger version of her mother, Hannah, who, next to Nicole, was the most beautiful woman Nir had ever seen. How his brother had managed to snatch her up, he'd never know. Eliana stopped on the bottom step and waited for him to come to her.

Nir smiled as he walked her way. "I'd lift my shirt and show you my Superman leotard, but I think I forgot to put it on. So, in the end, it would probably just end up being awkward."

Her ready smile spread across her face. "You are so weird. And a little gross." He reached her and she wrapped her arms around him. "We've missed you, *Dohd*. I'm so glad you came."

"You know us superheroes. Always out saving the world."

She stepped back and looked at him. Her hand reached up and touched a scuff mark on his forehead that Yaron had given him while they were sparring. "I think that's probably more true than you let on."

This girl is going to break a lot of hearts before she finds the right one.

He stretched out his hand behind her ear and came back with a package of plain M&M'S. "You didn't think I'd forget you."

"*Walla!* You're amazing," she said with an eye roll, taking the package.

"Pardon me, *habibti*. I didn't realize you were too old for candy." As he said this, he reached into his pocket and pulled out a 200-shekel note he had rolled up for her earlier. He passed it to her on the sly and whispered, "Happy Purim. Take this and go have fun with your friends, but don't tell your folks."

His niece wrapped her arms around his neck one more time before depositing the bill and the candy into her pocket. Sliding her arm through his, she said, "Come on, everyone is inside, except for *saba*, who is out back with his fruit trees, of course."

It was hard to believe that in less than six months, Eliana would begin her mandatory service in the IDF. Nir prayed that the conflicts in Gaza and up north would be done before that time arrived.

The front door opened to a wide room. His brother Michael sat on a couch talking with Shayna's husband, Elias Rochman.

"Nir," Michael said, lifting his bottle of Gold Star toward him. Despite the hugs of the children, Nir and his siblings hadn't grown up with a lot of physical touch. That continued into adulthood.

Elias nodded and said, "How goes it?" A CPA who leaned politically to the left, Nir had always felt that Shayna could have done much better. By all accounts, Elias had the same low opinion of his gun-toting brother-in-law.

"Doing okay," Nir answered. Then, before Nir could stop himself, he asked, "Attend any marches lately?"

The forced smile on Elias's face tightened even more. "No. Shoot anybody lately?"

"No. But the day's not over."

Nir felt a slap on his arm. He turned to see Eliana glaring at him. "It's Purim. Don't start things."

"What?" Nir pleaded with an innocent look on his face.

She pulled his arm and led him into the kitchen. His mother was stirring a pot on the stove, while Shayna and Hannah were both cutting vegetables at the kitchen island.

"Hey, *ima*," he said.

His mother turned. "Nir! So glad you came, even if you're a little late."

Both his sister and sister-in-law also greeted him warmly, although only Hannah put down her knife to come hug him.

"Good to see you, Nir," she said. Then, touching the scuff on his forehead, she added, "You look like you've been busy."

"Nah, just cut myself shaving," he said with a wink. "*Abba's* out back?"

"I'll take you," Eliana said, stepping toward the back door.

"Stop," said Hannah. "Give your *dohd* some room. Here, grab a bowl and start collecting these vegetables."

Nir's niece gave him an exasperated look of apology, then began to fill the proffered bowl.

Opening the back door to his father's small grove of orange trees always gave him a sense of déjà vu. He had done it so many times throughout his life, and, so often, when he did, he would see his father with his shears trimming and shaping what were his pride and joy.

"Hey, *abba*," Nir called out.

Without turning, his father said, "Ah, Nir, good. Grab that basket by the steps and come here."

Looking down, Nir spotted what his dad wanted. He carried it over.

"Now hold it there." Climbing onto the second step of a small ladder, his dad began to examine the oranges. Every fourth or fifth one, he would gently twist off and set in the basket. "It was good of you to show up. Your *ima* is always happy when you do."

There were several ways that Nir could interpret his father's words, but he figured it was best just to assume the best option. Like Eliana had warned, "Don't start things." Instead, he said, "The trees are looking great."

"No frost yet. Been a good year." The man continued to selectively harvest his fruit. "The Grebers three doors down lost a son in Gaza. Didn't know if you'd heard. Also, the Kantors' daughter is home from her reserve duty with a back injury. Don't know how it happened, but she's moving very slowly."

"That's a tragedy."

"What's a tragedy is that we're in this whole mess to begin with. Six months in, and we're still fighting in Gaza. What's the prime minister doing?"

"He's doing all he can, *abba*. From all I can tell, he won't stop until he finishes the job."

Nir's father backed down the two steps and leaned his elbow on the ladder. "That man better see it through or else he'll be out. He may be out anyway if the leftists, like that one in my house, have anything to do with it. If there was ever a time that should bring us together, this is it. But already the sharks are back in the water. The other day at work, I had to walk away from the table where I was having lunch with some coworkers because one idiot started spouting off how the prime minister was getting our kids killed in Gaza. Should we just give up? What does he want us to do about the hostages? If you ask him, he'd say, 'Negotiate.' Seriously? Negotiate with the ones who took them to begin with? I left the table because if I had stayed, I would have popped the man, and then I'd be out of a job."

Nir stayed silent, letting the man rant. He knew that if he agreed with him, it would extend the tirade indefinitely. And if he disagreed, it would be even worse. Then he'd be the target of his father's ire instead of Elias inside.

After half a minute of silence, his father grunted and climbed back up the ladder. "Take those in and give them to your *ima*."

Anxious to escape, Nir spun around and headed for the house. He was almost to the door when his father called out, "And how's that Christian girlfriend of yours?"

Nir stopped in his tracks. Once again, Eliana's words came back to him.

Don't start things.

"She's fine, *abba*. She's doing fine."

Hurrying up the steps, Nir walked back into the house, closing the door behind him.

CHAPTER 36

19:40 (7:40 PM) IST

Nir walked along the edge of the park. Up until a few minutes ago, Eliana had once again been holding on to his arm. It had been a little awkward, but he understood what she was doing. Hanging on to the arm of Nir Tavor gave her a little street cred, and he didn't want to deny that from her.

Rumors had legs of their own, especially in a country like Israel. Everyone had heard whispered stories of the Tavor boy who was now some special agent with the Mossad. The fact that his picture had shown up in the paper on several occasions hadn't helped matters. Few people, other than folks who had been around as he was growing up, said anything to him, and absolutely no one asked him about his work, which was a plus. For now, he would circle the park with Michael, watching the kids enjoy the Purim fair and pretending that no one was watching him.

Elias could have been with them also. However, he had made the mistake of voicing an offhand comment questioning the commitment of the present government to bring home the hostages. That had set Nir's father off. Their ensuing argument had ended with Elias gathering up Shayna and their two crying sons and driving off. The tension that remained at the table was thick as everyone just sat there.

Finally, Nir had reached across the table and said, "Since Elias is gone, mind if I have his brisket?" He lifted the man's plate and shoveled the food onto his own. "*Très magnifique, ima,*" he added, lifting his fingers to give a chef's kiss.

Everyone burst out laughing. At least, everyone except for his *abba*, who pushed his chair back and stormed away from the table. Nir's *ima* began to rise to follow him, but Michael stopped her. "Let him be, *ima*. He'll get over it or he won't. Let's not let him ruin our Purim."

After hesitating a moment, she sat back down. "I'm glad you like the beef, *matok*," she said, grabbing Nir's hand.

Maya, the youngest of Nir's nieces, began to sing:
Chag Purim, Chag Purim, Chag gadol layehudim…
Soon everyone had grabbed hands and joined in:
Masechot, ra'ashanim, shirim verikudim.
Hava narishah—rash, rash, rash…
As that line rang out they twisted their hands, pretending to spin the noisemakers they were singing about.
Hava narishah—rash, rash, rash,
Hava narishah—rash, rash, rash,
Bara'ashanim!
Grabbing hands again, they began the second verse of the Purim song. With his mother's hand in his right and little Maya's hand in his left, Nir couldn't remember the last time he had enjoyed his family quite so much.

Could it be because abba and Elias aren't here? Probably.

Leaving Hannah back at home with their mother, Michael and Nir had walked the girls up to the park for the fair. Reaching into his pocket, Michael pulled out a pack of Noblesse cigarettes. Turning the box upside down, he tapped it a couple times into his hand before opening it and pulling one out. He slipped it between his lips and said, "I'm not even going to offer you one."

"Good. When I die, I want it to be short and sweet."

Michael laughed as he traded the package for a lighter. He flicked it and took a drag on the cigarette. "I've quit these so many times. Even Hannah's convinced I gave them up a couple years ago."

Nir shook his head. "I doubt it. She just loves you too much to confront you. Besides, you've got prying little eyes all around you, and those little eyes are attached to big mouths."

Michael took another deep drag before chuckling. "Yeah, those girls love to talk. Hey, did I tell you I've been called back into the reserves?"

"Keep at them, Nir," cheered Mr. Levitz, who owned the Levitz Furniture store downtown. He gave a wave and a thumbs up. Nir nodded to him.

Turning back to his brother, Nir asked, "Aren't you too old to be called back?"

"In these times, it's all hands. They're digging deep for people. Besides, I'm not going to the front lines or anything. Apparently, I'm too old to hold a gun. Instead, they have me requisitioning cars from people."

That was something new. "How does that work?"

"They have me looking for SUVs to be used as transport by the IDF. If I see an SUV that looks like it's in good shape, I tell the owner, 'The military needs your vehicle.' We work out a reasonable deal, and I drive off in their car."

Nir was laughing. "*Sababa!* That definitely sounds like the IDF. You've got to have some people who are seriously angry at you."

"It all depends on the deal I get for them," Michael said with a wink.

Nir stopped and turned toward his brother. "Wait, didn't I park next to your SUV in the folks' front yard?" Nir could picture the white, late-model Chevy Equinox. It was his brother's pride and joy, and he kept it in pristine condition.

Michael grinned and flicked the butt of his cigarette away. "You did. Unfortunately, I determined that it wasn't up to the standards needed for the IDF."

Nir raised his eyebrows at his brother, then laughed and shook his head. They began walking again. It seemed that everyone in the country was running some sort of side hustle. Most were legit, but there were quite a few that balanced on that razor's edge between legal and maybe a step too far. Part of it came from living in what was still a relatively young nation. But the greater part was simply the history of the Jewish people. You always had to have something else going on, because you never knew when you would be banned from your livelihood or have it taken from you. This reminded Nir of a verse he had heard many years ago from Qoheleth, who said something like, "Sow your seed in the morning and at night keep working, because you don't know which will be successful, one or the other or both equally."

But even with those whose side hustles crossed the line into grifts, there were very few who ran them against fellow Jews. Most were directed at people outside of their race. That, too, seemed to come from history. When you were strangers in a foreign land, you had to band together and depend on one another. Besides, from what he could remember, there was a lot in the Mosaic law about not shafting other Jews—not that most Jews these days gave a rip about the Mosaic law.

After a few minutes, Michael spoke up again. "You keeping yourself safe out there? If anything happened to you, it would kill *ima*. Not sure how *abba* would react. I think the only thing that would kill him is if a frost took his trees."

Nir wondered how he should answer. Even though this was his own flesh and blood, most of his life was spent in a bubble that he couldn't talk about. "I'm trying," was the best he could come up with.

"And what about the rest of us? I hear the news. I know that the war is coming to the north eventually. Are we okay where we're at?"

"For now. If you were up around Mount Meron, I'd say to get your family down here to Afula. But at your home in Tiberias? You're good. There are no worries coming from Jordan, and there are enough targets around Golan to draw the enemy's fire."

Michael pulled out his box of cigarettes again and went through the ritual of lighting a fresh one. Once again, Nir raised his eyebrow.

"I don't want to hear it. Listen, I need to know. How did we miss it? How did we let hundreds of those maniacs over our border? You know that the parents of Hannah's sister's husband were slaughtered at Kibbutz Nir Oz?"

"Yeah, I know."

"Then how did it happen? We're supposed to have this great

military—and I think we do have a great military. But, my God, how could we miss this?"

Nir had a simple answer. "We underestimated them and overestimated ourselves."

When Nir said no more, Michael prodded him. "I'm listening."

"When you see a Palestinian on the street, what do you think? Uneducated. Simple. Someone fit for menial tasks. It's how so many of the Chinese view the Uyghurs, or the Europeans look at the Muslims, or the Americans treat the Mexicans. We took the Palestinians too lightly, not thinking that they'd actually be able to coordinate an attack across our border. But there were enough smart ones who watched us—not just for months, but for years. Eventually, they figured out a way to come across and kick us in the teeth. What they weren't smart enough to do was to sustain it. They had plans to keep pushing north, but as soon as the IDF got involved, they scurried back to their burrows."

"They were also expecting help, weren't they?"

"They were. This was all part of a grandiose plan overseen by—surprise, surprise—Iran. The ayatollahs were strategizing to launch a coordinated attack using their little axis of evil: Hezbollah, Hamas, and the Houthis, along with all their scrub militias in Iraq and Syria. They'd start with a massive barrage of rockets that would wear out the Iron Dome. Then the invasion would start. They figured we would be stretched so thin that we wouldn't be able to defend ourselves."

Michael took another long drag, then dropped his cigarette and stubbed it out with his shoe. "Would it have worked?"

"I don't know. Maybe. But we've been under worse odds before."

Nodding, Nir's brother asked, "So, what happened to this great plan of Khamenei's?"

Nir laughed quietly and shook his head. "The Palestinians happened. They decided they wanted the glory for themselves, so they launched prematurely, thinking that the others would jump in and back them. But the rest pretty much said, 'Screw you for not waiting. You got yourselves into this; now get yourselves out.' Hezbollah sent some rockets, and the militias did a little war dance, but that was pretty much it."

Michael was shaking his head. "Just when you think there might not be a God."

Surprised, Nir turned to him.

Michael continued, "No, seriously, Nir. How many times has it been now? Over and over, we're standing against impossible odds, and we come out on top. I don't know if the God of the Torah really is out there, but there sure as anything is something or someone out there looking out for us. Wasn't it David Ben-Gurion who said, 'With the Jews, anyone who doesn't believe in miracles isn't a realist'? And he was an atheist, or at least close to it."

"Calm down. I agree with you," Nir said. "I'm just surprised to hear you say it."

"So, you believe there's a God?"

How do I answer this? I'm pretty sure there is, but I don't know who He is. I certainly can't mention anything about Nicole's God.

"Let me just say that I've been in situations where only the supernatural kept me alive. Situations so close and timing so precise that you either believe the world is made up of continuously unexplainable circumstances, or there is a God watching over us. Now, don't ask me any more than that, because I can't answer you. I'm still trying to figure all this out myself. What I do know is that when I'm going into a dangerous situation, I no longer feel like I'm doing it on my own."

"Interesting," was all that Michael said as they continued their walk.

"Nir, we're all so proud of you!" It was Mrs. Goltz from his primary school's front office calling to him from a picnic table surrounded with people. Nir recognized her husband, but no one else. He waved to them and kept moving on, while she appeared to be giving them his full curriculum vitae.

Michael stopped and took Nir by the arm. "Just promise me that this is the last time this will happen. Little Maya still spends most nights in bed with Hannah and me. These kids are all growing up wondering when the bad men will appear to kill them or steal them away. I don't know, *achi*. It's like this is a damaged generation thanks to those pigs down in Gaza. Our children are going to carry this with them for the rest of their lives."

He reached for his pack of cigarettes again, but then stuffed it back into his shirt pocket. "Listen, I don't know what you do. I don't want to know because I'd probably freak out that my little brother was living that kind of life. Just swear to me that you are going to make those dogs who are responsible for this pay."

Nir knew he couldn't say anything. Instead, he just held his brother's eyes.

Finally, Michael began nodding. He put his hand on Nir's shoulder. "Good. Good. You get them, *achi*. And I can assure you that you have people back home who will be praying to whatever God is up there to keep you safe."

"Can't ask for more than that," said Nir. He turned, and the two of them went looking for Michael's kids.

CHAPTER 37

The battered and charred remains of a body filled the video screen. The face was completely unrecognizable, but Nir thought the hairline looked familiar. Straight cut across the sides with gray starting to frost the edges.

That's Lavie, sure as the day is long.

Lavie Bensoussan had been a Kidon team leader like Nir. Last year, a raid on four chemical weapons stashes in Damascus had gone all wrong when a massive earthquake hit the city. Now Damascus was in ruins, and the teams of Bensoussan and Zakai Abelman were wiped out. Nir had lost one of his own team members and two more who were on loan from Unit 504. The Damascus operation had turned into a bloodbath, and now seeing it replayed on television got his blood boiling. From the curses and oaths being spewed by the analysts and ops team around the table at CARL, Nir knew he wasn't the only one affected.

The picture changed, and Nir recognized the mangled profile.

Calev Furst. His older brother and I took our first jumps in the same class. Why is he showing us these?

President Vladimir Putin's voice began again, and Nir read the translation at the bottom of the screen.

"These are two Israeli operatives who were found amongst the rubble in Damascus. They were fully armed and had engaged the Syrian forces. And they weren't the only ones. We know of at least two, and maybe even three, other Israeli teams that were in Damascus at the time of the earthquake. Why were they there?"

To stop you from launching a chemical attack on our country, you aha-bal. To keep you from killing thousands of our people.

The Russian president raised an eyebrow as he continued. "The Jewish seismologists say that the earthquake originated along the Serghaya fault to the west of the city, but that seems far-fetched. No credible expert ever credited that line with such destructive power. We sent our own teams to examine the region, teams whose findings we could trust. When we did, we found these."

The screen now split into four rectangles, each featuring a picture of a cylindrical hole.

"What are those?" cried Imri, leaping to his feet. "He's surely not implying—"

"Shut up and listen," Nir chided. Imri settled mutely back into his chair.

"We found eight such holes along the Serghaya fault. What are they doing there? They certainly are not natural. These holes were made by human hands, and they are very, very deep. Of course, there are no notations on them, such as 'Made in Israel.'" The president smiled and paused as his unseen audience laughed at his joke. "But who else in the world would do such a thing to Syria? Is there any other country that was constantly flying sorties against Damascus in order to destroy their infrastructure? Is there any other people group, other than the Jews, who regularly kicks a wounded opponent when they are down, like they are doing to the Gazans? Every other nation is flying humanitarian aid into Syria. But the only items that Israel flies into Syria are missiles."

Once again, the president paused as his audience acknowledged his words with rousing applause. "This is why we are officially declaring two things tonight. First, we are condemning, in the strongest terms,

Israel's actions in Damascus and in the nation of Syria both before, during, and after last year's earthquake. Second, we are declaring a no-fly zone over the nation of Syria. If any plane crosses the border from Israel into Syria, it will be considered by the Russian people as an act of war. Mr. Prime Minister, Mr. Foreign Minister, and Mr. Secretary of State, you and your Israeli government are officially on notice. Do not test us in this, because we will act. And, I promise you that if you force us to act, you will pay an exorbitant price." The Russian president stared into the camera's lens for two beats longer before turning and walking off stage.

"Holy mother of Stalin, what was that?" asked Liora. She looked nervous, despite the fact Imri had his arm across the back of her chair.

"It was a confirmation of the Mossad party line on the so-called humanitarian aid in Beirut," answered Yariv. "He's been building up his supplies for an invasion. Everything is pointing toward it."

"Define for me 'everything,'" said Nir.

"There are currently 150,000 troops 'on leave' at Kamyshin," he answered, air-quoting the words *on leave*. "The runway at the air base that had been in disrepair has been fixed and extended so that they're able to land whatever they want there—Ilyushins, Tupolevs, even the Antonov An-124. All hands on deck, it would take them three days max to transport those troops down here. Then there are all the boxes that keep getting unloaded from Russian ships. They're taken off, then stored in an area that our people can't get to. From pictures, we can see that they are all labeled for humanitarian purposes, but they haven't moved in over a month. They're just sitting there rotting, if food is what's really in them. All of Russia's other stuff is being flown into Shayrat Airbase in Homs, where it is immediately trucked down the M5 to Damascus. The Red Crescent is overseeing the relief efforts there, so we know what's in those crates. But the ones coming off the ships in Beirut remain a mystery."

Nir leaned forward to grab a bag of whatever was in Liora's conference table snack bowl, but then he remembered that the bowl wasn't there because someone had forgotten to replace what he had borrowed on Purim. He quickly glanced at Liora, who glared at him, apparently knowing exactly what he had been about to do.

Dafna spared him the confrontation. "It still doesn't make sense to me, though. What do they think they're going to do? They're barely getting by fighting a one-front war in Ukraine. In fact, there are some who are saying that Russia's western advances are becoming unsustainable. Now they're looking to open a new front?"

Both Dima and Lahav began to speak. Dima nodded for Lahav to go ahead. "It's not about invasion. Once again, what do we do when we're looking for a motive?"

"Follow the money," replied Dafna, looking side-eyed down at the table. Nir could tell that her mind was racing.

Lahav continued, "Exactly. They may bring troops down here, but I doubt they'll cross our border. While our eyes are on the manpower, they'll launch their drones and take out our gas rigs."

"Wait—don't they want them?" asked Yariv.

Nir spoke up. "They do, but they are realizing that they can't get them. So instead of taking over their competition, they're taking them out."

"Time for our gas fields to sleep with the fishes," said Lahav.

"Didn't they try that last year and fail?" asked Yaron. "I know. I was there."

"If at first you don't succeed…" said Liora, letting the rest hang.

They all sat silently, which was a rarity for this group. Finally, Nir said, "I don't know. It feels like we're going back in time. You know, second verse same as the first. I need to hear what the *ramsad* and the others are saying about this."

Normally, there would have been protests about Nir seeking input from other sources. Not this time. The only one who seemed sure of Russia's big plot was the new guy—the weird one with the beanie and the tassels. He hadn't yet earned the right to stand out from the others.

Nir hated thinking of Yariv that stereotypical way, but he couldn't help it. The guy was brilliant, hardworking, and occasionally funny. But he was different. He was the round Orthodox peg trying to fit into their square secular hole. Nothing said he couldn't eventually do it, but there would always be gaps in the corners where he and the rest of the team wouldn't meet.

"Okay, good work, Yariv," Nir managed to say. "Keep at it. Girls, Iran?"

"Still sending explodey drones at the US," answered Dafna.

"Lahav, Turkey?"

"Still sucks."

"As always, I need a little more detail, please."

"Four days away from the election. Erdoğan's party is looking like it's going to get smacked. The economy is desperately searching for new ways to get worse. It's like the president is calling out threats against Israel while his country is curled up in a fetal position."

"And the sick man keeps getting sicker," said Imri.

"Exactly," answered Lahav, shooting two finger guns at the operative, then spinning them down into imaginary holsters on his hips.

Nir rolled his eyes at the analyst's antics.

Standing up, Nir said, "Okay, good work everyone. I've got a meeting with the *ramsad* and the muckety-mucks in about half an hour. I'll report back to you after."

As they broke up, he heard Liora impersonating him using an English accent. "Oh, I have a meeting with the *ramsad*," she said as she sipped from an imaginary teacup, her pinky extended.

Dafna lifted her own pretend cup and said, "Oh, how lovely. Maybe they'll have scones or some sort of digestive." They both laughed as they took their seats.

As he stared at them, he found himself thinking, *It's truly amazing how much I love this group of idiots.*

CHAPTER 38

In all Nir's years with the Mossad, he had been in this auditorium only once. That had been when he graduated from his training and received his credentials from the *ramsad*. Set up as a small amphitheater, the room had built-in seating for around 80 with chair room for another 20 or so. Nir didn't think they would need that many seats for this meeting, but he didn't know for sure. It wasn't his meeting.

About 20 people were scattered throughout. Never one to put himself forward, Nir didn't move down the steps, preferring to settle himself in the back row. He dropped into the theatre-style seat and waited for the show to begin. In front sat a table with seven microphones perched in front of seven chairs.

Lord, save me from ever being a microphone person. I like living in the shadows.

Nir noticed movement to his right. It was Irin Ehrlich, another Kidon team leader. The two men had experienced their differences in the past, but after two of their fellow leaders were killed and another retired, they were the only old guard left. Both had individually decided that they would do their best to put aside their differences and try to get along. It wasn't easy. Ehrlich had jerkness molded into him like dimples on a golfball. But when the man reached out his hand, Nir fist-bumped it.

As he settled into a seat one removed from Nir's, he said, "Heard you sold off your cash cow in Belgium."

That was the thing with Ehrlich. Great shooter, great strategist. He was a guy you wanted to have on your team in a firefight. But he always had to start talking.

"Yep."

I will not get baited into an argument. I will not get baited into an argument.

"Why would you want to do that? You've got more money than most of the people who'll be in this meeting. I always wondered how you pulled that off."

Nir kept looking straight ahead, hoping that his lack of eye contact would lessen his deep craving to tell the man to shut up. "It's good to be the teacher's pet."

"No doubt about that." Ehrlich leaned Nir's way so that he was half over the seat between them. "So, what are you thinking about this whole Russia thing?"

"Heck if I know. Could just be humanitarian aid, like the boxes say."

Ehrlich snorted. "*Chai b'seret!* Then why is it just sitting there? And why haven't they sent it to Homs like the rest of their crap?"

Nir kept looking forward. "I don't know. Hopefully, this meeting will give us a little insight."

"Yeah, whatever," sneered Ehrlich. "These stupid meetings are a waste of time."

"I'll make sure the *ramsad* knows you feel that way," said a new voice.

Nir looked over and saw Efraim walking up to Ehrlich. "Excuse me," he said, intentionally pushing into the Kidon leader's knees. Nir could tell that he was also making sure his backside was passing dangerously close to the other man's face. Once he cleared him, he plopped down in the seat between Nir and Ehrlich.

Surprised to see him, Nir asked, "*Achi,* what are you doing up here? Shouldn't you be down there behind one of those mics?"

"Alas, those microphones are for people whose pay grade is much higher than mine."

"Speaking of pay grades," said Ehrlich. "Now that Nir is back here, any chance you could set me up with some high-paying European gig like he managed to get?"

"As a matter of fact, we have an opening in Bulgaria for a colostomy technician. Of course, you'd have to start at the bottom and work your way up."

Ehrlich muttered a curse and shifted several seats to the right.

Still looking ahead, Nir said, "Sometimes working with you is like working with a thirteen-year-old."

"You're welcome."

"Seriously, though, shouldn't you at least be toward the front in case you're needed?"

"No. I get the feeling this is one of those informational meetings as opposed to a Q and A. The seven of them have been in a conference for the past two hours. All I know about this is the text I got saying to be here now. I'm assuming it's about Russia."

Nir was trying to count out the seven people in his head as his friend was talking. "Okay, I've got Katz, obviously. I'm figuring Asher Porush and Karin Friedman. Who else?"

"So, you're right on the first three. There's the *ramsad*, the deputy director of Mossad, and the assistant deputy director. But then you've got the government folk—Idan Snir, Shaul Arens, Dan Hurvitz, and Eli Rosen."

Nir ticked them off in his head—the prime minister, the foreign minister, the minister of defense, and the minister of interior. "Wow, that's quite a lineup."

"That's because anything having to do with Russia is a big deal. Oh, look who's walking in down there."

Nir followed the man's finger and saw Yoram Suissa, the director of Caesarea. He sat in the front row next to the two replacement Kidon leaders. "Interesting. Having him here along with Ehrlich, me, and the new guys tells me that we may be taking action."

A door on the right side of the platform opened, and six men and one woman walked out. Nir looked around and saw that the amphitheater was about half full. Probably 30 to 40 were in the audience. Nir recognized the heads of most departments, even though he couldn't remember all the names. The director of analytics, each division of intelligence gathering, and even the guy who led "future casting." Nir had shared a lunch with the man and was amazed at his grasp of national and global trends. The final group in attendance was the one to which he belonged—operations. Everyone had top-secret clearance, and each would be essential to whatever the chiefs on the platform were planning.

The men and woman on stage took their designated seats, and Prime Minister Snir began to speak. "Ladies and gentlemen, let me first thank you for being here. Let me also thank you for your hard work over these past few weeks analyzing the situation with Russia. Before we fill you in on any conclusions we've come to, let me have my colleagues tell you their concerns and where they are coming from." Turning to his left, he said, "Foreign Minister."

When Shaul Arens began to talk, Nir let out a silent sigh. At least he thought it was silent, but an elbow from Efraim and a glare from a woman two rows up told him that he was mistaken. He straightened up and pretended to be interested in what was being said. But the man's monotone delivery was somnambulic. Nir took a quick look at his watch and did the mental time-zone math between where he sat and Lisbon, Portugal, where Nicole was preparing for a smallish fashion show. With her face in his mind, he settled back in his chair to debate the best way to convince her to come to Israel.

Unfortunately, he didn't need her in Tel Aviv at the moment. He just wanted her there. His time with his family in Afula had been pleasant despite the annual row between his father and Elias. But it had also gotten him thinking about Nicole. Any other woman he would have married by now and probably had a couple ankle biters of his own. But Nicole had her Christian faith, and she wore it like a suit of armor that allowed him to get close, but not close enough.

If only she would compromise on that one thing, then we could be together. But then again, if she was the kind of girl who compromised on something that important, would you want to be with her? Face it—it's your own high standards that led you to fall for the one woman on earth who you can't have.

But Nir knew that wasn't totally true. There was one way he could have her. But that would mean buying in completely to her "Jesus as Messiah" belief system. Try as he might, he couldn't bring himself to that point. Something in his heart kept him from accepting it as truth. That block was aggravating, but he was also thankful for it. Whatever was keeping him from accepting Nicole's Jesus was part of what made him who he was.

Nir started. An elbow was pushing into his side. "Nir, wake up. He's talking to you," Efraim was whispering to him.

Sitting up straight, Nir said to the foreign minister, "Could you please repeat the question, Mr. Foreign Minister?"

Unfortunately, it was Defense Minister Hurvitz who answered. Nir quickly adjusted his attention.

"I said that since you are the one person in this room who has had the most recent deep dive with them, I wondered if you might have any insight."

Nir sat like a deer in headlights.

"He's talking about the Russians," whispered Efraim.

"Still?" Nir cleared his throat and said, "Sir, I don't trust the Russkis as far as I can throw them. But it's a different kind of distrust than I have for Hamas. I don't trust Hamas because I know exactly what they're going to do. They're going to try to kill me and my family. The Russians, though, have so many more layers that you never quite know where they're coming from. They're like Turkish baklava. Every layer you pull off reveals a new layer. Could they be preparing to invade us? Sure. I wouldn't put that past them. Could they just be trying a new route to ship aid to Damascus? Might be. Why not? Or could they be baiting us to do something like blow up a warehouse full of humanitarian aid so that we somehow look worse on the world stage than we already do? Definitely a possibility."

Hurvitz was about to follow up, but the *ramsad* cleared his throat, effectively taking the stage. In his low grumble, he said, "Tavor, if you were a betting man, where would you put your money?"

"I'd put it on Manchester City. But when it comes to the Russians, I wouldn't put it anywhere until I had a chance to look in those boxes."

The *ramsad* grunted, then leaned back in his chair. He turned and said something sotto voce to the prime minister.

"Cut the mics," said the prime minister. The seven people on stage began a discussion.

"Smooth, Tavor," said Ehrlich with a laugh.

"I thought this wasn't going to be Q and A," Nir whispered to Efraim, ignoring the Kidon team leader's dig.

"It wasn't supposed to be. But I also didn't think you'd treat it like nap time."

Ehrlich jumped in again. "He was probably thinking about that hot number he's got. The beautiful analyst with the smoking green eyes. Yeah, look at his face. He's turning all red."

A woman in front of Ehrlich turned around and shushed him. He quieted down, but he didn't stop grinning at Nir.

"Ignore him," Efraim said. But he had a subtle grin on his face. "Ehrlich's a jerk, but he's also not wrong. You either need to marry Nicole or cut her loose and hitch yourself to some *babushka* you can settle down with and make babies."

"Can we talk about this another time?" Nir pleaded. Now the woman shushed the two of them. Nir apologized, then said to Efraim, "See?"

The seven bigwigs talked for about ten minutes before the prime minister called out to turn the mics back on.

The defense minister began to speak. "We're facing two major problems with these boxes. First, learning what is in them. Then second, if they are weapons like we fear, we need to be ultra precise in destroying them. You all know what happened in 2020 when the ammonium nitrate exploded in the Port of Beirut. At least 218 people dead, more than 7,000 hurt, and over $15 billion in damages. If our missiles are off just a few meters and we set off something like that, we will be international pariahs for decades. And deservedly so. What that means is we need beacons placed in or on those boxes to guide our weapons precisely where they need to go."

The *ramsad* now spoke again. "Tavor, since you would like so much to see what is in those boxes, I am sending your team in."

Nir was about to protest that it was a near-impossible task, but Ehrlich was on his feet first.

"If he's not up for it, my team is."

The *ramsad* sighed. "Ehrlich, you are backup. If for some reason Tavor's team is not able to go or he is captured, you will step in. Tavor, your mission is twofold. First, examine the boxes. You won't be able to open all of them, but open enough to get a picture of what they contain. If you discover weapons, then place the beacons and get yourselves out. Do you understand?"

Nir stood. There was no way now that he was going to let Ehrlich take the lead. "I understand, *hamefaked*. But I'm going to need plenty of resources."

"All we have is at your disposal," said Defense Minister Hurvitz.

"Much appreciated. Director Suissa, I would like my team to spend some time with you to talk strategy," Nir said, addressing the head of Caesarea.

"I'm available," he replied.

The prime minister closed the meeting. "Okay, we're done here. Thank you all for coming. And, Tavor, Godspeed to you."

Nir nodded to the man, then turned toward the door. At least now he had his excuse to get Nicole back into the country.

CHAPTER 39

On his way back to CARL, Nir stopped by the cafeteria. Along one wall was a series of vending machines for people who either didn't want to wait in line for real food or who simply wanted a quick hit of sugar or caffeine. Of course, there was one machine that was committed to healthy options, but he figured those offerings remained on their racks until they expired and were replaced with fresh choices no one wanted to buy.

Nir pulled out his credit card and got to work. After a few tries, he developed a system to get three machines working on a rotating basis. He knew people had to be watching as he punched numbers and tapped his card on one pad after another, but he ignored them. Those who knew him would have figured he was just being his usual off-kilter self. Those who knew him only by reputation would have been too nervous to say anything. Once he had 30 or so packages of candy and bags of chips tossed into a pile, he laid his sweat jacket on the ground, filled it with the junk food, and hefted it up.

Turning, he saw that he had in fact drawn a crowd. "Movie night at CARL," he said with a sheepish smile before walking off. That explanation should satisfy most who heard it. They already thought that those working in CARL were freaks.

Once he reached his team's headquarters, he held his passcard up to the scanner and walked in. The analysts were hard at work at their stations, while the ops team had a chessboard set up on the conference table. It appeared that Dima was about to get checkmated by Yaron. The other two were giving Dima advice on how he might possibly escape.

"Meeting time," Nir called out, dumping his vending machine haul onto the table. Four or five candy bars skittered across the table, clearing half the remaining pieces from the chessboard.

Yaron swore, while Dima quickly stood and said, "Darn. Going to have to call that one a draw." Turning to Nir, he mouthed, "Thanks."

Nir winked in reply.

When Liora heard the clatter, she jumped from her chair and came bounding over. Seeing the pile, her face lit up and she gave Nir a kiss on the cheek. "You still owe me," she whispered in his ear.

"I'll have it to you tomorrow." As he sat, he snatched up a Twix bar, tore it open, removed one of the two pieces, and took a bite. Soon, the rest of the analysts were at the table, and Nir started the meeting.

"So, it seems me and the ops team are taking a little trip."

"Sweet, Sint Maarten?" asked Dima.

"Euro Disney?" said Imri.

"It's Disneyland Paris now, *motek*," corrected Liora, looking past Dafna to her fiancé.

"Yes, *motek*," mimicked the rest of the ops team, while Imri rolled his eyes.

Nir shook his head. "Your guesses are all so very close. We're actually taking an all-expenses-paid vacation to the Port of Beirut."

"Crap, I knew you were going to say that," grumbled Yaron before fitting half a Snickers bar into his mouth.

Nir caught them up on the details of the meeting, using his imagination to fill in the parts that he missed while he was dozing.

By the time he finished, Gil was waving his hands. "Whoa, whoa, whoa! So, there were more than thirty people in the auditorium listening while we were tasked with a secret mission? Are they going to headline it in the next edition of the *Mossad Post* too?"

"I know, I know. That bugged me also. But if you had seen the group that was there…it was the head of every department along with their lead assistants or heads of staff or some other big cheese dude or chick. If one of them is compromised, then we probably have a Philby-level problem on our hands," Nir said, referencing the infamous British MI6 agent who spied for the Russians from the 1940s to the 1960s before defecting to Moscow.

Gil leaned back. "Seems to me the fewer people who know what we're doing, the better off we are."

"I hear you, *achi*. But this is the hand we've been dealt. So, who can tell me about the Beirut port, other than that it appears to be somewhat flammable?"

Yariv raised his hand.

"You don't need to raise your hand, Yariv. You can just talk," said Nir.

"Okay. Well, I've done some digging into the port because of it being connected to Russia. The place is still a mess, even four years after the explosion. There are piles of rubble from old warehouses and burn marks from the blast. The investigation instituted by the government, along with the French, had steam in the beginning. But eventually it petered out."

"Eet was a beeg blast. Vat more can ve say?" said Dima in a poor French accent.

"Exactly. A group of German companies decided they were going to come in and begin reconstructing the port area in 2021, but the governmental red tape and the Hezbollah graft drove them away. It's those same two factors that have kept a lot of other countries away too—most of whom simply wanted to help. Instead, any renovation that has taken place has been piecemeal. A building here, a warehouse there—that kind of stuff."

"And the French were content to let the port sit like that?" asked Nir. "Lebanon has always been an important link for them into the Middle East. Has Hezbollah tainted the country that much?"

"Yes to your last question and no to your first. Hezbollah has tainted the country that much. It's like the country is mobbed up under layers of graft. And rather than it being like *The Godfather*, it's more like *Goodfellas* but with everyone playing the crazy Joe Pesci character."

"Perfect reference. But I thought you guys couldn't watch movies like that," said Gil.

Yariv put his finger to his lips. "Shhh!"

That was the first moment Nir thought maybe this guy could make it in CARL.

CHAPTER 40

Yariv finally appeared to be comfortable in his element. "So, you have all these crazies in the government with their hands out. Then you've got the terrorists with their hands out too. The only ones who know how to navigate them even somewhat decently are the French. That's why in 2022, the French CMA CGM Group were awarded a ten-year contract to clean up and rebuild the port."

"Do I care what CMA and CGM stand for?" asked Nir.

Yariv shook his head. "No. Just some French words that have to do with maritime stuff. So, they got to work and spent the last couple years planning. Then, just two weeks ago, Lebanon's caretaker Prime Minister Najib Mikati held a press conference with the leaders of the French group to reveal their new plan. Two French engineering companies, Artelia and Egis, have been given the task to reinvent the whole area for the twenty-first century."

Nir took the last bite of his Twix as he thought. Balling up the wrapper, he tossed it toward a trash can along the wall. But the foil wrapper sprung back open and dropped to the ground.

"*Walla*, you kinda suck," a disappointed Dafna said.

"The crosswinds got it," said Nir. "So, new guy, how does all this background help us? Based on what you know, tell me what we should know."

It was Yariv's turn to think. He picked up a Snickers bar, examined the label, then tore it open. But before he took a bite, he said, "Security is somewhat lax at the port because there is no overall system. It's like the times of the Judges. Everyone does as they see fit." He took a bite of his candy, then said between chews, "But I doubt that goes for the Russians. I would suspect that they have their warehouse locked up tight and guarded well."

"Yeah, I'm betting you're right," Nir said as he leaned forward and began sifting through the pile on the table looking for something a little healthier than candy or chips. Then he remembered that he had purposely avoided the machine with the healthy options. He leaned back.

"Yeah, snacks aren't as easy as you thought," said Liora, giving him an accusing look.

Nir glared at her. "Show me a picture of the Beirut port," he said to Yariv.

"I'll get it," said Dafna, spinning her chair and rolling to her workstation. Fifteen seconds later, a Google Earth image popped up on the screen. To the north was the Mediterranean. On the west was a series of warehouses. To the east was the blackened area of the blast zone, along with more warehouses. At the bottom of the screen was the Charles Helou Highway, and below that was downtown Beirut.

A cursor appeared, and Dafna drew a red circle around a building by the second roundabout on the left. "This is an older picture," she said. "The building here has been torn down and a new one has been built."

"Then why am I looking at this instead of the new one?" Nir demanded.

"Because you asked to see the port, not just a single warehouse. I went with Google Earth for the sake of expediency," Dafna said, air-quoting the end of her sentence. "Look it up if you don't understand the word."

Where was Nicole? She had a mediating calm that helped him get along even with the smart-mouthed girls. Without her, meetings tended to devolve into chaos.

He breathed deeply. "Dafna, would you kindly retrieve for me an updated picture showing the new building the Russians have erected in the port?"

"Of course, Mr. Tavor. All you had to do was ask."

About a minute later, a new image appeared on the screen. The trashed cement building was gone, replaced by a modern metal structure. Even from elevation, Nir was able to count 14 armed guards—two in the back, four on each side, and another four in the front.

"Lovely," grumbled Imri.

"We could try a candygram for Mongo," said Dima. But even he didn't laugh at his bad joke.

"That place is wrapped up tighter than a rabbi's purse," said Yaron.

There had to be a way in. "What do we know about it? This picture is during the day. Are there this many guards at night?" Nir asked.

Liora answered, "Because these guys are military, there's not much else for them to do other than to guard this building. At night, the sides are cut to two each, as is the front. So you're still looking at eight armed personnel with nothing to do except wait around to shoot people."

"Tell me about the building. How tall is it?"

Yariv flipped through some notes. "Ten meters. And, before you ask, the buildings to the west are also three stories. That's also true of the new construction across the street to the south."

"What about the security system? Can we hack into it?"

Again, Yariv read from his notes. "It's an autonomous system. Totally self-contained, so there's no getting into it. That's also true about all the electronics in the building. We can't touch the lights or the HVAC or anything."

"Beautiful," mumbled Nir.

"*Boker tov*, you guys are such idiots," said Lahav. All faces turned his way—the operators with scowls and Nir and the analysts with curiosity. "The answer is obvious. You can't get there on the ground, right? And you can't burrow in from underneath. So, go in from on top."

Gil dropped back into his chair. "Brilliant, analyst-boy. We'll just helicopter in. No one will hear that. Or, even better, we'll drop in with our magic camouflage parachutes and land perfectly on the roof of the building."

Lahav laughed. "You're so cute when you let your ignorance show."

Gil leaned toward the analyst, but Dima's large arm pushed him back. "Hear him out. We can pound him later."

"Dafna, can you go back to the Google Earth pic again?"

Dafna complied.

"Okay, now, check out the Russian building." This time Dafna circled the structure.

Nodding toward Yariv, Lahav continued. "Now, Curls here talked about the buildings to the west and to the south. All the same height. No good to anyone except a tightrope walker. But look farther south, across the parking lot. Check out the size of the cars next to those buildings compared to the Russian one, and tell me they're not taller."

Yariv looked closely. "He's right—probably four stories, possibly five."

Lahav was shaking his head. "No, they're not five stories. But you've got an extra three meters from that roof. You connect a line from that building to the Russian building, and you've got zip-line roof access."

"Dude, you're crazy," said Dima. "I'm no Tom Cruise, and three meters is not enough angle to zip anyone that far."

Lahav reached over and patted Dima on the arm. "Leave it to me, little man. I'll get you there."

CHAPTER 41

A hand rose from the hole. A whirring sound cut through the silence, then disappeared up toward the sky.

Two minutes later, Liora's voice sounded in Nir's coms. "All clear."

Nir slapped Dima's back. The Russian poked his head up and looked around. "Confirm clear."

The big man pulled himself up through the opening in the ground. Nir followed him, then laid flat as he waited for Gil, Imri, and Yaron to follow. Big deals were made about the tunnels Hezbollah and Hamas had dug into Israel. Much less was known about the very discreet underground passages that Israel had constructed going the other way.

The five men remained on the ground for three minutes, silently listening for voices or footsteps or snores. Once they were convinced they were alone, they stood and began moving forward. The tunnel had begun on the Israeli side just south of Metula, Israel, and terminated near the corner of an olive grove on the outskirts of Kfar Kila, Lebanon.

Nir carefully scanned for movement amongst the trees. These next four kilometers were when they would be at their most vulnerable. Farms and orchards were spread across the countryside. At any moment, a shepherd could bring his small flock of sheep around a corner or a property owner who had come out for a nighttime smoke could appear from between the trees. Slowly and carefully, the Kidon team wove their way through this semi-populated area so that they could reach the more sparsely populated hills that separated Kfar Kila to the east from Taybeh to the west. Higher ground didn't mean they were home free, but at least the likelihood of being spotted would greatly decrease.

Nir had initially argued for going in from the water. Doing so would have been quicker and far less physically taxing for his team. However, the higher-ups determined that the heightened tensions between Israel and Lebanon had led to the coastline being closely watched. So it was left to Nir's team to hoof it in, while Ehrlich's backup team waited out in the waters just in case.

Dima had taken point, while the rest followed in the same order they had exited the tunnel. Each man was similarly outfitted. Their base layer was all black, including the beanies they wore on their heads. Front and back plated body armor added extra weight to every stride they took, but the protection was worth the sweat. Each had a 9mm Jericho holstered on their hips and an IWI X95 strapped to their chests. In appropriate places on their vests and belts, they carried an assortment of loaded magazines, frag and flash-bang grenades, zip ties, a combat first aid kit, and various other necessities for killing some and keeping others alive. In addition, each had a fixed tactical blade strapped to a leg and several metal tubes to their backs, courtesy of Lahav's brainstorm.

Back at CARL, Lahav had said, "If all you need is more height, I can get you an extra fifteen meters, no problem. We've got strong, reinforced aluminum pipes that I could rig up so that you can carry them in pieces and assemble them on the roof. Easy peasy. That will give you enough angle to Ethan Hunt your way onto the rooftop."

Sure enough, three days later, Lahav had the sections ready. Initially, the team focused on assembling and disassembling what amounted to a tall pole. When the simplicity of that was proven, they each did target practice with a rope gun. Yaron was quickly named the shooter, but it was important that they all had the skill to accomplish the task in case they ran into trouble. Finally, the moment came for the first zip line down. As Nir climbed the narrow nubs that Lahav had designed to pop out after assembly, he remembered reading about how 60-plus Tom Cruise still did all his own stunts.

At least he gets paid millions to slide down these stupid lines. Hopefully, when I'm his age, the only stunt I'll be doing is dodging the Lego bricks my grandkids leave on the floor when I get up for another beer.

Forty zips down the line later, Nir felt a little more capable and a little less impressed with Tom Cruise. Lahav had examined the well-used pole and declared it to be good as new. They were ready to go.

Dima's hand went up and they all squatted. Nir clicked his coms twice, alerting Liora. Nir strained to hear anything beyond the normal night sounds of birds, dogs, and the wind rustling through the leaves of the olive trees. After a few moments, Liora said, "Clear from my view." Dima rose and began trekking forward again.

With all the starts and stops, it took nearly 30 minutes to clear the first one-and-a-half kilometers. But now that they were at the beginning of the incline, they were able to make up time. With Liora watching from above using infrared, it would be difficult for anyone to sneak up on them.

Twenty minutes later, they descended what passed for a peak in that area. Staying among the trees, they bridged the gap between Deir Mimas monastery and its namesake village. They reached a lookout point and dropped to the ground.

"I have one heat signature ahead at our designated meet point," Liora announced.

Nir clicked his acknowledgment. They slowly moved forward. As they did, a black minivan took shape. In two minutes, they were all in the vehicle with their driver, a short, bald Unit 504 man with a full beard and a fireplug physique.

CHAPTER 42

NEAR DEIR MIMAS, LEBANON—01:45 (1:45 AM) EEST

Warm and welcoming, the 504 man introduced himself as Stavro. While Nir didn't expect to hear the man's real name—that just wasn't Unit 504's way—the nom de guerre took him a little off guard. Stavro was the name of a famous Lebanese cartoonist who had laid blame for the war on all sides, including Israel. However, the middle of an operation in enemy territory was not the place to hold a political discussion.

It was nearing 04:00 when they approached the gates of a compound in the small village of Mechref, very near Rafik Hariri University. Still a good half-hour drive south of the Beirut port, this was about as far as they wanted to go until night fell once again.

A muscular man with a full head of black hair and a thick mustache pulled open the front gate, then closed it again once the van had gone through. Nir had already stepped out of the van and was stretching when the man reached him.

"It is good for you to be here," the man said. There was no clear expression on his face, but the tone of his voice and the slight squint of his eyes made it clear that he meant his words. "You are Tavor?"

Nir put out his hand and the man took it.

"Alif, who you lost last year, was a good friend of mine. He spoke quite highly of you," the man continued.

"Alif lived as a warrior, and he died as one. I think of him every day." As their hands separated, Nir asked, "What may I call you?"

"You may call me Farzat."

"Interesting. I hope your hands are in better shape." Syrian-born Ali Farzat was another political cartoonist who focused on events of the Middle East. In 2011, after hitting a little too close to home for Syrian president Bashar al-Assad's tastes, he was pulled from his car by masked gunmen while in Damascus. They then beat him and broke the bones in his hands as a warning for him to tame his pencil.

Winking, the pseudo-Farzat wiggled his fingers, then said, "Actually, all I need are these two fingers." He made a finger gun and pulled the trigger. "Now, introduce me to the rest of your team."

The rest were already out of the van. Nir gave their names one by one.

"You are all most welcome," Farzat said, his arm extended toward the house. "This is not my home. Let's just say that it belongs to all of us—the Israeli people. Please make yourselves comfortable. We will soon have a meal, then I will allow you to sleep before your operation tonight."

Nir heard a whirring sound and saw that Imri had just sent a fresh drone into the air. Moments later, another landed in his outstretched hand. Their small drone arsenal consisted of two mini-UAVs, with a pair of batteries for each. The three-hour batteries gave them a total run time of six hours, but that would get cut in half if they used the infrared function.

"Keep your eyes open," Imri said.

"You bet," came Liora's reply. The concern in her voice was evident.

They entered the house, and each man found a bed. As the food was cooked, the team went over their gear, checking loads, slides, batteries—anything that could get dirtied or fouled by their hike through the hills. The food was average, but there was plenty of it. When the time came, they hit their racks with stomachs full of lamb and pita.

Nir's sleep was restless. When he finally woke up, he checked his watch and saw that it was 11:37 a.m. He had been out for only two hours. Pulling out an encrypted phone, he texted:

how goes it there

Nicole's response was quick.

> *Okay. Ramsad came in earlier. Will be back*
> *for raid tonight. Lahav is driving everyone*
> *crazy telling them about the poles he designed*
> *for you guys and for Ehrlich's team.*

Nir smiled. He thumbed:

> *next time just tell him that even a trained*
> *monkey could put together a pole with*
> *climbing nubs. hes very proud of those*
> *climbing nubs. dinner at chichukai when i get*
> *back? a little white fish tamari to celebrate*

I'm in! What are we celebrating?

you

Nicole sent back a blushing emoji.

Liora's voice crashed through their little moment. "Three technicals are approaching your neighborhood. Two have guns mounted in the back."

Dafna broke in. "Three men in the bed of each. Assuming two to three in the cab. So, minimum of fifteen, maximum of eighteen."

Nir was up and running toward the front door. "It could be nothing. Are you sure they're coming our way?" His team ran up around him.

It was Nicole who answered. "I can see them. They're moving fast. They all look like they're ready for a fight. It's possible they're going somewhere else, but not probable."

"Farzat! Stavro!" Nir yelled. The two men burst through the door.

Nir pulled his Jericho and leveled it at Stavro. "Which one of you sold us out?"

Stavro's eyes were huge, but Farzat stepped in front of the gun. "What are you doing?"

Nir held the gun steady. "There are three pickups heading our way loaded with Hezbollah. How would they know we're here unless one of you said something?"

Farzat stepped forward so that Nir's pistol was pressed against his chest. "Listen, *ahabal*, we didn't tell anyone. Who knows how they found out? Maybe a neighbor saw you driving in. Maybe the woman in the next compound watched when an old man dressed in black took a leak on the orange tree out back?"

"Crap," said Yaron.

Farzat continued. "Listen, Tavor, we are on the same side, and we've got about three minutes to get underground before the guns on the back of those technicals light this place up."

The man was right. This was Unit 504. This was an elite squad. If he couldn't trust them, then who could he trust? He lowered his weapon and holstered it.

"Show me what you mean by underground," he said.

CHAPTER 43

CARL, switch out the drones," said Imri, reaching his hand out the front door.

"Swapping drones," replied Liora.

Yaron had snatched up Nir's gear, and Nir was strapping on his plate carrier when he saw the first drone shoot up into the sky. Moments later, the second landed on Imri's hand. He immediately popped open the back and swapped out a battery. He then stowed both the drone and the old battery into his tactical vest.

"Help us with this," called out Stavro. Nir turned and saw Dima and Gil racing toward the kitchen, where Stavro and Farzat had pushed aside the refrigerator. There were four handles imbedded in the cement floor. The two 504 men grabbed one set, lifting the heavy block up and to the side. Dima and Gil did the same with the other.

"Okay, everyone down. Now!" Farzat was waving Nir and Yaron over.

As Nir ran, he pulled out a small black case from his vest. Slapping Yaron on the back, he said, "Give me your backup coms."

When he reached the 504 guys, he passed the cases to them. "Coms," was all he said.

Both nodded as they hurried the men into the hole. Nir saw them opening the cases and placing the units into their ears as he took hold of the rebar ladder. He climbed three rungs down before he jumped the final couple meters to the ground. Dima, Imri, and Gil were waiting. Yaron followed Nir, trailed by Stavro and Farzat.

"How do we close the hole?" asked Nir.

"We don't. There's no time. Besides, it's Hezbollah. They'll shoot the house to tiny chunks before they breach the front door. They love to fire the big guns."

"The trucks have stopped out front," announced Nicole, who had apparently taken lead on coms. "You've got to get out back now."

"We're in a tunnel under the house," answered Nir.

"Gotta love me some 504." Sounded like Efraim was in the room listening in.

Nicole spoke up again. "Then you better follow the tunnel as far as it will go, because they're charging up their Brownings."

"I love a girl who knows her guns," said Farzat. Nir could barely see him grinning in the faint light. "Okay, follow me."

They ran, hunched over, under the ground. Nir focused on the back of Imri in front of him as the light faded to darkness. Through the hole in the kitchen, they heard a voice from outside the house call in Arabic, "Come out, Israelis! We know you are there! You have ten seconds!"

Suddenly, Imri stopped. Nir ran into his back, and Yaron plowed into Nir.

"Why'd we stop?" Nir called out in the black.

"The tunnel ended," answered Imri.

Nir was dumbfounded. "That's it? This is as far as we can go?"

"What can I say? We're not Gazan rats who spend their whole lives shoveling underground. We dug this just so we could get out of the house in case of an emergency. An emergency kind of like this," Farzat answered.

In the background, they could faintly hear the countdown reaching its end. The Brownings opened up. Even underground, the blast of the rounds and the power of the strikes rattled the brain.

"We'll wait here until they either get bored or run out of ammunition," Farzat yelled at Nir over the din.

"Where are we?"

"We are about ten meters beyond the back wall."

Nir tried to picture it. From what he remembered, it didn't look good.

"Ten meters? That's it?"

"It was a work in progress."

Nir pulled a small flashlight from his vest and turned it on. Imbedded into the dirt ahead of them was a rebar ladder. "If this tunnel is a work in progress, then why is this here?"

Farzat shrugged. "Our progress ended about three years ago."

The shooting began to let up, but then started up again.

Just changing belts, thought Nir. Farzat had turned to Gil, so Nir shook his arm to get his attention.

"When they stop shooting, they're going to start exploring. And when they start exploring, they're going to find this tunnel. How do we get out of here without being seen? I'm guessing by now the house is crumbling and the compound's rear wall is in ruins."

"Don't worry, *achi*. Escape will be easy. We just need to kill them all, then take their trucks."

Before Nir had a chance to question the man's sanity, Farzat held up a finger.

"Stavro, let's introduce them to our little friends."

Turning, Nir saw the other 504 man slide open a wide metal door that covered the top half of the tunnel wall. He had no idea it was there because he had already gone past it by the time he had turned on his light. From within the built-in cabinet Stavro pulled out an M16 rifle with an M203 grenade launcher attached to the underside of its barrel.

"Pass it up," the 504 man said, handing it to Yaron. The gun made its way into Farzat's hands. It was followed up by a bag that Nir could see held 40mm grenades, and finally, a pouch that felt heavy enough to contain nine or ten full 5.56x45mm 20-round magazines.

"They've paused the Brownings. Now they're sending an eight-man scout team toward the house," said Nicole.

"Remember, everyone, our goal is to blow them up without blowing up their trucks," said Stavro with a wide smile.

Okay, I knew it before, and this has only confirmed my suspicions. These 504 dudes are kinda nuts.

"Sweetheart, let us know when they're in the house," Farzat said. Nir knew that his words had likely grated on Nicole, but all credit to her—she let it go. The 504 man continued, "Now, before you think we're total idiots, there is a berm just outside this hole. It should give us enough cover to roll out and set up. Once we're ready, we'll fire the first grenades. Then you guys let them have it. But, remember, like Stavro said, we're trying to keep at least one truck drivable!"

"They're stacked in formation and about to enter the front door," said Nicole.

Farzat pushed hard on the ceiling above him. A thin beam of sunlight broke through the darkness of the tunnel. He pushed again, then slid the covering to the side.

"Okay, going out," he said, pulling himself up, then crawling to his right.

By the time Nir pulled himself into the light, he saw that the 504 men really had chosen their exit location well. The berm gave them good cover against both sight line and any rounds sent their way.

Suddenly, there was shouting from the house.

"Apparently, they spotted the tunnel," said Farzat. He fired off his grenade—*foomp*. Nir heard a second *foomp* from the other end of their line. Moments later, the projectiles exploded in the house.

It was great to go after the house, but for Nir it was the guys in the back of the trucks who were of the greatest concern. They were the ones who had the better sight lines and the bigger guns. "Gil, Imri, technical gunner right. Yaron, Dima, technical gunner left." Four shots rang out, and the men manning the large machine guns dropped to the ground. "Fire at will," Nir said.

Another two grenades dropped in the house. Screams carried across the open space.

"CARL, sitrep," he said.

"I can still see movement in the house where the ceiling has collapsed, but don't know how many. Everyone on the trucks is down, but I can't see what's happening behind them," Nicole answered.

Nir heard a bullet whistle past his head, and then another. He ducked down.

"Farzat, Stavro, keep pumping the grenades into the house. Everyone else, focus on the ones around the trucks. We've got to shut down their fire."

"*Root*," came the answers. Rising up just far enough to take aim, Nir sighted a gunner firing over the hood of one of the trucks. Nir pulled his trigger and saw the windshield next to the guy spiderweb. The man dropped down.

Patience...patience...wait the guy out.

The muzzle of the man's rifle peeked over the hood, followed by his head. Once again, Nir pulled the trigger. This time he didn't miss. Scanning the scene, he saw that the targets by the truck now appeared to be minimal. It was time to deal with the house.

CHAPTER 44

ima, Gil, on me. Everyone else, cover." Nir popped up and over the berm, his X95 readied and his eyes forward. Someone passed in front of a window to his right, but Dima put the man down before Nir could sight him in.

The rear compound wall had been shredded enough for them to simply step over it. Reaching the house, they flattened themselves against the back wall. There were two windows facing out, one on each side of them, and a back door. Nir pointed Dima to one and Gil to the other, then counted down with his fingers.

3…2…1

The two men moved, while Nir pushed down on the back door handle. There was no movement. Taking one step back, he kicked his right leg forward and connected just under the handle. The door swung open more easily than Nir had anticipated, throwing him off balance as he stumbled into the kitchen. A Hezbollah soldier stood beyond the doorway taking aim, but Dima leaned through a broken window and sent two rounds into the man's chest. He dropped.

Something metallic bounced into the room.

"Grenade!" Nir yelled. Still off balance, he fell across the kitchen, snatching hold of a table to use as a shield. The grenade went off, and the pressed-wood table exploded into tiny pieces. Splinters imbedded into his face and ricocheted off his body armor. Thankfully, the table had taken much of the force of the grenade, but still the air was driven from his lungs, and his head felt like someone had pinged an aluminum bat off his temple.

Stay in the game. Stay in the game.

Looking up, he spotted Dima and Gil, who were peeking through the back door into the kitchen. Both shook their heads. They didn't know where the grenade had come from either. Nir signaled for the two men to go opposite directions and clear the outside of the house.

"Lead, we're coming forward," said Yaron from back at the berm.

"Negative! Hold." He had to find where this other guy was. Then he heard the faintest sound. It was metallic. Like that of a pin being pulled from a grenade. And it came from down in the tunnel.

Leaping to his feet, Nir took three steps to the hole in the floor and opened fire. In the muzzle flashes, he saw what an up-close rifle round could do to a man's face. He immediately knew that this Lebanese fighter would join the long line of others who would sometimes visit him in his dreams.

A loud explosion from the terrorist's grenade sounded from below the ground. Nir stumbled backward as rocks and dirt flew up through the hole in the ground.

"Farzat, drop back into the tunnel and send a couple of those grenades rolling this way. I just took out someone down the hole and I don't know if he was alone."

"*Root*," said the 504 man.

Nir crossed to the other side of the kitchen, but kept his rifle trained on the hole. Soon there was a boom, and a dust cloud blew up out of the hole. That was followed by another. This time a voice cried out in Arabic, "I surrender! I surrender!"

First one hand rose above the floor, then a head and chest. It was a young Lebanese man no more than 20. Once he had pulled himself all the way out, he went to his knees and wrapped both hands behind his head. "I'm sorry! Please don't kill me! My mother depends upon me!"

The young man was shaking as he stared down at the floor. "Please, sir, I am so sorry! Spare my life! I left all my weapons in the tunnel. Come check me. I promise!"

"Who are you?" Nir demanded. He had been ready to advance on the man and pull him to the ground. But when the guy had said those last words, "Come check me," he almost seemed too eager.

"Please sir, do not hurt me. See, I have no weapons!"

Nir heard Gil and Dima both confirm the outside of the house was clear. "Okay, clear the rest of the inside." Turning back to the young man, he said, "I asked you your name."

"I am Kabbani. Wesalaam Kabbani. They came and took me when I was a teen. I didn't want to join them. They forced me. They threatened my mother." He was crying now.

"Open your shirt," Nir commanded in Arabic. The young man had said he left his weapons in the tunnel. Before Nir approached him, he was going to make sure.

Confused, the man asked, "Please, what do you want?"

"I want you to keep one hand above your head and use the other to open your shirt."

Kabbani seemed even more frightened now. "Please, sir, just let me go. My mother needs me. Please, come check me. No weapons."

Nir lifted his rifle and pointed it at the Hezbollah terrorist. "Open your shirt! Now!"

The man brought his hand down hard toward his chest, giving him just enough time to yell "Allahu akb—" before he blew up.

When the man started moving his hand, Nir dove toward the living room. The concussive wave caught him before he hit the ground and kept him airborne across the entire room. Because the front wall was so torn up by bullets, he burst through it and landed outside on the cement of the drive. The hard surface rejected his head's attempt to merge with it, and everything went black.

Nir may have passed out or maybe he didn't. He was never too sure even much later, after the ringing in his ears had stopped and he was able to piece together multiple coherent thoughts. For now, the first words that went through his mind were, *Voices. Who's talking? What's happening?*

As the fog began to clear, he saw Dima next to him, laid out on the ground and holding his head. The Russian had been clearing the room on the other side of the kitchen wall and, like Nir, had been tossed out onto the drive. Gil was kneeling over Nir, checking him for injuries.

"Nir, are you okay? Say something!"

"Well, that sucked," Nir tried to say, but he wasn't sure if he had actually formed real words.

To his left, Dima swore in some foreign tongue, then spat blood out of his mouth.

The rest of the team came running up. Along the way, Imri called out, "House is cleared. All are down."

Farzat dropped to his knees next to Nir. "You okay?"

"Never been better," Nir said before breaking into a coughing fit. This time, he was pretty sure his words made sense.

"That's good, *achi*, because Stavro and I have spent five years remodeling this house. Kidon comes by and destroys it in fifteen minutes. You people owe me some work."

Nir stared at him, trying to process the man's words. Then the 504 man began to laugh and slapped him on the shoulder, which Nir immediately discovered must have been the one he had landed on.

"Nir, coms. Listen to your coms," said Gil.

Reaching to his ear, he realized that he had lost his coms in the explosion. Farzat quickly pulled his out and handed it to Nir. He caught Nicole as she was saying, "...at least six vehicles. This isn't over yet. You've got to get out of there."

"Copy," he groaned.

"Hey, look here!" It was Stavro. He was out in the street standing next to one of the trucks. Next to him was Imri, who had his rifle trained on the neighbors, who had started exiting their homes now that the shooting was over. The 504 man continued, "The other two will never move again without donkeys towing them. But this one still seems good." Reaching in, he turned the key. It started up.

Unfortunately, it was the one without a machine gun.

"Okay, let's get moving," Nir croaked out as Gil helped him to his feet.

CHAPTER 45

12:20 (12:20 PM) EEST

They waited until Dima and Gil came back with the five packs of aluminum poles the team had carried into Lebanon. Farzat followed with three rifles and four heavy bags hanging from his shoulders. Nir had been recovering in the back of the truck, but he quickly jumped out and met the 504 man in the courtyard. He lifted three of the bags from the man, asking, "Is there anything in these that will blow me up?"

"Blow you up? No," Farzat answered as they began moving toward the truck again. "Others? We'll see."

"You've got to move now. We don't know how far out the enemy is," Nicole warned.

Stavro reached his hand outside the truck and slammed on the door several times. "Is everyone in?" he called out in Arabic.

"Go," answered Nir.

Stavro punched the accelerator and the engine revved, but they didn't move.

"Come on! Drive!" Yaron was in the cab sitting between the 504 man and Imri. He sounded desperate to take the wheel.

"I'm trying!" The gears ground as the man worked them back and forth. When he hit the accelerator again, the truck began to inch ahead. Slowly, the vehicle built up speed until they were nearly up to traffic level.

"Make a left! Left back into the hills," Nicole called. Stavro obeyed.

"Either of you still have an extra coms unit?" Nir asked Dima and Gil. The Russian pulled out a black case. "Give it to Farzat."

The gunfire had pulled a lot of people from their homes. Nir held his rifle at the ready, but it didn't seem as though anyone ahead was armed.

Nicole came back on. "Send up the second UAV so that I can follow you guys while Liora watches the house."

The truck slowed, then Imri put his hand out of the passenger window. A drone whizzed up into the air.

"Okay, I've got you guys. Keep going forward, up into the hills."

After about three minutes, Liora picked up the narration. "I've spotted the convoy. Six vehicles, three heavy. The troop trucks are open. All three are deuce-and-a-halves. Not fully packed. I'm counting six or seven a side, so say about 40 total. The other three are...what are those? Ivecos?"

Efraim answered, "Affirmative. Iveco LMVs. Each has a heavy gun on top. Can't tell yet what the caliber is, but it's ugly."

"Turn left! Left!" Nicole yelled. The truck swerved, and the four men in the back slammed against the side of the bed. "Sorry about that. Keep going straight. There are hills ahead."

"The lady is going to hurt us," said Farzat, rubbing the side of his head. "This road will take us toward Dmit. It is a good choice."

A few minutes later, Liora reported. "They've arrived at the house. Two trucks are unloading. I'm betting it won't be long before they find the tunnel...wait for it...there it is. Everyone is running back toward the truck. Now, they're starting to roll."

"Got it," said Nir. "Are they coming our way?" Nir figured that at least one of the people watching from their house had to have Hezbollah ties, although he hoped they'd get lucky and and everyone would keep their mouths shut.

There was a pause. "Turning left," said Liora. A couple minutes later, she added, "They're turning up the Dmit road."

Yaron spoke up. "Not good. We can't get more than sixty kilometers per hour out of this. A squadron on a pack of mules could catch us."

Nir asked, "CARL, how much of a lead do we have on them?"

"If they know where you are, I'd say ten minutes max. If they have to look for you, maybe a little more," answered Liora.

"Hey Efraim, if there's any air cover in the vicinity, it would be nice to get a visit," said Nir.

"I'll see what I can do," answered Efraim.

They had just executed a switchback, their second. As their angle increased, their speed did the opposite. He looked ahead over the roof of the truck at the smattering of small homes just ahead. When he did, he saw a pile of trash on the side of the road.

It seemed out of place. Random.

"Swerve right! Swerve right!" he cried.

Stavro pulled hard on the wheel. Still, when the IED went off, it was enough to lift the back of the truck and toss the four men through the air and onto the hard dirt below.

CHAPTER 46

OUTSIDE DMIT, LEBANON—12:35 (12:35 PM) EEST

When Nir came to, he saw Imri and Yaron working on Dima. He tried to speak, but instead threw up dirt and bile.

"Is he okay?" Nir managed to spit out.

Dima answered. "I'm fine. Just a couple metal splinters to my shoulder. Getting blown up once in a day sucks. Twice—*achi*, I need to find a new profession."

Nicole's harsh voice stopped the joking. "It's great everyone is okay and all, but you still have those vehicles coming your way. You need to get moving! Now!"

"Which way? We don't even know where we are," Nir shot back.

There was silence on the other end.

"Listen, we need to know now," he shouted.

Nicole sounded flustered. "I know! I know! Okay, go across the road and between the houses. Start up the hills. Your only hope now is high ground."

"*Root*! We're on it."

As they crossed the street, Nir saw two men with rifles sprawled out and obviously dead. Apparently, he had missed some action while he had been out. He looked over at Gil.

"They came from behind the shop," he said, using his head to indicate left. "Yaron put them down."

241

Nir nodded. The ringing in his ears was almost deafening, and he felt like someone had put his head in a heavy-duty vice. When he stumbled, he felt Gil's arm slip under his own. They moved unsteadily between the houses and out into open ground. There was yelling behind them, but it took just one quick high burst from Dima's X95 to send the people scurrying back into their homes.

"They're less than four minutes out," said Liora. "You can't outrun them, even off-road."

"Hang on! Hang on!" Nicole shouted. "Okay, there's a ridge about twenty kilometers up. It's not much, but it gives you high ground."

"*Root*," Nir replied. It wasn't that high, but he was thankful when he saw the perch. At least it would allow him to stretch out as he aimed. Being caught up in three blasts within 15 minutes of each other was a sure way to get a brain bleed. He prayed that wasn't what was happening to him.

When he and Gil reached the granite outcrop, he saw how little it truly was. They would have room to spread out at first, but a few minutes of fire from the oversized machine guns on the back of the LMVs would soon turn the granite to dust.

Farzat came and dropped next to him. "Remember the bags I brought with me?"

"Where are they?" Nir asked, looking behind the man.

A smile spread across the 504 man's face. "I left them down there. Turnabout is fair play, right? Mine just happen to be a lot bigger than theirs were."

The man turned away and used his scope to search for the enemy.

"One minute until the trucks are on you," said Liora.

"We see them," Nir said, removing the need for her to count down.

"Come to *abba*," whispered Farzat.

Nir could hear the vehicles racing up the winding road. The three LMVs were in the front, followed by the M35 deuce-and-a-halves loaded with Hezbollah soldiers.

"A little farther," said Farzat.

A blast echoed up the hill. The lead LMV flew up in the air. A second tactical vehicle slammed on its brakes, but not in time. The first

LMV landed on its hood with a crunch, instantly flattening its tires. The other vehicles screeched to a halt, which was exactly what Farzat was counting on. A second explosion tore open the side of the hill. Nir felt his short hair blow back from the concussive wave. There was a rumble, then a load roar as rocks broke free and showered the transport trucks.

Nir seized the opportunity. "Open fire!"

The guns on the ridge began sending bullets down at the confused Hezbollah terrorists. They tried to take cover but weren't sure from which direction the fire was coming. Nir's aim was not as good as it usually was. Still, he took down his share.

Then the tide turned. They had wiped out a heavy gun and maybe a third of the fighting force. That still left Nir and his men with a three-to-one disadvantage, minimum. The Brownings on top of the LMVs began firing their .50 BMG rounds up at the line of men. All seven rolled back to avoid the deadly shower of granite that began spewing into the air.

Dima broke left, while Yaron went right. Both were trying to get a good angle at the men behind the big guns. Unfortunately, the Hezbollah fighters were behind thick metal plates. There was no way to reach them.

"We're down to our last four grenades," said Farzat.

"Send them," Nir said, missing a shot as a man took cover behind a boulder.

Then, over the din, Nir's ears picked up a sound. It was growing louder by the second.

"Incoming," he called. Dropping to his face, he covered his head with his hands and curled into a ball.

Please be accurate! Please be accurate!

Four massive explosions sent dust, rock, and wood raining down on them. The blasts were soon followed by the sound of two very-low-flying F-35s. Nir looked up in time to see their engines burning hot as they angled back up into the skies. This was the fourth time he had been far too close to an explosion in the last hour. He prayed it would be his last.

Pulling himself to the edge of the ridgeline, he looked down. The road where the trucks had been was covered with twisted metal, body parts, and piles of rock.

"Imri, Dima, Gil, clear the site," he said.

"*Root*," the three men said as they began to sidestep their way down the steep hill. He would have gone with them, but he knew that his reaction time was practically nil.

"Lead, are you good?" It was Efraim.

Nir scanned the remaining team, who were all looking at him. Not a single man was free of blood and dirt, but they all held their thumbs up. "We're good. Thanks for the assist."

"No problem. You can buy me a round when you get back."

Nir laughed, feeling pain all over his body as he did so. "You got it. Speaking of…we need some alternate transportation to get up to the Beirut port. Got any ideas?"

Efraim turned serious. "Beirut? *Achi*, you guys aren't going to Beirut. Not after this."

Instantly, Nir's relief turned to anger. He was not going to allow his team to be cut out of the mission just because some Hezbollah goons stumbled onto them. "Nicole, switch Efraim and me to a separate line."

"Nir, he's…"

"Switch us."

"*Root*," she said curtly. As Nir waited, his anger continued to grow. This was his team's idea. They had prepared for this. This was his operation.

After a couple clicks, Nicole added, "You're clear."

"Efraim, we trained for this. We're ready to go."

"Brother, you just got chased halfway across central Lebanon. You've been blown up twice, at least by my calculation. You're being called off."

"On who's authority?"

"The *ramsad*'s. Face it, you were somehow compromised. Either someone saw you going in, or somebody from our office tipped off Hezbollah. I don't know. There will be some big investigation into it, I'm sure. All I know is that you guys are spent, done, out."

Nir looked up and saw all eyes on him. He walked away toward the woods. "So, are they calling the whole thing off?"

When Efraim paused, Nir knew exactly what he was going to say even before he said it.

"They're sending in Ehrlich, aren't they? They're sending him in by the water route—the route I said from the beginning we should have taken."

"Yes, it's by the water route, but no, it's not the better route. They have a much higher chance of being caught. Ehrlich and his team are going in at 22:00. That's nine hours from now. You'll probably be getting out of the tunnel at Metula by then."

Nir stood steaming. "You know he's going to screw it up somehow."

"Listen, Tavor, Ehrlich's a good agent and a good leader. He'll get it done. Now quit acting like a spoiled brat who's just had his lollipop stolen from him. This wasn't your day. It happens. Get over it and get out of there."

Nir switched back to the main line without responding. He stood, breathing in the air. It smelled like cedar and dust.

Efraim's right. This just wasn't our day. It happens. Don't pass your mood on to the guys. You've still got work to do to get back across the border.

He turned back to the men, who were all in the process of reloading and consolidating their unspent rounds. "Okay, guys, we've got to find our way back to the tunnel that brought us in here. They've passed the mission on to Ehrlich's team."

A groan sounded from one of his men. "Stow it," Nir commanded. "Ehrlich's a good agent and a good leader. He'll get it done." But even as he repeated the words Efraim had said to him, he didn't fully believe them. This whole operation didn't feel right, and he didn't trust anyone but himself to see it through. It was arrogant and obnoxious and likely totally wrong, but it was what his heart was telling him. Sadly, there was nothing he could do about it now.

Turning to Farzat, he asked, "You guys coming with us? I owe you a Gold Star."

Farzat reached out his hand, which Nir took. "I think we'll stay. We've got a little remodeling we need to do."

Nir grinned sheepishly. "Yeah, sorry about that."

Each man said his goodbyes, and the two Unit 504 men walked north, higher up into the hills. Nir and his team had a long journey south ahead of them, which would probably involve stealing at least one car. But would hopefully not include any gunplay.

"CARL, we're heading out. We'll hit you up when we need you."

"*Root*," acknowledged Nicole.

They all geared up and began walking.

"Ehrlich's going to totally botch it up," said Yaron, shaking his head.

This time, Nir let it go.

CHAPTER 47

CARL, MOSSAD HEADQUARTERS, TEL AVIV, ISRAEL— APRIL 4, 2024—01:15 (1:15 AM) IDT

Ehrlich's team approached the back of the building. Behind them was a long off-ramp from the Charles Helou Highway that exited up by the Statue of the Immigrant and skirted along south of the port area until it cut left under the major thoroughfare. Just before that bend in the road, Ehrlich's team huddled. One of the men raised a suppressed rifle and shot out the four lights that illuminated a stairway.

Now that it was dark, Nicole had a hard time spotting the men as they ascended the stairs. Because any action the team took would be out in the open, there was no need to use the infrared mode on the drone. Still, if Nicole had been controlling the UAV, she would have popped it into IR every few minutes, just to make sure no one was sneaking up through any back alleys or secret passages surrounding the building. Maybe she was a little paranoid, but you can never be too careful.

But Nicole wasn't controlling the UAV, nor was anyone in CARL. They were just along for the ride, watching a video-only feed as Ehrlich's analysts and operators carried out the plan that her team had created and perfected. She knew that it was aggravating to Nir to have lost this operation. But she wasn't disappointed. Too many Russians had crossed her path in the last year. She was happy to keep herself and those she cared about away from any of Putin's minions for a while.

She thumbed in a text:

They're on the roof.

Dots appeared on her screen, then resolved with:

time to see if lahavs contraption works

Nir was in a van with his team on his way back to CARL. She guessed he was still about an hour and a half out. The journey to the tunnel had taken longer than they had planned. The car they had stolen in Dmit had broken down after only 20 minutes. A two-hour hike later, they had come across a small parking lot of cars at some kind of cedar biosphere or something. Nir had been winded enough that Nicole couldn't fully understand his words. From the side talk between the team members, she picked up that he likely had a concussion and that his words weren't always making sense. Yaron had picked up the de facto lead of the operation.

Once they had the second car, they drove a couple hours south until they saw a roadblock. They abandoned the car and went on foot for another few hours. It was well past dark when they had arrived near the tunnel entrance, only to find that a shepherd had decided to let his goats bed down there for the night. After waiting for an hour, they became impatient. They tried quietly shooing the goats. They threw small rocks at them. It was only when Gil called out some surprisingly accurate coyote yips that the shepherd woke up and decided that this might not be the safest place for his flock. Once he was gone, the team passed through. On the Israeli side of the tunnel, they found a van waiting for them to bring them back to the Mossad headquarters.

Back in Beirut, Ehrlich's shooters were crawling to the front of the roof. During planning, the decision had been made to not kill the guards, if at all possible. Israelis killing Russians was a surefire way to incite an international incident, even if those guards were protecting weapons that would eventually be used to kill Israelis. The Mossad had been experimenting with a new kind of projectile that contained a very potent chemical agent and three dozen micro-darts. The theory was that the micro-darts would burst when they struck the target. They would puncture a person's skin, allowing the chemical to flow in subdermally. They worked on animals and the very few humans who had volunteered to take part in the testing. But they had never been used at this distance.

The Kidon men took their positions and aimed their weapons. Moments later, the guards at the back of the Russian building quickly lifted their hands, one to his neck and the other to his left cheek. They swayed for a moment, then they went down.

Rear guards are down.

Nir tagged the text with a thumbs-up emoji.

As those operators were taking out the guards, the rest of the team had been constructing the pole that Lahav had created, duplicate to the one Nir's team had carried in. Once the last piece was locked into place, it was lifted, pointing up into the sky. Members of the team began to run to opposing ends of the roof, each dragging a bundle made up of ten thin, reinforced wires. When they reached the edges of the roof, they set the hooks, one after another.

Back at the pole, the wires were attached to four spools with hand cranks. As a unit, they began turning the handles while one man held a level against the pole. Sometimes they'd have to turn one faster, other times, another. But once they were done, they had a solid, vertical post that wasn't going anywhere.

Now came the big test. One of Ehrlich's men went to the front of the roof. He took aim with a rifle chambered with a spike attached to a long line wire. He shot, and the spike imbedded itself in the target building's roof with an audible thud. The guards on the ground jumped and looked around. But when they saw nothing out of the ordinary, they went back to their stations.

Pole is set. E is climbing first.

does it look strong

> *Lahav did a good job. It doesn't*
> *look like it's going anywhere.*

Again, Nir dropped a thumbs-up on Nicole's most recent text.

Nicole watched as Ehrlich threaded the wire into the top of the pole. After tugging on it a few times, he hooked his vest to the lead. Then, with a thumbs-up to his team, he jumped. Over at the conference table, Lahav chanted, "Go! Go! Go!" The man sped from one roof, over another, and onto the Russian warehouse. Once there, he quickly unhooked himself, then gave the thumbs-up for the next guy to go.

Lahav let out a cheer and Liora and Dafna mobbed him, celebrating his victory. The only one who didn't join was Yariv, who called out "*L'chaim,*" but remained in his chair.

> *E is across safely. Rest of team are going.*

did he look cool doing it

> *Yeah, kinda*

Sigh

> *Maybe we can go to Costa Rica and you can*
> *do the zip lines there. You can pretend you're*
> *carrying a gun. It'll almost be the same.*

youre not helping

> *Wait... Lahav says you owe him a*
> *Kyojuro Rengoku figma. ????*

some weird anime thing. said if got this
to work i had to buy him one. dont even
know what it is. mind looking it up
and ordering it—ill pay you back

Nicole smiled and jotted herself a note. She dropped a thumbs-up on his last emoji and focused again on the screen.

Once the fifth team member crossed to the roof, the group moved to an access door. Not surprisingly, it appeared to be locked. They stood there watching one man work for about 30 seconds before the door popped open and they filed in, rifles in position.

The view on Nicole's screen switched to body cam. The feed said "Ehrlich" on the bottom, so she supposed it was his. He had one man in front of him, a guy named Andy or Anvi—she couldn't remember which. They went down the stairs. At the bottom, they peeked around the corner and saw that all was clear. Ehrlich turned and signaled for the rest to follow.

CHAPTER 48

Very quickly, Ehrlich's team was at another door. This one was unlocked, and it opened into an office. Nicole knew this was the office two flights up that gave a view of the warehouse floor. Ehrlich moved to the window and looked out. The floor was covered with boxes stacked five to seven meters high. Many of them certainly looked like what she thought boxes of guns would look like, although most of her experience with boxes of guns was from the movies.

She went back to her text thread with Nir.

> *There are a lot of boxes down there. Various sizes. A lot look like rifle boxes.*

> *is there anything that talks about humanitarian aid*

> *It all appears to be Cyrillic.*

Ehrlich was in the lead now, moving to the office door. Cracking it open, he stopped to listen. After a few moments, he moved forward and began descending the stairs.

> *whats happening*

*E is moving down the stairs with
team behind. No resistance so far.*

why not

                                        ???

*i expected there would be at least some guards
inside. youve got hundreds of thousands of
dollars of weapons inside and only place
guards outside? its as dumb as those Iranians
and their vaults that we cleared out.*

                        What are you saying?

*it just feels too easy. i dont know. wish
i could see what was happening*

Ehrlich was on the floor now. Three of his team took watch-over positions, while he and the maybe-Andy guy went to a box. They each pulled out crowbars they had sheathed to their legs and pried the lid on the box. Inside were what she had learned from Nir on a weapons crash course were AK-74Ms, the standard-issue rifle for the Russian army. Ehrlich lifted it out and held it at a distance so that his bodycam could get the full picture.

                *E just opened a box of AK-74s.
                They're moving to the next box.*

where is this box located

                        It's in the front corner. ???

*he needs to dig back. pull some out and
get to some of the boxes farther back in
the stack. the front is too easy. i wasnt
even going to mess with them.*

What are you saying?

*i dont know. if ivan is pulling a ruse
on us hes going to put guns easy access
and hidden stuff farther back*

What hidden stuff?

*humanitarian aid. its probably nothing. i
just want a look in boxes farther back*

Ehrlich checked another two boxes. One had more AKs and the second was filled with ammunition. Suddenly, Ehrlich stopped. He began directing his men toward the three entrance doors.

"Someone tell me what's happening," Nicole called out. Dafna and Liora were watching, but they were also getting updates from a friend on Ehrlich's analyst team.

"Vehicles are coming up Mar Mikhael with their lights on," answered Liora. "The team is looking to bug out."

*Police approaching.
E's team looking to get away.*

hes got to get deeper. not enough evidence

It's all they're going to get.

"They're looking to exit the front door. If they can make it past the grain silos, there'll be watercraft waiting for them," said Liora.

Nicole pulled up Google Earth and checked the map. That was quite the run. It all depended on how far back the police were.

Ehrlich pulled open the front door. Immediately, Nicole's screen switched back to drone view. Two of Ehrlich's men stepped through and took out the guards. Unfortunately, it didn't look like a less-lethal technique.

Putin's going to want answers for that one.

As they sprinted past a roundabout, the guards on the sides of the building came around the corners. They began firing. One of Ehrlich's men went down. Another man wrapped his arm under him and hauled him up. Together they limped ahead. Two more of the team turned and knelt. They began to fire with much better accuracy, and three of the guards went down.

whats happening

Nicole ignored the text. She needed to watch the action so she could report to Nir accurately. The police vehicles were just arriving on scene, and they cut to the right, plowing through the debris separating them from their quarry.

The five men were now by the grain silos. Three of them turned and fired at the police, causing the cruisers to slam on their brakes. The officers opened their doors, ducked behind them, and returned fire. Thankfully for Ehrlich's men, the cops were using pistols only, while the team was reaching rifle distance.

Just past the silos was a small inlet on the right. A rigid-hull inflatable boat was waiting there with a pilot and two gunners. The men on board began shooting, purposely aiming over the officers' heads. The last thing the IDF wanted was a Lebanese police massacre on their hands.

Ehrlich's men reached the boat and dove in. Ehrlich was the last on the rocks, pushing the boat away before joining his team. The watercraft floated backward until the pilot had enough room. Then he gunned it, spun the boat around, and headed out to sea.

E and his team are safe on the water.
Close call.

whats the pm going to do. did
they get enough evidence

Nicole put down her phone. She didn't know how to answer that question.

CHAPTER 49

Nir reached to the center of the table, grabbed a handful of fries, and dumped them on his plate. Sure, the coleslaw that came with his Schnitzelwich from Café Nona was good, but it was far from enough. He had just fled across Lebanon and escaped through a tunnel. No one could blame him for having an appetite.

There weren't many 24-hour cafes in Tel Aviv. But there didn't need to be, because no matter how many the CARL team stumbled across, they would always find their way back to Café Nona. The ops guys had texted their orders to Liora before they got to Tel Aviv, and she had called them in. When they arrived at the restaurant, three large bags were waiting for them. Now that they were all back at CARL, the whole gang surrounded the table, eating a meal that would be better suited for 7:00 at night instead of 4:00 in the morning.

Efraim had joined them and was making good work on his roast beef sandwich. Nir said to him, "Now, I know we're taking out that warehouse. Otherwise, we wouldn't be here watching on our big screen. Can you tell me how we got to this point? Because I don't know if I'm comfortable with it."

The assistant deputy director swallowed, then put down his sandwich. "I don't think I'm totally comfortable with it either, and I know the *ramsad* isn't happy about it."

"Then—"

Efraim held up his finger, stopping his friend. "But I don't know that we're in the wrong doing it either. My concern is just that I'd like to have more evidence."

"*Sababa*," said Nir as he dipped a fry and put it in his mouth. "I think it probably is a bunch of weapons and explosives in that warehouse. But I haven't seen enough that I'd risk a confrontation with Russia by raining missiles down on it."

"That's what the *ramsad* said."

"He's a smart man," Nir responded, waving around a few fries.

"I'll tell him you said so."

"So, then, why are we sending in the jets?" asked Nicole, unenthusiastically picking around her quinoa and feta salad.

"Because Defense Minister Hurvitz can be a very persuasive man. His fear of moving too slowly beat out the *ramsad*'s fear of moving too quickly. Better to be proactive than reactive."

Nicole lifted some sunflower sprouts and tomato with her fork, then put it back down with a grimace. "Yeah, this looked better in the picture. Anyway, all you're saying is that if someone is coming to kill you, get up and kill them first. Isn't that the way Israel has always operated?"

Efraim grinned around his mouthful of food. "I've told you before, you've got some Jewish blood in you. You're exactly right. It's better to hit first than to try to swing after someone just dropped you to the ground. The problem is that this is Russia. We're not talking about a militia or a third-rate military dictator. We're talking the most war-loving leader of our time, who has already invaded one country because doing so fits with his One Russia ideology."

Nir was nodding. "Yeah, if you hit Russia, they will hit back. They're as dangerous as we are when it comes to proportionality. Send a drone our way, and we'll blow up your drone factory. Shoot at some of our soldiers at a bus stop, and we'll tear down ten of your buildings. Send three thousand of your psycho warriors over the border, and we'll turn your entire land into rubble. And you know what? I'm glad we did it."

"Very good, Nir. But be quiet for a little bit while I talk to Nicole, because your concussion is showing." Turning to Nicole, Efraim continued, "The *ramsad* tried to convince the PM that waiting a bit to gather more evidence would be beneficial. Or at least giving a warning to Russia that we know what's going on."

"Makes sense."

"It does. So, we immediately contacted the Russian embassy, and they were thrilled at being woken up at two in the morning. We told them that we paid a visit to their warehouse, and we saw that they are breaking agreements by stockpiling weapons under the guise of humanitarian aid. They said, 'No, we're not.' We said, 'Yes, you are.' They said, 'Prove it.' We said, 'We were just there.' They said, 'All we have in there is humanitarian aid for the poor, suffering people of Damascus.' We said, 'Horse hockey.' They again said, 'Prove it.' We said, 'Okay, people will see what's in those boxes when they look through the charred remains of the warehouse.' They said, 'Bring it on, Jack. But know that you'll seriously regret it.'"

"Bring it on, Jack?" Nir asked through a mouth full of schnitzel. "What's with all the 'jacks' people are spouting off lately?"

"I editorialized. Now go back to sleep. Anyway, Nicole, Hurvitz's fear beat out the *ramsad*'s caution, and here we are."

"Speaking of…" Nir said, pointing to the screen. On it was a satellite view of the warehouse.

"Where are the guards?" Nicole asked.

"We let the Russians know when we were coming so that they could pull their people out," answered Efraim.

"How neighborly," she said.

The raucous atmosphere in the room faded to silence. Everyone's eyes were on the screen. Suddenly, a bright light burst from the warehouse, temporarily washing out the view. As it dissipated, Nir could make out the building. Flames were shooting up in the air.

"I'm assuming Ehrlich planted the directional beacons," he said.

Efraim was staring intensely at the screen. "He did. Are you not noticing what I'm not noticing?"

"Yeah. There're no secondary explosions. Just one big explosion followed by tons of smoke that I'm betting smells a lot like burning grain." Nir sat back and pushed his plate away.

Efraim did the same. "We won't know until we know," he said.

"Yeah, but we do know, don't we? We know. Russia set us up and we were played. We walked right into it." Nir noticed that everyone at the table was looking at him. "Well, what now, ladies and gentlemen? What can we expect in the next week?"

"Nuclear holocaust?" offered Dima.

"Not funny," said Yariv.

"Hmmm, kinda funny, new guy," said Imri. Then, to the rest, he said, "If this is all a big game by Putin, then this is just the beginning. Today's little charade is all done. Let's put it behind us. We need to figure out what his big game is."

"Good, good," said Nir. "You're right. If this is a big setup, which we're almost positive it is, we need to figure out what Putin is really up to."

Efraim patted Nir on the shoulder. "Nice job repeating exactly what Imri said, Concussion Boy. So, let's examine our playing field. Who are our big three enemies? Russia, Iran, Turkey. What's happening with them?"

Dafna answered, "We've gone over this while you were off hobnobbing with the tie-wearing crowd. Russia is gathering troops in Volgograd. I'd bet we'll start seeing some of them transferred down to Beirut."

Liora jumped in. "Through their proxies, Iran is creating a UAV rainstorm on the US bases in Syria and Iraq. Every night they're flying in. Ninety percent never even make it to the fence line. But the ten percent that do are causing great consternation in Washington, especially amongst the conservative crowd."

"And what about Turkey? Erdoğan is still having kittens about the killing of Mousa. But he doesn't appear to be doing a thing. Are they too busy drowning in their own debt to cause us any problems?" Dafna's question hung in the air.

Lahav leaned back in his chair and kicked his feet up on the table next to an open container of fries. Liora quickly moved them away. "You know, it's funny you should mention Turkey. The sick man might not be quite as infirmed as you think."

CHAPTER 50

04:35 (4:35 AM) IDT

All eyes turned to Lahav. In his right hand, he held a small bowl of hummus. On his chest, directly on his T-shirt, was a large piece of naan. With surprising dexterity, he tore off a corner one-handedly and popped it into his mouth.

"Is there more to that statement, or are you just throwing it out there as a conversation starter?" asked Nir.

"Oh, there's a lot more. I just wanted to be invited to talk. I don't want to be an intrusion." He tore off another piece of naan, dipped it, and tossed it in.

Nir knew this was part of Lahav's games. Experience also told him when he was this obnoxious, it was usually because he was holding on to something good. "I don't think you could be more intrusive than you are now with your feet in the middle of the table. We don't know where your toes have been."

"What? Oh, sorry," he said, pulling his feet off and sending the rest of the naan tumbling from his chest toward the floor. He made a quick swipe to catch it but failed. "Crud."

"It's remarkable that you don't have a girlfriend," said Gil.

Lahav voiced his dislike of Gil's remark using two words that drew a sharp look from Nicole.

After apologizing to Nicole, Lahav asked Nir, "So, should I speak?"

"Have you ever needed my permission before?"

Lahav thought a moment. "Not that I can remember. So, I'll take that as a yes." He reached across the table and pulled another piece of naan off a dwindling stack. Eating as he spoke, he said, "I was tasked with keeping my eye on Erdoğan and his sick old country. He had made his threats, and everyone thought that our next focus would be on Turkey. Pretty soon, though, his blustering became background noise. 'I'm going to kill you and blah blah blah.' No one paid attention anymore. That became doubly true when Russia started popping off with their troop movements and Iran started their militias shooting off rockets at us and at the US forces in Iraq and Syria. Suddenly, everyone's eyes were on them."

"But not yours," said Nir.

"But not mine, because you said to watch the old man. And I did. And it looked like he had settled in for a long winter's nap during which he'd occasionally bluster in his sleep." Lahav then spoke very softly. "But he wasn't sleeping."

Nir looked around and saw that everyone had been pulled in to Lahav's story—even the ops guys.

"I set up some algorithms." Turning to Nir, he said, "That's a fancy way of saying I set up some programs to track certain activities."

"I know what an algorithm is," Nir grumbled.

Lahav looked genuinely surprised. "Anyway, I was looking for movement of some kind. How do you tell whether someone is really asleep or if they're just pretending to be sleeping? You watch for any movement that gives them away."

"And you spotted something?" asked Nicole.

"I did. I saw a lot of things going on that weren't normal. But most of them I set aside as new projects or desperate actions to try to save their rapidly sinking ship. I mean, at the rate they're going down, not even Rose would stand a chance of survival."

"So those projects you categorized as being like involuntary twitches when we're sleeping—they're movement, but they don't really mean anything," said Nicole.

"Exactly! You are so smart, Nicole. It's no wonder Nir's in love with you."

Nir started to protest, then realized there was nothing he could say that wouldn't sound horrible. Thankfully, he was saved by Efraim, who said, "Well, that's today's awkward moment."

"Go on," Nir managed to say, knowing that his face was beet red. He didn't know whether Nicole was blushing also because he couldn't bring himself to look at her.

Lahav seemed a little put off. "I don't know what I said that's wrong. It's so obvious. Anyway, about two weeks after Mousa got his final rubdown, one of my algorithms pointed me to new activity in İskenderun. I had put special emphasis on areas down the eastern Mediterranean coast, just because of proximity to us."

"*Sababa*. What'd you see?" asked Efraim.

"Construction. A lot of it. We're talking a massive project with hundreds of people in a huge open field east of town. In a matter of one month, four huge warehouses were erected, each around two thousand square meters."

Efraim was sitting straight up now, jotting down notes. "How did we miss this?"

"We didn't. Once again, we were told it's for humanitarian aid. There are still a ton of refugees from the Turkey and Syria earthquake a year ago. And to prove their point, massive amounts of grain began to be shipped in as soon as the first building was finished. Inspectors came by and said, 'Yep, that's grain alright. Nothing to see here.' They gave it their stamp of approval, then turned their attention back to the noisy people—Russia and Iran."

Dima spoke up. "So you are saying that they filled the warehouses with grain? How will that hurt us? Are they going to overfeed us so that we become obese and die?"

"Nice try, you muddleheaded post-Soviet dolt. All I said was that they started filling them with grain. The grain came pouring in for a few weeks, but it never went out."

"So, it's just being kept in the warehouses?" asked Dafna.

"I didn't say that either."

"Then what?" asked Nir. "My head is hurting too much for riddles. Where is the grain?"

"I don't know for sure. But I do know that preparing the foundations for the other warehouses involved moving a lot of dirt. Yet if you look at the dirt piles behind the warehouses, they seem a little disproportionate—a little big."

It was Nicole's turn. "Are you saying that this starving country buried tons of grain in those dirt piles just so they could pull a switchy-fakey?"

Lahav pointed to his nose, but then added, "I mean, I can't give a definite answer, but that's what I believe."

CHAPTER 51

04:45 (4:45 AM) IDT

Nir stood. He had to think about this for a moment, and thinking wasn't exactly easy at the moment. "Who wants what to drink from the fridge?"

Nicole and Liora jumped up and followed him. He was glad they did, because to him, the drink orders shouted at him sounded like they were in Mandarin. Pulling a bottle of mineral water from the break area's refrigerator, Nir held it to his head.

"Do we need to take you anywhere?" asked Nicole, the concern evident in her eyes.

"No. I don't have any signs of a major concussion, other than fatigue. Trust me, I've had my brain jolted enough to know when to ask for help. I just need to get a little sleep. When we're done here, I'm going to crash in my office for a while."

Liora passed a few bottles to both of them, then directed their distribution when they returned to the table. After they sat down, Nicole reached over and took Liora's hand. "It's good to have you as our CARL *ima*." Liora blushed and looked down at the table.

Nir spoke. "Okay, Tabib, we're only halfway done with this. If these were just empty warehouses, you wouldn't be bothering us with this. So talk."

Imri broke in. "Wait just a second before you tell us anything else. What I don't get is this. If Erdoğan was planning something against us, then why doesn't he just shut up? You know, go undercover to work out his diabolical plan? Instead, he's out there every week, it seems, telling us how he's going to exact his great revenge against us."

"Mind if I take this?" asked Yariv. Lahav nodded his acquiescence. "Do you have younger brothers and sisters or maybe nieces and nephews?"

"My sister has three boys."

"They are the cutest," added Liora.

"Perfect. With three boys, it's got to be a total *balagan* around the house sometimes. Noise, kids running around, stuff getting knocked off of tables."

"So, you've been to my sister's house?"

Yariv laughed. "Noise and craziness is the foundational state of being for your family. What is the only time that your sister and her husband—I'm assuming she's married—what's the only time they get nervous?"

A smile spread across Imri's face. "They get nervous when all goes quiet. Because then they wonder what is going on."

Yariv spread his arms and leaned back in his chair.

Nir was nodding as he pointed at Yariv. "That's exactly right. If Erdoğan suddenly went quiet, we'd wonder what he was doing."

"Thank you for clearly stating the obvious conclusion that everyone had already figured out for themselves, Mr. Brainswell," said Efraim, patting Nir sympathetically on the arm. Turning to Lahav, he said, "Now, let's get back to what 'asleep-at-the-wheel' here was asking you before. This is about more than just four new warehouses."

Lahav got up and went to his workstation. Standing there, his fingers flew over his keyboard. Nir didn't think he had the dexterity to hit random keys as quickly as Lahav hit precise ones. After less than a minute, he walked back to the table carrying a remote.

"How many of you know about Baykar?" he asked.

"Tech company in Turkey. AI, UAVs, and C4I," answered Yariv.

"C4I?" asked Yaron.

"Defense and military systems. Typically weapons, combat management, command and control, national defense systems—that sort of stuff."

Yaron nodded thanks to the young man before biting off the end of a hummus-covered carrot.

Lahav picked up again. "Baykar is a diamond in a country of turds. While everyone else is struggling just to get by, Baykar is exporting products all over the world—countries like Ukraine, Azerbaijan, Ethiopia, Rwanda, Nigeria, Poland—we're talking everywhere. And it's because their products are so good. They're cutting edge, especially when it comes to UAVs. And their shining star is the Bayraktar TB2." He clicked the remote and a picture of a drone came up on the screen.

"It's a beautiful piece of work," said Yariv.

"Length is 6.5 meters. Wingspan is almost twice that. It can fly at a max speed of 222 kilometers per hour and cruise as high as 7,600 meters. It's a brilliant design that's changed the way a lot of countries do war. Even places like Burkina Faso and Djibouti can send a TB2 up into the sky and see what their enemies are doing."

Nir had opened his sparkling water but was once again resting the bottle against his forehead. "Okay, good for Baykar," he said. "Nice that it's the diamond amidst the…stuff. But what does that have to do with İskenderun and the warehouses? Are you saying that Baykar is turning them into factories?"

Efraim put his hand on Nir's arm. "That's not what he's saying. Just listen and let the non-addlebrained people talk." Turning to Lahav, he asked, "Do you have any evidence that Erdoğan is moving UAVs down to İskenderun?"

Moving drones to İskenderun? Did I miss a step here? Last I remember, we were talking about wingspans and Djibouti.

Nir was about to say something when Nicole put her arm around the back of his chair. She leaned toward him and whispered, "Shhh, just listen."

"Evidence, no. Suspicions, yes," Lahav answered. He clicked a button on the remote. This time the screen showed a satellite shot of four warehouses. "Here are trucks backed against the loading docks of the warehouses." Nir could see the semitrucks but couldn't understand the lettering on them. "These are official trucks from the Turkish department that gives out aid. They came directly from the center where the aid is doled out from."

"So, you're saying that it's aid," said Yaron, who seemed to be having as much trouble as Nir following Lahav's train of thought, only without a concussion.

"That's what I'm not so sure about." Lahav pressed the button again, and another picture appeared on the screen. It was a massive complex with trucks appearing to go in and out. "This is the central aid distribution center. Food is constantly passing through here. What I want you to notice are these four unmarked trucks that are in line to enter the complex." He circled the trucks with a red laser pointer. "They came in like all the rest and unloaded their cargo; they traveled back to their point of origin. What's interesting is where that point of origin is."

Once again, the screen changed to show a close-up of what appeared to be the same unmarked trucks backed against a loading dock. "Welcome, my dear friends, to Baykar." He pressed the button again, and a wide-angle shot appeared of a large complex with several factories and some nice office buildings.

Efraim was laughing now and applauding. "Dude, you are so good."

"Yes, I am," said Lahav, with a smirk.

"How long…?" Efraim began before cutting himself off. He pulled out his phone and read the screen. "Gotta go. The *ramsad* is calling us all in. Seems Putin actually got out of bed to present a statement. He has proof that we just destroyed many tons of humanitarian supplies. He's threatening severe retaliation. Get ready, everyone—this is going to be another long day."

Once the assistant deputy director was gone, Nir spoke. "Lahav, this is masterful work."

"I haven't even gotten to the three fuel trucks that are now parked outside of the warehouses. Every TB2 carries three hundred liters of gasoline to power it. These trucks pulled up two days ago and have not been unloaded."

A wave of lightheadedness felt like it floated Nir's brain in his skull.

He grabbed the table with both hands as he said to Lahav, "Fabulous. Fantastic. You're amazing. But, please, let's put this on hold for a little bit. I think we have something the *ramsad* needs to see, but until I get some rest, I won't be worth a thing."

"So what else is new?" said a female voice. The accent wasn't South African, so that was good. Whichever of the other two women was smack-talking him, Nir didn't care enough to find out.

"Everyone, take four hours rest. We're all going to need it. We'll reconvene here at 09:00. Until then, I don't want to see anyone at their workstation. Understood?"

There was grumbling and complaining, but eventually everyone except Nicole was out of the room. Nir had an old, threadbare couch in his office. He let Nicole lead him to it, where he stretched out and immediately fell asleep.

CHAPTER 52

11:23 (11:23 AM) IDT

Nir awoke to something tickling his face. He swatted at it, then realized it was the fringe of a blanket. The strange thing was that he didn't remember covering himself.

In the dark of his office, he reached around the floor for his phone. When his finger brushed the screen, it lit up.

11:23 a.m.

Nir jumped up off the couch and felt along the wall until he found the switch for the overhead light. The blanket that Nicole usually kept folded up in the corner of her workstation for when the workroom got especially chilly was now crumpled on the ground.

How did I sleep past our meet time?

He lifted the blanket off the ground and pulled his office door open to see the analysts working at their stations and the ops guys deep into a game of poker.

"Good morning, sunshine," said Liora, turning his way. Quickly, she grimaced. "You've got…" she paused, brushing at the corner of her mouth.

Nir lifted his hand to his face and felt a crusty residue trailing from the corner of his mouth down his cheek. He licked his fingers and scrubbed at the streak.

"Ugh, that somehow made it even more gross," Liora said, turning back to her station. Everyone else ignored Nir, except for Nicole, who waved him over. When he got there, she upended her water bottle on a tissue and gave the corner of his mouth a quick scrub.

As she did, he asked, "Why did you let me sleep so long?"

"Because you needed it after being blown up so many times. Maybe now you'll stop talking incessantly about leprechauns and unicorns."

"Wait, I was talking about...?" He trailed off when he saw the smirk on her face. She tossed away the tissue and pulled the blanket from his hand. After a quick fold, it went back into its usual spot.

"Thanks for that," he said, nodding at the blanket.

"No problem. Efraim came back for a few minutes. He asked us to call him once Prince Charming awoke from his beauty sleep, which I'm pretty sure is not how the story really goes."

"I'll give him a call." Raising his voice, he said, "Meeting in five minutes."

"Oh, now he wants a meeting after sleeping through half the day," said Yariv.

"Hey, new guy," Nir said harshly, pointing at the rookie. "Kudos on the sarcasm. Keep up the good work."

At first, Yariv wasn't sure if he was in trouble or not. But when Nicole gave him a thumbs-up, he smiled and turned back to his workstation.

"See you in a few," Nir said to Nicole, giving her arm a squeeze. Walking back into his office, he closed the door behind him. He swiped open his recent calls, and pressed Efraim's name.

"Prince Charming is awake."

"Nicole says that's not how the story goes. I think the prince got eaten by a wolf or something."

"Good to know. I'm glad you're awake, because we've got the bear after us."

Nir plopped down in his chair. "Russia is none too happy, huh?"

"They've already started airlifting troops down to Beirut."

"Amazing how quickly they were able to do that. It's almost like they were ready for it."

Efraim snorted. "*Sababa*. He's already put out pictures of the destruction of thousands of tons of food and medical supplies."

"Are they legit?"

"*Elef ahuz*. News crews, who just happened to be in the area, were there as soon as it was light enough to document the grain carnage."

"Stinking Hurvitz," Nir said, kicking his feet up onto his desk.

"Can't just blame the minister of defense. The PM went along with it. Besides, despite having our doubts, we all were thinking that the whole thing might be legit."

"Yeah, but instead, we got played like a Bach suite by Yo-Yo Ma."

"Listen to you, Mr. Culture. Hey, *achi*, how's your head? Earlier this morning I was about ready to force you into an ambulance and get you to Ichilov."

Nir was still a bit sore, but he wasn't about to admit that to anyone. The rest would fade through the day. "Glad you didn't. I wouldn't have been a happy patient. The sleep did me good. Feeling a lot better."

"Good."

There was a knock on Nir's door. "Come in."

Efraim stepped in and ended the call. "Started your way as soon as you called. I need to hear some more from Lahav and the rest of your gang about Turkey. The *ramsad* and the PM are looking for answers, and I can't help thinking that you guys are on the right track."

"Sounds like a plan," Nir said, getting up and following his friend out the door. "Let's go," he called when he entered the workroom.

Liora had just finished putting leftovers from earlier in the morning back out on the table, along with paper plates and some drinks from the fridge.

"Thank you, ma'am," Nir said, depositing some celery, peppers, and carrots onto his plate before following up with a couple scoops of hummus. He sat in his usual chair and waited.

Once everyone had a plate, he opened the meeting with one word. "Why?"

The question hung in the air.

Turning to Lahav, Nir said, "You think Turkey is preparing drones to hit us. Why?"

"Because we killed Mousa? Isn't this exactly what he said he'd do?"

"It is. But to me, that's too easy. That's like asking a kid, 'Why'd you hit your brother?' Then having them say, 'Because he hit me first.'"

Dima squinted his eyes as he turned to Nir. "Isn't that how it usually works? I still owe my brother a punch from the last time I saw him."

"You're right. That's usually how it works, especially with you Russians. But this is CARL. We don't think the usual way. What's Erdoğan really getting at? What's his endgame? Is this *mavi vatan*? Is this his ticket out of poverty? Is he working with anyone as part of a grand conspiracy? Or is this just some scraggly mustached doofus punching back because he got punched? And what's he going to do with the drones? Is he looking to hit Tel Aviv? Is he going after the gas fields? Does this have anything to do with Gaza or Hezbollah?"

Gil said, "Let's deal with the last part first. I don't think he's going after any civilian population. That would be severely disproportional. The only person killed on his soil was a Hamas leader who was born in Jordan. His pride was hurt, but not his people."

"He's right," said Yariv. "He knows that if he hits our civilians, we will hit back harder. He can't afford another humanitarian crisis on his soil. He's looking for ways to build up his economy, not crash it even farther."

"I agree. He's got to be going after the gas fields," said Efraim. "He had put so much stock into his *mavi vatan* philosophy, thinking that he was going to make huge profits off our pipeline with Cyprus. Now that we've told him to take a hike, he's reeling. He's either going to threaten to take the fields, extort from us a portion of the profits, or destroy the fields, hoping that the lack of gas profits will bring our economy down to his level."

Dafna was nodding. "Then, when we rebuild the fields, we will be forced to turn to Turkey for Mediterranean access or face a similar fate once again."

"I disagree, Efraim, with your first two options," said Nir. "He knows he's burned the bridge between us and them. He doesn't have the strength to take our gas fields, and he has nothing he can use to extort us. *Tachles*, I think he's going for destruction now. If he can't have part of the gas, no one will."

"*Yesh matzav.* Could be. Can these drones completely take out the fields?" asked Efraim.

Lahav answered. "Depending on their number, totally. Leviathan has four wells and one production platform. Tamar has eight wells and one platform. They're the big ones. Karish is definitely smaller." Bringing up a schematic on the big screen, Lahav continued, "Now, when you're talking about the Bayraktar TB2 drones—each has a max payload of one hundred and fifty kilograms, and they each have four hardpoints for attaching weapons."

"What kind of munitions do they carry?" asked Nir.

"Typically, they're loaded with MAMs, which stands for Mini Akıllı Mühimmat, or smart micro munitions. Those come in three sizes. The drones aren't designed for the biggest ones—the MAM-T. But they can handle the C or the L."

"Elaborate, please."

Lahav looked around at the open containers. He grabbed a french fry and a skewered lamb kebab. "Okay, the MAM-C is like this fry. It's just short of a meter long and it's about seventy millimeters wide. That thing blows up like a grenade. Frags everything around it." Holding up the kebab, he continued, "The MAM-L is a full meter long and twice the width of the C. It has multiple explosives, is armor-piercing, and can be fitted for thermobaric charges. Imagine what fifty of those drones firing four armor-piercing missiles each would do to a gas production platform."

"Where'd you get the number fifty?" Gil asked.

"Just did some quick math. Two-thousand-square-meter warehouse. Each drone is about eighty square meters. I had Turkey attacking Tamar and Leviathan, but not the Karish gas field because that might upset the Lebanese, who think part of that store belongs to them. But my numbers work only if the drones are laid out on the ground wing to wing. However, there's room for a whole lot more. The height is enough for four levels of UAVs. They could overlap wings or stagger them. I mean, there could be as many as four hundred UAVs at İskenderun. You heard what I said about the fuel trucks. That's just enough gas for all four hundred."

"Or you could be *chai b'seret*, just like we were in Lebanon," said Yaron.

"Or I could be living in a movie," agreed Lahav. He leaned over the table and pulled another handful of cold fries onto his plate. He dipped a few into a puddle of separated tahini, then put them in his mouth. As he chewed, he said, "But I don't think I am."

CHAPTER 53

TWO DAYS LATER
MOSSAD HEADQUARTERS, TEL AVIV, ISRAEL—
APRIL 6, 2024—08:55 (8:55 AM) IDT

You ready for this?" Nir asked Nicole, who was seated next to him. They were at a conference table in a room near the *ramsad*'s office. Seated to Nir's left were Ehrlich and the other two Kidon team leaders, Neeman and Libai. Spaced between the men were three females, the head analysts for each team. Nir wasn't sure of their names. Because of the size of the table, they were squeezed together enough so that Nir's hip was uncomfortably pressed against Ehrlich's head analyst—Hila or Hiba or Hili or something.

A stifled belch sounded from the other side of Nicole. It originated from the one other guest who had been invited to this meeting—Lahav Tabib.

"Excuse me," he muttered. There was a sound of plastic crinkling, then hitting the floor.

At least the chips are gone before the bigwigs come out.

"Hey, Ehrlich," Lahav said, causing a stab of dread in Nir's gut. Nir could think of no scenario in which this turned out well. "Dude, you looked awesome zip-lining from my pole. Totally had the Mission Impossible thing going on." Then he started humming the theme song from the movies.

Inside, Nir was torn between wanting Lahav to shut up and wanting him to keep on going. He had been at the meeting yesterday with the *ramsad* and some others when Ehrlich was chewed up and spat out for not recognizing the Lebanese warehouse was a trap. The whole mission was an incredibly sore spot for the man, and Lahav was unintentionally fanboying the scab right off the wound. Glancing to his left, Nir could see the other two team leaders had grins on their faces.

There was movement to his right, and he saw Nicole put her hand on Lahav's forearm. "Maybe he doesn't want to talk about it. It's always a little nerve-wracking when you get shot at."

"No doubt. I've been shot at. Hey, Nir, remember when I was shot at in Iran, then in Syria? But I'll tell you what I haven't done. I've never combat zip-lined over a building and landed on the roof of another. Hey, Ehrlich, was there any movement of the pole? I was sure my winch system would work."

Without looking over, Ehrlich replied, "It worked fine. No movement. You did a good job. Now, let's talk about something else."

"Like what? I've got to set you up on some other stunts. Maybe you drive a motorcycle off a cliff and land on a train."

Ehrlich's hand slammed down on the table. But then he took a deep breath. "No thank you, Lahav. Now let's talk about something else."

Leaning toward Nir, Lahav whispered, "Who peed in his coffee?"

"Just let it go, Lahav."

The door opened, and a line of people filed in, led by the prime minister. He was followed by Foreign Minister Arens, Minister of Defense Hurvitz, deputy director of Mossad Asher Porush, the assistant deputy director Karin Friedman, assistant deputy director of Caesarea Efraim Cohen, and finally, the *ramsad*. Nir noticed that the *ramsad* didn't take his usual place at the center of the table, leaving that for the prime minister. Instead, he seated himself at the end, across from Lahav.

The prime minister's voice was tight as he opened the meeting, as if he was struggling to keep his anger in check. "I have been on the phone all day yesterday and much of this morning apologizing and trying to explain away the Mossad's failures. Your poor intelligence led to one of the biggest international public-relations disasters that our nation has ever experienced."

"Excuse me, your highness." It was Lahav, and once again, Nir was torn. On the one hand, whatever the analyst was about to say would not go over well. But on the other, Prime Minister Snir deserved it because he was totally wrong and was acting like a jerk. Lahav continued, "That intelligence wasn't ours. Sure, we talked about it, but that information came from that guy's intel department." He pointed at Hurvitz, whose straight bearing became even more rigid at the accusation.

The prime minister wasn't having it, though. "Excuse me, junior analyst whatever-your-name-is. Wasn't it the Mossad who went into the building? Wasn't it your people who misunderstood what was contained in the warehouse?"

"*Sababa*. You're exactly right. Ehrlich botched that completely." Ehrlich whipped his head toward Lahav but held his tongue. "But did you see him zip-line in? It was amazing! A work of art. And that pole was my invention. Perfection on a plate!"

"Who is this guy, and why is he in here?" Snir asked the *ramsad*.

The *ramsad* began tapping a pen on a notebook that was in front of him. It looked like he was holding back a smile, but Nir couldn't be sure. "He is an analyst named Lahav Tabib. You may remember his work from years back when he shut down the power grid in Eilat just to prove a point."

"That was him? I thought he was in prison."

Nir spoke up. "He was, sir, but we brought him out. He's now semi-rehabilitated and has a brilliant mind."

"Thanks, Nir," said Lahav, reaching his fist over for a bump. Nir ignored it.

"But not great manners. I apologize for him, sir. We brought him here today because he is the one who developed the Turkey theory."

"Well, have him shut up until he's asked a question. I don't have much time here today," the prime minister said, purposefully looking at his watch.

"Rude," Lahav said quietly.

"Okay, so tell us about this theory," said the prime minister.

"Tavor," directed the *ramsad*.

"I want to start off by letting you know that all this information has been passed on to the other teams' analysts, who pored over it. You all agree that it is a viable threat, correct?"

The analysts nodded, as did the team leaders—all except for Ehrlich, who was still stewing.

"In our workroom, I set two of our analysts on Iran, one on Russia, and Lahav on Turkey. We had been especially concerned about what Erdoğan would do with his continuous threats. Russia and Iran had a flurry of activity, as you know. Turkey seemed to fall asleep, just with a very loud snore. Lahav, however, was able to determine that their slumber was actually a ruse. They were working quietly, behind the scenes. Lahav, take it from here."

The analyst proceeded to do an excellent job of laying out all the facts about Baykar, the Bayraktar TB2, the warehouses, the fuel trucks, and the heavy military guard that had just shown up yesterday. When he finished, Nicole stepped in. "Thank you, Lahav. Mr. Prime Minister, my job was to try to locate a paper trail, something in black and white that would show what was going on. The first item I found was a requisition for three hundred and fifty TB2 drones to be shipped down to İskenderun."

Nir opened a folder and fanned out a stack of papers. Each person took one. Nicole continued, "As you can see, they could fulfill only two hundred and seventy-five out of their present stock. So their factory went into hyperdrive, and they've been working 24/7 since then to fulfill the order. Our estimates are that they should be done and ready to ship within the week."

Foreign Minister Arens tapped the top of the paper with his finger. "There is no 'ship to' address on this requisition. How can you be sure that they are going to İskenderun?"

Nicole nodded even as he was still getting his words out. "Good question, sir, and it leads to one of our time concerns. Before, there had been a route whereby shipments would leave Baykar, unload at a humanitarian aid location, reload onto unmarked trucks, then travel the rest of the way to İskenderun. Two days ago, we saw the first trucks travel directly from Baykar to the warehouses for assembly. This tells us the timeline has been shortened."

"There is one more requisition that Nicole uncovered that has us concerned." Nir pulled another stack of papers out of the folder and spread them for everyone to take. "Nicole?"

Looking at the minister of defense, Nicole said, "Sir, you'll recognize what this is."

The man scanned the sheet. "I can't read the language, but it looks like a requisition for munitions."

"Exactly right. This is a request for fifteen hundred MAM-L bombs. You know what those are."

Hurvitz sat back in his chair. "Mini Akıllı Mühimmat—smart micro munitions. They're little bombs that pack an incredibly powerful punch."

"Correct. Each of these three hundred and fifty drones can carry four of them, and they added an extra hundred on the order just in case."

The defense minister swore. Then he turned to the prime minister. "Sir, this is a huge threat. We must act to neutralize it."

"And how would you propose we do that?"

Without hesitation, the minister said, "We need to destroy this warehouse before they have a chance to launch those drones, sir."

The prime minister spun on his chair until he was eye-to-eye with Hurvitz. "So, you want me to do exactly what we just did with the Russian warehouse? How do I know that it really isn't humanitarian aid in those warehouses? How do I know that Turkey isn't setting us up just like Russia did? How do I know that the two countries aren't working together to bring us down?"

Neeman's head analyst spoke up. "Sir, I think it's likely they are working together. And I think you need to add Iran in too."

CHAPTER 54

So, you're saying there's a grand conspiracy against us?" asked the prime minister.

Neeman responded, "Sir, there has always been a grand conspiracy against us, just like Kiva said."

Her name is Kiva. One down, two more to go, thought Nir.

Neeman continued. "Antisemitism has always been rampant around the world. It's just that sometimes it's stronger than at other times. After our independence in 1948, the fight came primarily to our border states, as you know. But now, it's expanding again. The states around us are too weak to come against us on their own. Iran tried using the militias and Hamas, Hezbollah, and the Houthis, but none of them have proven strong enough. But now there is a new axis of evil, and the center of it is Russia. Turkey is as sick as ever and desperately needs Russia, so it has joined the axis. As I said, Iran's allies have failed, so they are joining Russia also."

Nir raised his hand toward Neeman, who nodded for him to take over. "And each one of these countries is bringing its own allies. Belarus has threatened Israel. Why? Because Russia has. Once World War II was over, Turkey and the US became friends. They even became allies with us. But now Turkey is a member of NATO in name only, and we are at the top of their ten-most-hated list. Instead of their old alliances in the West, they are palling around with Russia, Libya, Somalia, and a bunch of other smaller states. And Iran has brought all their little minion states—Iraq, Syria, Yemen, and Lebanon—against us."

Neeman spoke up again. "*Sababa*. I know this is nothing new to you, Mr. Prime Minister. We're just trying to put it into context. Everyone at the United Nations hates us, but who cares? They'll keep passing resolutions, and we'll keep ignoring them. All the dirty little militias around us will keep shooting things at us, and we'll keep bombing the crap out of their explosives factories and launching sites. Who we truly need to be concerned about is the great bear lurking behind all this petty stuff."

"So, back to your earlier question, sir, yes, there is a conspiracy against us," Kiva said. Then looking at the row of team leaders and analysts, she added, "I think we all agree that Russia has created a distraction, and so has Iran. Russia wanted us to watch their growing troop accumulation near Volgograd and their pretend-weapons buildup down in Lebanon. Iran has been using their militias to bomb the US forces in Iraq and Syria, keeping the Pentagon looking that direction. They've also been shooting more and more rockets at us, keeping our attention on them."

"Meanwhile, you're saying that all this is happening so Turkey can build up for the true attack. And what are they going after?"

There were a number of answers on Nir's side of the table, ranging from Haifa to Tel Aviv to the gas fields.

Libai, the other team leader, answered, "As you can tell, that's a question we don't have the answer to. But when it comes down to it, that isn't what's most important."

Hurvitz put his elbows on the table and steepled his fingers. "What matters most are the warehouses."

"What do we do about them?" asked the prime minister.

"We destroy them," said Nir.

The prime minister pointed his finger and responded, "Back to that again. Listen, Tavor, destroying the warehouses is exactly what we are not going to do. That is what got us into this problem to begin with. It's that Mossad cowboy attitude that has had my phone ringing nonstop from the time our jets hit that Russian humanitarian aid station in Beirut until now. Nothing will happen until we have proof. And I'm talking real proof. Not some former criminal's musings and speculations."

"Hey," responded Lahav. But before he could say more, Nicole put her hand on his shoulder. Leaning back in his chair, he crossed his arms and scowled.

"Excuse me, sir, but we need to do something." Neeman's tone gave away that he was getting hot at the prime minister's response. "Our alternative to action is waiting until they hit us, then trying to find a way to respond."

Kiva interjected, "If someone is coming…"

The prime minister waved his hand. "Yeah, yeah, I know. If he's coming to kill you, kill him first."

Nir was getting frustrated with Prime Minister Snir. When the man had stepped into office last year, Nir had a lot of hope for him. He was from the Likud party and seemed to have a strong backbone. But it appeared as if October 7 had broken him. Nir knew that the man had lost a sister and brother-in-law during the attack. However, despite the violence perpetrated on his family and his country, Snir almost seemed gun-shy. Maybe it was all the personal attacks against him. Maybe he just couldn't stand up against the constant vitriol and lies of the left and of the press. Maybe he feared his government couldn't continue to stand if he was wrong again.

"Sir, if we got you more evidence, would you consider acting?" Nir asked.

Snir sat back and sighed. It was then that Nir could see the weight he was carrying on his shoulders. "Of course. If you get me incontrovertible proof that Erdoğan is planning an attack on us from those warehouses, I will make sure it doesn't happen, using whatever means are at my disposal. But if there is any room for doubt, *ein matzav*. It can't happen. Not now. Not after Lebanon."

Neeman turned to Nir. "Do you have something in mind? I don't see any way of getting into those warehouses with the large contingent of guards that have suddenly shown up."

"I do have a thought, but, Mr. Prime Minister, you aren't going to like it."

Snir suddenly stood up. "Then I don't want to hear about it. I already have too much dirt on my hands. Katz, if you think the idea is plausible, I can't stop you. But if it goes bust, I will stand by plausible deniability. I will tell the press that you went rogue, and I will insist on your resignation. So, you listen to Tavor and your gang here and decide whether it is worth your job." He walked out, with Hurvitz and Arens behind him.

All was quiet as the *ramsad* sat looking at the table, his pen tapping on his notebook. Then, with a grunt, he lifted himself up from his chair, walked over to the center of the table, and dropped himself back down. Another 30 seconds passed as he scanned the faces of the people across from him. Finally, he landed on Nir. "Okay, Tavor, let's hear your plan."

"Erdoğan has a fanatical bodyguard contingent around him. But his ministers don't. I was thinking that we might borrow a few ministers—say the defense minister, the foreign affairs guy, and maybe interior—and ask them if there is an attack on the horizon."

Katz started tapping his notebook again with his pen. Finally, the old man tossed his pen on the table, leaned back in his chair, and rubbed his face with his hands. "My God, son, you are brash. Do you ever think out logistics before you throw out ideas?" When his hands came down, Nir could see that there was a weary smile on the weathered face.

"Not really, *hamefaked*. I just figure that if we put enough brainpower to it, we can make it work."

The *ramsad*'s eyebrows went up. "Okay, just for fun. Let's think this through. How will Erdoğan react if we steal three of his ministers?"

Ehrlich's analyst answered, "He'll be extremely angry. But he's about to bomb our country, so does that really matter?"

"*Sababa*. What if it turns out that this is all a big hoax?"

Nicole answered, "Is that a risk you're willing to take? You've heard the evidence. You know we're right."

Reaching across the table, he patted Nicole's hand. "Yes, I know we're right. But we need to ask the questions. So, how do we think Russia will react?"

"This may start something big," said Lahav. "They're already moving troops down to Beirut after the warehouse attack. But they're in on this anyway. They know about the attack, and they are preparing their troops to follow up when we're down after Turkey's first move. We're going to end up facing the Putinistas one way or another."

"Iran too," said Ehrlich. "They're totally in on this. That's why they've stepped up their attacks on America's bases. If this Turkey attack takes place, expect hundreds of rockets to simultaneously launch from Syria and Iraq in order to keep our resources occupied."

"Hmmm, good, Ehrlich. You're right." Once again, the *ramsad* ran his hands over his face. "Are you folks confident enough to risk my job? Tavor, are you willing to get me fired if your gambit fails?"

Nir leaned onto the table and looked the old man in the eyes. "Sir, you have a boat moored in the bay and a lot of fishing line. If we fail, you'll be okay."

Their eyes held, then the *ramsad* burst out laughing. Everyone was a little shocked at first. It was a sound that was rarely heard coming out of the stern man.

"You all work it out and tell me what you need. Ehrlich, I want you in on the planning, but you won't be going. You're too toxic right now."

Ehrlich began to protest, but the *ramsad* held up his hand. He stood and walked out the door with his team following him, all except for Efraim.

CHAPTER 55

CARL—14:40 (2:40 PM) IDT

Nicole sat with her back to her workstation. All the way on the opposite end of the room was Nir's door. Closed, as usual lately. She turned back to her keyboard and began typing, but soon lost her train of thought. Spinning back around, she focused in on the door, willing it to open.

It didn't.

From her left, she heard Liora say, "Would you just go and say whatever you need to say to him? You're like the height of distraction right now."

She turned toward her fellow analyst but was greeted by the back of her head. Nicole's eyes returned to the door.

Forget it. He won't want to listen anyway.

She whirled around to her keyboard, put her fingers on the keys, but couldn't think of anything to type. She couldn't even remember the project she was working on.

Letting out a frustrated growl, she stood, picked up her phone, and crossed the floor to the office door.

"Finally," Liora said behind her.

Nicole paused a moment, smoothed her T-shirt, and used her fingers to fill out her curls.

"Jeez, it's just Nir," said Lahav from the workstation to the right of the door. Nicole glared at him until he turned away.

With a deep breath, she knocked.

"Come in," came the answer.

She had practiced a funny greeting while at her workstation, but now she couldn't remember it. It turned out to be fine, because Nir was on the phone. He waved her in and pointed to his couch. Then he pointed to the phone and held up his index finger.

Nicole smiled and waved her hand like it was no big deal. She sat and waited.

"Well, tell them we're going to need some help from another country. Our nearest exfil point is up in the Black Sea. We need some help from Bulgaria or Armenia or Georgia or someone."

Nir paused as he listened. "Well, then, we've got about forty-eight hours to make friends with them. Bribe them, extort them, promise them a free punch card for natural gas—I don't care. We need a way out. Turkey is too big to drive our way to safety. It's already going to be two hundred kilometers to reach the Black Sea. We won't have more time than that."

Another pause. "Sure, if Zelenskyy thinks he could pick us up and get us someplace safe without his boat or sub getting blown up, that's fine. Just find us someone, okay? Thanks, *achi.*"

Nir hung up the phone and set it on the desk. "It was Efraim. Getting in won't be the problem. Our two countries hate each other deep down, but diplomatically, we're still playing somewhat nice. Still, we won't be going in as Israelis. We'll all have Belgian passports and credentials from universities in the country. We'll be flying into Eskişehir as a group of history professors checking out the UNESCO heritage sites of the area."

"You guys look as much like history professors as I do a steelworker."

Nir tilted his head in agreement. "True. Our hope is that the agents at Hasan Polatkan Airport are a little sleepy at their jobs. Not a lot of purveyors of international intrigue flying into Eskişehir from Brussels."

"Well, make sure you bust out your corduroy jacket with the patches on the elbows."

Nir laughed. "Already have one coming up from costuming. Now, you didn't come in here to talk about my travel plans. Or, maybe you did. Why did you come in here?"

The question flustered Nicole, who had practiced this conversation quite a few times sitting at her desk. Unfortunately, none of her trial runs began with "Why are you here?"

Might as well just come out with it. Any roundabout way is going to sound disingenuous now.

"Okay, Nir. I need to talk about this with you at least once. All I'm asking is for you to please hear me out."

Nicole saw his eyes widen a touch and heard his intake of breath. He knew what was coming. Now it was just a matter of whether he'd listen.

"Please, Nir. All I'm asking for is the next ten minutes. After that, I'll have said my piece. Will you at least give me that?"

His internal turmoil was evident. She watched as he squinted his eyes a bit and set his jaw. But then his face softened. Getting up from behind his desk, he sat in the chair next to the couch. Taking her hands, he said, "Listen, you know I'm not a fan of the kinds of conversation that I'm pretty sure you're about to start. But I respect you too much to shut you down without even hearing you out. So, I'm yours for the next ten—heck, I'll even give you fifteen minutes."

Nicole put her hand on his. "Fifteen? Wow, I feel so special."

She inhaled deeply and slowly let her air out. "Okay, here goes. And trust me, it has everything to do with what we're about to do in Turkey."

"Interesting. Color me intrigued." Nir leaned back in the chair, crossed his legs, and waited.

"So, I've talked to you before about God's plans for the world, right?"

Nir smiled. "You mean Him snatching up His people and carrying them away before He rains fire and brimstone down on the planet?"

Nicole rolled her eyes. "Listen, I need you to be serious. I need you to hear what I'm about to say."

"Sorry. I'm listening."

"Okay, I know you've heard about the prophet Ezekiel, right?" Nir nodded his yes. "I don't know how much you remember from your studies as a kid, but there's a lot of weird stuff in it in the beginning—wheels and faces and freaky stuff like that. Then God goes on to talk about showing the world who He is. 'Then they will know that I'm the Lord,' and words to that effect."

"I remember."

"But then the chapters get into the thirties and things change. Suddenly, in 36 and 37, Ezekiel's talking about the Jews coming back into the land of Israel. In fact, a lot of church people in years past said those chapters were just stories or allegories because there was no Israel. Then suddenly 1948 came along, and Israel was back."

"*Esh!* Yea, us," said Nir. "Listen, Nicole, I know about all this stuff. It's part of what unites this country, this belief that God or something else bigger than us brought us back to our land to be a people. When has that ever happened in the past?"

Nicole dropped her hand on Nir's knee. "Exactly! But the thing is, so many people stop reading at chapter 37."

"*Sababa*, because I remember it gets really weird after that. A bunch of talk about wars and stuff."

"Again, you're exactly right. But it's those wars and stuff that are so important as we're looking at where we're at right now." She lifted her phone from the couch and began scrolling. "Hang on…okay, now, listen to these words directly from Ezekiel 38:

> Now the word of the LORD came to me, saying, "Son of man, set your face against Gog, of the land of Magog, the prince of Rosh, Meshech, and Tubal, and prophesy against him, and say, 'Thus says the Lord GOD: "Behold, I am against you, O Gog, the prince of Rosh, Meshech, and Tubal. I will turn you around, put hooks into your jaws, and lead you out, with all your army, horses, and horsemen, all splendidly clothed, a great company with bucklers and shields, all of them handling swords. Persia, Ethiopia, and Libya are with them, all of them with shield and helmet; Gomer and all its troops; the house of Togarmah from the far north and all its troops—many people are with you."'"

"Well, that's clear as mud. There are no such places anymore as Rosh, Meshech, and Tubal. And what's a Gog? I'm sure it all meant something at one time, but that time is past. We might as well be talking about Camelot now," said Nir.

"But are they really gone? Look a little later down in verse 15 at what Ezekiel says about Gog: 'Then you will come from your place out of the far north, you and many peoples with you, all of them riding on horses, a great company and a mighty army.' Gog, the prince of Rosh. That's Russia. Meshech, that's southern Russia. Tubal is northern Turkey. I've got it all on a map somewhere in my phone if you want me to find it."

Nir waved his hands. "No, *motek*, I believe you. But what does this…?"

"Hold on, let me finish. Persia—you know where that is."

"Iran."

"Yep, then you have Ethiopia, which is really more of Sudan these days. There's Libya, which recently became a huge ally of Turkey."

"Right, with the *mavi vatan* water agreement," Nir said. Nicole could tell that Nir was finally listening to her.

"And speaking of Turkey, you have Gomer and Togarmah. Never before in history have you had these nations all working together. Sudan is a huge ally of Russia. As you and I have talked about, Iran is desperate for friends now that Hezbollah, Hamas, and the Houthis are all busts. So, they've turned to Russia. And now we see both Russia and Iran running interference for Turkey so that Erdoğan can have his revenge."

So often, Nicole had heard Nir say that coincidence was an excuse for those not willing to step back and look at the big picture. What was he going to do with this? There was too much here.

"What about this hook in the jaws part? What's the hook in the jaws for Russia?"

Nicole rolled her eyes. "Come on, *motek*. You know the answer to that. The hook is gas. The Russkis had their troops down here in Syria and Lebanon. But the war in Ukraine forced them to pull their troops out so they could reinforce the front lines. However, since the warehouse attack, we're seeing Russian troops racing back toward our borders."

"But if the Russians are coming back for the gas, are they going to let the Turks blow up the fields in Leviathan and Tamar? Isn't that defeating their purpose?"

Nicole shook her head. "We have to think big picture. That kind of hit will cripple Israel's economy and cause major political turmoil, making the nation open for a takeover."

"Won't the United States stop them?"

"Who in the US will stop them? The president? Maybe the last one, but not this one. This one will shoot some missiles and slap some wrists, but there's no way he'll go to the wall for Israel. Besides, Russia just created the perfect excuse. Israel attacked first when it destroyed all that humanitarian aid in Syria."

Nir looked at the floor and thought.

"So, you're telling me that I should go to the *ramsad* and inform him that the more than 2,500-year-old predictions of a Hebrew prophet are telling us that we should prepare for a Russian attack."

Nicole dropped her head back on the couch and let out a groan of exasperation. "No, Nir. I'm not talking about Israel or the *ramsad* or anyone else. I'm talking about you. I believe that before this war happens, the rapture is coming. And as it stands right now, I'll be gone but you'll be left here."

"Oh, Lord, not the 'I'll fly away' talk again.'"

She slapped his leg a little harder than she intended. "Darnit, Nir, listen to me. I don't want you to patronize me, but I also don't want you to mock me. I'm telling you what I believe, and I expect you to respect it."

Nir put his hands up. "I'm sorry. You're right."

Nicole huffed out a breath, then reached out her hands and took his. They sat like that for a minute before she said, "I'm sorry too. I shouldn't have blown up at you. It's just that I can't bear the thought of going without you. I want you to come with me, to be with me, to believe with me."

She was suddenly emotional. Nir got up and pulled a couple tissues from a box behind his desk.

"Thanks," she said as she took them. "I'm so scared for you, Nir.

The prophet Zechariah said that two-thirds of the Jews are going to be wiped out in the years after the rapture. October 7 will look like nothing compared to what's coming."

"*Al hapanim.* That doesn't sound like a very loving God to me."

Nicole chuckled bitterly. "I know. I don't get it all. I just know that He's doing it to get the attention of those whose hearts will listen." Then, looking up into his eyes, she asked, "Why won't you let your heart listen?"

It was obvious that Nir didn't know what to say. She could see that he was wrestling with what she had said, but she knew that the veil she had heard her pastor talk about that covered the hearts of so many seemed to be especially thick with him.

Nir's phone rang. "That ring…it's Efraim. I need to take it, *motek*. We'll talk again."

As Nir picked up the phone, Nicole slowly got to her feet.

I hope we will, Nir. I truly hope we will.

CHAPTER 56

It was a beautiful day in Ankara. Nir wished he could have spent it outside lounging in the grass, rather than on the hard metal floor of a utility van. But this was not meant to be a relaxing vacation. This was a workday, and he and his team were about to put in some serious work.

Unfortunately, he felt like his guys were just doing due diligence. The Kidon teams had come to kidnap three ministers in the hopes that one would spill the beans about the UAV attack on Israel. His team's mission was to snatch the defense minister from out of his car. Definitely the most dangerous of the assignments, Nir had taken it because his guys had been together the longest and had much more experience. But the man they were taking was a battle-hardened veteran. He'd probably just swear and threaten and talk about how he would smile when they were shot.

Nir didn't think that Aryeh Neeman's kidnapping would work out either. At the last minute, the foreign minister of Turkey had decided to take a trip to Northern Cyprus. So Neeman and his four men were currently in North Nicosia trying to devise some way to grab the guy.

Nir had a feeling that the foreign minister would never even learn that they had been there for him.

Nir's money was on Tommy Libai. They were going for the minister of the interior, a man named Günes Kapanli, who appeared to all to be a good Muslim and a great family man. And he was, except for Tuesday evenings. That was the night he told his wife that he had late meetings with his leadership, which would usually end with time at a bath. How he actually spent the evening was by slipping off to a lavish apartment where he had set up a girlfriend to be at his beck and call. It was a good deal for her, since his beck and call came only once a week. She was content to pay the price if it meant the rest of the evenings were hers to spend as she wanted.

Cheaters cheat, and they never stop cheating. If he'll betray his wife, he'll betray his country. He'll talk.

Still, Nir and his guys had to do their part in rounding out the triumvirate of key ministers. And as time ran down toward 5:00 that afternoon, the adrenaline increased in his body. They were parked in the lot of TOBB University of Economics and Technology, just down Söğütözü thoroughfare from the Presidential Complex and the Congress. Minister of Defense Oltan Dogan was nothing if not punctual. Every afternoon, unless there was a military crisis, he would visit the president's office at 4:30 p.m., then head for home by 5:00 p.m. Always the same route. Always the same two-vehicle convoy.

Nothing kills you faster than routine. Except this guy isn't going to die. "Don't harm them," demanded the prime minister. I wonder what his definition of "harm" is.

At 5:03, Yaron, who was in an SUV parked further up toward the main street, pulled out. Imri put the van in gear and positioned behind him. As Dogan's lead car approached 22nd Road, Yaron gunned the gas. The SUV gained speed, then plowed into the side of the lead vehicle. The force of the blow sent the bodyguards' vehicle up onto the center divider before crashing hard into a tree.

The van carrying the rest of Nir's team screeched up next to Yaron's SUV. The doors flew open, and everyone jumped out. They were all wearing black with plate carriers over their chests and backs and balaclavas on their heads. Nir sprinted toward Dogan's SUV and fired five shots through the passenger window, instantly killing both men in the front seat. There had been debate about whether the Kidon teams had a green light to eliminate the bodyguards, but after coming to the conclusion that these men were guarding the people who were preparing to devastate Israel, the *ramsad* had given his okay. Not that he needed much convincing.

Dima had his gun pointed at the back window, while Gil was with Yaron dispatching the guards from the front vehicle. Imri stayed behind the wheel of the van, ready to take off as soon as everyone was in. Nir angled his rifle through the shattered side window and into the back seat. Dogan sat alone, a scowl on his face.

"*Eller yukarı,*" Nir yelled, telling the man to put his hands up. Slowly, the minister set down the file he had been reading and raised his hands. Nir reached into the car and unlocked the doors. As soon as he did, Dima yanked the rear door open. He took hold of the collar of the old man's jacket and pulled him out and to his feet.

Traffic was building behind them. Panicked drivers began to honk. They had to leave right away.

"Let's go!"

Nir heard one more shot from the lead vehicle, and Yaron and Gil came running. Dima already had Dogan in the back of the van. Everyone dove in and Imri hit the gas, running over the center divider and across opposing traffic. Tires screeched all around, and a small car hit the back of the van. Everyone inside flew across the floor, but Imri was able to keep going. Dima had been in the process of flex-cuffing their prisoner, but the jolt had separated them. Dogan dove toward the door, but Gil caught his foot and pulled him back. Dima pulled another pair of flex cuffs from his vest and cinched the man up.

"We have the package," Nir said into his coms.

CHAPTER 57

Nicole's body relaxed noticeably when she heard Nir say they had Dogan. Because of the proximity to Turkey's Presidential Complex, there was no way they could employ drones as an overwatch. They were having to go old school. All you could see was what was right around you.

"Any luck over there?" she called to Lahav.

"Nothing. Not even a laser pointer or a wayward Wii wand."

That didn't surprise her. She figured that nothing would show up unless and until the Turkish drones were sent.

Two days ago, the analysts were sitting at the conference table talking through whether there was any way to bring down the drones when they were launched.

"You realize that the Bayraktar TB2 is a laser-guided drone, don't you?" Yariv had asked.

Lahav rolled his eyes. "Is the pope Irish? It's a laser-guided UAV that uses line-of-sight propagation, giving it a range of more than three hundred kilometers."

"Leviathan is four hundred and fifty kilometers away from İskenderun."

That simple fact hung in the air like the funk from fake Chewbacca's decaying fur.

"My Lord, I'm an idiot," said Lahav.

"We're all idiots," said Dafna. "But I will agree with you that you are the biggest idiot."

"How are they doing it?" asked Nicole, staring down at the table. Turning to Yariv, she asked, "Does the primary signal need to be at the point of origin?"

"I don't know. Ask Lahav. I'm just here to do simple math."

Lahav laughed. "You know, I'm starting to like you. A bit. As far as I know, yes, the signal needs to be at point of origin. What I'm thinking is that they must have found a way to daisy-chain signals together. Bring up a map of the area."

Liora typed quickly, and a map of the eastern Mediterranean opened. "Give me control." A few more keystrokes, and Lahav's mouse was moving on the screen. He put a tag in the water just east-northeast of Haifa. "That's Leviathan. Tamar is right next to it. Again, we're assuming they aren't going after Karish because they need Hezbollah and Lebanon on their side."

Using his mouse, he took a quick measurement, then drew a wide circle around the gas field. "That's three hundred kilometers."

"Beautiful. So all we have to do is find a laser source in Cyprus, Lebanon, northern and central Israel, or somewhere in the eastern Med. No problem," Liora chided.

Nicole held up her hand. "Wait now. Let's narrow this down. This is line-of-sight propagation, so I'm guessing that anything inland or behind large structures is out."

"I'm taking control," Dafna said, then began blacking out the areas Nicole had mentioned.

"That leaves us beaches and the water," said Yariv. "But the other thing we need to remember is that this signal is for three hundred and fifty drones. We're not talking about simply popping a laser pointer out of your pocket and aiming it. It's a complex signal that has to be multiplied many times over."

Nicole was jotting down notes as he talked. She said, "Good. Now, are we talking box truck size? Semi size? Or VW Beetle size?"

"It'll be good sized, because there is computer equipment that will have to go along with it. I'm thinking troop transport size," said Lahav.

"Or just a plain old boat. A fishing trawler. A pleasure yacht. Any decent-sized watercraft," said Nicole. She tapped on her notes a few times with her pen. "That's what I would do. I wouldn't want to be cruising around on land, my escape limited by the roads that are around me. I'd want to be on the open sea, where I could run any direction I needed to."

"I don't know. I don't think I'd want all that open water around me. No place to hide," said Yariv.

That's how Yariv and the girls had ended up scouring for signals on land, while she and Lahav searched for laser signals of any type appearing over the Mediterranean. The Israeli Navy Ship *Atzmaut*, a 6-class corvette, and the INS *Sufa*, a Sa'ar 4.5-class missile boat, had shifted to the waters south of Cyprus and had given permission for the analysts to tap into their signals.

Having permission to dig into someone's signals is a whole lot easier. But it's definitely not as fun as breaking in.

Nicole had satisfied her hacker's need for stealth by sneaking into a number of different monitoring systems along the shores of Cyprus and Lebanon. She passed those leads on to the other three members of the team, and every now and then, they would bring her another source into which they wanted access.

Now, however, was one of those downtimes that she hated. Nothing was coming from the ships. The rest of the team was content listening to their sources. All of them understood that the greatest likelihood was that they would never hear anything because the Israeli Air Force would wipe out the drones before they launched, assuming they needed wiping out. CARL was part of the "just in case." As Asher Porush, the deputy director of Mossad, had told them, they were the "last-ditch effort to avoid an economy-crushing blow" that would hopefully never be set into action.

Nir and Nicole hadn't had any opportunity to talk again since that afternoon in his office. That broke her heart. No one could know the time when Jesus would return, but by all accounts, the time was short. While she was excited about the rapture and seeing Jesus face to face, she couldn't help feeling an emptiness in her heart knowing that Nir wouldn't be there with her. Then what would he have to endure? She just couldn't think about it.

Before Nir had left for Turkey, they had a quick moment for just the two of them. He had promised Nicole that when he was back, they would go to Aroma to get coffee together. There, they would both put their phones on silent and just talk. He promised her that he was thinking about what she had said, and she knew he didn't make such promises willy-nilly.

Taking her hands off her keyboard, she rested them in her lap.

Lord, please protect Nir. Watch over him and his team. Protect Your people in Israel from this attack. Bring Nir back home so we can talk. He belongs to You, and I trust You completely with him. Please, in Your time, bring him into Your kingdom.

"Nicole." It was Dafna. She had a piece of paper with a company name and coordinates. "These folks have a serious array of antennae and other stuff like that. They may be worth checking out. Mind opening a door for me?"

Taking the paper, Nicole said, "You bet." Then she began to type.

CHAPTER 58

ANKARA, TURKEY—17:10 (5:10 PM) EEST

They raced east on 22nd. Suddenly, the road split into a *T*. They went right, then made a quick left. Waiting for them was a cargo van with no back windows. The writing on the side advertised a moving company. Imri pulled in next to it, and everyone transferred from one van to another. Yaron slid into the driver's seat and started the engine.

"Everyone in?" Yaron called from the front.

"Go! Go," called Nir.

Yaron accelerated, but he didn't tear out. The goal now was not to rush past everybody, but to blend in. A few turns later, Yaron did just that as he merged in with the rush of the afternoon traffic.

In the back of the van, a dangling ceiling light swayed with the movement of the vehicle—casting erratic shadows that were disorienting enough that Nir had to pause for a moment before he began his interrogation. Dogan was propped up against a wall, sandwiched between Dima and Imri. Nir sat down cross-legged.

"Gil," he called out, holding out his hand. The operator stood and reached into a cooler he had been sitting on. He tossed a water bottle to Nir, who twisted the cap off. Nir offered it to the minister, but the man ignored him.

Dogan's dossier had shown that he graduated with a master's in political communication from the Université de Montréal. That intersected perfectly with the French that Nir had picked up while living in Belgium. But that also meant that when Nir spoke, it was in a language that only the two of them understood.

"Do you know who we are?"

"No. And I don't care. Whatever country you are from will pay for this, and you will die for your sins."

"It doesn't seem to me that we are the ones in danger of dying." Nir pulled off his balaclava and took a long swig from the bottle.

The minister stared at him for a long time, then said in an accusatory tone, "You are Israeli."

"Guilty as charged. And we're here because we've heard that you have some big plans for us. We're pretty sure we know what it is, and quite frankly, we already have assets in place to stop your president's little revenge plan. All I need to hear from you is, 'Yes, as a matter of fact, we are going to use drones to destroy your gas fields.'"

Nir could see surprise in the man's eyes at the extent of his knowledge. But the expression on his face never changed. "You are a fool to think that. And you are a fool to think that I would ever betray my country, even if that was true."

Nir drank some more water, then offered again to pour some into the man's mouth. Dogan sat mute. Nir drained the rest, then threw the bottle to a corner. "You know, Oltan, the first thing you said was a lie. 'Straight from the pit of hell,' a friend of mine would say. But that second part I think is true. In fact, I even told my higher-ups, 'Old Oltan, he won't say anything. He's too proud, too set in his ways.' So they said, 'You could torture him. Force him to talk.' But I said, 'No. He's probably already been shot and stabbed and all that sort of stuff already.' Am I right?"

The minister glared silently.

"Yeah, I've been shot and stabbed too. No fun at all. Anyway, the folks back home said, 'Maybe if you threaten his life, he'll talk.' Again, I said, 'No, not old Oltan. There's no better way for a soldier to go out than dying for his country.' So, why, you may be asking yourself, did I go through with this knowing you wouldn't talk? Two reasons. First, because we don't need your confirmation. I've got a group of friends with Günes Kapanli right now, your interior minister. Did you know he had a little honey on the side? Yeah, you knew. I can see it in your eyes. What do you think he'd be willing to tell to keep his secret from getting to his wife?"

A phone rang. Imri answered it, then walked over to Nir. "Yeah?… okay…okay…good work."

"Perfect timing," he said, passing the phone back to Imri. "Seems Günes couldn't wait to tell all about the drones and the MAM-Ls and the flight path to Leviathan and Tamar. Which means we don't need you anymore."

Nir stood, but then snapped his fingers and quickly dropped back down. Dogan continued to stare into Nir's eyes, but for the first time there was a hint of fear in them.

"I promised you two reasons why we snatched you up. The second is that I want you to pass a message on to your president. You tell him that no one is safe, and that Israelis never forget."

Nir pulled back his fist and drove it forward. Dogan was prepared for it, and slid down the van's back wall. The pain was electric as Nir's fist connected with the van's shell. At the same time Nir hit, Yaron slowed the van for a light. Off-balance after the miss, Nir tumbled on top of Dima.

With a surprising burst of speed for his age, Dogan rolled past where Nir had just been and got his feet under him. He took two steps and flew into Gil, who was on the cooler leaning against the rear doors. The force of the blow burst the doors open and the two men fell out backward into the middle of the road. Tires screeched as brakes slammed.

Not believing his eyes but acting on instinct, Nir shouted to Yaron, "Keep going. We'll catch up with you. Go!" Nir then took three steps across the van floor and dove out the back door.

CHAPTER 59

The phone next to Nicole began ringing. She saw that it was Efraim. "Hey," she said.

"Okay, I need you to listen closely, then pass this on to the team. First, the Turkish embassy called Prime Minister Snir. They know that Dogan, the defense minister, has been taken, and they are accusing us."

"Which is true."

"Well, yeah...right. They've reviewed the footage from the traffic cams and know that it was a snatch. They demanded him back immediately. Second, we've received confirmation from Libai's team that the UAVs in İskenderun are for us. Our fighters were waiting on the tarmac. They're now in the air. Full speed, it'll take twenty minutes for them to reach the warehouses."

"Nicole," called Yariv.

She held up her finger. "Do they know that we know about the drones?"

"Not sure."

"Nicole," Yariv called out again. "Now!"

That was as insistent as she had ever heard the young man. "Hang on," she told Efraim. Turning to Yariv, she said, "What?"

"The communications traffic in Turkey just exploded in activity. Everyone is calling everyone."

"Anything about the drone launches?"

"That's just it. It's all about the drone launches. At least all the important stuff. From what I can tell, they've sent the go signal to start sending them out."

"What a *balagan*," Nicole said. She repeated the information to Efraim.

He swore, then said, "Ask him how long it would take for them to get their drones in the air."

Nicole did, but Yariv responded, "*Ein li musag?* Ask the drone expert." He pointed to Lahav.

"Lahav! Lahav," she called out, but he had put on his noise-canceling headphones. Unfortunately, they worked a little too well, and she had made him promise to put them on only when he was deep into something and needed complete concentration.

This was a time, though, when she needed his complete concentration on her. Picking up her empty tea mug, she hurled it across the room. It hit the giant Wookie on the cheek, causing his head to teeter, then fall off.

Lahav's response was loud and profane and would have cost him big if they'd still had their swear jar out. Lucky for him, it had been stowed away once the ops guys had started spending more time in CARL.

"Tabib," Nicole shouted, mimicking lifting the headphones from his ears.

Lahav seemed genuinely shocked that the mug had come from her. He lifted his headphones and tossed them on his workstation, but before he could say anything, Dafna said, "You had your headphones on, *tembel*. Anything's broken, that's on you. Now listen to her."

Turning to Nicole with defiant eyes, he waited for her question.

"How long would it take for the Turks to get their UAVs up and flying?"

"Seriously? You broke Chewie for that?"

There were times when Nicole understood the frustration that Nir felt with this gang of misfits. This was one of those times. "Answer me, or the next mug is coming at your head."

Lahav's countenance changed from anger to hurt. "Jeez, Nicole.

Lighten up. I've had Chewie for a long time. Getting the UAVs flying all depends on the state of readiness. Could be as long as an hour. Could be as short as ten minutes."

As Nicole relayed the news to Efraim, she watched as the analyst squatted down and picked up the Wookie's head. He reached for Yossi's bucket hat and put it back on top.

"Let's pray we've got time," said Efraim. "You guys have got to find that laser relay."

Just then the door opened. The *ramsad* and Asher Porush walked through.

"Gotta go," Nicole said. Turning to the *ramsad*, she said, "*Ha'mefaked*, why are you here?"

"Not even a hello or a welcome?" the old man asked. He turned to watch as Lahav placed Chewie's head back on his body. It stayed for about four seconds, then tumbled to the ground. "Should I ask?"

"No. And I'm sorry. Welcome, *ramsad*. Mr. Porush. I'm just surprised to see you here."

The *ramsad* pulled out Nir's chair and sat down. Porush followed suit. "It was getting crowded in the war room. Besides, I figured if anyone were to find the laser relay, they would be in this room."

"Thank you, sir." Then after a brief pause, she added, "Speaking of that, do you mind if I get back to work?"

"Please, by all means."

Everyone else in the room was staring at the Mossad leader with big eyes. He had been there before, but it was still intimidating to have him in such close proximity. Nicole figured she had better take charge or else everyone would continue to sit there frozen.

"Okay, back to work. Dafna, Liora, Yariv, you all keep monitoring your land sources. Lahav, you and I will keep on our water input. Once the drones launch, if they launch, they've got a two-hour flight down to our gas fields. That gives us a huge window. But we've got a huge range. The more we can help the Iron Dome, the better chance we have. Got it?"

"*Root*," came the reply.

Nicole glanced at the *ramsad* as she turned toward her workstation. He gave her a quick nod before leaning in to talk with Porush.

She had just started going through her scans when her phone buzzed again. This time it was her Red Alert app. A rocket had been fired toward Kerem Shalom. Immediately, another alert popped up, warning that a rocket had been fired at Amka. Then another at Klil, another at Yarka, another at Julis, and another at Yanuh-Jat. Soon the app couldn't keep up with the alerts and she began receiving banners that proclaimed, "Five more notifications from Red Alert" and "Seven more notifications from Red Alert."

Nicole spun toward the *ramsad*, but the man hadn't moved. Looking her way, he said, "It seems that Hezbollah and Hamas are adding themselves into the mix. But you need to keep that out of your mind. You have one concern," he said, holding up a single finger. "You find me that laser relay."

CHAPTER 60

Nir rolled to a stop against the front of a small car. Steadying himself with the bumper, he pulled himself to his feet. Despite his best efforts, his head had taken a good jarring and his brain felt as if it was pounding against the back of his eyes, begging to come out. The world swayed around him as he tried to get his bearings.

Gil! Where is he?

Cars had stopped all around him and people were pouring out. Some were Good Samaritans, looking to help. Most had their cell phones out, looking to post an exciting story on their social media. A small group was kneeling to his left. Lying there in the middle of them was the minister of defense, his eyes wide open and his head cocked at an impossible angle. He was on his side, which exposed his zip-tied hands. Heads began to turn Nir's way.

Just past him, Gil was pulling himself together as he leaned against the hood of a car. Concerned hands were touching him, looking for injuries. But then the first accusatory-sounding words came from the defense minister crowd.

This is going to get ugly really fast.

"Gil," Nir shouted. His teammate turned, shocked to see Nir amongst the growing throng. "We gotta go! You good?"

"Little gimpy, but I'll be okay. Lost my gun in the roll."

Nir felt for his, but his sidearm was missing too.

Lovely.

A voice came over a loudspeaker. Everyone tensed, including the two Mossad agents. The Turkish police did not have a good reputation, especially when it came to crowd control. And, intentionally or not, the group outside of their cars had become a crowd.

Nir moved toward Gil. Once again, the voice spoke. There was authority in the words. Some of the men around Dogan began yelling, but their overlapping words were canceling each other out.

One of them moved toward Nir, reaching out his hand to grab his arm. Nir pushed him back hard, and the man stumbled to the ground. That one action turned the remainder of the crowd against them. Suddenly, Nir and Gil weren't victims; they were perpetrators.

Again, the police called out.

"Apparently, we're being beckoned," Nir said to Gil before turning toward the voice.

A police car must have been traveling several vehicles behind the van when Dagon took his plunge, because it was now wedged within all the stopped traffic, and the officers were out of their cars with their guns drawn.

"Ever had a desire to spend time in a Turkish prison?" Nir asked.

"Nope."

Nir dropped to his knees. Gil followed suit. Gunshots rang out.

These idiots have at least a dozen cars between them and us filled with innocents. What are they doing?

But Nir didn't have time to stay and ask. Staying low, he ran to the median and into the flow of opposing traffic. A driver in a Toyota that looked like it had been around when Atatürk still ruled the republic slammed his brakes. The front bumper glanced the side of Nir's knee and sent him sideways. He managed to keep his feet, but the pain was electric. Gil had raced ahead of him and was holding out his hands to stop the next two lanes of traffic.

Gunshots sounded behind them once again. The windshield of a BMW next to Gil spiderwebbed. Who knew where the rest of the shots went—whether into people or things?

Once across, Nir and Gil came to an intersection. Thankfully, the light was theirs, so there was no cross traffic. On their left was a long building with hanging banners that read "Alibaba." The gunshots had gotten the attention of two armed guards who manned the entrance to the store, as was typical in the nicer areas of town. Both were large men who looked like they could have medaled in the heavyweight division of the country's Olympic wrestling team. Making matters worse, each was holding a shotgun.

Nir and Gil were only meters away.

"*Durmak*," one of them yelled. Nir knew that word, but there was no way he was going to be able to stop in time.

"Down," Nir called to Gil.

As Nir dove forward, he watched as the front man pulled the trigger. Nothing happened. It was what Nir had hoped for. Rent-a-cops in front of never-robbed stores. Of course, the idiot had left the safety on. By the time the guard realized what had happened, Nir's entire body weight was folding the man's knees backward.

As Nir hit, the other guard's gun fired. But he was aiming at Gil, who, rather than going to the ground, had angled toward the street. The guard attempted to compensate for the angle change, but he wasn't fast enough. The blast from his shotgun shattered the passenger windows of a parked car. Spinning, he turned the barrel toward Nir, but found himself tottering backward as Nir caught the back of his leg with a kick.

Jumping from a crouch, Nir pounced at the man. But he was huge and incredibly strong. He grabbed hold of Nir and hefted him into the air. Then Nir saw the sidewalk below, approaching rapidly. But before he hit, Gil flew into the guy's side. Nir went tumbling end over end.

Sirens echoed down the street. They had to get rid of these guys and on their way fast. Gil was on the ground wrestling with the second behemoth. Nir turned back to the first man. He was on the ground groaning. Nir jumped to his feet, grabbed the man's shotgun, and whacked the side of his head with the stock. Quickly, he moved next to where the guard was now on top of Gil, ready to ground and pound the smaller man. Nir racked a shell into the chamber just for the sound effect, then placed the end of the barrel against the back of the man's head. The guard froze.

Moving to where the man could see him, Nir used the shotgun to motion him off. He moved over.

"Nir, behind!" shouted Gil.

Ducking, Nir felt a blow glance along the top of his head. Turning, he saw a bystander trying to regain his balance after whiffing on a punch. Reversing the shotgun so that it was like a club, Nir drove the stock into the civilian's forehead, sending him air-bound before he fell to the ground. Nir's momentum was the wrong direction for dealing with Gil's guard, so he called his teammate's name before tossing the shotgun. Gil caught it and swung it around in one fluid motion. A crack of wood against bone echoed in the busy street, and the beast fell to the ground.

Kneeling, Gil retrieved the other shotgun and tossed it to Nir. The sirens made it sound like the police were right on top of them, even though they couldn't see them yet through the traffic. They ran.

At the end of the block stood a big sign written in English. It read, "Next Level." Then below was the word "*Giriş*" with an arrow. *Giriş* was another of those basic Turkish words that Nir knew. The sign said that to the left was the entrance to the Next Level mall.

Whatever level they were on now, it was clear they were getting nowhere. Might as well try the Next Level. They cut to the left and spotted the three-story mall.

Perfect!

A very large building with lots of people and many stores where they could "borrow" clothes from retailers and blend in with the masses—what could be better? They both picked up their speed.

"We can't go in with shotguns," said Gil. He began racking out the shells, letting them drop to the cement sidewalk.

Nir followed suit, getting rid of the shells before dropping the shotgun into a street-corner trash bin. Next came the plate carriers. They tore open the Velcro as they ran and tossed them into some bushes. As they bypassed a Starbucks store, they slowed down and took deep breaths. Their goal was to look like they belonged there, not like fugitives from justice.

Nir pulled open a large glass door. There were no shouts, no gun-shots. So far, so good. Despite this being a high-end mall, the first smell that reached his nose was the greasy odor of KFC. But, seeing the stores around him, he realized that with a decent chunk of money, he could enjoy a nice shopping spree.

The mall seemed much smaller on the inside than it had from the exterior. There were quite a few people wandering around, but not as many as Nir would have liked. He still felt out of place, out in the open. Maybe it was the knot growing on his head, or Gil's bloody nose, which he kept dabbing with his shirt sleeve.

They were passing by the Rolex store when voices called out. Nir had no idea what the words meant, but he was pretty sure of their intention when he turned to see six policemen running toward them.

CHAPTER 61

CARL—17:29 (5:29 PM) IDT

The Red Alerts pinged on Nicole's phone app to the point of distraction. She pressed the mute button to silence the notifications. But in the semidarkness, the banners at the top of her phone screen kept flashing brightly. Flipping the phone over, she slid it to a corner of her desk.

As she worked, she thought back to October 7. The repeating tones from Red Alert had awakened her from a deep sleep in her bed in Milan. Rolling under the sheets toward the nightstand, she had grabbed her phone and was shocked at the number of notifications she had received. Dozens and dozens of Red Alert banners were layered on her lock screen. Reaching around more on the nightstand, she had found the television remote. The news had only the most basic information, but it was obvious that something very bad was happening in Israel. She had dialed Nir's number, but her calls had gone to his voicemail.

She had spent the morning sitting in bed, flipping from one news station to another. Never had she felt so helpless, so worthless. Her adopted family was under attack, and all she could do was watch from her luxurious apartment on the other side of the Mediterranean Sea. It was that day that she had determined to never again, as much as she could help it, be away from her second home when there was something she might be able to do to help.

Now the alerts were going off again, but this time she was in the right place at the right time. Unfortunately, she still felt helpless. Looking for a laser that wasn't lasering was like trying to find a white Lego in a stadium full of white Legos. The only chance anyone had of finding the one they were looking for was when it started glowing green or red or blue or whatever. And even then, a person could be on the lower section of the west side of the stadium while one tiny Lego started glowing in the upper section of the east side. How could someone possibly cover that distance in time to stop it before it does its lasery thing?

Still, she kept scanning the waters, hoping that some idiot on board a boat would think, *Hey, what does this switch do?* and accidentally turn it on.

Lahav suddenly called out. "Drones have started leaving the building. First wave has twenty, five from each building. The good news is that they've given me a signal range for the drones. I've been able to determine their frequency and signature so that we can recognize it when it's sent out."

"Send that to every analyst in the building," said the *ramsad*. "How long until our jets get there?"

"Another twelve minutes," answered Yariv. "A second wave of UAVs is now departing the warehouses."

Seconds later, Nicole got a ping and saw a message on her screen from Lahav. She copied down the numbers and honed in her search parameters.

"Great work, Lahav," she called out. "What's the time gap between waves?"

"I've got two minutes. Check me, Lahav," said Yariv.

"Two minutes. Check."

A phone on the conference table rang. Nicole heard the *ramsad* pick it up and answer, but he was speaking too low for her to make out the words. Then he spoke one less-than-pleasant word that was loud enough for everyone to hear. Nicole cringed.

"Le Roux," called the *ramsad*.

Hesitantly, Nicole turned her chair.

The old man's face was red. "It seems your boyfriend has managed to kill another of his hostages. Breaking Turkish media is saying that Israel has infiltrated the country and assassinated the defense minister by throwing him out of a moving vehicle."

Nicole didn't know what to say. "That doesn't sound…"

"Of course it doesn't sound like what Tavor would do. I have no idea what happened, but it certainly wasn't that. But there is more to what the media said. It informed the public that two Israeli agents exited the vehicle with the defense minister's body, and they are on the run. I have no doubt that your boyfriend is one of those who are now running wild through the streets of Ankara."

Nicole fought the urge to correct the *ramsad*'s constant use of the descriptor *boyfriend*. It was probably best to let the man vent. Besides, maybe his word choice was accurate.

"Did they give any updates on the fugitives?"

The *ramsad* snorted derisively. "We probably won't get any reliable details on those two until they are either arrested or dead."

Those words hit like a rock in her gut. She turned back around and began scanning her screens again. Less than a minute later, she felt a hand on her shoulder. She could tell by the small thatches of gray hair on the fingers that it belonged to the *ramsad*.

"Apologies from a gruff old man. But honestly, I hope that it's Nir out there on the streets. There is absolutely no one in Kidon that I would trust more to get himself out of this kind of jam than that man."

Nicole's eyes welled up. Without looking up, she placed her hand on his for a moment. Then she got back to work. After a few seconds of lingering, the hand left her shoulder.

Nir is going to make it back. He always does. He's like James Bond or Arnold Schwarzenegger or someone like that. No matter what situation they get in, they always find a way out.

"I've got a hit," called out Lahav. "A laser with the exact signature is beaming northward off a boat due south of Limassol, Cyprus. Latitude is 34.2240392; longitude, 33.1356642. He just turned the beam on." Lahav paused a moment, then added, "The IAF is sending two jets that direction."

If those jets can blow up that boat, that may take care of this whole situation. With no daisy-chain signal, the UAVs will have no target. Erdoğan's entire drone army will plunge into the sea.

Just in case, though, Nicole kept scanning the waters of the eastern Mediterranean.

CHAPTER 62

ANKARA, TURKEY—17:32 (5:32 PM) EEST

The two men started to run, but then Gil called out, "Hold on!"

Right across from the Rolex store was Guess. Gil bolted to the first display shelf, snatched a handful of sweatshirts from a pile, and took off. An alarm sounded as he passed through security. Voices shouted from in the store.

They rounded a right-hand corner and sprinted past an empty storefront and a lightly populated Nautica.

Crap! This mall is way smaller than I thought! Ahead of them stood three tiny stores leading to a dead end. They took another right.

The police must have been more familiar with the mall because half of them had swung around the corner ahead of them. No way forward. No way back.

They went up.

An escalator stretched to the second level. Despite sprinting up the steps two at a time, it still felt like forever. They were totally exposed. Shots rang out from below, and Nir saw a man at the top of the escalator collapse to the ground.

Ahabalim! *They're killing their own people!*

At the top, rather than having room to run, two burly and—judging by the open collars of their uniforms—hairy security agents waited for them. Gil came off the escalator first, and one of the guards smacked him in the ribs with his club. The agent doubled over and sprawled to the ground.

The club was still moving, spinning around for a replay against Nir's head. But Nir saw it coming. He ducked the blow and drove his knee into the other man's thigh, knocking him off balance. Then Nir drove his elbow up into the man's face, and, using the man's momentum, sent him tumbling down the escalator into the police officers who had begun to run up.

A hard blow caught Nir in the small of the back. It was the other guard. Nir raised his arm to deflect a second blow. The club hit, sending jolts of pain radiating up through his shoulder. From behind, Gil slammed a fist into the man's kidneys, causing him to buckle. Using his foot, Gil sent the second guard rolling into the police, who had just started making their way up the "down" escalator.

The Guess sweatshirts were spread all over the floor. Nir and Gil each grabbed one and slipped it over their head as they ran. Nir wore XXL, but the pale blue hoodie he tugged down his body felt like a medium.

"Really?" he said to Gil as they scanned their escape options.

"Sorry. I didn't have time to check sizes when I stole them off the shelf."

They hung a right and then a quick left toward where the entrance was a floor below. But rather than finding any steps down or some other way out, there was only a long coffee bar called Pure Black. The two men stopped, trying to figure out what to do next. Loud shouts behind them told them that the cops would be there any second.

Gil slapped Nir's shoulder and pointed to the right. Nestled between the coffee shop and a porcelain store sat an outdoor terrace. They were at least four-and-a-half meters from the ground, but going over the railing appeared to be the only option for getting back outside. They sprinted that direction.

More gunfire echoed through the mall. Nir knew that unless a person was well trained and had put thousands of rounds through a gun in combat settings, hitting targets when one's adrenaline was pumping was nearly impossible. Doing that on the run was even more so. Still, these idiot cops kept firing. Nir couldn't believe the lives the Turkish police were putting at risk for a one-in-a-million hit.

The two men sent one table spinning and a second tumbling over as they ran through the coffee shop. The sounds of somersaulting chairs and breaking ceramic accompanied their flight. Reaching the glass doors, they pushed through to the terrace. The late afternoon was too cool for anyone to be using the tables outside, but thankfully, the workers had unlocked the exit anyway. Reaching the rail, Nir and Gil looked over. Below was the valet entrance to the mall, with cars waiting to be parked. What looked like two BMWs, a Tesla, a McLaren, and a boxy silver Mercedes G-Wagen sat in a line. Nir pointed to the G-Wagen, and Gil nodded. Hopefully, the SUV would have just enough height to keep them from breaking any bones.

They heard glass getting punctured and felt the whiz of bullets go by. No time for second thoughts—they had to jump. They didn't look as glorious as Butch Cassidy and the Sundance Kid did when they jumped into a flowing river below, but Nir thought they had to look pretty cool as they flew down. They hit the Mercedes' roof with a crunch. Even though his head didn't strike anything, the pain in his recently concussed skull was excruciating. With a groan, he rolled down the windshield. Gil's voice got him into action.

"Nir! Let's go. We've got to go!"

The valets had circled the car to see if they were alright. Nir slid off the hood to join Gil, who had already dropped to the ground. Then shots rang out. Two of the valets went down. In the quick glance Nir was able to take, their wounds looked superficial. He prayed he was right.

Once again, they ran.

Up ahead was a large edifice. "Ufuk Üniversitesi," a sign read. An ambulance was parked out front by double doors.

"Let's skirt through the hospital grounds and see what's on the other side," said Nir, pointing ahead.

Either the people at the medical center were used to battered people running through their courtyard or they were too sick to care, because no one seemed to bat an eye at the two Israelis as they sprinted past. Sirens continued to sound in the streets around them, and Nir had no idea if they would exit the grounds to a phalanx of squad cars manned by gun-pointing cops. But when they burst through the trees on the other side of the hospital property, it seemed that no one else had made it there yet.

Nir slapped Gil in the chest and pointed ahead. "There's our ticket out!"

Across the road was a tall building, at least 15 stories. At its base was a Škoda car dealership. The two men ran across the street, getting honks and obscene gestures as they did. Spotting the service department, Nir angled that way. Reaching the building, they ran into a covered drop-off area. A man was standing next to the open door of his Octavia holding up a key fob.

"You drive," Nir called to Gil.

As Nir ran to the passenger side, Gil snatched the key fob from the owner's hand, spun him away from the door and into the service tech, and dove into the seat. Moments later, they were racing through the lot looking for an exit.

"That guy is not going to be happy with us," said Gil with a nervous laughter.

Nir ran his hands over the rich brown leather on the dashboard. "I don't blame him. This car is styling!"

They enjoyed the car for less than five minutes before they pulled into a public parking garage. There, they found an inconspicuous beater that they hoped wouldn't be noticed for a while.

Gil's phone had been destroyed when he flew out of the van. Nir's, however, was still intact. He dialed a number, which was answered by a very relieved Dima. After linking up with a local asset who knew all the back roads, they began their journey north to the Black Sea and safety.

CHAPTER 63

The room exploded with cheers. Nicole saw that even the *ramsad* pumped his fist. On the screen in front of them, they had watched the signal from an F-16I as it dropped two SPICE-guided Mark 84 bombs onto a large fishing trawler. The SPICE guidance system—standing for Strategic, Precise Impact, Cost-Effective—allowed Israel's Air Force to plug in the precise coordinates to ensure direct hits. The Mark 84 bombs were originally bound for a Hamas-controlled apartment building in Gaza, but after takeoff, the pilot of the F-16 was suddenly rerouted toward the blue waters of the Mediterranean to remove the laser-bearing ship from the playing field. After the first jet had dropped its bombs, the feed cut to one from a second jet flying behind "just in case." It was from this plane that the analysts watched the boat disintegrate.

Nicole's elation was cut short when she saw Lahav. He was taking no part in the celebration. Instead, he was typing away furiously at his keyboard while being watched intently by Chewie's head, which now sat on the corner of his desk. She walked over to him and tried to discern what he was working on, but without context, his screens looked like gibberish. On one of his second-tier screens, above and to the left of his primary, was a frozen shot of a boat on the Mediterranean. Nicole recognized it as the one that just blew up.

"Talk to me, Lahav. What's going on?"

"Go get me an apple juice," he said without looking up.

In the typical hierarchical structure of the intelligence service, a lead being ordered to fetch a juice for an underling would be met with strong consequences. But CARL was far from typical. Nicole walked to the fridge and pulled out a juice. She checked the date and saw it was marked for the end of March.

Two weeks past? Close enough.

When she set it next to him, he spun around. "I think we've been duped again."

"What are you talking about? We all saw the signal. We all watched the explosion."

"Exactly. We did precisely what Erdoğan wanted us to do."

The room had hushed when everyone else saw the two talking. The *ramsad* walked over. "Tell me what you're thinking, son."

"Okay. So, watch my screen up here." The screen with the boat rewound, then began to play forward at four times the speed. "The boat pulls up and anchors. Then a second boat shows up and the dudes from the first one join them and they all sail off to grab a beer, leaving the boat unmanned. Job well done."

Asher Porush, who had spoken only in whispers since he had arrived—and only to the *ramsad*—said, "But doesn't that make sense? If it's been rigged to be remotely controlled, then there's no reason to leave anyone on board."

"True. Hey, chips anyone?" Liora walked back to her desk and pulled a bag out of a drawer. Meanwhile, Lahav kept talking. "Of course, you're right. It just seems to me like Turkey wouldn't want to leave evidence behind of what they'd done. But who knows?"

Liora handed Lahav a bag of Doritos. His face lit up. "Taco flavored. Where'd you find these?"

"Is this all you have?" asked the *ramsad*.

"Heck no, your *ramsadness*. I just found that weird. What's really got me bothered is that the signal that was being sent out wasn't pinging."

Again, Porush spoke. "Translate that for us."

Taking four chips, Lahav stuffed them in his mouth. He began speaking through the crunch. "Okay, think of it this way. It's like me getting a new phone, but not getting a carrier for it. Wait, bad example. I'd just connect it to a carrier and use their service for free. It's like Yariv getting a new phone, but not getting a carrier for it. He could dial it all he wanted, but nothing would connect. It would just be sending out a random signal that no cell tower would recognize."

Lahav twisted the cap off his juice and took a long swig. "So, what I'm saying is that it was a dummy."

"I still don't get it," said Porush.

With a grin, Lahav looked at his team and whispered loudly, "Maybe it's not the only—"

"Lahav. Explain it to us," Nicole interrupted.

Lahav huffed. "What I'm telling you is that this boat sent out the signal to see if we were listening. Good grief, we've still got—what— an hour or so before the first wave needs to daisy-chain over? And I can promise you that they will wait until the very last second before they activate that laser. I mean, why send the signal now?"

"Running a test?" asked the deputy director of Mossad.

"Seriously, Porush? You're going to go with that?"

The *ramsad* clamped his hand down on Lahav's shoulder so hard that it made the analyst dip to the left. "Tabib, we are not running a daycare here. I am Ira Katz, not 'your *ramsadness*.' And this is my right-hand man, Mr. Porush. Do you understand?"

"I understand," Lahav croaked out under the pressure of the old man's grip. "Sorry, Mr. Katz. Mr. Porush."

The *ramsad* lifted his hand, and a chastened Lahav muttered, "Cheese and crackers, people. We're getting so serious all of a sudden. What I'm saying, sir, is that I think this was one more chance for Erdoğan to outsmart us. He wanted to know whether we were on to him. Now he knows."

Looking at the ground, the *ramsad* mulled over the analyst's words. "I think you're probably right."

Yariv said, "And before anyone asks, the reason the UAVs won't crash when we destroy the warehouses is because the signal is being generated from on top of one of the city's largest apartment buildings.

They took a page from the Hamas playbook and are using their own people as human shields."

"Speaking of…" said Dafna. She pointed to the room's large screen. On it was a satellite feed of the four warehouses. A new wave of UAVs emerged and began flying.

"Hurry," said Liora.

The screen flashed white. When the picture resolved, all four warehouses were cratered with bright white flames and dark black smoke rising up to the sky. This time, though, there were no cheers.

"Good work in helping us to get those warehouses. Now let's find our relay station," said the *ramsad*. Walking back to the conference table, he took his seat.

CHAPTER 64

Nicole's phone chimed. She ignored it as she scanned a grid of the Mediterranean designed to pick up any laser activity. It had been a while since the Red Alerts had stopped, but her silenced phone remained at the top corner of the desk. Her brain went through a moment of incongruity, until she realized the truth.

Nir!

Pulling her encrypted cell from her pocket, she read the one-word message.

safe

Quickly she thumbed back:

Thank God

getting updates from efraim. find that signal

Planning on it. Coffee when you're back?

count on it. get back to work

Tears came to Nicole's eyes as she slipped the phone back into her pocket. She grabbed a tissue and dabbed at her eyes. She felt such a huge sense of relief knowing that Nir was okay. No matter how much she concentrated on her work, she always wondered in the back of her mind, *Will I ever see him again?*

She had prayed that the answer to that question would be yes. They had unfinished business. Why couldn't he see the truth? Hope, peace, and salvation were just a prayer away for him. He had come so far since she had first told him about her radical conversion. But that final hump was turning into a wall.

Lord, please let him see. Let him come to know You before it's too late. Let him—

A sound from the conference table got her attention. It was the Red Alert app notification. Nicole picked up her phone and saw that silent banners were appearing on hers too. The first was followed by a second and a third. Soon, they were pinging in even greater numbers than before.

"Exactly what I would have done," said the *ramsad*. Then calling out to the room, he said, "Get ready, the UAVs are almost here."

On Nicole's screen, an indicator lit up. "Got a hit! In the Med, east of Larnaca! Sending coordinates!"

Liora called out, "Hit! Just inland from the water at Ayia Napa! Sending—"

Yariv interrupted, "Hit! Roof of Lebanese International University in Sidon!"

As the others spoke, Nicole saw eight, then a dozen, then two dozen signatures pop up on her screen.

"What's going on?" the *ramsad* thundered. "Somebody talk to me!"

"*Hamefaked*, they're flooding us with signals." She scrolled out the view on her screen so it wasn't only covering the territory she had carved out. "We have…hang on…we have at least eighty signatures registering."

"Tabib, are they pinging?"

"Every one of them, Mr. Katz. And they're latching on. They went out with one source, but they're daisy-chaining to multiple sources. I mean, they all are attaching to a single source. But they don't all have the same source."

Nicole looked down at her phone again. Well over 100 rockets had flown toward the border so far. The Iron Dome was doing its best, but some rockets appeared to be crossing into Israel.

When she turned back around, the *ramsad* was on his phone explaining to someone what was going on. After a pause, she heard him say, "What that means, Hurvitz, is that you need to have your air force scramble every plane to hunt these drones down. You also need to pull any Iron Dome resources available." He paused. "Yes, I know they are protecting our northern border. That's why I said any available. Whatever resources you have that you can shoot or scramble or laser beam, you get them to the Mediterranean. Destroy the sources. Take down the UAVs. We'll send your people all the coordinates. By our count, there are one hundred and twenty drones flying south, and they'll be hitting Leviathan and Tamar in about thirty minutes." The *ramsad* ended the call and dropped his phone onto the table.

"Tabib, compile all the information we have as far as targets and get them to Defense."

"*Root.*"

Less than ten minutes later, Nicole saw source indicators begin disappearing from her display. She typed in a quick code, and her computer monitor began mirroring on the main screen. It was a cluttered view, but the opposing enemies were evident.

Traveling south in a staggered formation were the drones, which showed up as red blips. On the water and near the coastlines were the daisy-chained laser sources, which were green. The planes of the Israeli Air Force were represented by blips colored blue. Both red and green indicators were sporadically disappearing as the jets either struck a signal source or shot down drones.

This was another one of those moments when Nicole felt completely helpless. She had done all she could in acquiring the targets. Now it was up to the IAF to destroy them.

Time passed, and more and more lights on the screen went out. But they weren't disappearing fast enough. She wasn't the only one to notice. The *ramsad* leaned over and said to Porush, "Make sure those men and women on the platforms are prepared for probable impact."

Porush didn't reply. Instead, he took his phone out of his pocket and dialed a number.

The IAF was putting on a valiant effort. Of the original 120 red blips on the screen, only 23 were left. But those 23 were getting closer and closer. A blue blip passed into a row of red blips. Four reds disappeared from the screen.

"That F-35 is using his 25mm guns to take down those UAVs. Incredible," said the *ramsad* to Nicole. There was awe in his voice, like a man obsessed with airplanes but who never had the time to learn how to fly.

More red dots disappeared over the next minutes, but in the end, it wasn't enough. The final eight UAVs disappeared from the screen, but they did so in the exact same locations as the Leviathan and Tamar gas production platforms.

CHAPTER 65

Nir checked his watch again. It was still over an hour before Nicole was scheduled to meet him. But he had gotten to their favorite Aroma coffee shop early because he had to think some things out. His gut seized just a bit, which he knew came from nerves. He was about to have a very important conversation with Nicole, one that could change both their lives and just might change his eternity.

Today was his first full day home after getting in the previous night following a circuitous route that had left him and his team hauling in nets for a Romanian fishing boat for four days. He didn't mind the work. It was a refreshing relief to be out on the water and away from bullets for a while. But he was also anxious to get back to Tel Aviv. There was a girl who was waiting for him.

He thumbed her a text:

ready to see you

Me 2

maybe if youre lucky ill buy you two espressos

*Good. I can finally drink one
myself before you steal it!*

possibly. but youll have to be quick

Draining the last from his cup, he motioned for the guy behind the counter to bring him another.

Better be careful. You might make yourself too jittery to even think straight.

But he was already too jittery to think straight. Besides, caffeine was his happy place. No one ever died of a caffeine overdose. Or, if they did, they certainly didn't have Jewish blood flowing through their veins.

After the days at sea, they had landed in the Bulgarian port city of Varna. From there, they drove through Bucharest and up to Budapest, a journey of well over 1,000 kilometers. Once in Hungary, they split up, which they were more than happy to do after being crammed together in a car across half of Eastern Europe. Each flew a different route, with all arriving within the last 36 hours.

Another reason he had enjoyed his time trapped out on the Black Sea so much was that the world was crazy inside of Israel. Leviathan had been hit by five UAVs, Tamar by three. The damage had been substantial, but it wasn't enough to shut down production completely. If Israel hadn't found a way to stop all the other drones, the gas fields would have been overwhelmed, and Israel's economy would have gone into a tailspin. It might take a month or two, but Israel's gas production would soon be back up and running at 100 percent.

Instead, it was Turkey's economy that had taken the brunt of the blowback. There is little that is less tolerated in the Turkish culture than failure. Erdoğan had the opportunity to be a hero or a goat. Leviathan and Tamar were burning, but they weren't destroyed. Thus, the Turkish president was being widely ridiculed in his own country and abroad. Rumors of early elections or even a military coup were surfacing.

But Turkey's pain did not mean any gain for Israel. Nir's people were still being massacred in the press for destroying the "humanitarian" aid that Russia was trying to send to the poor people in Syria. The war in Gaza continued to rage, and the leftist media couldn't get enough of saying the word *genocide*. Somehow, Prime Minister Snir was holding on, but who knew for how much longer?

Floating on the water. Hauling in nets. Staying up into the night drinking beer and telling old stories—some real, some made up. Yeah, that sounds pretty good. But not as good as seeing the woman who's about to walk through the doors of this café.

There was a loud crunch outside, followed by a hard smash. It was the type of metal-to-metal smack that said someone had gotten seriously careless with their car. The first responder in Nir had him instantly on his feet, racing for the doors.

Outside, he could immediately see what had happened. A midsized, white SUV had sideswiped a parked car, then careened into the intersection, where it had T-boned a second car. Victims and witnesses had already begun to exit their vehicles. Nir ran ahead to the T-boned car and pushed his way to the front.

An elderly man was behind the wheel and his wife was in the seat next to him. He was asking her, "Are you okay, *motek*? Are you okay?"

"Any broken bones? Any head trauma?" Nir asked through the open door.

The wife answered. "What? No, we're okay. Just shaken up."

"I'm so thankful they hit the rear of the car," the man said as he looked over his wife to make sure she wasn't hurt.

Nir turned his eyes to the offending vehicle. The rear of the elderly couple's sedan had been caved in by the SUV. A half-meter more, and the results could have been very different.

Weird. I wonder where the driver of the SUV is? Did they run? Was this a stolen car? A hit-and-run?

A quick scan of the people surrounding the cars didn't show anyone who looked like they had just stepped out of an accident scene.

Turning back to the couple, Nir said, "I'm sure emergency has been called. Are you two okay?"

The old man nodded and waved him away. "Go see how the other driver is."

The crowd around the SUV had expanded. Again, Nir tried to

spot the driver, but there was no one in the vehicle. The scene had an eerie feel to it. Most of the witnesses surrounding the accident were murmuring, except for a few who were trying to calm one hysterical woman. She was hyperventilating and her words weren't making sense.

Pushing his way through, Nir looked inside the SUV. It looked like a family car. Kids' toys in the back. Woman's purse on the floor in front of the passenger's seat. That made him think all the more that it was likely a stolen vehicle. But there was something off about the interior of the car. Something didn't make sense.

That's when he began to understand what the hysterical woman was saying.

"I was driving next to them. A little girl in the back seat was smiling at me. Then she just disappeared. They all just vanished. Everyone. The car veered and bounced off the parked car, then went into the intersection."

They just vanished? Could she have been the driver of the SUV and hit her head? Those sound like the rantings of a concussed mind, and I should know!

Then, in a flash, Nir realized what was wrong with the interior of the car. Looking inside again, he noticed the front passenger side. A full set of women's clothes were strewn on the seat and the floor. He looked down. The same was true on the driver's side, only this time it was men's clothing. Then he saw something else that made his blood chill. The seatbelts on both sides were still connected into their clasps.

Nir could feel his own panic swelling. He looked to the back, and what he saw confirmed his fears. Behind mom was a little dress held tight against the seat by the child restraint. Behind dad was a smaller dress, this one fashioned after some Disney princess. And in the middle was a sturdy child's seat. A red, white, and blue Avengers logo stared at him from the empty onesie that was trapped under the straps.

Nicole!

Less than a minute later, Nir was in his car, racing through traffic. All around him, people were acting like nothing had happened. Obviously, the news hadn't reached them yet because discovering that people had evaporated into thin air like in a Marvel movie is bound to shake anybody up.

Coming to a red light, he slowed his Mercedes until he saw a gap in the traffic. He gunned the accelerator and made a hard right. A horn blared behind him. He began weaving through cars until he saw the sign for the Marriott Courtyard. Cutting in front of a Land Cruiser, he bounced up into the parking lot, scraping the bottom of his chassis as he did so.

Nicole's suite could be accessed from the back, so Nir rounded the building and slammed on his brakes. Leaving the door open, he ran from the car to her room.

"Nicole! Nicole, you in there?" he called as he pounded on the door. He knew the answer, but forced himself to wait 30 seconds. "Nicole! I'll give you ten more seconds, then I'm kicking the door in."

A woman in her fifties stuck her head out of the next suite over. "What is wrong with you?"

"Get back inside," Nir roared. The woman quickly retreated. "Okay, *motek*, I'm coming in."

The lock was strong, but training had its benefits, and the door flew open when he kicked. He raced in.

"Nicole! Nicole, are you here?"

The place was immaculate, as he expected, except for a thin blanket that had been left bunched on one cushion of the couch. In the kitchen, he saw that a kettle was on the stove, but the burner appeared to be off.

Not in the living room. Not in the kitchen. There's only one place left to look.

Taking a deep breath, Nir walked toward the bedroom. The door was open, and the bed was made. He stepped inside. On one nightstand sat a magnetic phone charger and a second charger for an Apple Watch. The opposite nightstand held a Bible, black leather and worn along the edges. Nicole's cell phone sat on top of the book. There were no sounds coming from the bathroom, and the light was off.

There was only one place left to look. Very slowly, he walked around to the other side of the bed. On the ground at his feet were sweatpants and an old red T-shirt he had occasionally seen her wear with a logo for

the Cape Town Spurs Football Club. Next to the small pile of clothing was an empty mug and a spoon. An amber puddle had marred the
floor's tile.

She had warned him. She had said this was going to happen. Now
she was gone, and he was too late.

Nir sat on the corner of the bed and wept.

AUTHORS' NOTE

I t was very difficult to try to communicate the horrific events of October 7. The first part of this book went through many rewrites. Our goal was to be as brutally honest as possible, while still showing respect to the many victims, both living and dead. We settled with taking the reader into the experience of a Nova Music Festival attender, knowing that it was impossible to fully do so. There is no way that one can feel the terror as you run, knowing your killers are somewhere behind you gaining ground. It is impossible to take you into the mind and heart of a woman who is being assaulted time after time or the abject fear of staring into the business end of a rifle the moment before the trigger is pulled. Those things can only be experienced. And for so many, their precious lives were extinguished moments after.

Most of the survivors of October 7 remain deeply scarred today. Many have physical reminders that they have to endure each day. Others have emotional wounds. For some, those emotional scars have caused them to snap, leading them to harm themselves and, sometimes, others.

But it isn't only those who saw the terrorists face to face who have experienced a profound change in their lives. Israel is a damaged nation. Amir has spent many nights awake, listening for the footsteps of those breaking in to slaughter his family. Across the nation, children of this generation suffer greatly, with many living in fear that they will die at the hands of the invaders. Our hope is that this book reveals to the reader some of those scars.

Despite having been knocked down, the resulting effect of October 7 has buoyed this nation. Over the centuries, we Jews have learned to feed off our pain. Our woundedness is what has most Israelis determined to finish the job against the terrorist groups that surround our nation. Imagine you live in a country that has evil people living just across your borders. These malicious criminals have already proven their willingness, and their excitement, to cross your borders and slaughter your people. That is the experience of those of us who live in Israel.

It is true that there is a minority of people in this country who are seeking to appease the terrorists and, more importantly, the world stage. They want peace, no matter the price. Unfortunately, they are very vocal, and they have the media on their side. Thankfully, our prime minister has thus far stood strong and has promised to see this necessary battle through to the end.

The activities you read about in this book are from our own imagination. However, they find their genesis in the real operations of Israeli intelligence. Just ask Fuad Shukr and Ismail Haniyeh, who died within a day of each other in July 2024, one in Beirut and one in Tehran, about the power of the Mossad. The violent ends of Mohammed Deif and Mohammad Reza Zahedi and Razi Mousavi and a host of other men also laid the foundation for the actions of Nir Tavor and the other Kidon teams in this work of fiction. We were forced to avoid using the real names of terrorists because they were all getting removed from the playing board faster than we could write the book. Amir can remember texting Steve one day in January with the words "We better change our plans." Attached was a link to a story about the assassination of Saleh al-Arouri, who had originally been one of the Hamas terrorists killed in our Operation Amalek. That led to a rewrite and a change in philosophy.

There are a few real names we kept, but all are of national leaders or historical figures. These we kept in order to keep a tie in with the past, with today's news, and with the previous books in our series. This is not true, however, with the Israeli government. The prime minister in this book in no way is meant to represent Benjamin Netanyahu, and no one in our prime minister's cabinet or in other leadership positions is based on any specific person.

One of our purposes in writing this book is to show the growing alliances that fit directly into biblical prophecy. Ever since the time we published our first thriller, *Operation Joktan*, three years ago, the ties between Russia, Iran, and Turkey have only gotten stronger. Russia has very practically expressed its belligerence by invading Ukraine. Turkey is separating from its NATO allies and aligning with Russia and some northern African nations. Iran is finally recognizing that its great experiment with terrorist militias like Hezbollah, Hamas, and the Houthis has fallen flat. Now the ayatollahs are forced to look for new friends, and Russia and Turkey are there to welcome them with open arms.

The prophecies of the Bible are being played out on the world stage. Never in history have we seen Russia, Turkey, and Iran allied together. But now, as specifically talked about in Ezekiel 38, we find this three-nation axis of evil uniting under a single goal—the eventual pillaging and destruction of Israel. The Jewish people are now back in the land, as promised in Ezekiel 36–37. The alliance of Ezekiel 38 has formed against them. Some cry, "What an incredible coincidence!" We find ourselves agreeing with Nir Tavor that coincidence is only an excuse for those not willing to step back and see the big picture.

Which brings us to our conclusion. Neither one of us is a lover of cliffhangers. However, we agreed that in this case it was necessary. Not only does the ending of this book bring the current Nir Tavor Mossad Series to a close, but it whets the appetite for the next succession of thrillers, The Nir Tavor Tribulation Series, which will follow our hero as he navigates the seven years that God has planned as a time of chastening for His people, Israel. Watch for the first book in that series in the spring of 2026.

Not only will those seven years be a time of discipline for Israel, but they will be a period of punishment for the rest of the world that still remains. But you don't have to be one of those people forced to endure the ravages of the tribulation period. Salvation is promised to anyone who will simply believe Jesus is the Savior of this world and receive Him as their Lord. We are promised that if we do that, then when the event comes that whisked Nicole away to be with her Messiah, we, too, will be taken up to meet Jesus in the clouds. That day is drawing close. Don't be like Nir and find that you've waited too long.

Awaiting His return,
Amir Tsarfati
Steve Yohn

THE

NIR TAVOR

MOSSAD THRILLER

SERIES

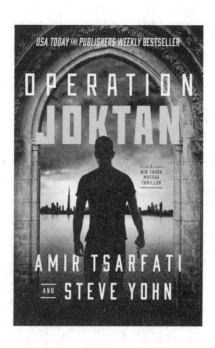

"IT WAS THE PERFECT DAY—UNTIL THE GUNFIRE."

Nir Tavor is an Israeli secret service operative turned talented Mossad agent.

Nicole le Roux is a model with a hidden skill.

A terrorist attack brings them together, and then work forces them apart—until they're unexpectedly called back into each other's lives.

But there's no time for romance. As violent radicals threaten chaos across the Middle East, the two must work together to stop these extremists, pooling Nicole's knack for technology and Nir's adeptness with on-the-ground missions. Each heart-racing step of their operation gets them closer to the truth—and closer to danger.

In this thrilling first book in the Nir Tavor Mossad thriller series, Amir Tsarfati and Steve Yohn draw on true events as well as tactical insights Amir learned from his time in the Israeli Defense Forces. For believers in God's life-changing promises, *Operation Joktan* is a suspense-filled page-turner that illuminates the blessing Israel is to the world.

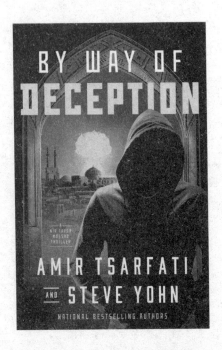

NUCLEAR DECEPTION

The Mossad has uncovered Iran's plans to smuggle untraceable weapons of mass destruction into Israel. The clock is ticking, and agents Nir Tavor and Nicole le Roux can't act quickly enough.

Nir and Nicole find themselves caught in a whirlwind plot of assassinations, espionage, and undercover recon, fighting against the clock to stop this threat against the Middle East. As they draw closer to danger—and closer to each other—they find themselves ensnared in a lethal web of secrets. Will they have to sacrifice their own lives to protect the lives of millions?

Inspired by real events, authors Amir Tsarfati and Steve Yohn reteam for this suspenseful follow-up to the bestselling *Operation Joktan*. Filled with danger, romance, and international intrigue, this Nir Tavor thriller reveals breathtaking true insights into the lives and duties of Mossad agents—and delivers a story that will have you on the edge of your seat.

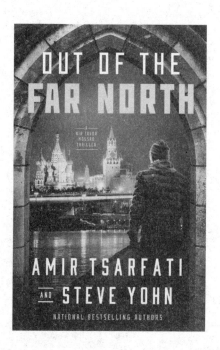

MOSCOW IS FURIOUS—AND PLOTTING REVENGE

Tensions are at a breaking point. The Western markets that once relied on Russian gas have turned to Israel for their energy needs. Furious, Russia surreptitiously moves to protect their interests by using their newfound ally, Iran, and Iran's proxy militias.

As Israel's elite fighting forces and the Mossad go undercover, they detect the Kremlin is planning a major attack against Israel. Hunting for clues, Mossad agents Nir Tavor and Nicole le Roux plunge themselves into the treacherous underworld of Russian oligarch money, power, and decadence.

With each danger they face, le Roux's newfound Christian faith grows stronger. And battle-weary Tavor—haunted by dreams from his past—must confront memories and pain he'd sought to bury.

In this electrifying thriller, hostilities explode as Tavor and le Roux fight to prevent a devastating conflict. Will they be able to outwit their enemies, or will their actions have catastrophic consequences? And how can Tavor's Kidon team possibly survive when forces beyond the Mossad's control step in and turn the whole operation upside down?